"Heads and tails above the majority of the 'definitive' type of horror anthologies which crop up every few years. It is recommended to everyone who needs to 'catch up' on the best of the best."

—Jessica Amanda Salmonson

"[An] exemplary collection."

—Brian Stableford

WORLDS OF FEAR

George R. R. Martin
Carlos Fuentes
Thomas Hardy
Thomas M. Disch
Violet Hunt
John W. Campbell
Theodore Sturgeon
Elizabeth Engstrom
Frederik Pohl
Gertrude Atherton

Tor anthologies edited by David G. Hartwell

The Ascent of Wonder (with Kathryn Cramer)
The Dark Descent
Foundations of Fear
Christmas Forever
Christmas Stars

WORLDS OF FEAR

FOUNDATIONS OF FEAR VOLUME II

EDITED BY

DAVID G. HARTWELL

TOR®
HORROR

A TOM DOHERTY ASSOCIATES BOOK
NEW YORK

WORLDS OF FEAR: FOUNDATIONS OF FEAR, VOLUME #2

Copyright © 1992 by David G. Hartwell

Cover art by Tom Canty

A Tor Book
Published by Tom Doherty Associates, Inc.
175 Fifth Avenue
New York, N.Y. 10010

Tor® is a registered trademark of Tom Doherty Associates, Inc.

ISBN: 0-812-55002-1

First Tor edition: September 1994

Printed in the United States of America

0 9 8 7 6 5 4 3 2 1

To the editors and anthologists who first gave the genre a canon in the 1920s–1940s;

To the publishers who stuck with it and gave the genre an identity for better or worse;

To the writers who often ignored them all and just wrote powerfully and well;

And finally, to my children, Alison and Geoffrey, without whom I couldn't have completed the book during difficult times.

Acknowledgments

This book continues the revaluation of horror literature I began in *The Dark Descent,* and so to the same people and books given credit there I continue my indebtedness. Discussions with Alfred Bendixen (and of course his books) have proven helpful, and with Robert Hadji, whose wide reading in and out of the genre and considered critical judgement have influenced several of my choices for inclusion herein. The support of those who were enthusiastic enough about *The Dark Descent* to demand that I continue working in this area—particularly Joanna Russ—carried me through a number of rough spots. Certainly the most important acknowledgment is to Kathryn Cramer, not only for discussion, critical commentary, and moral support, but for sharing with me her unfinished writings and researches on horror publishing and the distinctions between category and genre, and on Henry James, as well as her published work surveying influences among horror writers today. At every point her creative insights have been provocative and useful. The critical reconsideration of the evolution of horror in literature begun by Kathryn Cramer, Peter D. Pautz, and myself five years ago has borne a variety of fruits, including all our various anthologies. This is only the most recent.

No acknowledgment would be complete without proper recognition of the support of my publisher, Tor Books, who took a chance. To Tom Doherty, publisher, and Melissa Singer, editor, for patient enthusiasm, my sincere gratitude.

Contents

Introduction   *David G. Hartwell*   1
Introduction to *Worlds of Fear*   23

Sandkings   24
    George R. R. Martin (b. 1948)
Aura   76
    Carlos Fuentes (b. 1928)
Barbara, of the House of Grebe   115
    Thomas Hardy (1840–1928)
Torturing Mr. Amberwell   154
    Thomas M. Disch (b. 1940)
The Prayer   196
    Violet Hunt (1866–1942)
Who Goes There?   229
    John W. Campbell (1910–1971)
. . . and my fear is great   301
    Theodore Sturgeon (1918–1985)
When Darkness Loves Us   376
    Elizabeth Engstrom (b. 1951)
We Purchased People   437
    Frederik Pohl (b. 1919)
The Striding Place   456
    Gertrude Atherton (1857–1948)

I High and Low

There is no delight the equal of dread.

—Clive Barker, "Dread"

. . . if not the highest, certainly the most exacting form of literary art.

—L. P. Hartley on the ghost story

Taken as a whole, the output . . . stands in need of critical study, not to erect theories upon subterranean surmises, but by using direct observation and following educated taste . . . to enlarge for all readers the repertory of the well-wrought and the enjoyable.

—Jacques Barzun, Introduction to
*The Penguin Encyclopedia of
Horror and the Supernatural*

We dislike to predict the future of the horror story. We believe its powers are not yet exhausted. The advance of science proves this. It will lead us into unexplored labyrinths of terror and the human desire to experience new emotions will always be with us. . . . Some of the stories now being published in *Weird Tales* will live forever.

—editorial, *Weird Tales* (vol. 4, no. 2; 1924)

This anthology of horror literature is a companion volume to *The Dark Descent*, continuing a panorama of examples and an examination of the evolution of horror as a mode of literary expression from its roots in stories in the early Romantic period to the rich varieties of contemporary fiction. In *The Dark Descent*, it was observed that the short story has, until the 1970s, been the dominant literary genre of horror throughout its evolution (horror was in at the origination of the short story and has evolved with and through it); and that it is now evident that the horror novel is in a period of rapid development and proliferation, for the first time achieving dominance over the shorter forms. So it is a particularly appropriate historical moment for us to look back over the growth and spread of horror stories.

Furthermore, a general consideration of literary examples yields several conclusions about the nature of horror. First, that horror is not in the end either a marketing category or a genre, but a literary mode that has been used in every genre and category, the creation of an atmosphere and emotional environment that sparks a transaction between the reader and the text which yields the horrific response. Horrific poems and plays and novels predate the inception of the short story. There can and have been western horror stories, war horror stories, ghost stories, adventure stories, mystery stories, romances—the potential exists in every category.

But by the early twentieth century, horror began to spread and separate in two directions, in literary fiction and in popular literature, mirroring the Modernist distinction between high art and low, a distinction that is rapidly disintegrating today in the post–Modern period, but remains the foundation of marketing all literature in the twentieth century. For most of the century, horror has been considered narrowly as a marketing category or a popular genre, and dismissed by most serious readers and critics. In many ways, horror is associated with ghosts and the supernatural, which in a way stand for superstition and religion— and one of the great intellectual, cultural, and spiritual battles of the past 150 years has been on the part of intellectuals, to rid western civilization of the burdens of Medieval religion and superstition, especially in the wake of the great battles over Darwin and Evolution. The Modernist era, which began in the late nineteenth century, is an era of science.

The death of horror was widely announced by Modernist critics (particularly Edmund Wilson, who devoted two essays to demolishing it), the specialists such as Lovecraft and Blackwood denounced, and the psychological investigations of Henry James, Franz Kafka, Joseph Conrad, and D. H. Lawrence enshrined as the next stage in literary evolution, replacing superstition and the supernatural as the electric light had replaced the flame.

Yet it was precisely at that moment, in the 1920s and 1930s, that the first magazines devoted to horror began to appear, that the first major collections and anthologies of horror fiction from the previous hundred years were done, and the horror film came into prominence. Significantly, Lovecraft, in his classic study, *Supernatural Horror in Literature* (1936, revised), in examining the whole history of western literature concluded that over centuries and in a large preponderance of texts, the true sensations of horror occur rarely, and momentarily—in parts of works, not usually whole works. He wrote this during the generation when horror was actually becoming a genre, with an audience and a body of classic texts. A threshold had been reached after a century of literary evolution, in which a parallel evolution of the ghost story and the horror story had created a rich and varied body of tropes, conventions, texts, and passed, and the horror genre was established as a vigorous variety of popular literature, in rich interaction with the main body of the literature of this century ever since. One can speculate that, since the religious and superstitious beliefs had passed from overt currency in the reading public, their transformation into the subtext of horror fiction fulfilled certain desires, if not needs, in the audience and writers. As was noted in *The Dark Descent,* the most popular current of horror fiction for decades has been moral allegories of the power of evil.

The giant of the magazines of horror was *Weird Tales,* founded in 1923 and published until the 1950s (and recently revived). It was there that H. P. Lovecraft, Frank Belknap Long, Robert E. Howard, Clark Ashton Smith, and many others flourished. Davis Grubb, Tennessee Williams, Ray Bradbury, and many other literary writers also published early work in *Weird Tales,* which was hospitable to all forms of the weird and horrific and supernatural in literature. "Up to the day the first issue of *Weird Tales* was placed on the stands, stories of the sort you read between these covers each month were taboo in the publishing world. . . . Edgar Allan Poe . . . would have searched in vain for a publisher before the advent of this magazine," said the editorial of the first anniversary issue in 1924.

One of the conditions that favors genrification is an accessible category market, and *Weird Tales* provided this, along with a letter column in which the names and addresses of correspondents were published. This allowed readers and writers to get in touch with each other, and they did. The Lovecraft circle was composed of writers, poets, and readers, and generated thousands of letters among them over several decades, forming connections that lasted years after Lovecraft's death in 1937, some at least until the death of August Derleth in the 1960s. Some of the early correspondents were involved, as Lovecraft was, in the amateur journalism movement of the teens and twenties, and they generated amateur magazines and small press publications, which flourished from the 1930s to the 1960s—their descendents exist today. The World Fantasy Awards has a separate category award for excellence in fan publishing each year, and there are many nominees. So *Weird Tales* was seminal not only in creating a genre, but also in creating a field, a subculture of devotees.

In the 1940s and 1950s, the development of the popular form continued and, through a series of historical accidents, came under the protective umbrella of the science fiction field, as did the preponderance of fantasy literature. H. P. Lovecraft and many of his circle published in the science fiction magazines of the 1930s. And the letter-writing subcultures generated by the science fiction magazines interpenetrated with the horror field, creating one body, so that by the late 1930s the active fans commonly identified themselves as fans of the fantasy fiction field.

In 1939, the great science fiction editor, John W. Campbell, Jr., whose magazine, *Astounding Stories,* dominated science fiction, founded a companion magazine, *Unknown,* devoted to fantasy and horror, and to modernizing the style and atmosphere of the fiction. Campbell, who had written an influential science fiction horror story in 1938, encouraged his major science fiction writers to work for his new magazine, and in the five years of its existence, *Unknown* confirmed a bond between horror and science fiction that has not been broken, a bonding that yielded the flowering of SF horror movies in the fifties and encouraged a majority of the important horror writers for the next fifty years. Shirley Jackson once told me in conversation that she had a complete run of *Unknown.* "It's the best," she said. Several of Jackson's stories first appeared in the 1950s in *The Magazine of Fantasy and Science*

Fiction (as did, for instance, one of the earliest translations of Jorge Luis Borges). Since the 1930s, a majority of the horror stories in the English language have first appeared in genre magazines.

> In times when censorship or conventions operated to deter authors from dealing specifically with certain human situations, the occult provided a reservoir of images which could be used to convey symbolically what could not be presented literally.
>
> Glen St John Barclay, *Anatomy of Horror*

Meanwhile, from the 1890s onward, to a large extent under the influence of Henry James, writers such as Walter de la Mare, Edith Wharton, and others devoted significant portions of their careers to the literary ghost story. "In a certain sense, all of his stories are ghost stories—evocations of a tenuous past; and his most distinguished minor work is quite baldly cast in this rather vulgar, popular form. 'The "ghost story,"' he wrote in one of his prefaces, 'as we for convenience call it, has ever been for me the most possible form of the fairy tale.' But at a deeper level than he consciously sought in doing his intended stories of terror (he called, we remember, even 'The Turn of the Screw' a 'potboiler'), James was forever closing in on the real subject that haunted him always: the necrophilia that has always so oddly been an essential part of American romance," says critic Leslie Fiedler.

At the time of his death, Henry James was writing *The Sense of the Past,* a supernatural novel in which a character named Ralph becomes obsessed with a portrait and is translated into the past as a ghost from the future. The supernatural and ghosts were major strains in the work of this great and influential writer throughout his career and, under the pressure of his Modernist admirers, have often been ignored or banished from consideration by being considered only as psychological metaphors during most of the twentieth century. Virginia Woolf, for example, in defending the ghost stories, says the ghosts "have their origin within us. They are present whenever the significant overflows our powers of expressing it; whenever the ordinary appears ringed by the strange. . . . Can it be that we are afraid? . . . We are afraid of something unnamed, of something, perhaps, in ourselves." True, of course, but a defense of the metaphorical level of the text at the expense of the literal surface—which is often intentionally difficult to figure out.

Since the Modernists considered the supernatural a regressive and outmoded element in fiction, the contemporaries and followers of James who were strongly influenced by the literal level of his supernaturalism have been to a large extent banished from the literary canon. Most of them are women writers. A few, such as Edith Wharton, still have critical support, but not on the whole for their supernatural works. Those whose best work was largely in the supernatural, such as Violet Hunt and Gertrude Atherton, Harriet Prescott Spofford, and Mary Wilkins Freeman, have been consigned to literary history and biographical criticism, marginalized. In the recent volume, *Horror: 100 Best Books* (1988—covering literature from Shakespeare to Ramsey Campbell), five women writers were chosen for the list, omitting novelists such as Ann Radcliffe, Emily Brontë, and Anne Rice, and every short story collection by a woman—except Marjorie Bowen's and Lisa Tuttle's.

Horror, often cast as ghost story, was an especially useful mode for many woman writers, allowing them a freedom to explore the concerns of feminism symbolically and nonrhetorically with powerful effect. Alfred Bendixen, in the introduction to his scholarly anthology, *Haunted Women* (1985), says: "Supernatural fiction opened doors for American women writers, allowing them to move into otherwise forbidden regions. It permitted them to acknowledge the needs and fears of women, enabling them to examine such 'unladylike' subjects as sexuality, bad marriages, and repression." He goes on to identify stories rescued from virtual oblivion and observe that "most of the stories . . . come from the 1890s and early 1900s—a period when the feminist ghostly tale attracted the talents of the finest women writers in America and resulted in some of their most powerful and intriguing work." Alan Ryan, in his excellent anthology, *Haunting Women* (1988), adds the work of Ellen Glasgow, May Sinclair, Jean Rhys, and Isak Dinesen, extending the list into the present with works by Hortense Calisher, Muriel Spark, Ruth Rendell, and others. "One recurring theme," says Ryan, ". . . is a female character's fear of a domineering man, who may be father, husband, or lover."

Richard Dalby, in the preface to his *Victorian Ghost Stories by Eminent Women Writers* (1988—from Charlotte Brontë to Willa Cather), claims that "over the past 150 years Britain has led the world in the art of the classic ghost story, and it is no exaggeration to state that at least fifty percent of quality examples in the genre were by women writers." And in the introduction to that same volume, Jennifer Uglow observes, "although—perhaps because—they were written as unpretentious entertainments, ghost stories seemed to give their writers a license to experiment, to push the boundaries of fiction a little further. . . . Again and again we find that the machinery of this most conventional genre frees, rather than restricts, the women who use it."

An investigation of the horror fiction of the nineteenth and early twentieth centuries reveals that a preponderance of the supernatural fiction was written by women and that, buried in the works of a number of women writers whose fiction has been ignored or excluded from the literary canon, there exist significant landmarks in the evolution of horror. Harriet Prescott Spofford, for instance, is emerging as one of the major links between Poe and the later body of American women writers. Gertrude Atherton's "The Bell in the Fog" is both an homage to and critique of Henry James—and perhaps an influence on *The Sense of the Past*. It is provocative to wonder, since women were marginalized in English and American society, and since popular women writers were the most common producers of supernatural fiction, ghostly or horrific, whether supernatural fiction was not in part made marginal because of its association with women and feminine concerns. Just as James (except for "The Turn of the Screw") was forgotten as a writer of supernatural fiction for most of the Modernist era (although it was an important strain throughout his career), so were most of the women who wrote in that mode in the age of electricity. But the flame still burns, can illuminate, can heat the emotions.

In the contemporary period, much of the most popular horror is read by women (more than sixty percent of the adult audience is women in their thirties and forties, according to the most recent Gallup Poll surveys of reading). Best-selling horror most often addresses the traditional concerns of women (children, houses, the supernatural), as well as portraying vividly the place of women and their treatment in society.

Intriguingly, the same Gallup Poll indicates that in the teenage readership, an insignificant percentage ("0%") of girls read horror. The teenage audience is almost exclusively male. Perhaps this is because a very large amount of genre horror fiction (that is published in much smaller numbers of copies than best-selling horrific fiction) is extremely graphic and characteristically features extensive violence, often sexual abuse, torture, or mutilation of women alive, who then return for supernatural vengeance and hurt men. One wonders if this is characteristic of boys' concerns.

L. P. Hartley, in the introduction to Cynthia Asquith's anthology, *The Third Ghost Book* (1955), remarked, "Even the most impassioned devotee of the ghost story would admit that the taste for it is slightly abnormal, a survival, perhaps, from adolescence, a disease of deficiency suffered by those whose lives and imaginations do not react satisfactorily to normal experience and require an extra thrill." And a more recent comment: "Our fiction is not merely in flight from the physical data of the actual world . . . it is, bewilderingly and embarrassingly, a gothic fiction, nonrealistic and negative, sadist and melodramatic—a literature of darkness and the grotesque in a land of light and affirmation. . . . our classic [American] literature is a literature of horror for boys." So says Leslie Fiedler in his classic study, *Love and Death in the American Novel.* Still, one suspects that the subject of who reads horror, and why, and at what age, has been muddied by the establishment of genre and category marketing, and is more complex than has been illuminated by market research and interpretation to date.

II   The Sublime Transaction

The sublime provided a theory of terror in literature and the other arts.

—Carl Woodring, *The Penguin Encyclopedia of Horror and the Supernatural*

. . . confident skepticism is required by the genre that exploits the supernatural. To feel the unease aimed at in the ghost story, one must start by being certain that there is no such thing as a ghost.

—Jacques Barzun, Introduction to
*The Penguin Encyclopedia of Horror
and the Supernatural*

Supernatural horror, in all its bizarre constructions, enables a reader to taste a selection of treats at odds with his well-being. Admittedly, this is not an indulgence likely to find universal favor. True macabrists are as rare as poets and form a secret society unto themselves, if only because their memberships elsewhere were cancelled, some of them from the moment of birth. But those who have sampled these joys marginal to stable existence, once they have gotten a good whiff of other worlds, will not be able to stay away for long. They will loiter in moonlight, eyeing the entranceways to cemeteries, waiting for some terribly propitious moment to crash the gates.

—Thomas Ligotti, "Professor Nobody's
Little Lectures on Supernatural Horror"

The transaction between reader and text that creates the horrific is complex and to a certain extent subjective. Although the horrifying event may be quite overt, a death, a ghost, a monster, it is not the event itself but the style and atmosphere surrounding it that create horror, an atmosphere that suggests a greater awe and fear, wider and deeper than the event itself. "Because these ideas find proper expression in heightened language, the practiced reader of tales in our genre comes to feel not merely the shiver of fear, but the shiver of aesthetic seizure. In a superior story, there is a sentence, a word, a thing described, which is the high point of the preparation of the resolution. Here disquiet and vision unite to strike a powerful blow," said Jacques Barzun. M. R. James said that the core of the ghost story is "those things that can hardly be put into words and that sound rather foolish if they are not properly expressed." It is useful to examine literary history and criticism to illuminate some of the sources of horror's power.

We do know, from our study of history, that there was a time in our culture when the sublime was the goal of art, the Romantic era. Poetry, drama, prose fiction, painting strove to embody it. Horror was one of its components. Carl Woodring, summarizing the subject in *The Penguin Encyclopedia of Horror and the Supernatural*, says: "As did the scholars of tragedy, [Edmund] Burke and others who analyzed the sublime asked why such awesomeness gave pleasure when it might be expected to evoke only fear or abhorrence. Immanuel Kant, in his *Critique of Judgment* (1790), explained: "Whereas the beautiful is limited, the sublime is limitless, so that the mind in the presence of the sublime, attempting to imagine what it cannot, has pain in the failure but pleasure in contemplating the immensity of the attempt." Kant noted that the sublime could be mathematical—"whereby the mind imagines a magnitude by comparison with which everything in experience is small—or it could be dynamic—whereby power or might, as in hurricanes or volcanoes, can be pleasurable rather than frightening if we are safe from the threat of destruction."

One response to this aesthetic was the rise of Gothic fiction in England and America, and in Germany, "the fantastic." Jacques Barzun gives an eloquent summary of this period in his essay, "Romanticism," in the aforementioned Penguin *Encyclopedia.* "What is not in doubt is the influence of this literature. It established a taste for the uncanny that has survived all the temporary realisms and naturalisms and is once again in high favor, not simply in the form of tales of horror and fantasy, but also as an ingredient of the 'straight' novel." He goes on to discuss at length the fantastic, the Symbolist aspect of Romanticism, tracing its crucial import in the works of major literary figures in England, France, and America. Here, if anywhere, is the genesis of horror fiction.

> If the short story of the supernatural is often considered as an "inferior" literary genre, this is to a great extent due to the works of those authors to whom preternatural was synonymous with horror of the worst kind. To many writers the supernatural was merely a pretext for describing such things as they would never have dared to mention in terms of reality. To others the short story of the supernatural was but an outlet for unpleasant neurotic tendencies, and they chose unconsciously the most hideous symbols. . . . It is indeed a difficult task to rehabilitate the pure tale of horror and even harder, perhaps, for a lover of weird fiction, for pure horror has done much to discredit it.
>
> —Peter Penzoldt,
> *The Supernatural in Fiction*

Now that we have an historical and aesthetic background for the origins of horror literature, let us return to the nature of its power. Horror comes from material on the edge of repression, according to the French critic, Julia Kristeva, material we cannot confront directly because it is so threatening to our minds and emotional balances, material to which we can gain access only through literary indirection, through metaphor and symbol. Horror conjoins the cosmic or transcendental and the deeply personal. Individual reactions to horror fiction vary widely, since in some readers' minds the material is entirely repressed and therefore the emotional response entirely inaccessible.

But as Freud remarked in his essay on the uncanny, horror shares with humor the aspect of recognition—even if an individual does not respond with the intended emotional response, he or she recognizes that that material is supposed to be humorous or horrific. Indeed, one common response to horror that does not horrify is laughter. Note again the M. R. James comment above.

The experience of seeing an audience of teenage boys at the movies laugh uproariously at a brutal and grotesque horror film is not uncommon. I have taught horror literature to young students who confess some emotional disturbance late in the course as the authentic reaction of fear and awe begins to replace the dark humor that was previously their reaction to most horror.

Boris Karloff remarked, in discussing his preferred term for the genre, "horror carries with it a connotation of revulsion which has nothing to do with clean terror." Material on the edge of repression is often dismissed as dirty, pornographic. It is not unusual to see condemnations of genre horror on cultural or moral grounds. One need only look at the recent fuss over Bret Easton Ellis' novel, *American Psycho* (1990), to see these issues in the foreground in the mainstream. Certain horror material is banned in Britain.

And I have spoken to writers, such as David Morrell, who confess to laughing aloud during the process of composition when writing a particularly horrific scene —which I interpret as an essential psychological distancing device for individuals aware of confronting dangerous material. L. P. Hartley, in the introduction to his first collection, *Night Fears* (1924) said: "To put these down on paper gives relief. . . . It is a kind of insurance against the future. When we have imagined the worst that can happen, and embodied it in a story, we feel we have stolen a march on fate, inoculated ourselves, as it were, against disaster." Peter Penzoldt, in his book, *The Supernatural in Fiction,* concurs: ". . . the weird tale is primarily a means of overcoming certain fears in the most agreeable fashion. These fears are represented by the skillful author as pure fantasy, though in fact they are only too firmly founded in some repression. . . . Thus a healthy-minded even if very imaginative person will benefit more from the reading of weird fiction than a neurotic, to whom it will only be able to give a momentary relief."

There is a fine border between the horrific and the absurdly fantastic that generates much fruitful tension in the literature, and indeed deflates the effect when handled indelicately. Those who never read horror for pleasure, but feel the need to condemn those who do, like to point to the worst examples as representative of the genre. Others laugh. But the stories that have gained reputations for quality in the literature have for most readers generated that aesthetic seizure which is the hallmark of sublime horror.

III   Category, Genre, Mode

The modern imagination has indeed been well trained by psychiatry and avant-garde novels to accept the weird and horrible. Often, these works are themselves beyond rational comprehension. But stories of the supernatural—even the subtlest

—are accessible to the common reader; they make fewer demands on the intellect than on the sensibility.

> —Jacques Barzun, Introduction to
> *The Penguin Encyclopedia of Horror
> and the Supernatural*

Genres are essentially literary institutions, or social contracts between a writer and a specific public, whose function is to specify the proper use of a particular cultural artifact.

> —Frederic Jameson, *Magical Narratives*

A category is a contract between a publisher and a distribution system.

> —Kathryn Cramer,
> unpublished dissertation

. . . one thing we know is real: horror. It is so real, in fact, that we cannot quite be sure that it couldn't exist without us. Yes, it needs our imaginations and our awareness, but it does not ask or require our consent to use them. Indeed, both at the individual and collective levels, horror operates with an eerie autonomy.

> —Thomas Ligotti,
> "Professor Nobody's Little Lectures on
> Supernatural Horror"

Sir Walter Scott, to whom some attribute the creation of the first supernatural story in English, said, "The supernatural . . . is peculiarly subject to be exhausted by coarse handling and repeated pressure. It is also of a character which is extremely difficult to sustain and of which a very small proportion may be said to be better than the whole." This observation, while true, has certainly created an enduring environment in which critics can, if they choose, judge the literature by its worst examples. The most recent announcement of the death of horror literature occurs in Walter Kendrick's *The Thrill of Fear* (1991), which demise Kendrick attributes to the genrification of the literature as exemplified by the founding of *Weird Tales:* "*Weird Tales* helped to create the notion of an entertainment cult by publishing stories that only a few readers would like, hoping they would like them fiercely. There was nothing new to cultism, but it came fresh to horror. Now initiates learned to adore a sensation, not a person or a creed, and the ephemeral embarked on its strange journey from worthlessness to great price. . . . By about 1930, scary entertainment had amassed its full inventory of effects. It had recognized its history, begun to establish a canon, and even started rebelling against the stultification canons bring. Horrid stories would continue to flourish; they would spawn a score of sub-types, including science-fiction and fantasy tales. . . ." But three lines later he ends his discussion of literature, and his chapter, by declaring that by 1940, films had taken over from literature the job of scary entertainment. Thus evolution marches on and literature is no longer the fittest. It seems to me very like saying that lyric poetry is alive and well in pop music.

That an intelligent critic could find nothing worthwhile to say about horror in literature beyond the creation of the genre is astonishing in one sense (it betrays a certain ignorance), but in other ways not surprising. Once horror became a genre (as, under the influence of Dickens in the mid-nineteenth century, had the ghost story told at Christmas), it became in the hands of many writers a commercial exercise first and foremost. One might, upon superficial examination, not perceive the serious aesthetic debates raging among many of the better writers, from those of the Lovecraft circle, to Campbell's new vision in *Unknown,* to today's discussions among Stephen King, Peter Straub, Ramsey Campbell, David Morrell, Karl Edward Wagner, and others on such topics as violence, formal innovation, appropriate style (regardless of current literary fashion), and many others. That money and popularity was a serious consideration for Poe and Dickens, as well as King and Straub, does not devalue them aesthetically. Never mind that Henry James was distraught that he was not more popular and commercial, and expressed outrage at "those damned scribbling women" who outsold him—even his so-called "potboilers."

The curious lie concealed in James' last phrase (which he used to describe "The Turn of the Screw"), and in the public protestations of many writers before and since, up to Stephen King, today, is illuminated by Julia Briggs. In her *Night Visitors,* she states her opinion, based upon wide reading and study, that the supernatural horror story "appealed to serious writers largely because it invited a concern with the profoundest issues: the relationship between life and death, the body and the soul, man and his universe and the philosophical conditions of that universe, the nature of evil. . . . it could be made to embody symbolically hopes and fears too deep and too important to be expressed more directly." She then goes on to say, "The fact that authors often disclaimed any serious intention . . . may paradoxically support this view. The revealing nature of fantastic and imaginative writing has encouraged its exponents to cover their tracks, either by self-deprecation or other forms of retraction. The assertion of the author's detachment from his work may reasonably arouse the suspicion that he is less detached than he supposes."

To further complicate the matter, the marketing of literature in the twentieth century has become a matter of categories established by publishers upon analogy with the genre magazines. Whereas a piece of genre horror implies a contract between the writer and the audience, the marketing category of horror implies that the publisher will provide to the distribution system a certain quantity of product to fill certain display slots. Such material may or may not fulfill the genre contract. If it does not, it will be packaged to invoke its similarity to genre material and will be indistinguishable to the distribution system from material that does. As we discussed above, horror itself may exist in any genre as a literary mode, and, as a mode, is in the end an enemy of categorization and genrification. It is in part the purpose of this anthology to bring together works of fiction from within the horror genre together with works ordinarily labelled otherwise in contemporary publishing, from science fiction to thriller to "literature" (which is itself today a marketing category).

I have previously discussed, in the introduction to *The Dark Descent,* my observations that horror literature occurs in three main currents: the moral allegory, which deals with manifest evil; the investigation of abnormal psychology through metaphor and symbol; the fantastic, which creates a world of radical doubt and dread. Whether one or another of those currents is dominant in an individual work does not exclude the presence or intermingling of the others. Rather than taking the myopic stance that horror means what the marketing system says it does today, I have applied my perceptions of horror to the literature of the past two centuries to find accomplished and significant works that manifest the delights of horror and which mark signposts in the development of horror. Horror literature operates with an "eerie autonomy" not only without regard to the reader, but without regard to the marketing system. Critic Gary Wolfe's observation that "horror is the only genre named for its effect on the reader" should suggest that the normal usage of genre is somewhat suspect here.

IV   Short Forms

Why an ever-widening circle of connoisseurs and innocents seek out and read with delight stories about ghosts and other horrors has been accounted for on divers grounds, most of them presupposing complex motives in our hidden selves. That is what one might expect in a age of reckless psychologizing. It is surely simpler and sounder to adduce historical facts and literary traditions. . . .

> —Jacques Barzun, Introduction to
> *The Penguin Encyclopedia of Horror
> and the Supernatural*

It is all the more astonishing to find English weird fiction the property of the drama in Elizabethan days, and later see it confined to the Gothic novel. On first reflection this development seems strange because the supernatural appears to flow more easily into the short tale in verse or prose. The human mind cannot leave the solid basis of reality for long, and he who contemplates occult phenomena must sooner or later return to logical thinking in terms of reality lest his reason be endangered. . . .

> —Peter Penzoldt,
> *The Supernatural in Fiction*

A horror that is effective for thirty pages can seldom be sustained for three hundred, and there is no danger of confusing the bare scaffolding of the ghost story with the rambling mansion of the Gothic novel.

—Julia Briggs, *Night Visitors*

Commentators on horror agree that the short story has always been the form of the horror story: "Thus if it is to be successful the tale of the supernatural must be short, and it matters little whether we accept it as an account of facts or as a fascinating work of art," says Peter Penzoldt. At the same time, most of them have observed that some of the very best fiction in the history of horror writing occurs at the novella length. Julia Briggs, for instance, after having given the usual set of observations on the dominance of the short form, states: "There are, however, a number of full-length ghost stories of great importance. Most of these, written in the last century, are short in comparison to the standard Victorian three-volume novel, though their length would be quite appropriate for a modern novel. More accurately described as long–short stories, or novellas, they include [Robert Louis Stevenson, Vernon Lee, Oscar Wilde, Arthur Machen, Henry James]. They are quite distinct from the broad-canvas full-length novel of the period not only in being shorter, but also in using what is essentially a short-story structure, introducing only a few main characters within a strictly limited series of events. The greater length and complexity is often the result of a sophistocated narrative device or viewpoint. In each of these the angle or angles from which the story is told is of crucial importance to the total effect, while the action itself remains comparatively simple."

Only in a collection of this size could one gather a

significant selection of novellas, and I have included a number of them to emphasize the importance of that length. I have excluded familiar masterpieces such as Robert Louis Stevenson's "Dr. Jekyll and Mr. Hyde," Henry James' "The Turn of the Screw," and Conrad's "The Heart of Darkness" in favor of significant works such as Daphne Du Maurier's "Don't Look Now" and H. P. Lovecraft's sequel to Poe's *Narrative of Arthur Gordon Pym,* "At the Mountains of Madness," John W. Campbell, Jr.'s "Who Goes There?" (from which the classic horror film, *The Thing,* was made), Gerald Durrell's "The Entrance," and others.

I have included several examples of horror from the science fiction movement by writers such as Robert A. Heinlein, Frederik Pohl and Philip K. Dick, Octavia Butler and George R. R. Martin, wherein horror is the dominant emotional force for the fiction, and a sampling of horror stories by women often excluded from notice in the history and development of horror, such as Gertrude Atherton, Violet Hunt, Harriet Prescott Spofford, and Mary Wilkins Freeman. Contemporary masters and classic names in horror are the backbone of the book, Peter Straub and Arthur Machen, Clive Barker and E. T. A. Hoffmann, and many others, but for most readers there will be a few literary surprises. Horror literature is a literature of fear and wonder. Here, then, the *Foundations of Fear.*

This is the second of three volumes, published in paperback by Tor Books, that together comprise the entire contents of the large hardcover book, *Foundations of Fear*. The whole work, subtitled "An Exploration of Horror," is a sequel to *The Dark Descent*, the anthology that defines the nature of horror literature for contemporary times. Readers whose interests are piqued by the general introduction and the story notes in this book would do well to go back to *The Dark Descent*, in which similar concerns are addressed.

All of that having been said, the primary purpose of this book is to entertain. The devotee of the weird, horrific, and bizarre will find a feast herein, including much unfamiliar material. The general reader will also find a number of surprises and perhaps some unexpected illumination about literary types and literary politics. This work challenges the notion that the supernatural in fiction has in modern times been supplanted by the psychological, the idea that horror is dead.

Horror is one of the dominant literary modes of our time, a vigorous and living body of literature that continues to evolve and thrill us with the mystery and wonder of the unknown. This book explores where it has been and represents some of its finest accomplishments to date. Vampires, ghosts, and witches still plague us, along with many less nameable monsters—including, at times, ourselves.

Read on, in fear and wonder.

David G. Hartwell

George R. R. Martin (b. 1948)

SANDKINGS

George R. R. Martin gained wide popularity in the science-fiction field as a young writer in the 1970s, winning both the Hugo and Nebula Awards. In the 1980s, he moved into the horror genre with two novels, *Fevre Dream* (1982), an historical vampire novel, and *Armageddon Rag* (1983), a rock 'n' roll apocalypse of the 1960s, and a short story collection, *Songs the Dead Men Sing* (1983). Since then he has pursued a career as anthologist, television scriptwriter, and editor. "Sandkings" was the title story of his last science fiction collection (1979). It won the Hugo Award as best story of the year. One can see that Martin was already moving from science fiction to horror in this piece of uncanny, fantastic nightmare. It is both a literal and a psychological monster story, a social allegory and a moral one. The layering of meaning is deep and complex, the possibilities of reading many. Isaac Asimov said of this piece, "I can't help feeling what a terrific example of the horror story 'Sandkings' is . . . it just keeps hitting you harder as you go." Martin's contribution to horror in the 1980s is significant.

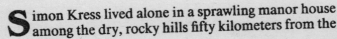 imon Kress lived alone in a sprawling manor house among the dry, rocky hills fifty kilometers from the

city. So, when he was called away unexpectedly on business, he had no neighbors he could conveniently impose on to take his pets. The carrion hawk was no problem; it roosted in the unused belfry and customarily fed itself anyway. The shambler Kress simply shooed outside and left to fend for itself; the little monster would gorge on slugs and birds and rockjocks. But the fish tank, stocked with genuine Earth piranhas, posed a difficulty. Kress finally just threw a haunch of beef into the huge tank. The piranhas could always eat each other if he were detained longer than expected. They'd done it before. It amused him.

Unfortunately, he was detained *much* longer than expected this time. When he finally returned, all the fish were dead. So was the carrion hawk. The shambler had climbed up to the belfry and eaten it. Simon Kress was vexed.

The next day he flew his skimmer to Asgard, a journey of some two hundred kilometers. Asgard was Baldur's largest city and boasted the oldest and largest starport as well. Kress liked to impress his friends with animals that were unusual, entertaining, and expensive; Asgard was the place to buy them.

This time, though, he had poor luck. Xenopets had closed its doors, t'Etherane the Petseller tried to foist another carrion hawk off on him, and Strange Waters offered nothing more exotic than piranhas, glowsharks, and spider-squids. Kress had had all those; he wanted something new.

Near dusk, he found himself walking down the Rainbow Boulevard, looking for places he had not patronized before. So close to the starport, the street was lined by importers' marts. The big corporate emporiums had impressive long windows, where rare and costly alien artifacts reposed on felt cushions against dark drapes that made the interiors of the stores a mystery. Between them were the junk shops; narrow, nasty little places whose display areas were crammed with all manner of offworld bric-a-brac. Kress tried both kinds of shop, with equal dissatisfaction.

Then he came across a store that was different.

It was quite close to the port. Kress had never been there before. The shop occupied a small, single-story building of moderate size, set between a euphoria bar and a temple-brothel of the Secret Sisterhood. Down this far, the Rainbow Boulevard grew tacky. The shop itself was unusual. Arresting.

The windows were full of mist; now a pale red, now the gray of true fog, now sparkling and golden. The mist swirled and eddied and glowed faintly from within. Kress glimpsed objects in the window—machines, pieces of art, other things he could not recognize—but he could not get a good look at any of them. The mists flowed sensuously around them, displaying a bit of first one thing and then another, then cloaking all. It was intriguing.

As he watched, the mist began to form letters. One word at a time. Kress stood and read.

WO. AND. SHADE. IMPORTERS.
ARTIFACTS. ART. LIFE-FORMS. AND. MISC.

The letters stopped. Through the fog, Kress saw something moving. That was enough for him, that and the "life-forms" in their advertisement. He swept his walking cloak over his shoulder and entered the store.

Inside, Kress felt disoriented. The interior seemed vast, much larger than he would have guessed from the relatively modest frontage. It was dimly lit, peaceful. The ceiling was a starscape, complete with spiral nebulae, very dark and realistic, very nice. The counters all shone faintly, to better display the merchandise within. The aisles were carpeted with ground fog. It came almost to his knees in places, and swirled about his feet as he walked.

"Can I help you?"

She almost seemed to have risen from the fog. Tall and gaunt and pale, she wore a practical gray jumpsuit and a strange little cap that rested well back on her head.

"Are you Wo or Shade?" Kress asked. "Or only sales help?"

"Jala Wo, ready to serve you," she replied. "Shade does not see customers. We have no sales help."

"You have quite a large establishment," Kress said. "Odd that I have never heard of you before."

"We have only just opened this shop on Baldur," the woman said. "We have franchises on a number of other worlds, however. What can I sell you? Art, perhaps? You have the look of a collector. We have some fine Nor T'alush crystal carvings."

"No," Simon Kress said. "I own all the crystal carvings I desire. I came to see about a pet."

"A life-form?"

"Yes."

"Alien?"

"Of course."

"We have a mimic in stock. From Celia's World. A clever little simian. Not only will it learn to speak, but eventually it will mimic your voice, inflections, gestures, even facial expressions."

"Cute," said Kress. "And common. I have no use for either, Wo. I want something exotic. Unusual. And not cute. I detest cute animals. At the moment I own a shambler. Imported from Cotho, at no mean expense. From time to time I feed him a litter of unwanted kittens. This is what I think of *cute*. Do I make myself understood?"

Wo smiled enigmatically. "Have you ever owned an animal that worshiped you?" she asked.

Kress grinned. "Oh, now and again. But I don't require worship, Wo. Just entertainment."

"You misunderstand me," Wo said, still wearing her strange smile. "I meant worship literally."

"What are you talking about?"

"I think I have just the thing for you," Wo said. "Follow me."

She led Kress between the radiant counters and down a long, fog-shrouded aisle beneath false starlight. They passed through a wall of mist into another section of the store, and stopped before a large plastic tank. An aquarium, thought Kress.

Wo beckoned. He stepped closer and saw that he was wrong. It was a terrarium. Within lay a miniature desert about two meters square. Pale sand bleached scarlet by wan red light. Rocks: basalt and quartz and granite. In each corner of the tank stood a castle.

Kress blinked, and peered, and corrected himself; actually only three castles stood. The fourth leaned; a crumbled, broken ruin. The other three were crude but intact, carved of stone and sand. Over their battlements and through their rounded porticos, tiny creatures climbed and scrambled. Kress pressed his face against the plastic. "Insects?" he asked.

"No," Wo replied. "A much more complex life-form. More intelligent as well. Smarter than your shambler by a considerable amount. They are called sandkings."

"Insects," Kress said, drawing back from the tank. "I don't care how complex they are." He frowned. "And kindly don't try to gull me with this talk of intelligence. These things are far too small to have anything but the most rudimentary brains."

"They share hiveminds," Wo said. "Castle minds, in this case. There are only three organisms in the tank, actually. The fourth died. You see how her castle has fallen."

Kress looked back at the tank. "Hiveminds, eh?

Interesting." He frowned again. "Still, it is only an oversized ant farm. I'd hoped for something better."

"They fight wars."

"Wars? Hmmm." Kress looked again.

"Note the colors, if you will," Wo told him. She pointed to the creatures that swarmed over the nearest castle. One was scrabbling at the tank wall. Kress studied it. It still looked like an insect to his eyes. Barely as long as his fingernail, six-limbed, with six tiny eyes set all around its body. A wicked set of mandibles clacked visibly, while two long fine antennae wove patterns in the air. Antennae, mandibles, eyes, and legs were sooty black, but the dominant color was the burnt orange of its armor plating. "It's an insect," Kress repeated.

"It is not an insect," Wo insisted calmly. "The armored exoskeleton is shed when the sandking grows larger. *If* it grows larger. In a tank this size, it won't." She took Kress by the elbow and led him around the tank to the next castle. "Look at the colors here."

He did. They were different. Here the sandkings had bright-red armor; antennae, mandibles, eyes, and legs were yellow. Kress glanced across the tank. The denizens of the third live castle were off-white, with red trim. "Hmmm," he said.

"They war, as I said," Wo told him. "They even have truces and alliances. It was an alliance that destroyed the fourth castle in this tank. The blacks were getting too numerous, so the others joined forces to destroy them."

Kress remained unconvinced. "Amusing, no doubt. But insects fight wars too."

"Insects do not worship," Wo said.

"Eh?"

Wo smiled and pointed at the castle. Kress stared. A face had been carved into the wall of the highest tower. He recognized it. It was Jala Wo's face. "How . . . ?"

"I projected a holograph of my face into the tank, kept it there for a few days. The face of god, you see? I feed them, I am always close. The sandkings have a rudimentary psionic sense. Proximity telepathy. They sense me, and worship me by using my face to decorate their buildings. All the castles have them, see?" They did.

On the castle, the face of Jala Wo was serene and peaceful, and very lifelike. Kress marveled at the workmanship. "How do they do it?"

"The foremost legs double as arms. They even have fingers of a sort: three small, flexible tendrils. And they cooperate well, both in building and in battle. Remember, all the mobiles of one color share a single mind."

"Tell me more," Kress said.

Wo smiled. "The maw lives in the castle. Maw is my name for her. A pun, if you will; the thing is mother and stomach both. Female, large as your fist, immobile. Actually, sandking is a bit of a misnomer. The mobiles are peasants and warriors, the real ruler is a queen. But that analogy is faulty as well. Considered as a whole, each castle is a single hermaphroditic creature."

"What do they eat?"

"The mobiles eat pap, predigested food obtained inside the castle. They get it from the maw after she has worked on it for several days. Their stomachs can't handle anything else, so if the maw dies, they soon die as well. The maw . . . the maw eats anything. You'll have no special expense there. Table scraps will do excellently."

"Live food?" Kress asked.

Wo shrugged. "Each maw eats mobiles from the other castles, yes."

"I am intrigued," he admitted. "If only they weren't so small."

"Yours can be larger. These sandkings are small because their tank is small. They seem to limit their growth to fit available space. If I moved these to a larger tank, they'd start growing again."

"Hmmm. My piranha tank is twice this size, and vacant. It could be cleaned out, filled with sand . . ."

"Wo and Shade would take care of the installation. It would be our pleasure."

"Of course," said Kress, "I would expect four intact castles."

"Certainly," Wo said.

They began to haggle about the price.

Three days later Jala Wo arrived at Simon Kress's estate, with dormant sandkings and a work crew to take charge of the installation. Wo's assistants were aliens unlike any Kress was familiar with; squat, broad bipeds with four arms and bulging, multifaceted eyes. Their skin was thick and leathery, and twisted into horns and spines and protrusions at odd spots upon their bodies. But they were very strong, and good workers. Wo ordered them about in a musical tongue that Kress had never heard.

In a day it was done. They moved his piranha tank to the center of his spacious living room, arranged couches on either side of it for better viewing, scrubbed it clean and filled it two-thirds of the way up with sand and rock. Then they installed a special lighting system, both to provide the dim red illumination the sandkings preferred and to project holographic images into the tank. On top they mounted a sturdy plastic cover, with a feeder mechanism built in. "This way you can feed your sandkings without removing the top of the tank," Wo explained. "You would not want to take any chances on the mobiles escaping."

The cover also included climate control devices, to condense just the right amount of moisture from the air. "You want it dry, but not too dry," Wo said.

Finally one of the four-armed workers climbed into

the tank and dug deep pits in the four corners. One of his companions handed the dormant maws over to him, removing them one-by-one from their frosted cryonic traveling cases. They were nothing to look at. Kress decided they resembled nothing so much as a mottled, half-spoiled chunk of raw meat. With a mouth.

The alien buried them, one in each corner of the tank. Then they sealed it all up and took their leave.

"The heat will bring the maws out of dormancy," Wo said. "In less than a week, mobiles will begin to hatch and burrow to the surface. Be certain to give them plenty of food. They will need all their strength until they are well established. I would estimate that you will have castles rising in about three weeks."

"And my face? When will they carve my face?"

"Turn on the hologram after about a month," she advised him. "And be patient. If you have any questions, please call. Wo and Shade are at your service." She bowed and left.

Kress wandered back to the tank and lit a joy stick. The desert was still and empty. He drummed his fingers impatiently against the plastic, and frowned.

On the fourth day, Kress thought he glimpsed motion beneath the sand, subtle subterranean stirrings.

On the fifth day, he saw his first mobile, a lone white.

On the sixth day, he counted a dozen of them, whites and reds and blacks. The oranges were tardy. He cycled through a bowl of half-decayed table scraps. The mobiles sensed it at once, rushed to it, and began to drag pieces back to their respective corners. Each color group was very organized. They did not fight. Kress was a bit disappointed, but he decided to give them time.

The oranges made their appearance on the eighth day. By then the other sandkings had begun to carry small stones and erect crude fortifications. They still did not war. At the moment they were only half the size of those he had seen at Wo and Shade's, but Kress thought they were growing rapidly.

The castles began to rise midway through the second week. Organized battalions of mobiles dragged heavy chunks of sandstone and granite back to their corners, where other mobiles were pushing sand into place with mandibles and tendrils. Kress had purchased a pair of magnifying goggles so he could watch them work, wherever they might go in the tank. He wandered around and around the tall plastic walls, observing. It was fascinating. The castles were a bit plainer than Kress would have liked, but he had an idea about that. The next day he cycled through some obsidian and flakes of colored glass along with the food. Within hours, they had been incorporated into the castle walls.

The black castle was the first completed, followed by the white and red fortresses. The oranges were last, as usual. Kress took his meals into the living room and ate seated on the couch, so he could watch. He expected the first war to break out any hour now.

He was disappointed. Days passed, the castles grew taller and more grand, and Kress seldom left the tank except to attend to his sanitary needs and answer critical business calls. But the sandkings did not war. He was getting upset.

Finally he stopped feeding them.

Two days after the table scraps had ceased to fall from their desert sky, four black mobiles surrounded an orange and dragged it back to their maw. They maimed it first, ripping off its mandibles and antennae and limbs, and carried it through the shadowed main gate of their miniature castle. It never emerged. Within an hour, more than forty orange mobiles marched across the sand and attacked the blacks' corner. They were outnumbered by the blacks that came rushing up from the depths. When the fighting was over, the attackers had been slaughtered. The dead and dying were taken down to feed the black maw.

Kress, delighted, congratulated himself on his genius.

When he put food into the tank the following day, a three-cornered battle broke out over its possession. The whites were the big winners.

After that, war followed war.

Almost a month to the day after Jala Wo had delivered the sandkings, Kress turned on the holographic projector, and his face materialized in the tank. It turned, slowly, around and around, so his gaze fell on all four castles equally. Kress thought it rather a good likeness; it had his impish grin, wide mouth, full cheeks. His blue eyes sparkled, his gray hair was carefully arrayed in a fashionable sidesweep, his eyebrows were thin and sophisticated.

Soon enough, the sandkings set to work. Kress fed them lavishly while his image beamed down at them from their sky. Temporarily, the wars stopped. All activity was directed toward worship.

His face emerged on the castle walls.

At first all four carvings looked alike to him, but as the work continued and Kress studied the reproductions, he began to detect subtle differences in technique and execution. The reds were the most creative, using tiny flakes of slate to put the gray in his hair. The white idol seemed young and mischievous to him, while the face shaped by the blacks—although virtually the same, line for line—struck him as wise and beneficent. The orange sandkings, as ever, were last and least. The wars had not gone well for them, and their castle was sad compared to the others. The image they carved was crude and cartoonish and they seemed to intend to leave it that way. When they stopped work on the face, Kress grew quite piqued with them, but there was really nothing he could do.

When all of the sandkings had finished their Kress-faces, he turned off the holograph and decided that it was time to have a party. His friends would be impressed. He could even stage a war for them, he thought. Humming happily to himself, he began to draw up a guest list.

The party was a wild success.

Kress invited thirty people; a handful of close friends who shared his amusements, a few former lovers, and a collection of business and social rivals who could not afford to ignore his summons. He knew some of them would be discomfited and even offended by his sandkings. He counted on it. Simon Kress customarily considered his parties a failure unless at least one guest walked out in a high dudgeon.

On impulse he added Jala Wo's name to his list. "Bring Shade if you like," he added when dictating her invitation.

Her acceptance surprised him just a bit. "Shade, alas, will be unable to attend. He does not go to social functions," Wo added. "As for myself, I look forward to the chance to see how your sandkings are doing."

Kress ordered them up a sumptuous meal. And when at last the conversation had died down, and most of his guests had gotten silly on wine and joy sticks, he shocked them by personally scraping their table leavings into a large bowl. "Come, all of you," he told them. "I want to introduce you to my newest pets." Carrying the bowl, he conducted them into his living room.

The sandkings lived up to his fondest expectations. He had starved them for two days in preparation, and they were in a fighting mood. While the guests ringed the tank, looking through the magnifying glasses Kress had thoughtfully provided, the sandkings waged a glorious battle over the scraps. He counted almost sixty dead mobiles when the struggle was over. The reds and whites, who had recently formed an alliance, emerged with most of the food.

"Kress, you're disgusting," Cath m'Lane told him. She had lived with him for a short time two years before, until her soppy sentimentality almost drove him mad. "I was a fool to come back here. I thought perhaps you'd changed, wanted to apologize." She had never forgiven him for the time his shambler had eaten an excessively cute puppy of which she had been fond. "Don't *ever* invite me here again, Simon." She strode out, accompanied by her current lover and a chorus of laughter.

His other guests were full of questions.

Where did the sandkings come from? they wanted to know. "From Wo and Shade, Importers," he replied, with a polite gesture toward Jala Wo, who had remained quiet and apart through most of the evening.

Why did they decorate their castles with his likeness? "Because I am the source of all good things. Surely you know that?" That brought a round of chuckles.

Will they fight again? "Of course, but not tonight. Don't worry. There will be other parties."

Jad Rakkis, who was an amateur xenologist, began talking about other social insects and the wars they fought. "These sandkings are amusing, but nothing really. You ought to read about Terran soldier ants, for instance."

"Sandkings are not insects," Jala Wo said sharply, but Jad was off and running, and no one paid her the slightest attention. Kress smiled at her and shrugged.

Malada Blane suggested a betting pool the next time they got together to watch a war, and everyone was taken with the idea. An animated discussion about rules and odds ensued. It lasted for almost an hour. Finally the guests began to take their leave.

Jala Wo was the last to depart. "So," Kress said to her

when they were alone, "it appears my sandkings are a hit."

"They are doing well," Wo said. "Already they are larger than my own."

"Yes," Kress said, "except for the oranges."

"I had noticed that," Wo replied. "They seem few in number, and their castle is shabby."

"Well, someone must lose," Kress said. "The oranges were late to emerge and get established. They have suffered for it."

"Pardon," said Wo, "but might I ask if you are feeding your sandkings sufficiently?"

Kress shrugged. "They diet from time to time. It makes them fiercer."

She frowned. "There is no need to starve them. Let them war in their own time, for their own reasons. It is their nature, and you will witness conflicts that are delightfully subtle and complex. The constant war brought on by hunger is artless and degrading."

Simon Kress repaid Wo's frown with interest. "You are in my house, Wo, and here I am the judge of what is degrading. I fed the sandkings as you advised, and they did not fight."

"You must have patience."

"No," Kress said. "I am their master and their god, after all. Why should I wait on their impulses? They did not war often enough to suit me. I corrected the situation."

"I see," said Wo. "I will discuss the matter with Shade."

"It is none of your concern, or his," Kress snapped.

"I must bid you good night, then," Wo said with resignation. But as she slipped into her coat to depart, she fixed him with a final disapproving stare. "Look to your faces, Simon Kress," she warned him. "Look to your faces."

Puzzled, he wandered back to the tank and stared at

the castles after she had taken her departure. His faces were still there, as ever. Except— He snatched up his magnifying goggles and slipped them on. Even then it was hard to make out. But it seemed to him that the expression on the face of his images had changed slightly, that his smile was somehow twisted so that it seemed a touch malicious. But it was a very subtle change, if it was a change at all. Kress finally put it down to his suggestibility, and resolved not to invite Jala Wo to any more of his gatherings.

Over the next few months, Kress and about a dozen of his favorites got together weekly for what he liked to call his "war games." Now that his initial fascination with the sandkings was past, Kress spent less time around his tank and more on his business affairs and his social life, but he still enjoyed having a few friends over for a war or two. He kept the combatants sharp on a constant edge of hunger. It had severe effects on the orange sandkings, who dwindled visibly until Kress began to wonder if their maw was dead. But the others did well enough.

Sometimes at night, when he could not sleep, Kress would take a bottle of wine into the darkened living room, where the red gloom of his miniature desert was the only light. He would drink and watch for hours, alone. There was usually a fight going on somewhere, and when there was not he could easily start one by dropping in some small morsel of food.

They took to betting on the weekly battles, as Malada Blane had suggested. Kress won a good amount by betting on the whites, who had become the most powerful and numerous colony in the tank, with the grandest castle. One week he slid the corner of the tank top aside, and dropped the food close to the white castle instead of on the central battleground as usual, so the others had to attack the whites in their stronghold to get any food at all. They tried. The whites were brilliant in defense. Kress won a hundred standards from Jad Rakkis.

Rakkis, in fact, lost heavily on the sandkings almost every week. He pretended to a vast knowledge of them and their ways, claiming that he had studied them after the first party, but he had no luck when it came to placing his bets. Kress suspected that Jad's claims were empty boasting. He had tried to study the sandkings a bit himself, in a moment of idle curiosity, tying in to the library to find out what world his pets were native to. But there was no listing for them. He wanted to get in touch with Wo and ask her about it, but he had other concerns, and the matter kept slipping his mind.

Finally, after a month in which his losses totaled more than a thousand standards, Jad Rakkis arrived at the war games carrying a small plastic case under his arm. Inside was a spiderlike thing covered with fine golden hair.

"A sand spider," Rakkis announced. "From Cathaday. I got it this afternoon from t'Etherane the Petseller. Usually they remove the poison sacs, but this one is intact. Are you game, Simon? I want my money back. I'll bet a thousand standards, sand spider against sandkings."

Kress studied the spider in its plastic prison. His sandkings had grown—they were twice as large as Wo's, as she'd predicted—but they were still dwarfed by this thing. It was venomed, and they were not. Still, there were an awful lot of them. Besides, the endless sandking wars had begun to grow tiresome lately. The novelty of the match intrigued him. "Done," Kress said. "Jad, you are a fool. The sandkings will just keep coming until this ugly creature of yours is dead."

"You are the fool, Simon," Rakkis replied, smiling. "The Cathadayn sand spider customarily feeds on burrowers that hide in nooks and crevices and—well, watch—it will go straight into those castles, and eat the maws."

Kress scowled amid general laughter. He hadn't counted on that. "Get on with it," he said irritably. He went to freshen his drink.

The spider was too large to cycle conveniently through the food chamber. Two of the others helped Rakkis slide the tank top slightly to one side, and Malada Blane handed him up his case. He shook the spider out. It landed lightly on a miniature dune in front of the red castle, and stood confused for a moment, mouth working, legs twitching menacingly.

"Come on," Rakkis urged. They all gathered round the tank. Simon Kress found his magnifiers and slipped them on. If he was going to lose a thousand standards, at least he wanted a good view of the action.

The sandkings had seen the invader. All over the castle, activity had ceased. The small scarlet mobiles were frozen, watching.

The spider began to move toward the dark promise of the gate. On the tower above, Simon Kress's countenance stared down impassively.

At once there was a flurry of activity. The nearest red mobiles formed themselves into two wedges and streamed over the sand toward the spider. More warriors erupted from inside the castle and assembled in a triple line to guard the approach to the underground chamber where the maw lived. Scouts came scuttling over the dunes, recalled to fight.

Battle was joined.

The attacking sandkings washed over the spider. Mandibles snapped shut on legs and abdomen, and clung. Reds raced up the golden legs to the invader's back. They bit and tore. One of them found an eye, and ripped it loose with tiny yellow tendrils. Kress smiled and pointed.

But they were *small,* and they had no venom, and the

spider did not stop. Its legs flicked sandkings off to either side. Its dripping jaws found others, and left them broken and stiffening. Already a dozen of the reds lay dying. The sand spider came on and on. It strode straight through the triple line of guardians before the castle. The lines closed around it, covered it, waging desperate battle. A team of sandkings had bitten off one of the spider's legs, Kress saw. Defenders leapt from atop the towers to land on the twitching, heaving mass.

Lost beneath the sandkings, the spider somehow lurched down into the darkness and vanished.

Jad Rakkis let out a long breath. He looked pale. "Wonderful," someone else said. Malada Blane chuckled deep in her throat.

"Look," said Idi Noreddian, tugging Kress by the arm.

They had been so intent on the struggle in the corner that none of them had noticed the activity elsewhere in the tank. But now the castle was still, the sands empty save for dead red mobiles, and now they saw.

Three armies were drawn up before the red castle. They stood quite still, in perfect array, rank after rank of sandkings, orange and white and black. Waiting to see what emerged from the depths.

Simon Kress smiled. "A *cordon sanitaire*," he said. "And glance at the other castles, if you will, Jad."

Rakkis did, and swore. Teams of mobiles were sealing up the gates with sand and stone. If the spider somehow survived this encounter, it would find no easy entrance at the other castles. "I should have brought four spiders," Jad Rakkis said. "Still, I've won. My spider is down there right now, eating your damned maw."

Kress did not reply. He waited. There was motion in the shadows.

All at once, red mobiles began pouring out of the gate. They took their positions on the castle, and began repairing the damage the spider had wrought. The other armies dissolved and began to retreat to their respective corners.

"Jad," said Simon Kress, "I think you are a bit confused about who is eating who."

The following week Rakkis brought four slim silver snakes. The sandkings dispatched them without much trouble.

Next he tried a large black bird. It ate more than thirty white mobiles, and its thrashing and blundering virtually destroyed that castle, but ultimately its wings grew tired, and the sandkings attacked in force wherever it landed.

After that it was a case of insects, armored beetles not too unlike the sandkings themselves. But stupid, stupid. An allied force of oranges and blacks broke their formation, divided them, and butchered them.

Rakkis began giving Kress promissory notes.

It was around that time that Kress met Cath m'Lane again, one evening when he was dining in Asgard at his favorite restaurant. He stopped at her table briefly and told her about the war games, inviting her to join them. She flushed, then regained control of herself and grew icy. "Someone has to put a stop to you, Simon. I guess it's going to be me," she said. Kress shrugged and enjoyed a lovely meal and thought no more about her threat.

Until a week later, when a small, stout woman arrived at his door and showed him a police wristband. "We've had complaints," she said. "Do you keep a tank full of dangerous insects, Kress?"

"Not insects," he said, furious. "Come, I'll show you."

When she had seen the sandkings, she shook her head. "This will never do. What do you know about these creatures, anyway? Do you know what world they're from? Have they been cleared by the ecological board? Do you have a license for these things? We have a report that they're carnivores, possibly dangerous. We also have a report that they are semisentient. Where did you get these creatures, anyway?"

"From Wo and Shade," Kress replied.

"Never heard of them," the woman said. "Probably smuggled them in, knowing our ecologists would never approve them. No, Kress, this won't do. I'm going to confiscate this tank and have it destroyed. And you're going to have to expect a few fines as well."

Kress offered her a hundred standards to forget all about him and his sandkings.

She tsked. "Now I'll have to add attempted bribery to the charges against you."

Not until he raised the figure to two thousand standards was she willing to be persuaded. "It's not going to be easy, you know," she said. "There are forms to be altered, records to be wiped. And getting a forged license from the ecologists will be time-consuming. Not to mention dealing with the complainant. What if she calls again?"

"Leave her to me," Kress said. "Leave her to me."

He thought about it for a while. That night he made some calls.

First he got t'Etherane the Petseller. "I want to buy a dog," he said. "A puppy."

The round-faced merchant gawked at him. "A puppy? That is not like you, Simon. Why don't you come in? I have a lovely choice."

"I want a very specific *kind* of puppy," Kress said. "Take notes. I'll describe to you what it must look like."

Afterward he punched for Idi Noreddian. "Idi," he said, "I want you out here tonight with your holo equipment. I have a notion to record a sandking battle. A present for one of my friends."

* * *

The night after they made the recording, Simon Kress stayed up late. He absorbed a controversial new drama in his sensorium, fixed himself a small snack, smoked a joy stick or two, and broke out a bottle of wine. Feeling very happy with himself, he wandered into the living room, glass in hand.

The lights were out. The red glow of the terrarium made the shadows flushed and feverish. He walked over to look at his domain, curious as to how the blacks were doing in the repairs on their castle. The puppy had left it in ruins.

The restoration went well. But as Kress inspected the work through his magnifiers, he chanced to glance closely at the face. It startled him.

He drew back, blinked, took a healthy gulp of wine, and looked again.

The face on the walls was still his. But it was all wrong, all *twisted*. His cheeks were bloated and piggish, his smile was a crooked leer. He looked impossibly malevolent.

Uneasy, he moved around the tank to inspect the other castles. They were each a bit different, but ultimately all the same.

The oranges had left out most of the fine detail, but the result still seemed monstrous, crude: a brutal mouth and mindless eyes.

The reds gave him a satanic, twitching kind of smile. His mouth did odd, unlovely things at its corners.

The whites, his favorites, had carved a cruel idiot god.

Simon Kress flung his wine across the room in rage. "You *dare*," he said under his breath. "Now you won't eat for a week, you damned . . ." His voice was shrill. "I'll teach you." He had an idea. He strode out of the room, returned a moment later with an antique iron throwing-sword in his hand. It was a meter long, and the point was still sharp. Kress smiled, climbed up and moved the tank cover aside just enough to give him working room, opening one corner of the desert. He leaned down, and jabbed the sword at the white castle below him. He waved it back and forth, smashing towers and ramparts and walls. Sand and stone collapsed, burying the scrambling mobiles. A flick of his wrist obliterated the features of the insolent, insulting caricature the sandkings had made of his face. Then he poised the point of the sword above the dark mouth that opened down into the maw's chamber, and thrust with all his strength. He heard a soft, squishing sound, and met resistance. All of the mobiles trembled and collapsed. Satisfied, Kress pulled back.

He watched for a moment, wondering whether he'd killed the maw. The point of the throwing-sword was wet and slimy. But finally the white sandkings began to move again. Feebly, slowly, but they moved.

He was preparing to slide the cover back in place and move on to a second castle when he felt something crawling on his hand.

He screamed and dropped the sword, and brushed the sandking from his flesh. It fell to the carpet, and he ground it beneath his heel, crushing it thoroughly long after it was dead. It had crunched when he stepped on it. After that, trembling, he hurried to seal the tank up again, and rushed off to shower and inspect himself carefully. He boiled his clothing.

Later, after several fresh glasses of wine, he returned to the living room. He was a bit ashamed of the way the sandking had terrified him. But he was not about to open the tank again. From now on, the cover stayed sealed permanently. Still, he had to punish the others.

Kress decided to lubricate his mental processes with another glass of wine. As he finished it, an inspiration came to him. He went to the tank smiling, and made a few adjustments to the humidity controls.

By the time he fell asleep on the couch, his wine glass

still in his hand, the sand castles were melting in the rain.

Kress woke to angry pounding on his door.

He sat up, groggy, his head throbbing. Wine hangovers were always the worst, he thought. He lurched to the entry chamber.

Cath m'Lane was outside. "You monster," she said, her face swollen and puffy and streaked by tears. "I cried all night, damn you. But no more, Simon, no more."

"Easy," he said, holding his head. "I've got a hangover."

She swore and shoved him aside and pushed her way into his house. The shambler came peering round a corner to see what the noise was. She spat at it and stalked into the living room, Kress trailing ineffectually after her. "Hold on," he said, "where do you . . . you can't . . ." He stopped, suddenly horror-struck. She was carrying a heavy sledgehammer in her left hand. "No," he said.

She went directly to the sandking tank. "You like the little charmers so much, Simon? Then you can live with them."

"Cath!" he shrieked.

Gripping the hammer with both hands, she swung as hard as she could against the side of the tank. The sound of the impact set his head to screaming, and Kress made a low blubbering sound of despair. But the plastic held.

She swung again. This time there was a *crack,* and a network of thin lines sprang into being.

Kress threw himself at her as she drew back her hammer for a third swing. They went down flailing, and rolled. She lost her grip on the hammer and tried to throttle him, but Kress wrenched free and bit her on the arm, drawing blood. They both staggered to their feet, panting.

"You should see yourself, Simon," she said grimly. "Blood dripping from your mouth. You look like one of your pets. How do you like the taste?"

"Get out," he said. He saw the throwing-sword where it had fallen the night before, and snatched it up. "Get out," he repeated, waving the sword for emphasis. "Don't go near that tank again."

She laughed at him. "You wouldn't dare," she said. She bent to pick up her hammer.

Kress shrieked at her, and lunged. Before he quite knew what was happening, the iron blade had gone clear through her abdomen. Cath m'Lane looked at him wonderingly, and down at the sword. Kress fell back whimpering. "I didn't mean . . . I only wanted . . ."

She was transfixed, bleeding, dead, but somehow she did not fall. "You monster," she managed to say, though her mouth was full of blood. And she whirled, impossibly, the sword in her, and swung with her last strength at the tank. The tortured wall shattered, and Cath m'Lane was buried beneath an avalanche of plastic and sand and mud.

Kress made small hysterical noises and scrambled up on the couch.

Sandkings were emerging from the muck on his living room floor. They were crawling across Cath's body. A few of them ventured tentatively out across the carpet. More followed.

He watched as a column took shape, a living, writhing square of sandkings, bearing something, something slimy and featureless, a piece of raw meat big as a man's head. They began to carry it away from the tank. It pulsed.

That was when Kress broke and ran.

* * *

It was late afternoon before he found the courage to return.

He had run to his skimmer and flown to the nearest city, some fifty kilometers away, almost sick with fear. But once safely away, he had found a small restaurant, put down several mugs of coffee and two antihangover tabs, eaten a full breakfast, and gradually regained his composure.

It had been a dreadful morning, but dwelling on that would solve nothing. He ordered more coffee and considered his situation with icy rationality.

Cath m'Lane was dead at his hand. Could he report it, plead that it had been an accident? Unlikely. He had run her through, after all, and he had already told that policer to leave her to him. He would have to get rid of the evidence, and hope that she had not told anyone where she was going this morning. That was probable. She could only have gotten his gift late last night. She said that she had cried all night, and she had been alone when she arrived. Very well: he had one body and one skimmer to dispose of.

That left the sandkings. They might prove more of a difficulty. No doubt they had all escaped by now. The thought of them around his house, in his bed and his clothes, infesting his food—it made his flesh crawl. He shuddered and overcame his revulsion. It really shouldn't be too hard to kill them, he reminded himself. He didn't have to account for every mobile. Just the four maws, that was all. He could do that. They were large, as he'd seen. He would find them and kill them.

Simon Kress went shopping before he flew back to his home. He bought a set of skinthins that would cover him from head to foot, several bags of poison pellets for rockjock control, and a spray canister of illegally strong pesticide. He also bought a magnalock towing device.

When he landed, he went about things methodically.

First he hooked Cath's skimmer to his own with the magnalock. Searching it, he had his first piece of luck. The crystal chip with Idi Noreddian's holo of the sandking fight was on the front seat. He had worried about that.

When the skimmers were ready, he slipped into his skinthins and went inside for Cath's body.

It wasn't there.

He poked through the fast-drying sand carefully, but there was no doubt of it; the body was gone. Could she have dragged herself away? Unlikely, but Kress searched. A cursory inspection of his house turned up neither the body nor any sign of the sandkings. He did not have time for a more thorough investigation, not with the incriminating skimmer outside his front door. He resolved to try later.

Some seventy kilometers north of Kress's estate was a range of active volcanoes. He flew there, Cath's skimmer in tow. Above the glowering cone of the largest, he released the magnalock and watched it vanish in the lava below.

It was dusk when he returned to his house. That gave him pause. Briefly he considered flying back to the city and spending the night there. He put the thought aside. There was work to do. He wasn't safe yet.

He scattered the poison pellets around the exterior of his house. No one would find that suspicious. He'd always had a rockjock problem. When that task was completed, he primed the canister of pesticide and ventured back inside.

Kress went through the house room by room, turning on lights everywhere he went until he was surrounded by a blaze of artificial illumination. He paused to clean up in the living room, shoveling sand and plastic fragments back into the broken tank. The sandkings were all gone, as he'd feared. The castles were shrunken and distorted, slagged by the watery bombardment

Kress had visited upon them, and what little remained was crumbling as it dried.

He frowned and searched on, canister of pest spray strapped across his shoulders.

Down in his deepest wine cellar, he came upon Cath m'Lane's corpse.

It sprawled at the foot of a steep flight of stairs, the limbs twisted as if by a fall. White mobiles were swarming all over it, and as Kress watched, the body moved jerkily across the hard-packed dirt floor.

He laughed, and twisted the illumination up to maximum. In the far corner, a squat little earthen castle and a dark hole were visible between two wine racks. Kress could make out a rough outline of his face on the cellar wall.

The body shifted once again, moving a few centimeters toward the castle. Kress had a sudden vision of the white maw waiting hungrily. It might be able to get Cath's foot in its mouth, but no more. It was too absurd. He laughed again, and started down into the cellar, finger poised on the trigger of the hose that snaked down his right arm. The sandkings—hundreds of them moving as one—deserted the body and formed up battle lines, a field of white between him and their maw.

Suddenly Kress had another inspiration. He smiled and lowered his firing hand. "Cath was always hard to swallow," he said, delighted at his wit. "Especially for one your size. Here, let me give you some help. What are gods for, after all?"

He retreated upstairs, returning shortly with a cleaver. The sandkings, patient, waited and watched while Kress chopped Cath m'Lane into small, easily digestible pieces.

Simon Kress slept in his skinthins that night, the pesticide close at hand, but he did not need it. The whites, sated, remained in the cellar, and he saw no sign of the others.

In the morning he finished cleanup in the living room. After he was through, no trace of the struggle remained except for the broken tank.

He ate a light lunch, and resumed his hunt for the missing sandkings. In full daylight, it was not too difficult. The blacks had located in his rock garden, and built a castle heavy with obsidian and quartz. The reds he found at the bottom of his long-unused swimming pool, which had partially filled with wind-blown sand over the years. He saw mobiles of both colors ranging about his grounds, many of them carrying poison pellets back to their maws. Kress decided his pesticide was unnecessary. No use risking a fight when he could just let the poison do its work. Both maws should be dead by evening.

That left only the burnt-orange sandkings unaccounted for. Kress circled his estate several times, in ever-widening spirals, but found no trace of them. When he began to sweat in his skinthins—it was a hot, dry day—he decided it was not important. If they were out here, they were probably eating the poison pellets along with the reds and blacks.

He crunched several sandkings underfoot, with a certain degree of satisfaction, as he walked back to the house. Inside he removed his skinthins, settled down to a delicious meal, and finally began to relax. Everything was under control. Two of the maws would soon be defunct, the third was safely located where he could dispose of it after it had served his purposes, and he had no doubt that he would find the fourth. As for Cath, all trace of her visit had been obliterated.

His reverie was interrupted when his viewscreen began to blink at him. It was Jad Rakkis, calling to brag about some cannibal worms he was bringing to the war games tonight.

Kress had forgotten about that, but he recovered quickly. "Oh, Jad, my pardons. I neglected to tell you. I grew bored with all that, and got rid of the sandkings. Ugly little things. Sorry, but there'll be no party tonight."

Rakkis was indignant. "But what will I do with my worms?"

"Put them in a basket of fruit and send them to a loved one," Kress said, signing off. Quickly he began calling the others. He did not need anyone arriving at his doorstep now, with the sandkings alive and about the estate.

As he was calling Idi Noreddian, Kress became aware of an annoying oversight. The screen began to clear, indicating that someone had answered at the other end. Kress flicked off.

Idi arrived on schedule an hour later. She was surprised to find the party canceled, but perfectly happy to share an evening alone with Kress. He delighted her with his story of Cath's reaction to the holo they had made together. While telling it, he managed to ascertain that she had not mentioned the prank to anyone. He nodded, satisfied, and refilled their wine glasses. Only a trickle was left. "I'll have to get a fresh bottle," he said. "Come with me to my wine cellar, and help me pick out a good vintage. You've always had a better palate than I."

She came along willingly enough, but balked at the top of the stairs when Kress opened the door and gestured for her to precede him. "Where are the lights?" she said. "And that smell—what's that peculiar smell, Simon?"

When he shoved her, she looked briefly startled. She screamed as she tumbled down the stairs. Kress closed the door and began to nail it shut with the boards and air-hammer he had left for that purpose. As he was finishing, he heard Idi groan. "I'm hurt," she called.

"Simon, what is this?" Suddenly she squealed, and shortly after that the screaming started.

It did not cease for hours. Kress went to his sensorium and dialed up a saucy comedy to blot it out of his mind.

When he was sure she was dead, Kress flew her skimmer north to his volcanoes and discarded it. The magnalock was proving a good investment.

Odd scrabbling noises were coming from beyond the wine cellar door the next morning when Kress went down to check it out. He listened for several uneasy moments, wondering if Idi Noreddian could possibly have survived and be scratching to get out. It seemed unlikely; it had to be the sandkings. Kress did not like the implications of that. He decided that he would keep the door sealed, at least for the moment, and went outside with a shovel to bury the red and black maws in their own castles.

He found them very much alive.

The black castle was glittering with volcanic glass, and sandkings were all over it, repairing and improving. The highest tower was up to his waist, and on it was a hideous caricature of his face. When he approached, the blacks halted in their labors, and formed up into two threatening phalanxes. Kress glanced behind him and saw others closing off his escape. Startled, he dropped the shovel and sprinted out of the trap, crushing several mobiles beneath his boots.

The red castle was creeping up the walls of the swimming pool. The maw was safely settled in a pit, surrounded by sand and concrete and battlements. The reds crept all over the bottom of the pool. Kress watched them carry a rockjock and a large lizard into the castle. He stepped back from the poolside, horrified, and felt something crunch. Looking down, he saw three mobiles climbing up his leg. He brushed them off and stamped them to death, but others were approaching quickly. They were larger than he remembered. Some were almost as big as his thumb.

He ran. By the time he reached the safety of the house, his heart was racing and he was short of breath. The door closed behind him, and Kress hurried to lock it. His house was supposed to be pest-proof. He'd be safe in here.

A stiff drink steadied his nerve. So poison doesn't faze them, he thought. He should have known. Wo had warned him that the maw could eat anything. He would have to use the pesticide. Kress took another drink for good measure, donned his skinthins, and strapped the canister to his back. He unlocked the door.

Outside, the sandkings were waiting.

Two armies confronted him, allied against the common threat. More than he could have guessed. The damned maws must be breeding like rockjocks. They were everywhere, a creeping sea of them.

Kress brought up the hose and flicked the trigger. A gray mist washed over the nearest rank of sandkings. He moved his hand side to side.

Where the mist fell, the sandkings twitched violently and died in sudden spasms. Kress smiled. They were no match for him. He sprayed in a wide arc before him and stepped forward confidently over a litter of black and red bodies. The armies fell back. Kress advanced, intent on cutting through them to their maws.

All at once the retreat stopped. A thousand sandkings surged toward him.

Kress had been expecting the counterattack. He stood his ground, sweeping his misty sword before him in great looping strokes. They came at him and died. A few got through; he could not spray everywhere at once. He felt them climbing up his legs, sensed their mandibles biting futilely at the reinforced plastic of his skinthins. He ignored them, and kept spraying.

Then he began to feel soft impacts on his head and shoulders.

Kress trembled and spun and looked up above him. The front of his house was alive with sandkings. Blacks and reds, hundreds of them. They were launching themselves into the air, raining down on him. They fell all around him. One landed on his faceplate, its mandibles scraping at his eyes for a terrible second before he plucked it away.

He swung up his hose and sprayed the air, sprayed the house, sprayed until the airborne sandkings were all dead or dying. The mist settled back on him, making him cough. He coughed, and kept spraying. Only when the front of the house was clean did Kress turn his attention back to the ground.

They were all around him, on him, dozens of them scurrying over his body, hundreds of others hurrying to join them. He turned the mist on them. The hose went dead. Kress heard a loud *hiss* and the deadly fog rose in a great cloud from between his shoulders, cloaking him, choking him, making his eyes burn and blur. He felt for the hose, and his hand came away covered with dying sandkings. The hose was severed; they'd eaten it through. He was surrounded by a shroud of pesticide, blinded. He stumbled and screamed, and began to run back to the house, pulling sandkings from his body as he went.

Inside, he sealed the door and collapsed on the carpet, rolling back and forth until he was sure he had crushed them all. The canister was empty by then, hissing feebly. Kress stripped off his skinthins and showered. The hot spray scalded him and left his skin reddened and sensitive, but it made his flesh stop crawling.

He dressed in his heaviest clothing, thick workpants and leathers, after shaking them out nervously. "Damn," he kept muttering, "damn." His throat was dry. After searching the entry hall thoroughly to make certain it was clean, he allowed himself to sit and pour a drink. "Damn," he repeated. His hand shook as he poured, slopping liquor on the carpet.

The alcohol settled him, but it did not wash away the fear. He had a second drink, and went to the window furtively. Sandkings were moving across the thick plastic pane. He shuddered and retreated to his communications console. He had to get help, he thought wildly. He would punch through a call to the authorities, and policers would come out with flamethrowers and . . .

Simon Kress stopped in mid-call, and groaned. He couldn't call in the police. He would have to tell them about the whites in his cellar, and they'd find the bodies there. Perhaps the maw might have finished Cath m'Lane by now, but certainly not Idi Noreddian. He hadn't even cut her up. Besides, there would be bones. No, the police could be called in only as a last resort.

He sat at the console, frowning. His communications equipment filled a whole wall; from here he could reach anyone on Baldur. He had plenty of money, and his cunning; he had always prided himself on his cunning. He would handle this somehow.

Briefly he considered calling Wo, but he soon dismissed the idea. Wo knew too much, and she would ask questions, and he did not trust her. No, he needed someone who would do as he asked *without* questions.

His frown faded, and slowly turned into a smile. Simon Kress had contacts. He put through a call to a number he had not used in a long time.

A woman's face took shape on his viewscreen: white-haired, bland of expression, with a long hook nose. Her voice was brisk and efficient. "Simon," she said. "How is business?"

"Business is fine, Lissandra," Kress replied. "I have a job for you."

"A removal? My price has gone up since last time, Simon. It has been ten years, after all."

"You will be well paid," Kress said. "You know I'm generous. I want you for a bit of pest control."

She smiled a thin smile. "No need to use euphemisms, Simon. The call is shielded."

"No, I'm serious. I have a pest problem. Dangerous pests. Take care of them for me. No questions. Understood?"

"Understood."

"Good. You'll need . . . oh, three or four operatives. Wear heat-resistant skinthins, and equip them with flamethrowers, or lasers, something on that order. Come out to my place. You'll see the problem. Bugs, lots and lots of them. In my rock garden and the old swimming pool you'll find castles. Destroy them, kill everything inside them. Then knock on the door, and I'll show you what else needs to be done. Can you get out here quickly?"

Her face was impassive. "We'll leave within the hour."

Lissandra was true to her word. She arrived in a lean black skimmer with three operatives. Kress watched them from the safety of a second-story window. They were all faceless in dark plastic skinthins. Two of them wore portable flamethrowers, a third carried lasercannon and explosives. Lissandra carried nothing; Kress recognized her by the way she gave orders.

Their skimmer passed low overhead first, checking out the situation. The sandkings went mad. Scarlet and ebony mobiles ran everywhere, frenetic. Kress could see the castle in the rock garden from his vantage point. It stood tall as a man. Its ramparts were crawling with black defenders, and a steady stream of mobiles flowed down into its depths.

Lissandra's skimmer came down next to Kress's and the operatives vaulted out and unlimbered their weapons. They looked inhuman, deadly.

The black army drew up between them and the castle. The reds— Kress suddenly realized that he could not see the reds. He blinked. Where had they gone?

Lissandra pointed and shouted, and her two flamethrowers spread out and opened up on the black sandkings. Their weapons coughed dully and began to roar, long tongues of blue-and-scarlet fire licking out before them. Sandkings crisped and blackened and died. The operatives began to play the fire back and forth in an efficient, interlocking pattern. They advanced with careful, measured steps.

The black army burned and disintegrated, the mobiles fleeing in a thousand different directions, some back toward the castle, others toward the enemy. None reached the operatives with the flamethrowers. Lissandra's people were very professional.

Then one of them stumbled.

Or seemed to stumble. Kress looked again, and saw that the ground had given way beneath the man. Tunnels, he thought with a tremor of fear; tunnels, pits, traps. The flamer was sunk in sand up to his waist, and suddenly the ground around him seemed to erupt, and he was covered with scarlet sandkings. He dropped the flamethrower and began to claw wildly at his own body. His screams were horrible to hear.

His companion hesitated, then swung and fired. A blast of flame swallowed human and sandkings both. The screaming stopped abruptly. Satisfied, the second flamer turned back to the castle and took another step forward, and recoiled as his foot broke through the ground and vanished up to the ankle. He tried to pull it back and retreat, and the sand all around him gave way. He lost his balance and stumbled, flailing, and the sandkings were everywhere, a boiling mass of them, covering him as he writhed and rolled. His flamethrower was useless and forgotten.

Kress pounded wildly on the window, shouting for attention. "The castle! Get the castle!"

Lissandra, standing back by her skimmer, heard and gestured. Her third operative sighted with the laser-cannon and fired. The beam throbbed across the grounds and sliced off the top of the castle. He brought it down sharply, hacking at the sand and stone parapets. Towers fell. Kress's face disintegrated. The laser bit into the ground, searching round and about. The castle crumbled; now it was only a heap of sand. But the black mobiles continued to move. The maw was buried too deeply; they hadn't touched her.

Lissandra gave another order. Her operative discarded the laser, primed an explosive, and darted forward. He leapt over the smoking corpse of the first flamer, landed on solid ground within Kress's rock garden, and heaved. The explosive ball landed square atop the ruins of the black castle. White-hot light seared Kress's eyes, and there was a tremendous gout of sand and rock and mobiles. For a moment dust obscured everything. It was raining sandkings and pieces of sandkings.

Kress saw that the black mobiles were dead and unmoving.

"The pool," he shouted down through the window. "Get the castle in the pool."

Lissandra understood quickly; the ground was littered with motionless blacks, but the reds were pulling back hurriedly and reforming. Her operative stood uncertain, then reached down and pulled out another explosive ball. He took one step forward, but Lissandra called him and he sprinted back in her direction.

It was all so simple then. He reached the skimmer, and Lissandra took him aloft. Kress rushed to another window in another room to watch. They came swooping in just over the pool, and the operative pitched his bombs down at the red castle from the safety of the skimmer. After the fourth run, the castle was unrecognizable, and the sandkings stopped moving.

Lissandra was thorough. She had him bomb each castle several additional times. Then he used the lasercannon, crisscrossing methodically until it was certain that nothing living could remain intact beneath those small patches of ground.

Finally they came knocking at his door. Kress was grinning manically when he let them in. "Lovely," he said, "lovely."

Lissandra pulled off the mask of her skinthins. "This will cost you, Simon. Two operatives gone, not to mention the danger to my own life."

"Of course," Kress blurted. "You'll be well paid, Lissandra. Whatever you ask, just so you finish the job."

"What remains to be done?"

"You have to clean out my wine cellar," Kress said. "There's another castle down there. And you'll have to do it without explosives. I don't want my house coming down around me."

Lissandra motioned to her operative. "Go outside and get Rajk's flamethrower. It should be intact."

He returned armed, ready, silent. Kress led them down to the wine cellar.

The heavy door was still nailed shut, as he had left it. But it bulged outward slightly, as if warped by some tremendous pressure. That made Kress uneasy, as did the silence that held reign about them. He stood well away from the door as Lissandra's operative removed his nails and planks. "Is that safe in here?" he found himself muttering, pointing at the flamethrower. "I don't want a fire, either, you know."

"I have the laser," Lissandra said. "We'll use that for the kill. The flamethrower probably won't be needed. But I want it here just in case. There are worse things than fire, Simon."

He nodded.

The last plank came free of the cellar door. There was still no sound from below. Lissandra snapped an order, and her underling fell back, took up a position behind her, and leveled the flamethrower square at the door. She slipped her mask back on, hefted the laser, stepped forward, and pulled open the door.

No motion. No sound. It was dark down there.

"Is there a light?" Lissandra asked.

"Just inside the door," Kress said. "On the right-hand side. Mind the stairs, they're quite steep."

She stepped into the door, shifted the laser to her left hand, and reached up with her right, fumbling inside for the light panel. Nothing happened. "I feel it," Lissandra said, "but it doesn't seem to . . ."

Then she was screaming, and she stumbled backward. A great white sandking had clamped itself around her wrist. Blood welled through her skinthins where its mandibles had sunk in. It was fully as large as her hand.

Lissandra did a horrible little jig across the room and began to smash her hand against the nearest wall. Again and again and again. It landed with a heavy, meaty thud. Finally the sandking fell away. She whimpered and fell to her knees. "I think my fingers are broken," she said softly. The blood was still flowing freely. She had dropped the laser near the cellar door.

"I'm not going down there," her operative announced in clear firm tones.

Lissandra looked up at him. "No," she said. "Stand

in the door and flame it all. Cinder it. Do you understand?"

He nodded.

Simon Kress moaned. "My *house*," he said. His stomach churned. The white sandking had been so *large*. How many more were down there? "Don't," he continued. "Leave it alone. I've changed my mind. Leave it alone."

Lissandra misunderstood. She held out her hand. It was covered with blood and greenish-black ichor. "Your little friend bit clean through my glove, and you saw what it took to get it off. I don't care about your house, Simon. Whatever is down there is going to die."

Kress hardly heard her. He thought he could see movement in the shadows beyond the cellar door. He imagined a white army bursting forth, all as large as the sandking that had attacked Lissandra. He saw himself being lifted by a hundred tiny arms, and dragged down into the darkness where the maw waited hungrily. He was afraid. "Don't," he said.

They ignored him.

Kress darted forward, and his shoulder slammed into the back of Lissandra's operative just as the man was bracing to fire. The operative grunted, lost his balance, and pitched forward into the black. Kress listened to him fall down the stairs. Afterward there were other noises; scuttlings and snaps and soft squishing sounds.

Kress swung around to face Lissandra. He was drenched in cold sweat, but a sickly kind of excitement was on him. It was almost sexual.

Lissandra's calm cold eyes regarded him through her mask. "What are you doing?" she demanded as Kress picked up the laser she had dropped. *"Simon!"*

"Making a peace," he said, giggling. "They won't hurt god, no, not so long as god is good and generous. I was cruel. Starved them. I have to make up for it now, you see."

"You're insane," Lissandra said. It was the last thing she said. Kress burned a hole in her chest big enough to put his arm through. He dragged the body across the floor and rolled it down the cellar stairs. The noises were louder; chitinous clackings and scrapings and echoes that were thick and liquid. Kress nailed up the door once again.

As he fled, he was filled with a deep sense of contentment that coated his fear like a layer of syrup. He suspected it was not his own.

He planned to leave his home, to fly to the city and take a room for a night, or perhaps for a year. Instead Kress started drinking. He was not quite sure why. He drank steadily for hours, and retched it all up violently on his living room carpet. At some point he fell asleep. When he woke, it was pitch-dark in the house.

He cowered against the couch. He could hear *noises*. Things were moving in the walls. They were all around him. His hearing was extraordinarily acute. Every little creak was the footstep of a sandking. He closed his eyes and waited, expecting to feel their terrible touch, afraid to move lest he brush against one.

Kress sobbed, and was very still.

After a while, nothing happened.

He opened his eyes again. He trembled. Slowly the shadows began to soften and dissolve. Moonlight was filtering through the high windows. His eyes adjusted.

The living room was empty. Nothing there, nothing, nothing. Only his drunken fears.

Simon Kress steeled himself, and rose, and went to a light.

Nothing there. The room was quiet, deserted.

He listened. Nothing. No sound. Nothing in the walls. It had all been his imagination, his fear.

The memories of Lissandra and the thing in the cellar returned to him unbidden. Shame and anger washed over him. Why had he done that? He could have helped her burn it out, kill it. *Why* . . . he knew why. The maw had done it to him, put fear in him. Wo had said it was psionic, even when it was small. And now it was large, so large. It had feasted on Cath, and Idi, and now it had two more bodies down there. It would keep growing. And it had learned to like the taste of human flesh, he thought.

He began to shake, but he took control of himself again and stopped. It wouldn't hurt him, he was god, the whites had always been his favorites.

He remembered how he had stabbed it with his throwing-sword. That was before Cath came. Damn her anyway.

He couldn't stay here. The maw would grow hungry again. Large as it was, it wouldn't take long. Its appetite would be terrible. What would it do then? He had to get away, back to the safety of the city while it was still contained in his wine cellar. It was only plaster and hard-packed earth down there, and the mobiles could dig and tunnel. When they got free . . . Kress didn't want to think about it.

He went to his bedroom and packed. He took three bags. Just a single change of clothing, that was all he needed; the rest of the space he filled with his valuables, with jewelry and art and other things he could not bear to lose. He did not expect to return.

His shambler followed him down the stairs, staring at him from its baleful glowing eyes. It was gaunt. Kress realized that it had been ages since he had fed it. Normally it could take care of itself, but no doubt the pickings had grown lean of late. When it tried to clutch at his leg, he snarled at it and kicked it away, and it scurried off, offended.

Kress slipped outside, carrying his bags awkwardly, and shut the door behind him.

For a moment he stood pressed against the house, his heart thudding in his chest. Only a few meters between him and his skimmer. He was afraid to take them. The moonlight was bright, and the front of his house was a scene of carnage. The bodies of Lissandra's two flamers lay where they had fallen, one twisted and burned, the other swollen beneath a mass of dead sandkings. And the mobiles, the black and red mobiles, they were all around him. It was an effort to remember that they were dead. It was almost as if they were simply waiting, as they had waited so often before.

Nonsense, Kress told himself. More drunken fears. He had seen the castles blown apart. They were dead, and the white maw was trapped in his cellar. He took several deep and deliberate breaths, and stepped forward onto the sandkings. They crunched. He ground them into the sand savagely. They did not move.

Kress smiled, and walked slowly across the battleground, listening to the sounds, the sounds of safety.

Crunch. Crackle. Crunch.

He lowered his bags to the ground and opened the door to his skimmer.

Something moved from shadow into light. A pale shape on the seat of his skimmer. It was as long as his forearm. Its mandibles clacked together softly, and it looked up at him from six small eyes set all around its body.

Kress wet his pants and backed away slowly.

There was more motion from inside the skimmer. He had left the door open. The sandking emerged and came toward him, cautiously. Others followed. They had been hiding beneath his seats, burrowed into the upholstery. But now they emerged. They formed a ragged ring around the skimmer.

Kress licked his lips, turned, and moved quickly to Lissandra's skimmer.

He stopped before he was halfway there. Things were moving inside that one too. Great maggoty things half-seen by the light of the moon.

Kress whimpered and retreated back toward the house. Near the front door, he looked up.

He counted a dozen long white shapes creeping back and forth across the walls of the building. Four of them were clustered close together near the top of the unused belfry where the carrion hawk had once roosted. They were carving something. A face. A very recognizable face.

Simon Kress shrieked and ran back inside.

A sufficient quantity of drink brought him the easy oblivion he sought. But he woke. Despite everything, he woke. He had a terrific headache, and he smelled, and he was hungry. Oh so very hungry. He had never been so hungry.

Kress knew it was not his *own* stomach hurting.

A white sandking watched him from atop the dresser in his bedroom, its antennae moving faintly. It was as big as the one in the skimmer the night before. He tried not to shrink away. "I'll . . . I'll feed you," he said to it. "I'll feed you." His mouth was horribly dry, sandpaper dry. He licked his lips and fled from the room.

The house was full of sandkings; he had to be careful where he put his feet. They all seemed busy on errands of their own. They were making modifications in his house, burrowing into or out of his walls, carving things. Twice he saw his own likeness staring out at him from unexpected places. The faces were warped, twisted, livid with fear.

He went outside to get the bodies that had been rotting in the yard, hoping to appease the white maw's hunger. They were gone, both of them. Kress remembered how easily the mobiles could carry things many times their own weight.

It was terrible to think that the maw was *still* hungry after all of that.

When Kress reentered the house, a column of sandkings was wending its way down the stairs. Each carried a piece of his shambler. The head seemed to look at him reproachfully as it went by.

Kress emptied his freezers, his cabinets, everything, piling all the food in the house in the center of his kitchen floor. A dozen whites waited to take it away. They avoided the frozen food, leaving it to thaw in a great puddle, but they carried off everything else.

When all the food was gone, Kress felt his own hunger pangs abate just a bit, though he had not eaten a thing. But he knew the respite would be short-lived. Soon the maw would be hungry again. He had to feed it.

Kress knew what to do. He went to his communicator. "Malada," he began casually when the first of his friends answered, "I'm having a small party tonight. I realize this is terribly short notice, but I hope you can make it. I really do."

He called Jad Rakkis next, and then the others. By the time he had finished, nine of them had accepted his invitation. Kress hoped that would be enough.

Kress met his guests outside—the mobiles had cleaned up remarkably quickly, and the grounds looked almost as they had before the battle—and walked them to his front door. He let them enter first. He did not follow.

When four of them had gone through, Kress finally worked up his courage. He closed the door behind his latest guest, ignoring the startled exclamations that soon turned into shrill gibbering, and sprinted for the skimmer the man had arrived in. He slid in safely, thumbed the startplate, and swore. It was programmed to lift only in response to its owner's thumbprint, of course.

Jad Rakkis was the next to arrive. Kress ran to his

skimmer as it set down, and seized Rakkis by the arm as he was climbing out. "Get back in, quickly," he said, pushing. "Take me to the city. Hurry, Jad. *Get out of here!*"

But Rakkis only stared at him, and would not move. "Why, what's wrong, Simon? I don't understand. What about your party?"

And then it was too late, because the loose sand all around them was stirring, and the red eyes were staring at them, and the mandibles were clacking. Rakkis made a choking sound, and moved to get back in his skimmer, but a pair of mandibles snapped shut about his ankle, and suddenly he was on his knees. The sand seemed to boil with subterranean activity. Jad thrashed and cried terribly as they tore him apart. Kress could hardly bear to watch.

After that, he did not try to escape again. When it was all over, he cleaned out what remained in his liquor cabinet, and got extremely drunk. It would be the last time he would enjoy that luxury, he knew. The only alcohol remaining in the house was stored down in the wine cellar.

Kress did not touch a bite of food the entire day, but he fell asleep feeling bloated, sated at last, the awful hunger vanquished. His last thoughts before the nightmares took him were on who he could ask out tomorrow.

Morning was hot and dry. Kress opened his eyes to see the white sandking on his dresser again. He shut them again quickly, hoping the dream would leave him. It did not, and he could not go back to sleep, and soon he found himself staring at the thing.

He stared for almost five minutes before the strangeness of it dawned on him; the sandking was not moving.

The mobiles could be preternaturally still, to be sure. He had seen them wait and watch a thousand times.

But always there was some motion about them; the mandibles clacked, the legs twitched, the long fine antennae stirred and swayed.

But the sandking on his dresser was completely still.

Kress rose, holding his breath, not daring to hope. Could it be dead? Could something have killed it? He walked across the room.

The eyes were glassy and black. The creature seemed swollen, somehow; as if it were soft and rotting inside, filling up with gas that pushed outward at the plates of white armor.

Kress reached out a trembling hand and touched it.

It was warm; hot even, and growing hotter. But it did not move.

He pulled his hand back, and as he did, a segment of the sandking's white exoskeleton fell away from it. The flesh beneath was the same color, but softer-looking, swollen and feverish. And it almost seemed to throb.

Kress backed away, and ran to the door.

Three more white mobiles lay in his hall. They were all like the one in his bedroom.

He ran down the stairs, jumping over sandkings. None of them moved. The house was full of them, all dead, dying, comatose, whatever. Kress did not care what was wrong with them. Just so they could not move.

He found four of them inside his skimmer. He picked them up one by one, and threw them as far as he could. Damned monsters. He slid back in, on the ruined half-eaten seats, and thumbed the startplate.

Nothing happened.

Kress tried again, and again. Nothing. It wasn't fair. This was *his* skimmer, it ought to start, why wouldn't it lift, he didn't understand.

Finally he got out and checked, expecting the worst. He found it. The sandkings had torn apart his gravity grid. He was trapped. He was still trapped.

Grimly Kress marched back into the house. He went to his gallery and found the antique axe that had hung next to the throwing sword he had used on Cath m'Lane. He set to work. The sandkings did not stir even as he chopped them to pieces. But they splattered when he made the first cut, the bodies almost bursting. Inside was awful; strange half-formed organs, a viscous reddish ooze that looked almost like human blood, and the yellow ichor.

Kress destroyed twenty of them before he realized the futility of what he was doing. The mobiles were nothing, really. Besides, there were so *many* of them. He could work for a day and night and still not kill them all.

He had to go down into the wine cellar and use the axe on the maw.

Resolute, he started down. He got within sight of the door, and stopped.

It was not a door anymore. The walls had been eaten away, so the hole was twice the size it had been, and round. A pit, that was all. There was no sign that there had ever been a door nailed shut over that black abyss.

A ghastly choking fetid odor seemed to come from below.

And the walls were wet and bloody and covered with patches of white fungus.

And worst, it was *breathing*.

Kress stood across the room and felt the warm wind wash over him as it exhaled, and he tried not to choke, and when the wind reversed direction, he fled.

Back in the living room, he destroyed three more mobiles, and collapsed. What was *happening?* He didn't understand.

Then he remembered the only person who might understand. Kress went to his communicator again, stepped on a sandking in his haste, and prayed fervently that the device still worked.

When Jala Wo answered, he broke down and told her everything.

She let him talk without interruption, no expression save for a slight frown on her gaunt, pale face. When Kress had finished, she said only, "I ought to leave you there."

Kress began to blubber. "You can't. Help me. I'll pay . . ."

"I ought to," Wo repeated, "but I won't."

"Thank you," Kress said. "Oh, thank . . ."

"Quiet," said Wo. "Listen to me. This is your own doing. Keep your sandkings well, and they are courtly ritual warriors. You turned yours into something else, with starvation and torture. You were their god. You made them what they are. That maw in your cellar is sick, still suffering from the wound you gave it. It is probably insane. Its behavior is . . . unusual.

"You have to get out of there quickly. The mobiles are not dead, Kress. They are dormant. I told you the exoskeleton falls off when they grow larger. Normally, in fact, it falls off much earlier. I have never heard of sandkings growing as large as yours while still in the insectoid stage. It is another result of crippling the white maw, I would say. That does not matter.

"What matters is the metamorphosis your sandkings are now undergoing. As the maw grows, you see, it gets progressively more intelligent. Its psionic powers strengthen, and its mind becomes more sophisticated, more ambitious. The armored mobiles are useful enough when the maw is tiny and only semisentient, but now it needs better servants, bodies with more capabilities. Do you understand? The mobiles are all going to give birth to a new breed of sandking. I can't say exactly what it will look like. Each maw designs its own, to fit its perceived needs and desires. But it will be biped, with four arms, and opposable thumbs. It will be able to construct and operate advanced machinery.

The individual sandkings will not be sentient. But the maw will be very sentient indeed."

Simon Kress was gaping at Wo's image on the viewscreen. "Your workers," he said, with an effort. "The ones who came out here . . . who installed the tank . . ."

Jala Wo managed a faint smile. "Shade," she said.

"Shade is a sandking," Kress repeated numbly. "And you sold me a tank of . . . of . . . infants, ah . . ."

"Do not be absurd," Wo said. "A first-stage sandking is more like a sperm than an infant. The wars temper and control them in nature. Only one in a hundred reaches second stage. Only one in a thousand achieves the third and final plateau, and becomes like Shade. Adult sandkings are not sentimental about the small maws. There are too many of them, and their mobiles are pests." She sighed. "And all this talk wastes time. That white sandking is going to waken to full sentience soon. It is not going to need you any longer, and it hates you, and it will be very hungry. The transformation is taxing. The maw must eat enormous amounts both before and after. So you have to get out of there. Do you understand?"

"I *can't,*" Kress said. "My skimmer is destroyed, and I can't get any of the others to start. I don't know how to reprogram them. Can you come out for me?"

"Yes," said Wo. "Shade and I will leave at once, but it is more than two hundred kilometers from Asgard to you, and there is equipment we will need to deal with the deranged sandking you've created. You cannot wait there. You have two feet. Walk. Go due east, as near as you can determine, as quickly as you can. The land out there is pretty desolate. We can find you easily with an aerial search, and you'll be safely away from the sandkings. Do you understand?"

"Yes," said Simon Kress. "Yes, oh, yes."

They signed off, and he walked quickly toward the

door. He was halfway there when he heard the noise; a sound halfway between a pop and a crack.

One of the sandkings had split open. Four tiny hands covered with pinkish-yellow blood came up out of the gap, and began to push the dead skin aside.

Kress began to run.

He had not counted on the heat.

The hills were dry and rocky. Kress ran from the house as quickly as he could, ran until his ribs ached and his breath was coming in gasps. Then he walked, but as soon as he had recovered he began to run again. For almost an hour he ran and walked, ran and walked, beneath the fierce hot sun. He sweated freely, and wished that he had thought to bring some water, and he watched the sky in hopes of seeing Wo and Shade.

He was not made for this. It was too hot, and too dry, and he was in no condition. But he kept himself going with the memory of the way the maw had breathed, and the thought of the wriggling little things that by now were surely crawling all over his house. He hoped Wo and Shade would know how to deal with them.

He had his own plans for Wo and Shade. It was all their fault, Kress had decided, and they would suffer for it. Lissandra was dead, but he knew others in her profession. He would have his revenge. He promised himself that a hundred times as he struggled and sweated his way east.

At least he hoped it was east. He was not that good at directions, and he wasn't certain which way he had run in his initial panic, but since then he had made an effort to bear due east, as Wo had suggested.

When he had been running for several hours, with no sign of rescue, Kress began to grow certain that he had gone wrong.

When several more hours passed, he began to grow afraid. What if Wo and Shade could not find him? He would die out here. He hadn't eaten in two days, he was weak and frightened, his throat was raw for want of water. He couldn't keep going. The sun was sinking now, and he'd be completely lost in the dark. What was wrong? Had the sandkings eaten Wo and Shade? The fear was on him again, filling him, and with it a great thirst and a terrible hunger. But Kress kept going. He stumbled now when he tried to run, and twice he fell. The second time he scraped his hand on a rock, and it came away bloody. He sucked at it as he walked, and worried about infection.

The sun was on the horizon behind him. The ground grew a little cooler, for which Kress was grateful. He decided to walk until last light and settle in for the night. Surely he was far enough from the sandkings to be safe, and Wo and Shade would find him come morning.

When he topped the next rise, he saw the outline of a house in front of him.

It wasn't as big as his own house, but it was big enough. It was habitation, safety. Kress shouted and began to run toward it. Food and drink, he had to have nourishment, he could taste the meal now. He was aching with hunger. He ran down the hill toward the house, waving his arms and shouting to the inhabitants. The light was almost gone now, but he could still make out a half-dozen children playing in the twilight. "Hey there," he shouted. "Help, help."

They came running toward him.

Kress stopped suddenly. "No," he said, "Oh, no. Oh, no." He backpedaled, slipped on the sand, got up, and tried to run again. They caught him easily. They were ghastly little things with bulging eyes and dusky-orange skin. He struggled, but it was useless. Small as they were, each of them had four arms, and Kress had only two.

They carried him toward the house. It was a sad,

shabby house built of crumbling sand, but the door was quite large, and dark, and it breathed. That was terrible, but it was not the thing that set Simon Kress to screaming. He screamed because of the others, the little orange children who came crawling out from the castle, and watched impassively as he passed.

All of them had his face.

Carlos Fuentes (b. 1928)

AURA

Carlos Fuentes is the foremost living Mexican novelist and one of the world's great living writers. The son of a diplomat, he has lived in several countries and spent much time in Paris, in particular. His novella, "Aura," is one of the masterpieces of horror of the twentieth century and an important work of contemporary fiction. In an essay "On Reading and Writing Myself: How I Wrote 'Aura,'" Fuentes traces the genesis of the piece to a moment in Paris in the summer of 1961, and the concatenation of circumstances surrounding a moment when he saw a woman enter his bedroom in the mirror, illuminated by the light of the city, and perceived a second person in the mirror: ". . . that threshold between the parlor and the bedroom became the lintel between all the ages of this girl: the light that had been struggling against the clouds also fought against her flesh, took it, sketched it, granted her a shadow of years, sculpted a death in her eyes, tore the smile from her lips, waned through her hair with the floating melancholy of madness. . . . I was only, that afternoon, 'a strange guest in the kingdom of love,' and knew that the eyes of love can also see us with—once more I quote Quevedo—'a beautiful Death.'"

"The next morning I started writing 'Aura' in a cafe near my hotel. . . ." Fuentes names his conscious influences as Henry James' "The Aspern Papers," Charles Dickens' *Great Expectations*, Pushkin's *The Queen of Spades*, Michelet's medieval sorceress, and Circe, saying "Aura came into this world to increase the secular descent of witches." What more need one say about this powerful novella's place in the evolution of horror?

> *Man hunts and struggles.*
> *Woman intrigues and dreams;*
> *she is the mother of fantasy,*
> *the mother of the gods.*
> *She has second sight,*
> *the wings that enable her to fly*
> *to the infinite of*
> *desire and the imagination . . .*
> *The gods are like men:*
> *they are born and they die*
> *on a woman's breast . . .*
> —Jules Michelet

I

You're reading the advertisement: an offer like this isn't made every day. You read it and reread it. It seems to be addressed to you and nobody else. You don't even notice when the ash from your cigarette falls into the cup of tea you ordered in this cheap, dirty café. You read it again. "Wanted, young historian, conscientious, neat. Perfect knowledge colloquial French." Youth . . . knowledge of French, preferably after living in France for a while . . . "Four thousand pesos a month, all meals, comfortable bedroom-study." All that's missing is your name. The advertisement should have two more words, in bigger, blacker type: Felipe Montero, Wanted, Felipe Montero, formerly on scholarship at the Sorbonne, historian full of useless facts, accustomed to digging among yellowed documents, part-time teacher in private schools, nine hundred pesos a month. But if you read that, you'd be suspicious, and take it as a joke. "Address, Donceles 815." No telephone. Come in person.

You leave a tip, reach for your briefcase, get up. You wonder if another young historian, in the same situation you are, has seen the same advertisement, has got ahead of you and taken the job already. You walk down to the corner, trying to forget this idea. As you wait for the bus, you run over the dates you must have on the tip of your tongue so that your sleepy pupils will respect you. The bus is coming now, and you're staring at the tips of your black shoes. You've got to be prepared. You put your hand in your pocket, search among the coins, and finally take out thirty centavos. You've got to be prepared. You grab the handrail—the bus slows down but doesn't stop—and jump aboard. Then you shove your way forward, pay the driver the thirty centavos, squeeze yourself in among the passengers already standing in the aisle, hang onto the overhead rail, press your briefcase tighter under your left arm, and automatically put your left hand over the back pocket where you keep your billfold.

This day is just like any other day, and you don't remember the advertisement until the next morning, when you sit down in the same café and order breakfast and open your newspaper. You come to the advertising section and there it is again: *young historian*. The job is still open. You reread the advertisement, lingering over the final words: four thousand pesos.

It's surprising to know that anyone lives on Donceles Street. You always thought that nobody lived in the old center of the city. You walk slowly, trying to pick out the number 815 in that conglomeration of old colonial mansions, all of them converted into repair shops, jewelry shops, shoe stores, drugstores. The numbers have been changed, painted over, confused. A 13 next to a 200. An old plaque reading 47 over a scrawl in blurred charcoal: *Now 924*. You look up at the second stories. Up there, everything is the same as it was. The jukeboxes don't disturb them. The mercury streetlights don't shine in. The cheap merchandise on sale along the street doesn't have any effect on that upper level; on the baroque harmony of the carved stones; on the battered stone saints with pigeons clustering on their shoulders; on the latticed balconies, the copper gutters, the sandstone gargoyles; on the greenish curtains that darken the long windows; on that window from which someone draws back when you look at it. You gaze at the fanciful vines carved over the doorway, then lower your eyes to the peeling wall and discover *815, formerly 69*.

You rap vainly with the knocker, that copper head of a dog, so worn and smooth that it resembles the head of a canine foetus in a museum of natural science. It seems as if the dog is grinning at you and you let go of the cold metal. The door opens at the first light push of your fingers, but before going in you give a last look over your shoulder, frowning at the long line of stalled cars that growl, honk, and belch out the unhealthy fumes of their impatience. You try to retain some single image of that indifferent outside world.

You close the door behind you and peer into the darkness of a roofed alleyway. It must be a patio of some sort, because you can smell the mold, the dampness of the plants, the rotting roots, the thick drowsy aroma. There isn't any light to guide you, and you're searching in your coat pocket for the box of matches when a sharp, thin voice tells you, from a distance: "No, it isn't necessary. Please. Walk thirteen steps forward and you'll come to a stairway at your right. Come up, please. There are twenty-two steps. Count them."

Thirteen. To the right. Twenty-two.

The dank smell of the plants is all around you as you

count out your steps, first on the paving-stones, then on the creaking wood, spongy from the dampness. You count to twenty-two in a low voice and then stop, with the matchbox in your hand, and the briefcase under your arm. You knock on a door that smells of old pine. There isn't any knocker. Finally you push it open. Now you can feel a carpet under your feet, a thin carpet, badly laid. It makes you trip and almost fall. Then you notice the grayish filtered light that reveals some of the humps.

"Señora," you say, because you seem to remember a woman's voice. "Señora . . ."

"Now turn to the left. The first door. Please be so kind."

You push the door open: you don't expect any of them to be latched, you know they all open at a push. The scattered lights are braided in your eyelashes, as if you were seeing them through a silken net. All you can make out are the dozens of flickering lights. At last you can see that they're votive lights, all set on brackets or hung between unevenly spaced panels. They cast a faint glow on the silver objects, the crystal flasks, the gilt-framed mirrors. Then you see the bed in the shadows beyond, and the feeble movement of a hand that seems to be beckoning to you.

But you can't see her face until you turn your back on that galaxy of religious lights. You stumble to the foot of the bed, and have to go around it in order to get to the head of it. A tiny figure is almost lost in its immensity. When you reach out your hand, you don't touch another hand, you touch the ears and thick fur of a creature that's chewing silently and steadily, looking up at you with its glowing red eyes. You smile and stroke the rabbit that's crouched beside her hand. Finally you shake hands, and her cold fingers remain for a long while in your sweating palm.

"I'm Felipe Montero. I read your advertisement."

"Yes, I know. I'm sorry, there aren't any chairs."

"That's all right. Don't worry about it."

"Good. Please let me see your profile. No, I can't see it well enough. Turn toward the light. That's right. Excellent."

"I read your advertisement . . ."

"Yes, of course. Do you think you're qualified? *Avez-vous fait des études?*"

"*A Paris, madame.*"

"*Ah, oui, ça me fait plaisir, toujours, toujours, d'entendre . . . oui . . . vous savez . . . on était telle-ment habitué . . . et après . . .*"

You move aside so that the light from the candles and the reflections from the silver and crystal show you the silk coif that must cover a head of very white hair, and that frames a face so old it's almost childlike. Her whole body is covered by the sheets and the feather pillows and the high, tightly buttoned white collar, all except for her arms, which are wrapped in a shawl, and her pallid hands resting on her stomach. You can only stare at her face until a movement of the rabbit lets you glance furtively at the crusts and bits of bread scattered on the worn-out red silk of the pillows.

"I'll come directly to the point. I don't have many years ahead of me, Señor Montero, and therefore I decided to break a life-long rule and place an advertisement in the newspaper."

"Yes, that's why I'm here."

"Of course. So you accept."

"Well, I'd like to know a little more."

"Yes. You're wondering."

She sees you glance at the night table, the different-colored bottles, the glasses, the aluminum spoons, the row of pillboxes, the other glasses—all stained with whitish liquids—on the floor within reach of her hand.

Then you notice that the bed is hardly raised above the level of the floor. Suddenly the rabbit jumps down and disappears in the shadows.

"I can offer you four thousand pesos."

"Yes, that's what the advertisement said today."

"Ah, then it came out."

"Yes, it came out."

"It has to do with the memoirs of my husband, General Llorente. They must be put in order before I die. I want them to be published. I decided that a short time ago."

"But the General himself? Wouldn't he be able to . . ."

"He died sixty years ago, Señor. They're his unfinished memoirs. They have to be completed before I die."

"But . . ."

"I can tell you everything. You'll learn to write in my husband's own style. You'll only have to arrange and read his manuscripts to become fascinated by his style . . . his clarity . . . his . . ."

"Yes, I understand."

"Saga, Saga. Where are you? *Ici,* Saga!"

"Who?"

"My companion."

"The rabbit?"

"Yes. She'll come back."

When you raise your eyes, which you've been keeping lowered, her lips are closed but you can hear her words again—"She'll come back"—as if the old lady were pronouncing them at that instant. Her lips remain still. You look in back of you and you're almost blinded by the gleam from the religious objects. When you look at her again you see that her eyes have opened very wide, and that they're clear, liquid, enormous, almost the same color as the yellowish whites around them, so that only the black dots of the pupils mar that clarity. It's lost a moment later in the heavy folds of her lowered eyelids, as if she wanted to protect that glance which is now hiding at the back of its dry cave.

"Then you'll stay here. Your room is upstairs. It's sunny there."

"It might be better if I didn't trouble you, Señora. I can go on living where I am and work on the manuscripts there."

"My conditions are that you have to live here. There isn't much time left."

"I don't know if . . ."

"Aura . . ."

The old woman moves for the first time since you entered her room. As she reaches out her hand again, you sense that agitated breathing beside you, and another hand reaches out to touch the Señora's fingers. You look around and a girl is standing there, a girl whose whole body you can't see because she's standing so close to you and her arrival was so unexpected, without the slightest sound—not even these sounds that can't be heard but are real anyway because they're remembered immediately afterwards, because in spite of everything they're louder than the silence that accompanies them.

"I told you she'd come back."

"Who?"

"Aura. My companion. My niece."

"Good afternoon."

The girl nods and at the same instant the old lady imitates her gesture.

"This is Señor Montero. He's going to live with us."

You move a few steps so that the light from the candles won't blind you. The girl keeps her eyes closed, her hands at her sides. She doesn't look at you at first, then little by little she opens her eyes as if she were afraid of the light. Finally you can see that those eyes are sea green and that they surge, break to foam, grow calm again, then surge again like a wave. You look into them and tell yourself it isn't true, because they're beautiful green eyes just like all the beautiful green eyes you've ever known. But you can't deceive yourself: those eyes do surge, do change, as if offering you a landscape that only you can see and desire.

"Yes. I'm going to live with you."

II

The old woman laughs sharply and tells you that she is grateful for your kindness and that the girl will show you to your room. You're thinking about the salary of four thousand pesos, and how the work should be pleasant because you like these jobs of careful research that don't include physical effort or going from one place to another or meeting people you don't want to meet. You're thinking about this as you follow her out of the room, and you discover that you've got to follow her with your ears instead of your eyes: you follow the rustle of her skirt, the rustle of taffeta, and you're anxious now to look into her eyes again. You climb the stairs behind that sound in the darkness, and you're still unused to the obscurity. You remember it must be about six in the afternoon, and the flood of light surprises you when Aura opens the door to your bedroom—another door without a latch—and steps aside to tell you: "This is your room. We'll expect you for supper in an hour."

She moves away with that same faint rustle of taffeta, and you weren't able to see her face again.

You close the door and look up at the skylight that serves as a roof. You smile when you find that the evening light is blinding compared with the darkness in the rest of the house, and smile again when you try out the mattress on the gilded metal bed. Then you glance around the room: a red wool rug, olive and gold wallpaper, an easy chair covered in red velvet, an old walnut desk with a green leather top, an old Argand lamp with its soft glow for your nights of research, and a bookshelf over the desk in reach of your hand. You walk over to the other door, and on pushing it open you discover an outmoded bathroom: a four-legged bathtub with little flowers painted on the porcelain, a blue hand basin, an old-fashioned toilet. You look at yourself in the large oval mirror on the door of the wardrobe—it's also walnut—in the bathroom hallway. You move your heavy eyebrows and wide thick lips, and your breath fogs the mirror. You close your black eyes, and when you open them again the mirror has cleared. You stop holding your breath and run your hand through your dark, limp hair; you touch your fine profile, your lean cheeks; and when your breath hides your face again you're repeating her name: "Aura."

After smoking two cigarettes while lying on the bed, you get up, put on your jacket, and comb your hair. You push the door open and try to remember the route you followed coming up. You'd like to leave the door open so that the lamplight could guide you, but that's impossible because the springs close it behind you. You could enjoy playing with that door, swinging it back and forth. You don't do it. You could take the lamp down with you. You don't do it. This house will always be in darkness, and you've got to learn it and relearn it by touch. You grope your way like a blind man, with your arms stretched out wide, feeling your way along the wall, and by accident you turn on the light-switch. You stop and blink in the bright middle of that long, empty hall. At the end of it you can see the bannister and the spiral staircase.

You count the stairs as you go down: another custom you've got to learn in Señora Llorente's house. You take a step backward when you see the reddish eyes of the rabbit, which turns its back on you and goes hopping away.

You don't have time to stop in the lower hallway because Aura is waiting for you at a half-open stained-glass door, with a candelabrum in her hand. You walk toward her, smiling, but you stop when you hear the painful yowling of a number of cats—yes, you stop to listen, next to Aura, to be sure that they're cats—and then follow her to the parlor.

"It's the cats," Aura tells you. "There are lots of rats in this part of the city."

You go through the parlor: furniture upholstered in faded silk; glass-fronted cabinets containing porcelain figurines, musical clocks, medals, glass balls; carpets with Persian designs; pictures of rustic scenes; green velvet curtains. Aura is dressed in green.

"Is your room comfortable?"

"Yes. But I have to get my things from the place where . . ."

"It won't be necessary. The servant has already gone for them."

"You shouldn't have bothered."

You follow her into the dining room. She places the candelabrum in the middle of the table. The room feels damp and cold. The four walls are paneled in dark wood, carved in Gothic style, with fretwork arches and large rosettes. The cats have stopped yowling. When you sit down, you notice that four places have been set. There are two large, covered plates and an old, grimy bottle.

Aura lifts the cover from one of the plates. You breathe in the pungent odor of the liver and onions she serves you, then you pick up the old bottle and fill the cut-glass goblets with that thick red liquid. Out of curiosity you try to read the label on the wine bottle, but the grime has obscured it. Aura serves you some whole broiled tomatoes from the other plate.

"Excuse me," you say, looking at the two extra places, the two empty chairs, "but are you expecting someone else?"

Aura goes on serving the tomatoes. "No. Señora Consuelo feels a little ill tonight. She won't be joining us."

"Señora Consuelo? Your aunt?"

"Yes. She'd like you to go in and see her after supper."

You eat in silence. You drink that thick wine, occasionally shifting your glance so that Aura won't catch you in the hypnotized stare that you can't control. You'd like to fix the girl's features in your mind. Every time you look away you forget them again, and an irresistible urge forces you to look at her once more. As usual, she has her eyes lowered. While you're searching for the pack of cigarettes in your coat pocket, you run across that big key, and remember, and say to Aura: "Ah! I forgot that one of the drawers in my desk is locked. I've got my papers in it."

And she murmurs: "Then you want to go out?" She says it as a reproach.

You feel confused, and reach out your hand to her with the key dangling from one finger.

"It isn't important. The servant can go for them tomorrow."

But she avoids touching your hand, keeping her own hands on her lap. Finally she looks up, and once again you question your senses, blaming the wine for your bewilderment, for the dizziness brought on by those shining, clear green eyes, and you stand up after Aura does, running your hand over the wooden back of the Gothic chair, without daring to touch her bare shoulder or her motionless head.

You make an effort to control yourself, diverting your attention away from her by listening to the imperceptible movement of a door behind you—it must lead to the kitchen—or by separating the two different elements that make up the room: the compact circle of light around the candelabrum, illuminating the table and one carved wall, and the larger circle of darkness surrounding it. Finally you have the courage to go up to her, take her hand, open it, and place your key-ring in her smooth palm as a token.

She closes her hand, looks up at you, and murmurs, "Thank you." Then she rises and walks quickly out of the room.

You sit down in Aura's chair, stretch your legs, and light a cigarette, feeling a pleasure you've never felt before, one that you knew was part of you but that only now you're experiencing fully, setting it free, bringing it out because this time you know it'll be answered and won't be lost . . . And Señora Consuelo is waiting for you, as Aura said. She's waiting for you after supper . . .

You leave the dining room, and with the candelabrum in your hand you walk through the parlor and the hallway. The first door you come to is the old lady's. You rap on it with your knuckles, but there isn't any answer. You knock again. Then you push the door open because she's waiting for you. You enter cautiously, murmuring: "Señora . . . Señora . . ."

She doesn't hear you, for she's kneeling in front of that wall of religious objects, with her head resting on her clenched fists. You see her from a distance: she's kneeling there in her coarse woolen nightgown, with her head sunk into her narrow shoulders; she's thin, even emaciated, like a medieval sculpture; her legs are like two sticks, and they're inflamed with erysipelas. While you're thinking of the continual rubbing of that rough wool against her skin, she suddenly raises her fists and strikes feebly at the air, as if she were doing battle against the images you can make out as you tiptoe closer: Christ, the Virgin, St. Sebastian, St.

Lucia, the Archangel Michael, and the grinning demons in an old print, the only happy figures in that iconography of sorrow and wrath, happy because they're jabbing their pitchforks into the flesh of the damned, pouring cauldrons of boiling water on them, violating the women, getting drunk, enjoying all the liberties forbidden to the saints. You approach that central image, which is surrounded by the tears of Our Lady of Sorrows, the blood of Our Crucified Lord, the delight of Lucifer, the anger of the Archangel, the viscera preserved in bottles of alcohol, the silver heart: Señora Consuelo, kneeling, threatens them with her fists, stammering the words you can hear as you move even closer: "Come, City of God! Gabriel, sound your trumpet! Ah, how long the world takes to die!"

She beats her breast until she collapses in front of the images and candles in a spasm of coughing. You raise her by the elbow, and as you gently help her to the bed you're surprised at her smallness: she's almost a little girl, bent over almost double. You realize that without your assistance she would have had to get back to bed on her hands and knees. You help her into that wide bed with its bread crumbs and old feather pillows, and cover her up, and wait until her breathing is back to normal, while the involuntary tears run down her parchment cheeks.

"Excuse me . . . excuse me, Señor Montero. Old ladies have nothing left but . . . the pleasures of devotion . . . Give me my handkerchief, please."

"Señorita Aura told me . . ."

"Yes, of course. I don't want to lose any time. We should . . . we should begin working as soon as possible. Thank you."

"You should try to rest."

"Thank you . . . Here . . ."

The old lady raises her hand to her collar, unbuttons it, and lowers her head to remove the frayed purple ribbon that she hands to you. It's heavy because there's a copper key hanging from it.

"Over in that corner . . . Open that trunk and bring me the papers at the right, on top of the others . . . They're tied with a yellow ribbon."

"I can't see very well . . ."

"Ah, yes . . . it's just that I'm so accustomed to the darkness. To my right . . . Keep going till you come to the trunk. They've walled us in, Señor Montero. They've built up all around us and blocked off the light. They've tried to force me to sell, but I'll die first. This house is full of memories for us. They won't take me out of here till I'm dead! Yes, that's it. Thank you. You can begin reading this part. I will give you the others later. Good night, Señor Montero. Thank you. Look, the candelabrum has gone out. Light it outside the door, please. No, no, you can keep the key. I trust you."

"Señora, there's a rat's nest in that corner."

"Rats? I never go over there."

"You should bring the cats in here."

"The cats? What cats? Good night. I'm going to sleep. I'm very tired."

"Good night."

III

That same evening you read those yellow papers written in mustard-colored ink, some of them with holes where a careless ash had fallen, others heavily fly-specked. General Llorente's French doesn't have the merits his wife attributed to it. You tell yourself you can make considerable improvements in the style, can tighten up his rambling account of past events: his childhood on a hacienda in Oaxaca, his military studies in France, his friendship with the duc de Morny and the intimates of Napoleon III, his return to Mexico on the staff of Maximilian, the imperial ceremonies and gatherings, the battles, the defeat in 1867, his exile in France. Nothing that hasn't been described before. As you undress you think of the old lady's distorted notions, the value she attributes to these memoirs. You smile as you get into bed, thinking of the four thousand pesos.

You sleep soundly until a flood of light wakes you up at six in the morning: that glass roof doesn't have any curtain. You bury your head under the pillow and try to go back to sleep. Ten minutes later you give it up and walk into the bathroom, where you find all your things neatly arranged on a table and your few clothes hanging in the wardrobe. Just as you finish shaving the early morning silence is broken by that painful, desperate yowling.

You try to find out where it's coming from: you open the door to the hallway, but you can't hear anything from there: those cries are coming from up above, from the skylight. You jump up on the chair, from the chair onto the desk, and by supporting yourself on the bookshelf you can reach the skylight. You open one of the windows and pull yourself up to look out at that side garden, that square of yew trees and brambles where five, six, seven cats—you can't count them, can't hold yourself up there for more than a second—are all twined together, all writhing in flames and giving off a dense smoke that reeks of burnt fur. As you get down again you wonder if you really saw it: perhaps you only imagined it from those dreadful cries that continue, grow less, and finally stop.

You put on your shirt, brush off your shoes with a piece of paper, and listen to the sound of a bell that seems to run through the passageways of the house until it arrives at your door. You look out into the hallway. Aura is walking along it with a bell in her hand. She turns her head to look at you and tells you that breakfast is ready. You try to detain her but she goes down the spiral staircase, still ringing that black-painted bell as if she were trying to wake up a whole asylum, a whole boarding-school.

You follow her in your shirt-sleeves, but when you reach the downstairs hallway you can't find her. The door of the old lady's bedroom opens behind you and you see a hand that reaches out from behind the partly opened door, sets a chamberpot in the hallway and disappears again, closing the door.

In the dining room your breakfast is already on the table, but this time only one place has been set. You eat quickly, return to the hallway, and knock at Señora Consuelo's door. Her sharp, weak voice tells you to come in. Nothing has changed: the perpetual shadows, the glow of the votive lights and the silver objects.

"Good morning, Señor Montero. Did you sleep well?"

"Yes. I read till quite late."

The old lady waves her hand as if in a gesture of dismissal. "No, no, no. Don't give me your opinion. Work on those pages and when you've finished I'll give you the others."

"Very well. Señora, would I be able to go into the garden?"

"What garden, Señor Montero?"

"The one that's outside my room."

"This house doesn't have any garden. We lost our garden when they built up all around us."

"I think I could work better outdoors."

"This house has only got that dark patio where you came in. My niece is growing some shade plants there. But that's all."

"It's all right, Señora."

"I'd like to rest during the day. But come to see me tonight."

"Very well, Señora."

You spend all morning working on the papers, copying out the passages you intend to keep, rewriting the ones you think are especially bad, smoking one cigarette after another and reflecting that you ought to space your work so that the job lasts as long as possible. If you can manage to save at least twelve thousand pesos, you can spend a year on nothing but your own work, which you've postponed and almost forgotten. Your great, inclusive work on the Spanish discoveries and conquests in the New World. A work that sums up all the scattered chronicles, makes them intelligible, and discovers the resemblances among all the undertakings and adventures of Spain's Golden Age, and all the human prototypes and major accomplishments of the Renaissance. You end up by putting aside the General's tedious pages and starting to compile the dates and summaries of your own work. Time passes and you don't look at your watch until you hear the bell again. Then you put on your coat and go down to the dining room.

Aura is already seated. This time Señora Llorente is at the head of the table, wrapped in her shawl and nightgown and coif, hunching over her plate. But the fourth place has also been set. You note it in passing. It doesn't bother you anymore. If the price of your future creative liberty is to put up with all the manias of this old woman, you can pay it easily. As you watch her eating her soup you try to figure out her age. There's a time after which it's impossible to detect the passing of the years, and Señora Consuelo crossed that frontier a long time ago. The General hasn't mentioned her in what you've already read of the memoirs. But if the General was forty-two at the time of the French invasion, and died in 1901, forty years later, he must have died at the age of eighty-two. He must have married the

Señora after the defeat at Querétaro and his exile. But she would only have been a girl at that time . . .

The dates escape you because now the Señora is talking in that thin, sharp voice of hers, that birdlike chirping. She's talking to Aura and you listen to her as you eat, hearing her long list of complaints, pains, suspected illnesses, more complaints about the cost of medicines, the dampness of the house and so forth. You'd like to break in on this domestic conversation to ask about the servant who went for your things yesterday, the servant you've never even glimpsed and who never waits on table. You're going to ask about him but you're suddenly surprised to realize that up to this moment Aura hasn't said a word and is eating with a sort of mechanical fatality, as if she were waiting for some outside impulse before picking up her knife and fork, cutting a piece of liver—yes, it's liver again, apparently the favorite dish in this house—and carrying it to her mouth. You glance quickly from the aunt to the niece, but at that moment the Señora becomes motionless, and at the same moment Aura puts her knife on her plate and also becomes motionless, and you remember that the Señora put down her knife only a fraction of a second earlier.

There are several minutes of silence: you finish eating while they sit there rigid as statues, watching you. At last the Señora says, "I'm very tired. I ought not to eat at the table. Come, Aura, help me to my room."

The Señora tries to hold your attention: she looks directly at you so that you'll keep looking at her, although what she's saying is aimed at Aura. You have to make an effort in order to evade that look, which once again is wide, clear, and yellowish, free of the veils and wrinkles that usually obscure it. Then you look at Aura, who is staring fixedly at nothing and silently moving her lips. She gets up with a motion like those you associate with dreaming, takes the arm of the bent old lady, and slowly helps her from the dining room.

Alone now, you help yourself to the coffee that has been there since the beginning of the meal, the cold coffee you sip as you wrinkle your brow and ask yourself if the Señora doesn't have some secret power over her niece: if the girl, your beautiful Aura in her green dress, isn't kept in this dark old house against her will. But it would be so easy for her to escape while the Señora was asleep in her shadowy room. You tell yourself that her hold over the girl must be terrible. And you consider the way out that occurs to your imagination: perhaps Aura is waiting for you to release her from the chains in which the perverse, insane old lady, for some unknown reason, has bound her. You remember Aura as she was a few moments ago, spiritless, hypnotized by her terror, incapable of speaking in front of the tyrant, moving her lips in silence as if she were silently begging you to set her free; so enslaved that she imitated every gesture of the Señora, as if she were permitted to do only what the Señora did.

You rebel against this tyranny. You walk toward the other door, the one at the foot of the staircase, the one next to the old lady's room: that's where Aura must live, because there's no other room in the house. You push the door open and go in. This room is dark also, with whitewashed walls, and the only decoration is an enormous black Christ. At the left there's a door that must lead into the widow's bedroom. You go up to it on tiptoe, put your hands against it, then decide not to open it: you should talk with Aura alone.

And if Aura wants your help she'll come to your room. You go up there for a while, forgetting the yellowed manuscripts and your own notebooks, thinking only about the beauty of your Aura. And the more you think about her, the more you make her yours, not only because of her beauty and your desire, but also because you want to set her free: you've found a moral basis for your desire, and you feel innocent and self-satisfied. When you hear the bell again you don't go down to supper because you can't bear another scene like the one at the middle of the day. Perhaps Aura will realize it, and come up to look for you after supper.

You force yourself to go on working on the papers. When you're bored with them you undress slowly, get into bed, and fall asleep at once, and for the first time in years you dream, dream of only one thing, of a fleshless hand that comes toward you with a bell, screaming that you should go away, everyone should go away; and when that face with its empty eye-sockets comes close to yours, you wake up with a muffled cry, sweating, and feel those gentle hands caressing your face, those lips murmuring in a low voice, consoling you and asking you for affection. You reach out your hands to find that other body, that naked body with a key dangling from its neck, and when you recognize the key you recognize the woman who is lying over you, kissing you, kissing your whole body. You can't see her in the black of the starless night, but you can smell the fragrance of the patio plants in her hair, can feel her smooth, eager body in your arms; you kiss her again and don't ask her to speak.

When you free yourself, exhausted, from her embrace, you hear her first whisper: "You're my husband." You agree. She tells you it's daybreak, then leaves you, saying that she'll wait for you that night in her room. You agree again, and then fall asleep, relieved, unburdened, emptied of desire, still feeling the touch of Aura's body, her trembling, her surrender.

It's hard for you to wake up. There are several knocks on the door, and at last you get out of bed, groaning and still half-asleep. Aura, on the other side of the door, tells you not to open it: she says that Señora Consuelo wants to talk with you, is waiting for you in her room.

Ten minutes later you enter the widow's sanctuary. She's propped up against the pillows, motionless, her eyes hidden by those drooping, wrinkled, dead-white lids; you notice the puffy wrinkles under her eyes, the utter weariness of her skin.

Without opening her eyes she asks you, "Did you bring the key to the trunk?"

"Yes, I think so . . . Yes, here it is."

"You can read the second part. It's in the same place. It's tied with a blue ribbon."

You go over to the trunk, this time with a certain disgust: the rats are swarming around it, peering at you with their glittering eyes from the cracks in the rotted floorboards, galloping toward the holes in the rotted walls. You open the trunk and take out the second batch of papers, then return to the foot of the bed. Señora Consuelo is petting her white rabbit. A sort of croaking laugh emerges from her buttoned-up throat, and she asks you, "Do you like animals?"

"No, not especially. Perhaps because I've never had any."

"They're good friends. Good companions. Above all when you're old and lonely."

"Yes, they must be."

"They're always themselves, Señor Montero. They don't have any pretensions."

"What did you say his name is?"

"The rabbit? She's Saga. She's very intelligent. She follows her instincts. She's natural and free."

"I thought it was a male rabbit."

"Oh? Then you still can't tell the difference."

"Well, the important thing is that you don't feel all alone."

"They want us to be alone, Señor Montero, because

they tell us that solitude is the only way to achieve saintliness. They forget that in solitude the temptation is even greater."

"I don't understand, Señora."

"Ah, it's better that you don't. Get back to work now, please."

You turn your back on her, walk to the door, leave her room. In the hallway you clench your teeth. Why don't you have courage enough to tell her that you love the girl? Why don't you go back and tell her, once and for all, that you're planning to take Aura away with you when you finish the job? You approach the door again and start pushing it open, still uncertain, and through the crack you see Señora Consuelo standing up, erect, transformed, with a military tunic in her arms: a blue tunic with gold buttons, red epaulettes, bright medals with crowned eagles—a tunic the old lady bites ferociously, kisses tenderly, drapes over her shoulders as she performs a few teetering dance steps. You close the door.

"She was fifteen years old when I met her," you read in the second part of the memoirs. *"Elle avait quinze ans lorsque je l'ai connue et, si j'ose le dire, ce sont ses yeux verts qui ont fait ma perdition."* Consuelo's green eyes, Consuelo who was only fifteen in 1867, when General Llorente married her and took her with him into exile in Paris. *"Ma jeune poupée,"* he wrote in a moment of inspiration, *"ma jeune poupée aux yeux verts; je t'ai comblée d'amour."* He described the house they lived in, the outings, the dances, the carriages, the world of the Second Empire, but all in a dull enough way. *"J'ai même supporté ta haine des chats, moi qu'aimais tellement les jolies bêtes . . ."* One day he found her torturing a cat: she had it clasped between her legs, with her crinoline skirt pulled up, and he didn't know how to attract her attention because it seemed to him that *"tu faisais ça d'une façon si* innocent, *par pur enfantillage,"* and in fact it excited him so much that if you can believe what he wrote, he made love to her that night with extraordinary passion, *"parce que tu m'avais dit que torturer les chats était ta manière a toi de rendre notre amour favorable, par un sacrifice symbolique . . ."* You've figured it up: Señora Consuelo must be 109. Her husband died fifty-nine years ago. *"Tu sais si bien t'habiller, ma douce Consuelo, toujours drappé dans de velours verts, verts comme tes yeux. Je pense que tu seras toujours belle, même dans cent ans . . ."* Always dressed in green. Always beautiful, even after a hundred years. *"Tu es si fière de ta beauté; que ne ferais-tu pas pour rester toujours jeune?"*

IV

Now you know why Aura is living in this house: to perpetuate the illusion of youth and beauty in that poor, crazed old lady. Aura, kept here like a mirror, like one more icon on that votive wall with its clustered offerings, preserved hearts, imagined saints and demons.

You put the manuscript aside and go downstairs, suspecting there's only one place Aura could be in the morning—the place that greedy old woman has assigned to her.

Yes, you find her in the kitchen, at the moment she's beheading a kid: the vapor that rises from the open throat, the smell of spilt blood, the animal's glazed eyes, all give you nausea. Aura is wearing a ragged, blood-stained dress and her hair is disheveled; she looks at you without recognition and goes on with her butchering.

You leave the kitchen: this time you'll really speak to the old lady, really throw her greed and tyranny in her face. When you push open the door she's standing behind the veil of lights, performing a ritual with the empty air, one hand stretched out and clenched, as if holding something up, and the other clasped around an invisible object, striking again and again at the same place. Then she wipes her hands against her breast, sighs, and starts cutting the air again, as if—yes, you can see it clearly—as if she were skinning an animal . . .

You run through the hallway, the parlor, the dining room, to where Aura is slowly skinning the kid, absorbed in her work, heedless of your entrance or your words, looking at you as if you were made of air.

You climb up to your room, go in, and brace yourself against the door as if you were afraid someone would follow you: panting, sweating, victim of your horror, of your certainty. If something or someone should try to enter, you wouldn't be able to resist, you'd move away from the door, you'd let it happen. Frantically you drag the armchair over to that latchless door, push the bed up against it, then fall onto the bed, exhausted, drained of your will-power, with your eyes closed and your arms wrapped around your pillow—the pillow that isn't yours. Nothing is yours.

You fall into a stupor, into the depths of a dream that's your only escape, your only means of saying No to insanity. "She's crazy, she's crazy," you repeat again and again to make yourself sleepy, and you can see her again as she skins the imaginary kid with an imaginary knife. "She's crazy, she's crazy . . ."

in the depths of the dark abyss, in your silent dream with its mouths opening in silence, you see her coming toward you from the blackness of the abyss, you see her crawling toward you.

in silence,

moving her fleshless hand, coming toward you until

her face touches yours and you see the old lady's bloody gums, her toothless gums, and you scream and she goes away again, moving her hand, sowing the abyss with the yellow teeth she carries in her blood-stained apron:

your scream is an echo of Aura's, she's standing in front of you in your dream, and she's screaming because someone's hands have ripped her green taffeta skirt in two, and then

she turns her head toward you

with the torn folds of the skirt in her hands, turns toward you and laughs silently, with the old lady's teeth superimposed on her own, while her legs, her naked legs, shatter into bits and fly toward the abyss . . .

There's a knock at the door, then the sound of the bell, the supper bell. Your head aches so much that you can't make out the hands on the clock, but you know it must be late: above your head you can see the night clouds beyond the skylight. You get up painfully, dazed and hungry. You hold the glass pitcher under the faucet, wait for the water to run, fill the pitcher, then pour it into the basin. You wash your face, brush your teeth with your worn toothbrush that's clogged with greenish paste, dampen your hair—you don't notice you're doing all this in the wrong order—and comb it meticulously in front of the oval mirror on the walnut wardrobe. Then you tie your tie, put on your jacket and go down to the empty dining room, where only one place has been set—yours.

Beside your plate, under your napkin, there's an object you start caressing with your fingers: a clumsy little rag doll, filled with a powder that trickles from its badly sewn shoulder; its face is drawn with India ink, and its body is naked, sketched with a few brush strokes. You eat the cold supper—liver, tomatoes, wine—with your right hand while holding the doll in your left.

You eat mechanically, without noticing at first your own hypnotized attitude, but later you glimpse a reason for your oppressive sleep, your nightmare, and finally identify your sleep-walking movements with those of Aura and the old lady. You're suddenly disgusted by that horrible little doll, in which you begin to suspect a secret illness, a contagion. You let it fall to the floor. You wipe your lips with the napkin, look at your watch, and remember that Aura is waiting for you in her room.

You go cautiously up to Señora Consuelo's door, but there isn't a sound from within. You look at your watch again: it's barely nine o'clock. You decide to feel your way down to that dark, roofed patio you haven't been in since you came through it, without seeing anything, on the day you arrived here.

You touch the damp, mossy walls, breathe the perfumed air, and try to isolate the different elements you're breathing, to recognize the heavy, sumptuous aromas that surround you. The flicker of your match lights up the narrow, empty patio, where various plants are growing on each side in the loose, reddish earth. You can make out the tall, leafy forms that cast their shadows on the walls in the light of the match. But it burns down, singeing your fingers, and you have to light another one to finish seeing the flowers, fruits and plants you remember reading about in old chronicles, the forgotten herbs that are growing here so fragrantly and drowsily: the long, broad, downy leaves of the henbane; the twining stems with flowers that are yellow outside, red inside; the pointed, heart-shaped leaves of the nightshade; the ash-colored down of the grape-mullein with its clustered flowers; the bushy gatheridge with its white blossoms; the belladonna. They come to life in the flare of your match, swaying gently with their shadows, while you recall the uses of these herbs that dilate the pupils, alleviate pain, reduce the pangs of childbirth, bring consolation, weaken the will, induce a voluptuous calm.

You're all alone with the perfumes when the third match burns out. You go up to the hallway slowly, listen again at Señora Consuelo's door, then tiptoe on to Aura's. You push it open without knocking and go into that bare room, where a circle of light reveals the bed, the huge Mexican crucifix, and the woman who comes toward you when the door is closed. Aura is dressed in green, in a green taffeta robe from which, as she approaches, her moon-pale thighs reveal themselves. The woman, you repeat as she comes close, the woman, not the girl of yesterday: the girl of yesterday—you touch Aura's fingers, her waist—couldn't have been more than twenty; the woman of today—you caress her loose black hair, her pallid cheeks—seems to be forty. Between yesterday and today, something about her green eyes has turned hard; the red of her lips has strayed beyond their former outlines, as if she wanted to fix them in a happy grimace, a troubled smile; as if, like that plant in the patio, her smile combined the taste of honey and the taste of gall. You don't have time to think of anything more.

"Sit down on the bed, Felipe."

"Yes."

"We're going to play. You don't have to do anything. Let me do everything myself."

Sitting on the bed, you try to make out the source of that diffuse, opaline light that hardly lets you distinguish the objects in the room, and the presence of Aura, from the golden atmosphere that surrounds them. She sees you looking up, trying to find where it comes from. You can tell from her voice that she's kneeling down in front of you.

"The sky is neither high nor low. It's over us and under us at the same time."

She takes off your shoes and socks and caresses your bare feet.

You feel the warm water that bathes the soles of your feet, while she washes them with a heavy cloth, now and then casting furtive glances at that Christ carved from black wood. Then she dries your feet, takes you by the hand, fastens a few violets in her loose hair, and begins to hum a melody, a waltz, to which you dance with her, held by the murmur of her voice, gliding around to the slow, solemn rhythm she's setting, very different from the light movements of her hands, which unbutton your shirt, caress your chest, reach around to your back and grasp it. You also murmur that wordless song, that melody rising naturally from your throat: you glide around together, each time closer to the bed, until you muffle the song with your hungry kisses on Aura's mouth, until you stop the dance with your crushing kisses on her shoulders and breasts.

You're holding the empty robe in your hands. Aura, squatting on the bed, places an object against her closed thighs, caressing it, summoning you with her hand. She caresses that thin wafer, breaks it against her thighs, oblivious of the crumbs that roll down her hips: she offers you half of the wafer and you take it, place it in your mouth at the same time she does, and swallow it with difficulty. Then you fall on Aura's naked body, you fall on her naked arms, which are stretched out from one side of the bed to the other like the arms of the crucifix hanging on the wall, the black Christ with that scarlet silk wrapped around his thighs, his spread knees, his wounded side, his crown of thorns set on a tangled black wig with silver spangles. Aura opens up like an altar.

You murmur her name in her ear. You feel the woman's full arms against your back. You hear her warm voice in your ear: "Will you love me forever?"

"Forever, Aura. I'll love you forever."

"Forever? Do you swear it?"

"I swear it."

"Even though I grow old? Even though I lose my beauty? Even though my hair turns white?"

"Forever, my love, forever."

"Even if I die, Felipe? Will you love me forever, even if I die?"

"Forever, forever. I swear it. Nothing can separate us."

"Come, Felipe, come . . ."

When you wake up, you reach out to touch Aura's shoulder, but you only touch the still-warm pillow and the white sheet that covers you.

You murmur her name.

You open your eyes and see her standing at the foot of the bed, smiling but not looking at you. She walks slowly toward the corner of the room, sits down on the floor, places her arms on the knees that emerge from the darkness you can't peer into, and strokes the wrinkled hand that comes forward from the lessening darkness: she's sitting at the feet of the old lady, of Señora Consuelo, who is seated in an armchair you hadn't noticed earlier: Señora Consuelo smiles at you, nodding her head, smiling at you along with Aura, who moves her head in rhythm with the old lady's: they both smile at you, thanking you. You lie back, without any will, thinking that the old lady has been in the room all the time;

you remember her movements, her voice, her dance, though you keep telling yourself she wasn't there.

The two of them get up at the same moment, Consuelo from the chair, Aura from the floor. Turning their backs on you, they walk slowly toward the door that leads to

the widow's bedroom, enter that room where the lights
are forever trembling in front of the images, close the
door behind them, and leave you to sleep in Aura's bed.

V

Your sleep is heavy and unsatisfying. In your dreams
you had already felt the same vague melancholy, the
weight on your diaphragm, the sadness that won't stop
oppressing your imagination. Although you're sleeping
in Aura's room, you're sleeping all alone, far from the
body you believe you've possessed.

When you wake up, you look for another presence in
the room, and realize it's not Aura who disturbs you but
rather the double presence of something that was
engendered during the night. You put your hands on
your forehead, trying to calm your disordered senses:
that dull melancholy is hinting to you in a low voice,
the voice of memory and premonition, that you're
seeking your other half, that the sterile conception last
night engendered your own double.

And you stop thinking, because there are things even
stronger than the imagination: the habits that force you
to get up, look for a bathroom off this room without
finding one, go out into the hallway rubbing your
eyelids, climb the stairs tasting the thick bitterness of
your tongue, enter your own room feeling the rough
bristles on your chin, turn on the bath faucets and then
slide into the warm water, letting yourself relax into
forgetfulness.

But while you're drying yourself, you remember the
old lady and the girl as they smiled at you before
leaving the room arm in arm; you recall that whenever
they're together they always do the same things: they
embrace, smile, eat, speak, enter, leave, at the same
time, as if one were imitating the other, as if the will of

one depended on the existence of the other . . . You cut yourself lightly on one cheek as you think of these things while you shave; you make an effort to get control of yourself. When you finish shaving you count the objects in your traveling case, the bottles and tubes which the servant you've never seen brought over from your boarding house: you murmur the names of these objects, touch them, read the contents and instructions, pronounce the names of the manufacturers, keeping to these objects in order to forget that other one, the one without a name, without a label, without any rational consistency. What is Aura expecting of you? you ask yourself, closing the traveling case. What does she want, what does she want?

In answer you hear the dull rhythm of her bell in the corridor telling you breakfast is ready. You walk to the door without your shirt on. When you open it you find Aura there: it must be Aura because you see the green taffeta she always wears, though her face is covered with a green veil. You take her by the wrist, that slender wrist which trembles at your touch . . .

"Breakfast is ready," she says, in the faintest voice you've ever heard.

"Aura, let's stop pretending."

"Pretending?"

"Tell me if Señora Consuelo keeps you from leaving, from living your own life. Why did she have to be there when you and I . . . Please tell me you'll go with me when . . ."

"Go away? Where?"

"Out of this house. Out into the world, to live together. You shouldn't feel bound to your aunt forever . . . Why all this devotion? Do you love her that much?"

"Love her?"

"Yes. Why do you have to sacrifice yourself this way?"

"Love her? She loves me. She sacrifices herself for me."

"But she's an old woman, almost a corpse. You can't . . ."

"She has more life than I do. Yes, she's old and repulsive . . . Felipe, I don't want to become . . . to be like her . . . another . . ."

"She's trying to bury you alive. You've got to be reborn, Aura."

"You have to die before you can be reborn . . . No, you don't understand. Forget about it, Felipe. Just have faith in me."

"If you'd only explain."

"Just have faith in me. She's going to be out today for the whole day."

"She?"

"Yes, the other."

"She's going out? But she never . . ."

"Yes, sometimes she does. She makes a great effort and goes out. She's going out today. For all day. You and I could . . ."

"Go away?"

"If you want to."

"Well . . . perhaps not yet. I'm under contract. But as soon as I can finish the work, then . . ."

"Ah, yes. But she's going to be out all day. We could do something."

"What?"

"I'll wait for you this evening in my aunt's bedroom. I'll wait for you as always."

She turns away, ringing her bell like the lepers who use a bell to announce their approach, telling the unwary: "Out of the way, out of the way." You put on your shirt and coat and follow the sound of the bell calling you to the dining room. In the parlor the widow Llorente comes toward you, bent over, leaning on a knobby cane; she's dressed in an old white gown with a stained and tattered gauze veil. She goes by without looking at you, blowing her nose into a handkerchief, blowing her nose and spitting. She murmurs, "I won't be at home today, Señor Montero. I have complete confidence in your work. Please keep at it. My husband's memoirs must be published."

She goes away, stepping across the carpets with her tiny feet, which are like those of an antique doll, and supporting herself with her cane, spitting and sneezing as if she wanted to clear something from her congested lungs. It's only by an effort of the will that you keep yourself from following her with your eyes, despite the curiosity you feel at seeing the yellowed bridal gown she's taken from the bottom of that old trunk in her bedroom.

You scarcely touch the cold coffee that's waiting for you in the dining room. You sit for an hour in the tall, archback chair, smoking, waiting for the sounds you never hear, until finally you're sure the old lady has left the house and can't catch you at what you're going to do. For the last hour you've had the key to the trunk clutched in your hand, and now you get up and silently walk through the parlor into the hallway, where you wait for another fifteen minutes—your watch tells you how long—with your ear against Señora Consuelo's door. Then you slowly push it open until you can make out, beyond the spider's web of candle, the empty bed on which her rabbit is gnawing at a carrot: the bed that's always littered with scraps of bread, and that you touch gingerly as if you thought the old lady might be hidden among the rumples of the sheets. You walk over to the corner where the trunk is, stepping on the tail of one of those rats; it squeals, escapes from your foot, and scampers off to warn the others. You fit the copper key into the rusted padlock, remove the padlock, and then raise the lid, hearing the creak of the old, stiff hinges. You take out the third portion of the memoirs—it's tied with a red ribbon—and under it you discover those photographs, those old, brittle, dog-eared photographs. You pick them up without looking at them, clutch the whole treasure to your breast, and hurry out of the room without closing the trunk, forgetting the hunger of the rats. You close the door, lean against the wall in the hallway till you catch your breath, then climb the stairs to your room.

Up there you read the new pages, the continuation, the events of an agonized century. In his florid language General Llorente describes the personality of Eugenia de Montijo, pays his respects to Napoleon the Little, summons up his most martial rhetoric to proclaim the Franco-Prussian War, fills whole pages with his sorrow at the defeat, harangues all men of honor about the Republican monster, sees a ray of hope in General Boulanger, sighs for Mexico, believes that in the Dreyfus affair the honor—always that word "honor"— of the army has asserted itself again.

The brittle pages crumble at your touch: you don't respect them now, you're only looking for a reappearance of the woman with green eyes. "I know why you weep at times, Consuelo. I have not been able to give you children, although you are so radiant with life . . ." And later: "Consuelo, you should not tempt God. We must reconcile ourselves. Is not my affection enough? I know that you love me; I feel it. I am not asking you for resignation, because that would offend you. I am only asking you to see, in the great love which you say you have for me, something sufficient, something that can fill both of us, without the need of turning to sick imaginings . . ." On another page: "I told Consuelo that those medicines were utterly useless. She insists on growing her own herbs in the garden. She says she is not deceiving herself. The herbs are not to strengthen the body, but rather the soul." Later: "I found her in a delirium, embracing the pillow. She cried, 'Yes, yes,

yes, I've done it, I've re-created her! I can invoke her, I can give her life with my own life!' It was necessary to call the doctor. He told me he could not quiet her, because the truth was that she was under the effects of narcotics, not of stimulants." And finally: "Early this morning I found her walking barefooted through the hallways. I wanted to stop her. She went by without looking at me, but her words were directed to me. 'Don't stop me,' she said. 'I'm going toward my youth, and my youth is coming toward me. It's coming in, it's in the garden, it's come back . . .' Consuelo, my poor Consuelo! Even the devil was an angel once."

There isn't any more. The memoirs of General Llorente end with that sentence: *"Consuelo, le démon aussi était un ange, avant . . ."*

And after the last page, the portraits. The portrait of an elderly gentleman in a military uniform, an old photograph with these words in one corner: *"Moulin, Photographe, 35 Boulevard Haussmann"* and the date *"1894."* Then the photograph of Aura, of Aura with her green eyes, her black hair gathered in ringlets, leaning against a Doric column with a painted landscape in the background: the landscape of a Lorelei in the Rhine. Her dress is buttoned up to the collar, there's a handkerchief in her hand, she's wearing a bustle: Aura, and the date *"1876"* in white ink, and on the back of the daguerreotype, in spidery handwriting: *"Fait pour notre dixième anniversaire de mariage,"* and a signature in the same hand, *"Consuelo Llorente."* In the third photograph you see both Aura and the old gentleman, but this time they're dressed in outdoor clothes, sitting on a bench in a garden. The photograph has become a little blurred: Aura doesn't look as young as she did in the other picture, but it's she, it's he, it's . . . it's you. You stare and stare at the photographs, then hold them up to the skylight. You cover General Llorente's beard with your finger, and imagine him with black hair, and you only discover yourself: blurred, lost, forgotten, but you, you, you.

Your head is spinning, overcome by the rhythms of that distant waltz, by the odor of damp, fragrant plants: you fall exhausted on the bed, touching your cheeks, your eyes, your nose, as if you were afraid that some invisible hand had ripped off the mask you've been wearing for twenty-seven years, the cardboard features that hid your true face, your real appearance, the appearance you once had but then forgot. You bury your face in the pillow, trying to keep the wind of the past from tearing away your own features, because you don't want to lose them. You lie there with your face in the pillow, waiting for what has to come, for what you can't prevent. You don't look at your watch again, that useless object tediously measuring time in accordance with human vanity, those little hands marking out the long hours that were invented to disguise the real passage of time, which races with a mortal and insolent swiftness no clock could ever measure. A life, a century, fifty years: you can't imagine those lying measurements any longer, you can't hold that bodiless dust within your hands.

When you look up from the pillow, you find you're in darkness. Night has fallen.

Night has fallen. Beyond the skylight the swift black clouds are hiding the moon, which tries to free itself, to reveal its pale, round, smiling face. It escapes for only a moment, then the clouds hide it again. You haven't got any hope left. You don't even look at your watch. You hurry down the stairs, out of that prison cell with its old papers and faded daguerreotypes, and stop at the door of Señora Consuelo's room, and listen to your own voice, muted and transformed after all those hours of silence: "Aura . . ."

Again: "Aura . . ."

You enter the room. The votive lights have gone out.

You remember that the old lady has been away all day: without her faithful attention the candles have all burned up. You grope forward in the darkness to the bed.

And again: "Aura . . ."

You hear a faint rustle of taffeta, and the breathing that keeps time with your own. You reach out your hand to touch Aura's green robe.

"No. Don't touch me. Lie down at my side."

You find the edge of the bed, swing up your legs, and remain there stretched out and motionless. You can't help feeling a shiver of fear: "She might come back any minute."

"She won't come back."

"Ever?"

"I'm exhausted. She's already exhausted. I've never been able to keep her with me for more than three days."

"Aura . . ."

You want to put your hand on Aura's breasts. She turns her back: you can tell by the difference in her voice.

"No . . . Don't touch me . . ."

"Aura . . . I love you."

"Yes. You love me. You told me yesterday that you'd always love me."

"I'll always love you, always. I need your kisses, your body . . ."

"Kiss my face. Only my face."

You bring your lips close to the head that's lying next to yours. You stroke Aura's long black hair. You grasp that fragile woman by the shoulders, ignoring her sharp complaint. You tear off her taffeta robe, embrace her, feel her small and lost and naked in your arms, despite her moaning resistance, her feeble protests, kissing her face without thinking, without distinguishing, and you're touching her withered breasts when a ray of moonlight shines in and surprises you, shines in through a chink in the wall that the rats have chewed open, an eye that lets in a beam of silvery moonlight. It falls on Aura's eroded face, as brittle and yellowed as the memoirs, as creased with wrinkles as the photographs. You stop kissing those fleshless lips, those toothless gums: the ray of moonlight shows you the naked body of the old lady, of Señora Consuelo, limp, spent, tiny, ancient, trembling because you touch her. You love her, you too have come back . . .

You plunge your face, your open eyes, into Consuelo's silver-white hair, and you'll embrace her again when the clouds cover the moon, when you're both hidden again, when the memory of youth, of youth re-embodied, rules the darkness.

"She'll come back, Felipe. We'll bring her back together. Let me recover my strength and I'll bring her back . . ."

*—Translated from the Spanish
by Lysander Kemp*

Thomas Hardy (1840–1928)

BARBARA, OF THE HOUSE OF GREBE

Thomas Hardy, one of the finest British novelists and poets, wrote a small number of stories of high quality relevant to horror literature, for the most part macabre pieces. Critics often refer to his poetry as an influence on the development of horror fiction as well. Moreover, individual scenes in his novels, such as the children's suicide in *Jude the Obscure*, are horrific. His most clearly supernatural piece, "The Withered Arm," is a story of witchcraft with a strongly psychological subtext. Less familiar, but stronger in impact, is "Barbara, of the House of Grebe." T.S. Eliot, in *After Strange Gods*, described it as revealing "a world of pure evil." It is certainly not what we would consider a genre horror tale, but it develops through one horrific scene after another a powerful effect without any overt supernatural trappings. As a moral and psychological tale of horror it is often overlooked. It is for stories such as this that the Penguin *Encyclopedia* says his "neglected short tales constitute one of the key contributions to horror literature by a distinguished writer." While perhaps an overstatement, Hardy somehow holds a place of influence in the evolution of the mode in the late nineteenth and early twentieth century.

It was apparently an idea, rather than a passion, that inspired Lord Uplandtowers' resolve to win her. Nobody ever knew when he formed it, or whence he got his assurance of success in the face of her manifest dislike of him. Possibly not until after that first important act of her life which I shall presently mention. His matured and cynical doggedness at the age of nineteen, when impulse mostly rules calculation, was remarkable, and might have owed its existence as much to his succession to the earldom and its accompanying local honours in childhood, as to the family character; an elevation which jerked him into maturity, so to speak, without his having known adolescence. He had only reached his twelfth year when his father, the fourth Earl, died, after a course of the Bath waters.

Nevertheless, the family character had a great deal to do with it. Determination was hereditary in the bearers of that escutcheon; sometimes for good, sometimes for evil.

The seats of the two families were about ten miles apart, the way between them lying along the now old, then new, turnpike-road connecting Havenpool and Warborne with the city of Melchester; a road which, though only a branch from what was known as the Great Western Highway, is probably, even at present, as it has been for the last hundred years, one of the finest examples of a macadamized turnpike-track that can be found in England.

The mansion of the Earl, as well as that of his neighbour, Barbara's father, stood back about a mile from the highway, with which each was connected by an ordinary drive and lodge. It was along this particular highway that the young Earl drove on a certain evening at Christmastide some twenty years before the end of the last century, to attend a ball at Chene Manor, the home of Barbara and her parents Sir John and Lady Grebe. Sir John's was a baronetcy created a few years before the breaking out of the Civil War, and his lands were even more extensive than those of Lord Uplandtowers himself, comprising this Manor of Chene, another on the coast near, half the Hundred of Cockdene, and well-enclosed lands in several other parishes, notably Warborne and those contiguous. At this time Barbara was barely seventeen, and the ball is the first occasion on which we have any tradition of Lord Uplandtowers attempting tender relations with her; it was early enough, God knows.

An intimate friend—one of the Drenkhards—is said to have dined with him that day, and Lord Uplandtowers had, for a wonder, communicated to his guest the secret design of his heart.

"You'll never get her—sure; you'll never get her!" this friend had said at parting. "She's not drawn to your lordship by love: and as for thought of a good match, why, there's no more calculation in her than in a bird."

"We'll see," said Lord Uplandtowers impassively.

He no doubt thought of his friend's forecast as he travelled along the highway in his chariot; but the sculptural repose of his profile against the vanishing daylight on his right hand would have shown his friend that the Earl's equanimity was undisturbed. He reached the solitary wayside tavern called Lornton Inn—the rendezvous of many a daring poacher for operations in the adjoining forest; and he might have observed, if he had taken the trouble, a strange post-chaise standing in the halting-space before the inn. He duly sped past it, and half-an-hour after through the little town of Warborne. Onward, a mile further, was the house of his entertainer.

At this date it was an imposing edifice—or, rather, congeries of edifices—as extensive as the residence of the Earl himself, though far less regular. One wing showed extreme antiquity, having huge chimneys, whose substructures projected from the external walls like towers; and a kitchen of vast dimensions, in which (it was said) breakfasts had been cooked for John of Gaunt. Whilst he was yet in the forecourt he could hear the rhythm of French horns and clarionets, the favourite instruments of those days at such entertainments.

Entering the long parlour, in which the dance had just been opened by Lady Grebe with a minuet—it being now seven o'clock, according to the tradition— he was received with a welcome befitting his rank, and looked round for Barbara. She was not dancing, and seemed to be preoccupied—almost, indeed, as though she had been waiting for him. Barbara at this time was a good and pretty girl, who never spoke ill of anyone, and hated other pretty women the very least possible. She did not refuse him for the country-dance which followed, and soon after was his partner in a second.

The evening wore on, and the horns and clarionets tootled merrily. Barbara evinced towards her lover neither distinct preference nor aversion; but old eyes would have seen that she pondered something. However, after supper she pleaded a headache, and disappeared. To pass the time of her absence, Lord Uplandtowers went into a little room adjoining the long gallery, where some elderly ones were sitting by the fire—for he had a phlegmatic dislike of dancing for its own sake,—and, lifting the window-curtains, he looked out of the window into the park and wood, dark now as a cavern. Some of the guests appeared to be leaving even so soon as this, two lights showing themselves as turning away from the door and sinking to nothing in the distance.

His hostess put her head into the room to look for partners for the ladies, and Lord Uplandtowers came out. Lady Grebe informed him that Barbara had not returned to the ball-room: she had gone to bed in sheer necessity.

"She has been so excited over the ball all day," her mother continued, "that I feared she would be worn out early. . . . But sure, Lord Uplandtowers, you won't be leaving yet?"

He said that it was near twelve o'clock, and that some had already left.

"I protest nobody has gone yet," said Lady Grebe.

To humour her he stayed till midnight, and then set out. He had made no progress in his suit; but he had assured himself that Barbara gave no other guest the preference, and nearly everybody in the neighbourhood was there.

"'Tis only a matter of time," said the calm young philosopher.

The next morning he lay till near ten o'clock, and he had only just come out upon the head of the staircase when he heard hoofs upon the gravel without; in a few moments the door had been opened, and Sir John Grebe met him in the hall, as he set foot on the lowest stair.

"My lord—where's Barbara—my daughter?"

Even the Earl of Uplandtowers could not repress amazement. "What's the matter, my dear Sir John," says he.

The news was startling, indeed. From the Baronet's disjointed explanation Lord Uplandtowers gathered that after his own and the other guests' departure Sir John and Lady Grebe had gone to rest without seeing any more of Barbara; it being understood by them that she had retired to bed when she sent word to say that she could not join the dancers again. Before then she had told her maid that she would dispense with her services for this night; and there was evidence to show that the young lady had never lain down at all, the bed remaining unpressed. Circumstances seemed to prove that the deceitful girl had feigned indisposition to get an excuse for leaving the ball-room, and that she had left the house within ten minutes, presumably during the first dance after supper.

"I saw her go," said Lord Uplandtowers.

"The devil you did!" says Sir John.

"Yes." And he mentioned the retreating carriage-lights, and how he was assured by Lady Grebe that no guest had departed.

"Surely that was it!" said the father. "But she's not gone alone, d'ye know!"

"Ah—who is the young man?"

"I can on'y guess. My worst fear is my most likely guess. I'll say no more. I thought—yet I would not believe—it possible that you was the sinner. Would that you had been! But 'tis t'other, 'tis t'other, by Heaven! I must e'en up and after 'em!"

"Whom do you suspect?"

Sir John would not give a name, and, stultified rather than agitated, Lord Uplandtowers accompanied him back to Chene. He again asked upon whom were the Baronet's suspicions directed; and the impulsive Sir John was no match for the insistence of Uplandtowers.

He said at length, "I fear 'tis Edmond Willowes."

"Who's he?"

"A young fellow of Shottsford-Forum—a widow-woman's son," the other told him, and explained that Willowes's father, or grandfather, was the last of the old glass-painters in that place, where (as you may know) the art lingered on when it had died out in every other part of England.

"By God that's bad—mighty bad!" said Lord Uplandtowers, throwing himself back in the chaise in frigid despair.

They despatched emissaries in all directions; one by the Melchester Road, another by Shottsford-Forum, another coastwards.

But the lovers had a ten-hours' start; and it was

apparent that sound judgment had been exercised in choosing as their time of flight the particular night when the movements of a strange carriage would not be noticed, either in the park or on the neighbouring highway, owing to the general press of vehicles. The chaise which had been seen waiting at Lornton Inn was, no doubt, the one they had escaped in; and the pair of heads which had planned so cleverly thus far had probably contrived marriage ere now.

The fears of her parents were realized. A letter sent by special messenger from Barbara, on the evening of that day, briefly informed them that her lover and herself were on the way to London, and before this communication reached her home they would be united as husband and wife. She had taken this extreme step because she loved her dear Edmond as she could love no other man, and because she had seen closing round her the doom of marriage with Lord Uplandtowers, unless she put that threatened fate out of possibility by doing as she had done. She had well considered the step beforehand, and was prepared to live like any other country-townsman's wife if her father repudiated her for her action.

"Damn her!" said Lord Uplandtowers, as he drove homeward that night. "Damn her for a fool!"—which shows the kind of love he bore her.

Well; Sir John had already started in pursuit of them as a matter of duty, driving like a wild man to Melchester, and thence by the direct highway to the capital. But he soon saw that he was acting to no purpose; and by and by, discovering that the marriage had actually taken place, he forebore all attempts to unearth them in the City, and returned and sat down with his lady to digest the event as best they could.

To proceed against this Willowes for the abduction of our heiress was, possibly, in their power; yet, when they considered the now unalterable facts, they refrained from violent retribution. Some six weeks passed, during which time Barbara's parents, though they keenly felt her loss, held no communication with the truant, either for reproach or condonation. They continued to think of the disgrace she had brought upon herself; for, though the young man was an honest fellow, and the son of an honest father, the latter had died so early, and his widow had had such struggles to maintain herself, that the son was very imperfectly educated. Moreover, his blood was, as far as they knew, of no distinction whatever, whilst hers, through her mother, was compounded of the best juices of ancient baronial distillation, containing tinctures of Maundeville, and Mohun, and Syward, and Peverell, and Culliford, and Talbot, and Plantagenet, and York, and Lancaster, and God knows what besides, which it was a thousand pities to throw away.

The father and mother sat by the fireplace that was spanned by the four-centred arch bearing the family shields on its haunches, and groaned aloud—the lady more than Sir John.

"To think this should have come upon us in our old age!" said he.

"Speak for yourself!" she snapped through her sobs, "I am only one-and-forty! . . . Why didn't ye ride faster and overtake 'em!"

In the meantime the young married lovers, caring no more about their blood than about ditch-water, were intensely happy—happy, that is, in the descending scale which, as we all know, Heaven in its wisdom has ordained for such rash cases; that is to say, the first week they were in the seventh heaven, the second in the sixth, the third week temperate, the fourth reflective, and so on; a lover's heart after possession being comparable to the earth in its geologic stages, as described to us sometimes by our worthy President; first a hot coal, then a warm one, then a cooling cinder, then chilly—

the simile shall be pursued no further. The long and the short of it was that one day a letter, sealed with their daughter's own little seal, came into Sir John and Lady Grebe's hands; and, on opening it, they found it to contain an appeal from the young couple to Sir John to forgive them for what they had done, and they would fall on their naked knees and be most dutiful children for evermore.

Then Sir John and his lady sat down again by the fireplace with the four-centred arch, and consulted, and re-read the letter. Sir John Grebe, if the truth must be told, loved his daughter's happiness far more, poor man, than he loved his name and lineage; he recalled to his mind all her little ways, gave vent to a sigh; and, by this time acclimatized to the idea of the marriage, said that what was done could not be undone, and that he supposed they must not be too harsh with her. Perhaps Barbara and her husband were in actual need; and how could they let their only child starve?

A slight consolation had come to them in an unexpected manner. They had been credibly informed that an ancestor of plebeian Willowes was once honoured with intermarriage with a scion of the aristocracy who had gone to the dogs. In short, such is the foolishness of distinguished parents, and sometimes of others also, that they wrote that very day to the address Barbara had given them, informing her that she might return home and bring her husband with her; they would not object to see him, would not reproach her, and would endeavour to welcome both, and to discuss with them what could best be arranged for their future.

In three or four days a rather shabby post-chaise drew up at the door of Chene Manor-house, at sound of which the tender-hearted baronet and his wife ran out as if to welcome a prince and princess of the blood. They were overjoyed to see their spoilt child return safe and sound—though she was only Mrs. Willowes, wife of Edmond Willowes of nowhere. Barbara burst into penitential tears, and both husband and wife were contrite enough, as well they might be, considering that they had not a guinea to call their own.

When the four had calmed themselves, and not a word of chiding had been uttered to the pair, they discussed the position soberly, young Willowes sitting in the background with great modesty till invited forward by Lady Grebe in no frigid tone.

"How handsome he is!" she said to herself. "I don't wonder at Barbara's craze for him."

He was, indeed, one of the handsomest men who ever set his lips on a maid's. A blue coat, murrey waistcoat, and breeches of drab set off a figure that could scarcely be surpassed. He had large dark eyes, anxious now, as they glanced from Barbara to her parents and tenderly back again to her; observing whom, even now in her trepidation, one could see why the *sang froid* of Lord Uplandtowers had been raised to more than lukewarmness. Her fair young face (according to the tale handed down by old women) looked out from under a gray conical hat, trimmed with white ostrich-feathers, and her little toes peeped from a buff petticoat worn under a puce gown. Her features were not regular; they were almost infantine, as you may see from miniatures in possession of the family, her mouth showing much sensitiveness, and one could be sure that her faults would not lie on the side of bad temper unless for urgent reasons.

Well, they discussed their state as became them, and the desire of the young couple to gain the good-will of those upon whom they were literally dependent for everything induced them to agree to any temporizing measure that was not too irksome. Therefore, having been nearly two months united, they did not oppose Sir John's proposal that he should furnish Edmond Willowes with funds sufficient for him to travel a year on the Continent in the company of a tutor, the young man undertaking to lend himself with the utmost diligence to the tutor's instructions, till he became polished outwardly and inwardly to the degree required in the husband of such a lady as Barbara. He was to apply himself to the study of languages, manners, history, society, ruins, and everything else that came under his eyes, till he should return to take his place without blushing by Barbara's side.

"And by that time," said worthy Sir John, "I'll get my little place out at Yewsholt ready for you and Barbara to occupy on your return. The house is small and out of the way; but it will do for a young couple for a while."

"If 'twere no bigger than a summer-house it would do!" says Barbara.

"If 'twere no bigger than a sedan-chair!" says Willowes. "And the more lonely the better."

"We can put up with the loneliness," said Barbara, with less zest. "Some friends will come, no doubt."

All this being laid down, a travelled tutor was called in—a man of many gifts and great experience—and on a fine morning away tutor and pupil went. A great reason urged against Barbara accompanying her youthful husband was that his attentions to her would naturally be such as to prevent his zealously applying every hour of his time to learning and seeing—an argument of wise prescience, and unanswerable. Regular days for letter-writing were fixed, Barbara and her Edmond exchanged their last kisses at the door, and the chaise swept under the archway into the drive.

He wrote to her from Le Havre, as soon as he reached that port, which was not for seven days, on account of adverse winds; he wrote from Rouen, and from Paris; described to her his sight of the King and Court at Versailles, and the wonderful marble-work and mirrors in that palace; wrote next from Lyons; then, after a comparatively long interval, from Turin, narrating his fearful adventures in crossing Mont Cenis on mules, and how he was overtaken with a terrific snowstorm, which had well-nigh been the end of him, and his tutor, and his guides. Then he wrote glowingly of Italy; and Barbara could see the development of her husband's mind reflected in his letters month by month; and she much admired the forethought of her father in suggesting this education for Edmond. Yet she sighed sometimes—her husband being no longer in evidence to fortify her in her choice of him—and timidly dreaded what mortifications might be in store for her by reason of this *mésalliance*. She went out very little; for on the one or two occasions on which she had shown herself to former friends she noticed a distinct difference in their manner, as though they should say, "Ah, my happy swain's wife; you're caught!"

Edmond's letters were as affectionate as ever; even more affectionate, after a while, than hers were to him. Barbara observed this growing coolness in herself; and like a good and honest lady was horrified and grieved, since her only wish was to act faithfully and uprightly. It troubled her so much that she prayed for a warmer heart, and at last wrote to her husband to beg him, now that he was in the land of Art, to send her his portrait, ever so small, that she might look at it all day and every day, and never for a moment forget his features.

Willowes was nothing loth, and replied that he would do more than she wished: he had made friends with a sculptor in Pisa, who was much interested in him and his history; and he had commissioned this artist to make a bust of himself in marble, which when finished he would send her. What Barbara had wanted was something immediate; but she expressed no objection to the delay; and in his next communication Edmond told her that the sculptor, of his own choice, had decided to extend the bust to a full-length statue, so anxious was he to get a specimen of his skill introduced to the notice of the English aristocracy. It was progressing well, and rapidly.

Meanwhile, Barbara's attention began to be occupied at home with Yewsholt Lodge, the house that her kind-hearted father was preparing for her residence when her husband returned. It was a small place on the plan of a large one—a cottage built in the form of a mansion, having a central hall with a wooden gallery running round it, and rooms no bigger than closets to support this introduction. It stood on a slope so solitary, and surrounded by trees so dense, that the birds who inhabited the boughs sang at strange hours, as if they hardly could distinguish night from day.

During the progress of repairs at this bower Barbara frequently visited it. Though so secluded by the dense growth, it was near the high road, and one day while looking over the fence she saw Lord Uplandtowers riding past. He saluted her courteously, yet with mechanical stiffness, and did not halt. Barbara went home, and continued to pray that she might never cease to love her husband. After that she sickened, and did not come out of doors again for a long time.

The year of education had extended to fourteen months, and the house was in order for Edmond's return to take up his abode there with Barbara, when, instead of the accustomed letter for her, came one to Sir John Grebe in the handwriting of the said tutor, informing him of a terrible catastrophe that had occurred to them at Venice. Mr. Willowes and himself had attended the theatre one night during the Carnival of the preceding week, to witness the Italian comedy, when owing to the carelessness of one of the candle-snuffers, the theatre had caught fire, and been burnt to the ground. Few persons had lost their lives, owing to the superhuman exertions of some of the audience in getting out the senseless sufferers; and, among them all, he who had risked his own life the most heroically was Mr. Willowes. In re-entering for the fifth time to save his fellow-creatures some fiery beams had fallen upon him, and he had been given up for lost. He was, however, by the blessing of Providence, recovered, with the life still in him, though he was fearfully burnt; and by almost a miracle he seemed likely to survive, his constitution being wondrously sound. He was, of course, unable to write, but he was receiving the attention of several skilful surgeons. Further report would be made by the next mail or by private hand.

The tutor said nothing in detail of poor Willowes's sufferings, but as soon as the news was broken to Barbara she realized how intense they must have been, and her immediate instinct was to rush to his side, though, on consideration, the journey seemed impossible to her. Her health was by no means what it had been, and to post across Europe at that season of the year, or to traverse the Bay of Biscay in a sailing-craft, was an undertaking that would hardly be justified by the result. But she was anxious to go till, on reading to the end of the letter, her husband's tutor was found to hint very strongly against such a step if it should be contemplated, this being also the opinion of the surgeons. And though Willowes's comrade refrained from giving his reasons, they disclosed themselves plainly enough in the sequel.

The truth was that the worst of the wounds resulting from the fire had occurred to his head and face—that handsome face which had won her heart from her,—and both the tutor and the surgeons knew that for a sensitive young woman to see him before his wounds had healed would cause more misery to her by the shock than happiness to him by her ministrations.

Lady Grebe blurted out what Sir John and Barbara had thought, but had had too much delicacy to express.

"Sure, 'tis mighty hard for you, poor Barbara, that

the one little gift he had to justify your rash choice of him—his wonderful good looks—should be taken away like this, to leave 'ee no excuse at all for your conduct in the world's eyes. . . . Well, I wish you'd married t'other—that do I!" And the lady sighed.

"He'll soon get right again," said her father soothingly.

Such remarks as the above were not often made; but they were frequent enough to cause Barbara an uneasy sense of self-stultification. She determined to hear them no longer; and the house at Yewsholt being ready and furnished, she withdrew thither with her maids, where for the first time she could feel mistress of a home that would be hers and her husband's exclusively, when he came.

After long weeks Willowes had recovered sufficiently to be able to write himself, and slowly and tenderly he enlightened her upon the full extent of his injuries. It was a mercy, he said, that he had not lost his sight entirely; but he was thankful to say that he still retained full vision in one eye, though the other was dark for ever. The sparing manner in which he meted out particulars of his condition told Barbara how appalling had been his experience. He was grateful for her assurance that nothing could change her; but feared she did not fully realize that he was so sadly disfigured as to make it doubtful if she would recognize him. However, in spite of all, his heart was as true to her as it ever had been.

Barbara saw from his anxiety how much lay behind. She replied that she submitted to the decrees of Fate, and would welcome him in any shape as soon as he could come. She told him of the pretty retreat in which she had taken up her abode, pending their joint occupation of it, and did not reveal how much she had sighed over the information that all his good looks were gone. Still less did she say that she felt a certain strangeness in awaiting him, the weeks they had lived together having been so short by comparison with the length of his absence.

Slowly drew on the time when Willowes found himself well enough to come home. He landed at Southampton, and posted thence towards Yewsholt. Barbara arranged to go out to meet him as far as Lornton Inn—the spot between the Forest and the Chase at which he had waited for night on the evening of their elopement. Thither she drove at the appointed hour in a little pony-chaise, presented her by her father on her birthday for her especial use in her new house; which vehicle she sent back on arriving at the inn, the plan agreed upon being that she should perform the return journey with her husband in his hired coach.

There was not much accommodation for a lady at this wayside tavern; but, as it was a fine evening in early summer, she did not mind—walking about outside, and straining her eyes along the highway for the expected one. But each cloud of dust that enlarged in the distance and drew near was found to disclose a conveyance other than his post-chaise. Barbara remained till the appointment was two hours passed, and then began to fear that owing to some adverse wind in the Channel he was not coming that night.

While waiting she was conscious of a curious trepidation that was not entirely solicitude, and did not amount to dread; her tense state of incertitude bordered both on disappointment and on relief. She had lived six or seven weeks with an imperfectly educated yet handsome husband whom now she had not seen for seventeen months, and who was so changed physically by an accident that she was assured she would hardly know him. Can we wonder at her compound state of mind?

But her immediate difficulty was to get away from Lornton Inn, for her situation was becoming embarrassing. Like too many of Barbara's actions, this drive had been undertaken without much reflection. Expecting to wait no more than a few minutes for her husband in his post-chaise, and to enter it with him, she had not hesitated to isolate herself by sending back her own little vehicle. She now found that, being so well known in this neighbourhood, her excursion to meet her long-absent husband was exciting great interest. She was conscious that more eyes were watching her from the inn-windows than met her own gaze. Barbara had decided to get home by hiring whatever kind of conveyance the tavern afforded, when, straining her eyes for the last time over the now darkening highway, she perceived yet another dust-cloud drawing near. She paused; a chariot ascended to the inn, and would have passed had not its occupant caught sight of her standing expectantly. The horses were checked on the instant.

"You here—and alone, my dear Mrs. Willowes?" said Lord Uplandtowers, whose carriage it was.

She explained what had brought her into this lonely situation; and, as he was going in the direction of her own home, she accepted his offer of a seat beside him. Their conversation was embarrassed and fragmentary at first; but when they had driven a mile or two she was surprised to find herself talking earnestly and warmly to him: her impulsiveness was in truth but the natural consequence of her late existence—a somewhat desolate one by reason of the strange marriage she had made; and there is no more indiscreet mood than that of a woman surprised into talk who has long been imposing upon herself a policy of reserve. Therefore her ingenuous heart rose with a bound into her throat when, in response to his leading questions, or rather hints, she allowed her troubles to leak out of her. Lord Uplandtowers took her quite to her own door, although he had driven three miles out of his way to do so; and in handing her down she heard from him a whisper of stern reproach: "It need not have been thus if you had listened to me!"

She made no reply, and went indoors. There, as the evening wore away, she regretted more and more that she had been so friendly with Lord Uplandtowers. But he had launched himself upon her so unexpectedly: if she had only foreseen the meeting with him, what a careful line of conduct she would have marked out! Barbara broke into a perspiration of disquiet when she thought of her unreserve, and, in self-chastisement, resolved to sit up till midnight on the bare chance of Edmond's return; directing that supper should be laid for him, improbable as his arrival till the morrow was.

The hours went past, and there was dead silence in and round about Yewsholt Lodge, except for the soughing of the trees; till, when it was near upon midnight, she heard the noise of hoofs and wheels approaching the door. Knowing that it could only be her husband, Barbara instantly went into the hall to meet him. Yet she stood there not without a sensation of faintness, so many were the changes since their parting! And, owing to her casual encounter with Lord Uplandtowers, his voice and image still remained with her, excluding Edmond, her husband, from the inner circle of her impressions.

But she went to the door, and the next moment a figure stepped inside, of which she knew the outline, but little besides. Her husband was attired in a flapping black cloak and slouched hat, appearing altogether as a foreigner, and not as the young English burgess who had left her side. When he came forward into the light of the lamp, she perceived with surprise, and almost with fright, that he wore a mask. At first she had not noticed this—there being nothing in its colour which would lead a casual observer to think he was looking on anything but a real countenance.

He must have seen her start of dismay at the unexpectedness of his appearance, for he said hastily: "I did not mean to come in to you like this—I thought you would have been in bed. How good you are, dear Barbara!" He put his arm round her, but he did not attempt to kiss her.

"O Edmond—it *is* you?—it must be?" she said, with clasped hands, for though his figure and movement were almost enough to prove it, and the tones were not unlike the old tones, the enunciation was so altered as to seem that of a stranger.

"I am covered like this to hide myself from the curious eyes of the inn-servants and others," he said, in a low voice. "I will send back the carriage and join you in a moment."

"You are quite alone?"

"Quite. My companion stopped at Southampton."

The wheels of the post-chaise rolled away as she entered the dining-room, where the supper was spread; and presently he rejoined her there. He had removed his cloak and hat, but the mask was still retained; and she could now see that it was of special make, of some flexible material like silk, coloured so as to represent flesh; it joined naturally to the front hair, and was otherwise cleverly executed.

"Barbara—you look ill," he said, removing his glove, and taking her hand.

"Yes—I have been ill," said she.

"Is this pretty little house ours?"

"O—yes." She was hardly conscious of her words, for the hand he had ungloved in order to take hers was contorted, and had one or two of its fingers missing; while through the mask she discerned the twinkle of one eye only.

"I would give anything to kiss you, dearest, now at this moment!" he continued, with mournful passionateness. "But I cannot—in this guise. The servants are abed, I suppose?"

"Yes," said she. "But I can call them? You will have some supper?"

He said he would have some, but that it was not necessary to call anybody at that hour. Thereupon they approached the table, and sat down, facing each other.

Despite Barbara's scared state of mind, it was forced upon her notice that her husband trembled, as if he feared the impression he was producing, or was about to produce, as much as, or more than, she. He drew nearer, and took her hand again.

"I had this mask made at Venice," he began, in evident embarrassment. "My darling Barbara—my dearest wife—do you think you—will mind when I take it off? You will not dislike me—will you?"

"O Edmond, of course I shall not mind," said she. "What has happened to you is our misfortune; but I am prepared for it."

"Are you sure you are prepared?"

"O yes! You are my husband."

"You really feel quite confident that nothing external can affect you?" he said again, in a voice rendered uncertain by his agitation.

"I think I am—quite," she answered faintly.

He bent his head. "I hope, I hope you are," he whispered.

In the pause which followed, the ticking of the clock in the hall seemed to grow loud; and he turned a little aside to remove the mask. She breathlessly awaited the operation, which was one of some tediousness, watching him one moment, averting her face the next; and when it was done she shut her eyes at the dreadful spectacle that was revealed. A quick spasm of horror had passed through her; but though she quailed she forced herself to regard him anew, repressing the cry that would naturally have escaped from her ashy lips. Unable to look at him longer, Barbara sank down on the floor beside her chair, covering her eyes.

"You cannot look at me!" he groaned in a hopeless way. "I am too terrible an object even for you to bear! I knew it; yet I hoped against it. O, this is a bitter fate—curse the skill of those Venetian surgeons who saved me alive! . . . Look up, Barbara," he continued beseechingly; "view me completely; say you loathe me, if you do loathe me, and settle the case between us for ever!"

His unhappy wife pulled herself together for a desperate strain. He was her Edmond; he had done her no wrong; he had suffered. A momentary devotion to him helped her, and lifting her eyes as bidden she regarded this human remnant, this *écorché*, a second time. But the sight was too much. She again involuntarily looked aside and shuddered.

"Do you think you can get used to this?" he said. "Yes or no! Can you bear such a thing of the charnel-house near you? Judge for yourself, Barbara. Your Adonis, your matchless man, has come to this!"

The poor lady stood beside him motionless, save for the restlessness of her eyes. All her natural sentiments of affection and pity were driven clean out of her by a sort of panic; she had just the same sense of dismay and fearfulness that she would have had in the presence of an apparition. She could nohow fancy this to be her chosen one—the man she had loved; he was metamorphosed to a specimen of another species. "I do not loathe you," she said with trembling. "But I am so horrified—so overcome! Let me recover myself. Will you sup now? And while you do so may I go to my room to—regain my old feeling for you? I will try, if I may leave you awhile? Yes, I will try!"

Without waiting for an answer from him, and keeping her gaze carefully averted, the frightened woman crept to the door and out of the room. She heard him sit down to the table, as if to begin supper; though, Heaven knows, his appetite was slight enough after a reception which had confirmed his worst surmises. When Barbara had ascended the stairs and arrived in her chamber she sank down, and buried her face in the coverlet of the bed.

Thus she remained for some time. The bed-chamber was over the dining-room, and presently as she knelt Barbara heard Willowes thrust back his chair, and rise to go into the hall. In five minutes that figure would probably come up the stairs and confront her again; it,—this new and terrible form, that was not her husband's. In the loneliness of this night, with neither maid nor friend beside her, she lost all self-control, and at the first sound of his footstep on the stairs, without so much as flinging a cloak round her, she flew from the room, ran along the gallery to the back staircase, which she descended, and, unlocking the back door, let herself out. She scarcely was aware what she had done till she found herself in the greenhouse, crouching on a flower-stand.

Here she remained, her great timid eyes strained through the glass upon the garden without, and her skirts gathered up, in fear of the field-mice which sometimes came there. Every moment she dreaded to hear footsteps which she ought by law to have longed for, and a voice that should have been as music to her soul. But Edmond Willowes came not that way. The nights were getting short at this season, and soon the dawn appeared, and the first rays of the sun. By daylight she had less fear than in the dark. She thought she could meet him, and accustom herself to the spectacle.

So the much-tried young woman unfastened the door of the hot-house, and went back by the way she had emerged a few hours ago. Her poor husband was probably in bed and asleep, his journey having been long; and she made as little noise as possible in her entry. The house was just as she had left it, and she looked about in the hall for his cloak and hat, but she could not see them; nor did she perceive the small trunk which had been all that he brought with him, his heavier baggage having been left at Southampton for the road-waggon. She summoned courage to mount the stairs; the bedroom-door was open as she had left it. She fearfully peeped round; the bed had not been pressed. Perhaps he had lain down on the dining-room sofa. She descended and entered; he was not there. On the table beside his unsoiled plate lay a note, hastily written on the leaf of a pocket-book. It was something like this:

> MY EVER-BELOVED WIFE,—The effect that my forbidding appearance has produced upon you was one which I foresaw as quite possible. I hoped against it, but foolishly so. I was aware that no *human* love could survive such a catastrophe. I confess I thought yours *divine;* but, after so long an absence, there could not be left sufficient warmth to overcome the too natural first aversion. It was an experiment, and it has failed. I do not blame you; perhaps, even, it is better so. Good-bye. I leave England for one year. You will see me again at the expiration of that time, if I live. Then I will ascertain your true feeling; and, if it be against me, go away for ever.
>
> E.W.

On recovering from her surprise, Barbara's remorse was such that she felt herself absolutely unforgiveable. She should have regarded him as an afflicted being, and not have been this slave to mere eyesight, like a child. To follow him and entreat him to return was her first thought. But on making inquiries she found that nobody had seen him: he had silently disappeared.

More than this, to undo the scene of last night was impossible. Her terror had been too plain, and he was a man unlikely to be coaxed back by her efforts to do her duty. She went and confessed to her parents all that had occurred; which, indeed, soon became known to more persons than those of her own family.

The year passed, and he did not return; and it was doubted if he were alive. Barbara's contrition for her unconquerable repugnance was now such that she longed to build a church-aisle, or erect a monument, and devote herself to deeds of charity for the remainder of her days. To that end she made inquiry of the excellent parson under whom she sat on Sundays, at a vertical distance of a dozen feet. But he could only adjust his wig and tap his snuff-box; for such was the lukewarm state of religion in those days, that not an aisle, steeple, porch, east window, Ten-Commandment board, lion-and-unicorn, or brass candlestick, was required anywhere at all in the neighbourhood as a votive offering from a distracted soul—the last century contrasting greatly in this respect with the happy times in which we live, when urgent appeals for contributions to such objects pour in by every morning's post, and nearly all churches have been made to look like new pennies. As the poor lady could not ease her conscience this way, she determined at least to be charitable, and soon had the satisfaction of finding her porch thronged every morning by the raggedest, idlest, most drunken, hypocritical, and worthless tramps in Christendom.

But human hearts are as prone to change as the leaves of the creeper on the wall, and in the course of time, hearing nothing of her husband, Barbara could sit unmoved whilst her mother and friends said in her hearing, "Well, what has happened is for the best." She began to think so herself, for even now she could not summon up that lopped and mutilated form without a shiver, though whenever her mind flew back to her early wedded days, and the man who had stood beside her then, a thrill of tenderness moved her, which if quickened by his living presence might have become strong. She was young and inexperienced, and had hardly on his late return grown out of the capricious fancies of girlhood.

But he did not come again, and when she thought of his word that he would return once more, if living, and how unlikely he was to break his word, she gave him up for dead. So did her parents; so also did another person—that man of silence, of irresistible incisiveness, of still countenance, who was as awake as seven sentinels when he seemed to be as sound asleep as the figures on his family monument. Lord Uplandtowers, though not yet thirty, had chuckled like a caustic fogey of threescore when he heard of Barbara's terror and flight at her husband's return, and of the latter's prompt departure. He felt pretty sure, however, that Willowes, despite his hurt feelings, would have reappeared to claim his bright-eyed property if he had been alive at the end of the twelve months.

As there was no husband to live with her, Barbara had relinquished the house prepared for them by her father, and taken up her abode anew at Chene Manor, as in the days of her girlhood. By degrees the episode with Edmond Willowes seemed but a fevered dream, and as the months grew to years Lord Uplandtowers' friendship with the people at Chene—which had somewhat cooled after Barbara's elopement—revived considerably, and he again became a frequent visitor there. He could not make the most trivial alteration or improvement at Knollingwood Hall, where he lived, without riding off to consult with his friend Sir John at Chene; and thus putting himself frequently under her eyes, Barbara grew accustomed to him, and talked to him as freely as to a brother. She even began to look up to him as a person of authority, judgment, and prudence; and though his severity on the bench towards poachers, smugglers, and turnip-stealers was matter of common notoriety, she trusted that much of what was said might be misrepresentation.

Thus they lived on till her husband's absence had stretched to years, and there could be no longer any doubt of his death. A passionless manner of renewing his addresses seemed no longer out of place in Lord Uplandtowers. Barbara did not love him, but hers was essentially one of those sweet-pea or with-wind natures which require a twig of stouter fibre than its own to hang upon and bloom. Now, too, she was older, and admitted to herself that a man whose ancestor had run scores of Saracens through and through in fighting for the site of the Holy Sepulchre was a more desirable husband, socially considered, than one who could only claim with certainty to know that his father and grandfather were respectable burgesses.

Sir John took occasion to inform her that she might legally consider herself a widow; and, in brief, Lord Uplandtowers carried his point with her, and she married him, though he could never get her to own that she loved him as she had loved Willowes. In my childhood I knew an old lady whose mother saw the wedding, and she said that when Lord and Lady Uplandtowers drove away from her father's house in the evening it was in a coach-and-four, and that my lady was dressed in green and silver, and wore the gayest hat and feather that ever were seen; though whether it was that the green did not suit her complexion, or otherwise, the Countess looked pale, and the reverse of blooming. After their marriage her husband took her to London, and she saw the gaieties of a season there; then they returned to Knollingwood Hall, and thus a year passed away.

Before their marriage her husband had seemed to care but little about her inability to love him passionately. "Only let me win you," he had said, "and I will submit to all that." But now her lack of warmth seemed to irritate him, and he conducted himself towards her with a resentfulness which led to her passing many hours with him in painful silence. The heir-presumptive to the title was a remote relative, whom Lord Uplandtowers did not exclude from the dislike he entertained towards many persons and things besides, and he had set his mind upon a lineal successor. He blamed her much that there was no promise of this, and asked her what she was good for.

On a particular day in her gloomy life a letter, addressed to her as Mrs. Willowes, reached Lady Uplandtowers from an unexpected quarter. A sculptor in Pisa, knowing nothing of her second marriage, informed her that the long-delayed life-size statue of Mr. Willowes, which, when her husband left that city, he had been directed to retain till it was sent for, was still in his studio. As his commission had not wholly been paid, and the statue was taking up room he could ill spare, he should be glad to have the debt cleared off, and directions where to forward the figure. Arriving at a time when the Countess was beginning to have little secrets (of a harmless kind, it is true) from her husband, by reason of their growing estrangement, she replied to this letter without saying a word to Lord Uplandtowers, sending off the balance that was owing to the sculptor, and telling him to despatch the statue to her without delay.

It was some weeks before it arrived at Knollingwood Hall, and, by a singular coincidence, during the interval she received the first absolutely conclusive tidings of her Edmond's death. It had taken place years before, in a foreign land, about six months after their parting, and had been induced by the sufferings he had already undergone, coupled with much depression of spirit, which had caused him to succumb to a slight ailment. The news was sent her in a brief and formal letter from some relative of Willowes's in another part of England.

Her grief took the form of passionate pity for his misfortunes, and of reproach to herself for never having been able to conquer her aversion to his latter image by recollection of what Nature had originally made him. The sad spectacle that had gone from earth had never been her Edmond at all to her. O that she could have met him as he was at first! Thus Barbara thought. It was only a few days later that a waggon with two horses, containing an immense packing-case, was seen at breakfast-time both by Barbara and her husband to drive round to the back of the house, and by-and-by they were informed that a case labelled "Sculpture" had arrived for her ladyship.

"What can that be?" said Lord Uplandtowers.

"It is the statue of poor Edmond, which belongs to me, but has never been sent till now," she answered.

"Where are you going to put it?" asked he.

"I have not decided," said the Countess. "Anywhere, so that it will not annoy you."

"Oh, it won't annoy me," says he.

When it had been unpacked in a back room of the house, they went to examine it. The statue was a full-length figure, in the purest Carrara marble, representing Edmond Willowes in all his original beauty, as he had stood at parting from her when about to set out on his travels; a specimen of manhood almost perfect in every line and contour. The work had been carried out with absolute fidelity.

"Phœbus-Apollo, sure," said the Earl of Uplandtowers, who had never seen Willowes, real or represented, till now.

Barbara did not hear him. She was standing in a sort of trance before the first husband, as if she had no consciousness of the other husband at her side. The mutilated features of Willowes had disappeared from her mind's eye; this perfect being was really the man she had loved, and not that later pitiable figure; in whom tenderness and truth should have seen this image always, but had not done so.

It was not till Lord Uplandtowers said roughly, "Are you going to stay here all the morning worshipping him?" that she roused herself.

Her husband had not till now the least suspicion that Edmond Willowes originally looked thus, and he thought how deep would have been his jealousy years ago if Willowes had been known to him. Returning to the Hall in the afternoon he found his wife in the gallery, whither the statue had been brought.

She was lost in reverie before it, just as in the morning.

"What are you doing?" he asked.

She started and turned. "I am looking at my husb— my statue, to see if it is well done," she stammered. "Why should I not?"

"There's no reason why," he said. "What are you going to do with the monstrous thing? It can't stand here forever."

"I don't wish it," she said. "I'll find a place."

In her boudoir there was a deep recess, and while the Earl was absent from home for a few days in the following week, she hired joiners from the village, who under her directions enclosed the recess with a panelled door. Into the tabernacle thus formed she had the statue placed, fastening the door with a lock, the key of which she kept in her pocket.

When her husband returned he missed the statue from the gallery, and, concluding that it had been put away out of deference to his feelings, made no remark. Yet at moments he noticed something on his lady's face which he had never noticed there before. He could not construe it; it was a sort of silent ecstasy, a reserved beatification. What had become of the statue he could not divine, and growing more and more curious, looked about here and there for it till, thinking of her private room, he went towards that spot. After knocking he heard the shutting of a door, and the click of a key; but when he entered his wife was sitting at work, on what was in those days called knotting. Lord Uplandtowers' eye fell upon the newly painted door where the recess had formerly been.

"You have been carpentering in my absence then, Barbara," he said carelessly.

"Yes, Uplandtowers."

"Why did you go putting up such a tasteless enclosure as that—spoiling the handsome arch of the alcove?"

"I wanted more closet-room; and I thought that as this was my own apartment—"

"Of course," he returned. Lord Uplandtowers knew now where the statue of young Willowes was.

One night, or rather in the smallest hours of the morning, he missed the Countess from his side. Not being a man of nervous imaginings he fell asleep again before he had much considered the matter, and the next morning had forgotten the incident. But a few nights later the same circumstances occurred. This time he fully roused himself; but before he had moved to search for her she returned to the chamber in her dressing-gown, carrying a candle, which she extinguished as she approached, deeming him asleep. He could discover from her breathing that she was strangely moved; but not on this occasion either did he reveal that he had seen her. Presently, when she had lain down, affecting to wake, he asked her some trivial questions. "Yes, *Edmond,*" she replied absently.

Lord Uplandtowers became convinced that she was in the habit of leaving the chamber in this queer way more frequently than he had observed, and he determined to watch. The next midnight he feigned deep sleep, and shortly after perceived her stealthily rise and let herself out of the room in the dark. He slipped on some clothing and followed. At the further end of the corridor, where the clash of flint and steel would be out of the hearing of one in the bed-chamber, she struck a light. He stepped aside into an empty room till she had lit a taper and had passed on to her boudoir. In a minute or two he followed. Arrived at the door of the boudoir, he beheld the door of the private recess open, and Barbara within it, standing with her arms clasped tightly round the neck of her Edmond, and her mouth on his. The shawl which she had thrown round her nightclothes had slipped from her shoulders, and her long white robe and pale face lent her the blanched appearance of a second statue embracing the first. Between her kisses, she apostrophized it in a low murmur of infantine tenderness:

"My only love—how could I be so cruel to you, my perfect one—so good and true—I am ever faithful to you, despite my seeming infidelity! I always think of you—dream of you—during the long hours of the day, and in the night-watches! O Edmond, I am always yours!" Such words as these, intermingled with sobs, and streaming tears, and dishevelled hair, testified to an intensity of feeling in his wife which Lord Uplandtowers had not dreamed of her possessing.

"Ha, ha!" says he to himself. "This is where we evaporate—this is where my hopes of a successor in the title dissolve—ha! ha! This must be seen to, verily!"

Lord Uplandtowers was a subtle man when once he set himself to strategy; though in the present instance he never thought of the simple stratagem of constant tenderness. Nor did he enter the room and surprise his wife as a blunderer would have done, but went back to his chamber as silently as he had left it. When the Countess returned thither, shaken by spent sobs and sighs, he appeared to be soundly sleeping as usual. The next day he began his countermoves by making inquiries as to the whereabouts of the tutor who had travelled with his wife's first husband; this gentleman, he found, was now master of a grammar-school at no great distance from Knollingwood. At the first convenient moment Lord Uplandtowers went thither and obtained an interview with the said gentleman. The schoolmaster was much gratified by a visit from such an influential neighbour, and was ready to communicate anything that his lordship desired to know.

After some general conversation on the school and its progress, the visitor observed that he believed the schoolmaster had once travelled a good deal with the unfortunate Mr. Willowes, and had been with him on the occasion of his accident. He, Lord Uplandtowers, was interested in knowing what had really happened at that time, and had often thought of inquiring. And then the Earl not only heard by word of mouth as much as he wished to know, but, their chat becoming more intimate, the schoolmaster drew upon paper a sketch of the disfigured head, explaining with bated breath various details in the representation.

"It was very strange and terrible!" said Lord Uplandtowers, taking the sketch in his hand. "Neither nose nor ears, nor lips scarcely!"

A poor man in the town nearest to Knollingwood Hall, who combined the art of sign-painting with ingenious mechanical occupations, was sent for by Lord Uplandtowers to come to the Hall on a day in that week when the Countess had gone on a short visit to her parents. His employer made the man understand that the business in which his assistance was demanded was to be considered private, and money insured the observance of this request. The lock of the cupboard was picked, and the ingenious mechanic and painter, assisted by the schoolmaster's sketch, which Lord Uplandtowers had put in his pocket, set to work upon the god-like countenance of the statue under my lord's direction. What the fire had maimed in the original the

chisel maimed in the copy. It was a fiendish disfigure-
ment, ruthlessly carried out, and was rendered still
more shocking by being tinted to the hues of life, as life
had been after the wreck.

Six hours after, when the workman was gone, Lord
Uplandtowers looked upon the result, and smiled grimly, and said:

"A statue should represent a man as he appeared in
life, and that's as he appeared. Ha! ha! But 'tis done to
good purpose, and not idly."

He locked the door of the closet with a skeleton key,
and went his way to fetch the Countess home.

That night she slept, but he kept awake. According to
the tale, she murmured soft words in her dream; and he
knew that the tender converse of her imaginings was
held with one whom he had supplanted but in name. At
the end of her dream the Countess of Uplandtowers
awoke and arose, and then the enactment of former
nights was repeated. Her husband remained still and
listened. Two strokes sounded from the clock in the
pediment without, when, leaving the chamber-door
ajar, she passed along the corridor to the other end,
where, as usual, she obtained a light. So deep was the
silence that he could even from his bed hear her softly
blowing the tinder to a glow after striking the steel. She
moved on into the boudoir, and he heard, or fancied he
heard, the turning of the key in the closet-door. The
next moment there came from that direction a loud and
prolonged shriek, which resounded to the furthest
corners of the house. It was repeated, and there was the
noise of a heavy fall.

Lord Uplandtowers sprang out of bed. He hastened
along the dark corridor to the door of the boudoir,
which stood ajar, and, by the light of the candle within,
saw his poor young Countess lying in a heap in her
nightdress on the floor of the closet. When he reached
her side he found that she had fainted, much to the

relief of his fears that matters were worse. He quickly shut up and locked in the hated image which had done the mischief, and lifted his wife in his arms, where in a few instants she opened her eyes. Pressing her face to his without saying a word, he carried her back to her room, endeavouring as he went to disperse her terrors by a laugh in her ear, oddly compounded of causticity, predilection, and brutality.

"Ho—ho—ho!" says he. "Frightened, dear one, hey? What a baby 'tis! Only a joke, sure, Barbara—a splendid joke! But a baby should not go to closets at midnight to look for the ghost of the dear departed! If it do it must expect to be terrified at his aspect—ho— ho—ho!"

When she was in her bed-chamber, and had quite come to herself, though her nerves were still much shaken, he spoke to her more sternly. "Now, my lady, answer me: do you love him—eh?"

"No—no!" she faltered, shuddering, with her expanded eyes fixed on her husband. "He is too terrible— no, no!"

"You are sure?"

"Quite sure!" replied the poor broken-spirited Countess.

But her natural elasticity asserted itself. Next morning he again inquired of her: "Do you love him now?" She quailed under his gaze, but did not reply.

"That means that you do still, by God!" he continued.

"It means that I will not tell an untruth, and do not wish to incense my lord," she answered, with dignity.

"Then suppose we go and have another look at him?" As he spoke, he suddenly took her by the wrist, and turned as if to lead her towards the ghastly closet.

"No—no! O—no!" she cried, and her desperate wriggle out of his hand revealed that the fright of the night had left more impression upon her delicate soul than superficially appeared.

"Another dose or two, and she will be cured," he said to himself.

It was now so generally known that the Earl and Countess were not in accord, that he took no great trouble to disguise his deeds in relation to this matter. During the day he ordered four men with ropes and rollers to attend him in the boudoir. When they arrived, the closet was open, and the upper part of the statue tied up in canvas. He had it taken to the sleeping-chamber. What followed is more or less matter of conjecture. The story, as told to me, goes on to say that, when Lady Uplandtowers retired with him that night, she saw facing the foot of the heavy oak four-poster, a tall dark wardrobe, which had not stood there before; but she did not ask what its presence meant.

"I have had a little whim," he explained when they were in the dark.

"Have you?" says she.

"To erect a little shrine, as it may be called."

"A little shrine?"

"Yes; to one whom we both equally adore—eh? I'll show you what it contains."

He pulled a cord which hung covered by the bed-curtains, and the doors of the wardrobe slowly opened, disclosing that the shelves within had been removed throughout, and the interior adapted to receive the ghastly figure, which stood there as it had stood in the boudoir, but with a wax candle burning on each side of it to throw the cropped and distorted features into relief. She clutched him, uttered a low scream, and buried her head in the bedclothes. "O, take it away—please take it away!" she implored.

"All in good time; namely, when you love me best," he returned calmly. "You don't quite yet—eh?"

"I don't know—I think—O Uplandtowers, have mercy—I cannot bear it—O, in pity, take it away!"

"Nonsense; one gets accustomed to anything. Take another gaze."

In short, he allowed the doors to remain unclosed at the foot of the bed, and the wax-tapers burning; and such was the strange fascination of the grisly exhibition that a morbid curiosity took possession of the Countess as she lay, and, at his repeated request, she did again look out from the coverlet, shuddered, hid her eyes, and looked again, all the while begging him to take it away, or it would drive her out of her senses. But he would not do so yet, and the wardrobe was not locked till dawn.

The scene was repeated the next night. Firm in enforcing his ferocious correctives, he continued the treatment till the nerves of the poor lady were quivering in agony under the virtuous tortures inflicted by her lord, to bring her truant heart back to faithfulness.

The third night, when the scene had opened as usual, and she lay staring with immense wild eyes at the horrid fascination, on a sudden she gave an unnatural laugh; she laughed more and more, staring at the image, till she literally shrieked with laughter: then there was silence, and he found her to have become insensible. He thought she had fainted, but soon saw that the event was worse: she was in an epileptic fit. He started up, dismayed by the sense that, like many other subtle personages, he had been too exacting for his own interests. Such love as he was capable of, though rather a selfish gloating than a cherishing solicitude, was fanned into life on the instant. He closed the wardrobe with the pulley, clasped her in his arms, took her gently to the window, and did all he could to restore her.

It was a long time before the Countess came to herself, and when she did so, a considerable change seemed to have taken place in her emotions. She flung her arms around him, and with gasps of fear abjectly kissed him many times, at last bursting into tears. She had never wept in this scene before.

"You'll take it away, dearest—you will!" she begged plaintively.

"If you love me."

"I do—oh, I do!"

"And hate him, and his memory?"

"Yes—yes!"

"Thoroughly?"

"I cannot endure recollection of him!" cried the poor Countess slavishly. "It fills me with shame—how could I ever be so depraved! I'll never behave badly again, Uplandtowers; and you will never put the hated statue again before my eyes?"

He felt that he could promise with perfect safety. "Never," said he.

"And then I'll love you," she returned eagerly, as if dreading lest the scourge should be applied anew. "And I'll never, never dream of thinking a single thought that seems like faithlessness to my marriage vow."

The strange thing now was that this fictitious love wrung from her by terror took on, through mere habit of enactment, a certain quality of reality. A servile mood of attachment to the Earl became distinctly visible in her contemporaneously with an actual dislike for her late husband's memory. The mood of attachment grew and continued when the statue was removed. A permanent revulsion was operant in her, which intensified as time wore on. How fright could have effected such a change of idiosyncrasy learned physicians alone can say; but I believe such cases of reactionary instinct are not unknown.

The upshot was that the cure became so permanent as to be itself a new disease. She clung to him so tightly that she would not willingly be out of his sight for a moment. She would have no sitting-room apart from his, though she could not help starting when he entered suddenly to her. Her eyes were well-nigh always fixed upon him. If he drove out, she wished to go with him; his slightest civilities to other women made her frantically jealous; till at length her very fidelity became a burden to him, absorbing his time, and curtailing his liberty, and causing him to curse and swear. If he ever spoke sharply to her now, she did not revenge herself by flying off to a mental world of her own; all that affection for another, which had provided her with a resource, was now a cold black cinder.

From that time the life of this scared and enervated lady—whose existence might have been developed to so much higher purpose but for the ignoble ambition of her parents and the conventions of the time—was one of obsequious amativeness towards a perverse and cruel man. Little personal events came to her in quick succession—half a dozen, eight, nine, ten such events, —in brief, she bore him no less than eleven children in the nine following years, but half of them came prematurely into the world, or died a few days old; only one, a girl, attained to maturity; she in after years became the wife of the Honourable Mr. Beltonleigh, who was created Lord d'Almaine, as may be remembered.

There was no living son and heir. At length, completely worn out in mind and body, Lady Uplandtowers was taken abroad by her husband, to try the effect of a more genial climate upon her wasted frame. But nothing availed to strengthen her, and she died at Florence, a few months after her arrival in Italy.

Contrary to expectation, the Earl of Uplandtowers did not marry again. Such affection as existed in him—strange, hard, brutal as it was—seemed untransferable, and the title, as is known, passed at his death to his nephew. Perhaps it may not be so generally known that, during the enlargement of the Hall for the sixth Earl, while digging in the grounds for the new foundations, the broken fragments of a marble statue were unearthed. They were submitted to various antiquaries, who said that, so far as the damaged pieces would allow them to form an opinion, the statue seemed to be that of a mutilated Roman satyr; or, if not, an allegorical figure of Death. Only one or two old inhabitants guessed whose statue those fragments had composed.

I should have added that, shortly after the death of the Countess, an excellent sermon was preached by the Dean of Melchester, the subject of which, though names were not mentioned, was unquestionably suggested by the aforesaid events. He dwelt upon the folly of indulgence in sensuous love for a handsome form merely; and showed that the only rational and virtuous growths of that affection were those based upon intrinsic worth. In the case of the tender but somewhat shallow lady whose life I have related, there is no doubt that an infatuation for the person of young Willowes was the chief feeling that induced her to marry him; which was the more deplorable in that his beauty, by all tradition, was the least of his recommendations, every report bearing out the inference that he must have been a man of steadfast nature, bright intelligence, and promising life.

Thomas M. Disch (b. 1940)

TORTURING MR. AMBERWELL

Thomas M. Disch began his writing career as a science fiction writer in the revolutionary "New Wave" days of the 1960s, but is a diverse writer of many talents that no genre can quite contain. Poet, essayist, dramatist, critic, novelist, and short story writer, he excels. *Newsweek* called him the most underrated major writer in America. He is a frequent contributor to *The Nation*, in which his abilities as a biting social satirist are given their full play. He wrote a controversial play called *The Cardinal Detoxes*. The Catholic Church, landlord of the theater in which it was performed, took such strong exception to the play that it tried to evict the theater company. His children's book *The Brave Little Toaster* is the basis for a Disney movie. Throughout his career he has written stories in the horror mode, and is one of the finest living writers of horrific fiction, often darkly humorous. He has the stylistic polish of a Jamesian and ironic vision similar to Philip K. Dick (in whose memory Disch founded a literary award). He has published a number of short story collections with horrific content, and edited a distinguished anthology, *Strangeness* (1977), devoted to the Poesian and the bizarre. His horror novels include *The Businessman: A Tale of Terror*, and *The M.D.: A Tale of Horror*. "Torturing Mr. Amberwell" was published only in a limited edition by a small press. This is the first time it has been reprinted.

January 30, 1983

Amberwell is installed in the basement, fully conscious and indignant as Donald Duck. What do I think I'm doing, he wants to know.

"That's a question," I replied, "that I hope we'll be able to discuss at length, Mr. Amberwell."

Then it was Quack! Quack! Quack! until I called a halt, forcing his mouth open by crimping his nostrils till he had to take a breath, then wedging in a gag that kept him quiet. He did not try hard to resist. He seems to understand the need for ready compliance. I left him with the tape of "That's Entertainment" (Boston Pops directed by John Williams, Philips 6302 124) blaring tinnily from the cassette player. The tape is one of three with which Amberwell's limousine was supplied.

Eleven o'clock. Nothing to be done now but reduce my own excitement to a slow simmer. For half an hour I worked on a new 1000-piece jigsaw of King Ludwig's megalomaniacal Neuschwanstein, all its turrets and battlements edged with snow. The urge to go down to the basement and get going on Amberwell was intense. But I resisted it, got the sky assembled, steeped in the tub, jotted down these few lines, and called it a day.

January 31

Amberwell was already awake when I went downstairs at 7 A.M. "Mmmrff! Mmmrff! Mmmrff!" said Amberwell.

"That's one way to look at it," I teased. "But if you took a somewhat larger view, as I do, you'd see that there is a real opportunity for personal growth in the situation. People too often let personal anxieties get in the way of the Big Picture. Like getting your thumb in front of the lens when you're taking a photograph. Which reminds me, I need film."

He attempted a defiant stare—but I knew better. For there at the corner of each eye tears of pure fear were forming. I hunkered down in front of the chair into which Amberwell was bound, took his chin in my hand, and tilted his head to the right and to the left, like an appraiser judging a prize Toby mug. "Tears! Oh, there's nothing so apt to melt the cruelty of my nature as the sight of genuine liquid tears. Especially in a man. Men are brought up to hide their vulnerability. Their feelings are all bottled up, until after a while they get so atrophied you wouldn't recognize them as feelings, and it takes the emotional equivalent of an earthquake to produce one single—" Just before it rolled down his cheek I caught the tear on the end of my finger and showed it to Amberwell. "—teardrop."

"But now to be practical—" I wiped the teardrop off on the cuff of my jacket. "—I suppose you would like an explanation of why I've abducted you and made you a prisoner here in the basement of my house. Hmm?"

He nodded.

"That's a legitimate curiosity. There you were, about to fly off to . . . Where was it? Cleveland? Omaha? Toledo? . . . and instead you find yourself bound and gagged in the basement of someone who doesn't even have the decency to offer an explanation of his behavior. Naturally, you must be wondering what I have in mind. Am I some kind of sex maniac, for instance, who's got tired of luring teenage drifters to his den of unspeakable vice and has started hunting for bigger game? I'm sure that possibility must have occurred to you by now. And even though the idea is a bit self-aggrandizing in a man of your years, still you can never entirely discount the sexual component. It's always bound to be present in any relationship as intimate as that between a torturer and his victim."

Amberwell contemplated that statement a moment, then strained against his bonds and produced the loudest and most emphatic of Mmmrff's: "MMMRFF!!" The chair, anchored by each leg to a 6'-square sheet of plywood, seemed proof against any amount of lurching about, so I felt no qualms in leaving Amberwell to his thoughts.

Though not to those exclusively. Before I left I plugged some earphones into my new AIWA cassette recorder, taped the earphones to Amberwell's ears, made sure no amount of head-twisting could loosen the wires, and left Amberwell to the endlessly autoreversing strains of "That's Entertainment." I can't lay claim to any originality in that. The idea came from General Dozier's captors, and before that from Billy Wilder's cold-war comedy, *One, Two, Three.*

Then I had breakfast, wrote the above entry while the events were still fresh, and set off for work.

For obvious reasons I'm obliged to censor a good many details of my day-to-day life, so that the authorities, at some future date when this memoir is published, won't be able to track me to my lair. Enough to say that my job is respectable without being glamorous. Basically I english the pronouncements of corporate executives of two- and three-star rank and otherwise run rhetorical interference—without, however, making decisions. It's a job that brings me into contact regularly with the Amberwells of the world (with, indeed, Amberwell himself, though only at the remove of two switchboards), though none of them would ever mistake me for a peer. To say any more than this would be compromising, so regretfully (for I have, as much as any poet or painter, a natural desire to be credited for the work I've accomplished) I must restrict this narrative to the events of my life at home with Amberwell.

It's a bit ironic that I thereby find myself observing one of the standard protocols of conventional fiction.

I got home, as usual, just in time to turn on the 7 O'Clock News, where who to my wondering eyes should appear but Brigadier-General James "Speak of the Devil" Dozier, who'd gone to Rome to hand out medals to the policemen who'd rescued him from the Red Brigade. Then Reagan came on to deliver his Budget Message ("To arms! To arms!"), and I went downstairs to find Amberwell asleep despite all that music could do. The air was thick with the smell of his urine, though the pool that had formed between his shackled feet had almost entirely evaporated.

This seemed the right time to accustom myself and Amberwell to the formal requirements of our relationship, and so I spent the next fifteen minutes torturing him, starting at the soles of his feet and working up to the eyelids. Having no basis for comparison, it's hard to say whether I tortured Amberwell mildly, moderately, or severely. I thought it important that his punishments should exceed those commonly meted out in the classic pornographic narratives of de Sade, et al, since I wanted to emphasize the point I'd made that morning, that ours was not to be an erotic association. On the other hand I didn't wish, this soon, to precipitate a medical crisis.

Then upstairs to cook dinner. Already the shock of this radically new experience was unsettling accustomed perceptions. The chuck I sliced into two-inch cubes for stewing was no longer the innocent cellophane-wrapped commodity I'd picked out of the grocer's meat cooler. It was a cross-section of recently living tissue with a strong family resemblance to what might be laid bare under my own, or Amberwell's, skin—beneath, you might say, our beauty.

While the stew bubbled, I went back downstairs, stripped off Amberwell's clothes, and hosed him clean.

Then I took out his gag and let him plead for water (granted), his life, my mercy, an explanation, a chance to get out of the chair. He assured me that his wife would readily pay any ransom I demanded and with the utmost secrecy.

"I have no intention of asking for ransom, Mr. Amberwell. There's no likelier way to get caught. In any case, profit isn't my motive."

"Then what is?" he asked in a throaty whisper that mingled outrage and fear and a tremor of something unpinpointable that might have been the dawning of a sense of what was in store for him or maybe only the start of a cold.

I unfolded a metal chair, set it down in front of him, sat down, and lighted a cigarette. "I'll explain as best I can, Mr. Amberwell. My original idea, about a year ago, came from seeing you on "Sixty Minutes." Toxic waste disposal is the one issue in the news that always gets my blood boiling. And there you were trying to wave the camera out of existence and answering every question with the same smirking 'No Comment.' My first furious fantasy was to rent a cropduster and phone a bomb threat to the Unitask office, and then while you were all out in the parking lot fly over and douse the lot of you with your own medicine. A cocktail of dioxin and toluene and maybe some trichloroethylene for impaired memory function. But obviously that's just a wish-fulfillment fantasy and requires a budget and skills I simply don't possess. Whereas this costs less than a weekend skiing in the Catskills. Some chloroform from a hobby shop, a few gadgets from a sex boutique, odds and ends from a hardware store, four hours of carpentry, and I was ready to open shop."

"You mean to tell me that you're doing this because . . . because you're a god-damned *environmentalist?*"

"That's what I mean to tell you."

"But—" He shook his head briskly, as who would say, "You've got to be kidding."

"Of course, I haven't been what you'd call an activist. Unless this counts as activism. I never could get over my feeling of hopelessness of ever accomplishing anything against people like you. Like Unitask. I mean, there you are, monolithically in control. You've got the money. You've bought the politicians and the judges. The A.B.A. is your harem. You don't care *how* you mess up the world for anyone else so long as your net assets increase and multiply. And even when the government gets you for tax evasion or some such, the most that happens is that you get fined. And the fine probably entitles you to a tax deduction the next year. It's so frustrating to people like me."

"To the lunatics, you mean," said Amberwell.

It's wonderful how basic a sense of contentiousness is to human nature. Here was Amberwell still quivering from what he'd been through, and he could not resist putting in his two cents. Lucky for him I'm not so small-minded (or short-sighted) as to revenge myself on a taunt.

"I suppose on the face of it I would be considered a lunatic. A fanatic at the very least. On the other hand, it may be that I'm just a step ahead of the crowd."

Amberwell made a sort of snorting sound to express his derision.

"No, seriously. Consider Argentina. Unitask has strong ties with Argentina. You'll be building a plant there soon, I understand."

"What's this have to do with Argentina?" Amberwell demanded in the tone of a defendant preparing to plead the Fifth Amendment.

"Argentina is an example of a country governed by torture," I said, dropping the ash of my cigarette on the back of Amberwell's hand. "And not even the most extreme example. Now it's my contention that what the government can do, individuals can do just as effectively. With respect to torture, that is. The larger deterrents, like missiles, still require forces on a grand scale. So you might think of this as a counter-cultural, human-scale penitentiary. The first of who knows how many? Indeed, who knows if it's the first?"

"Listen, if you're some kind of . . . terrorist, you're making a mistake. I've got no connection with Argentina. That's another branch of Unitask entirely. I'm just an ordinary business executive. As for the allegations on that god-damned TV program, the government decided on its own not to prosecute. No one knew that that [expletive deleted] toluene——"

I pressed the burning tip of the cigarette against the back of Amberwell's hand and, when he was done screaming, explained:

"Please, Mr. Amberwell, don't use obscene language. I want our discussions to be frank and open, and you will not be punished for expressing any opinion you have. But don't use language you wouldn't use before a TV camera. When the tapes of our meetings are aired, I don't want them to have an X-rated tone. I've always thought one of the reasons Watergate made so little lasting impact among the namby-pamby-minded was that just because of all the foul language they discounted the whole affair as a kind of dirty joke."

"You think a TV station would agree to . . ."

"A radio station, more likely. It would probably do wonders for their ratings. Remember how hard Nixon fought—and still is fighting—to keep *his* tapes from being broadcast? And this has the added drama of your being tortured from time to time."

"You are really demented," said Amberwell.

I poised the cigarette over his hand. "What do you want to bet, Mr. Amberwell, that you will beg to have our tapes broadcast by all the radio stations in the country?"

"Please," he said. "Don't."

I brought the cigarette closer to his hand, so the ginger hairs began to shrivel, crisp, and smell.

"You will *implore* radio stations everywhere to make you a celebrity. Will you not, Mr. Amberwell?"

"Yes," he said.

"Yes what?"

"Yes, I will . . . implore them."

"Then begin, sir, begin. We're recording: implore."

I won't bother to transcribe that part of the session. When I had satisfied myself as to Amberwell's complete abjection, I went upstairs. Just in time to keep the stew from burning and to catch the beginning of the movie version of *Pennies from Heaven*. But before two songs had been sung, the old Sony finally conked out.

February 1

The repair shop called me at work to advise me that I'll be without a TV till Friday. Woe's me: TV is my most reliable tranquilizer. So, after work, to compensate for my affliction, I went to *Gandhi*. I don't understand Pauline Kael. Can't she get off on anything but horror movies anymore? The movie was nothing like the dud she'd made it out to be. I can't imagine anyone leaving the theater without feeling ennobled. Long live humanity! Peace now! We *shall* overcome! Of course, I wasn't convinced that passive resistance is the most effective way to deal with the bad guys of history, but then I didn't expect to be. It's still a terrific movie.

On the homebound train, mulling over the movie and my own domestic situation, I had an inspiration for a further turn of the screw. I'm leery, on principle, of deviating from the scenario already under way, but this would add a dimension of drollery (of kinkiness?) that will be hard to resist. Maybe I won't resist it.

Down in the dungeon I transferred a groaning Amberwell from the chair into a canvas straitjacket that I'd bought at Nymphomania's Special January White Sale. There's enough slack in the chains mooring him to the anchorbolts in the floor so that now he can sit up or stretch out as he chooses.

He was too weak to put up more than token resistance as I fit him into the straitjacket. He cried and mumbled and seemed more or less out of his mind. It seems a bit early in the game for him to have reached that stage of collapse. I told him to buck up and got what was left of last night's stew from the refrigerator and spoonfed it to him. By the time the pot was empty, Amberwell was almost his old self, promising me the open sesames to all four of his clandestine bank accounts: *if* I would let him go. I praised him for his more cooperative spirit and announced he would not be tortured tonight, by courtesy of Mahatma Gandhi. When I left he begged me not to turn off the light.

February 2

On my lunch hour I found all things needful to carry out my new change of plan. Encountered, as well, an Omen in the form of a magazine abandoned in a trash can, which the wind had opened to an article headlined:

> SHOULD WE TRY
> TO CHANGE
> OTHER PEOPLE?

No comment, in Amberwell's words.

Tonight instead of using insidious-type tortures I

simply beat Amberwell with a rubber truncheon (they seem to be a popular item these days at army surplus stores; there was a barrel full of them where I got mine) until he'd given me all the relevant information on the bank accounts he's spoken of. Then, postponing the use of today's purchases, I set Amberwell the task, as per the established scenario, of singing nursery rhymes for the rest of the night in harmony with the Mother Goose Consort (Merritime Records XG352 900).

I spent the rest of the evening alternating between the jigsaw (the lighter-toned bricks of the castle are mostly in place) and Erik Erikson's *Gandhi's Truth* (Norton, 1969). Meanwhile, Amberwell serenaded me, over the rewired stereo, with a medley of "Bye, baby bunting," "Ding, dong, bell," "Mary had a little lamb," and a counting rhyme that he never could seem to get right, even though I would go downstairs each time he goofed and clobber him with the truncheon. Here's how it goes:

> One-ery, two-ery, tickery, seven,
> Hallibo, crackibo, ten and eleven,
> Spin, span, muskidan,
> Twiddle-um, twaddle-um, twenty-one.
> Eeerie, orie, ourie,
> You, are, out!

February 3

Having laid the groundwork yesterday with dark hints and muffled coughs, I phoned in sick to work this morning, then went through a charade of dish clattering and door banging to simulate my departure. When Amberwell judged me to be out of earshot, he set into baying "Please! Somebody! Help me! Please!" and similar litanies of hopelessness, all quite inaudible, I'm pleased to say, except over the audio system.

When he appeared to be shouted out, I went downstairs with my parcel of yesterday's purchases.

"Oh, Mr. Amberwell," I said reproachfully. "You're going to catch it now."

Amberwell slumped sideways, curling his knees to his chest, as though waiting to be kicked, and squeezing his eyes tight shut.

On the concrete wall behind Amberwell I taped the posters I had bought at the Aghora Panthis Meditation Center. One showed Shiva wearing a tiger skin and holding out, invitingly, a skull-shaped bowl adorned with snakes. The second represented Ganesh, Shiva's fat, elephant-headed son, whose specialty is guaranteeing success to new undertakings.

I then persuaded Amberwell to open his eyes and study a photograph in B.K.S. Iyengar's *Light on Yoga* (Schocken, 1966) representing a yogi in the *padmasana,* or lotus, position. Fortunately for Amberwell he belongs to the new breed of business executives who jog, and he was able, with only a small assist from me and a modest amount of surgical tape, to assume the lotus position. With a new dhoti, a necklace of rudraksha berries, a clean-shaven head, and a dab of white paint in the middle of his forehead, he looked the spit-and-image of Ben Kingsley.

The dicey part came when I removed the straitjacket so that Amberwell might extend his arms in the manner illustrated in the book. Would he have the strength and the will to struggle once his arms were free? Admittedly, his lower body was secured to the bolt in the floor by a belt (also from Nymphomania) hidden beneath his dhoti. Admittedly, too, I had the truncheon on the ready. But if Amberwell weren't willing to cooperate, then all this elaborate scene-setting would be in vain.

I needn't have worried. Amberwell spread out his arms just so, and curled his finger to his thumb in a gesture of prayer. He even smiled for the camera upon command. It could not be said to have been a very warm smile, but any sense of strain could be accounted for by the difficulty of the position for a neophyte.

When the two Polariod pictures had developed themselves, I showed them to Amberwell, who was once again straitjacketed.

He stared at them gloomily. "This is some kind of religious cult, isn't it?"

"Yes, Mr. Amberwell, now you know. This is how we indoctrinate all our new members. It may seem cruel to you at first, but once your heart opens to accept our gods, you will know the joy that can only come after the ego has been destroyed and the mind cleansed."

"What . . . gods?" Amberwell asked, as a suspicious diner might ask to know the ingredients of some anomalous dish at a Chinese restaurant.

I pressed my hands together, church-steeple-style, and made an obeisance to the garishly-colored, elephant-headed god. "This is our god Ganesh. Say hi to Ganesh."

Amberwell gave me a look halfway between horror and incredulous amusement. Then he turned to the poster and said, "Hi . . . Ganesh."

"And this—" Tapping the other poster. "—is Shiva, the Destroyer."

Amberwell did not say hi to Shiva, nor did I suggest he should. He regarded the snake-festooned skull that Shiva held out to him with respectful silence. Then he closed his eyes and his jaw dropped open and his breathing became slower and deeper.

In what we are about to undertake, O Ganesh, make us truly successful!

February 4

A postcard from the library has notified me that they have got in the copy of Leni Riefenstahl's *The Last of the Nuba* that I'd put in a request for two months ago. Too late, now that Amberwell is so far along the path to becoming a Hindoo, to terrorize him with the prospect of having his face decoratively welted like his black brothers in Africa. There's something much more serious, and accordingly scarier, about a world-class religion. People are known to *believe* in religions. You can see them at airports selling their records or marvel at the troops of them hippity-hopping up the street. They've become one of life's real possibilities. Whereas, unless you know who Leni Riefenstahl *was*, the Nuba and their scarifications come off as little more than a coffee-table book, ethnology for punk rockers.

This evening, after a light repast, Amberwell, assuming the lotus position, chanted the following mantra for two hours:

> Mary had a little lamb,
> Its fleece was white as snow,
> And everywhere that Mary went
> The lamb was sure to go.
> Hari Mary,
> Rama lamb-a,
> Amberwell loves Ganesh.

Upstairs on my born-again TV I watched a cable broadcast of *The Atomic Cafe,* a montage of old Civil Defense instruction films that does for the defense industry what *Reefer Madness* did for narcs. From time to time I would tune in to Amberwell's progress in the basement. Only twice did he flag and require correction.

February 5

Saturday. My soon-to-be-ex-wife dropped by unannounced at lunchtime, letting herself in with the key she'd assured me she didn't have.

"Whatever are you listening to?" Adelle asked, as she set down her matching ("The Bag") canvas totes and I hastened to turn off the broadcast of Amberwell's noontide mantra from the torture chamber.

"Oh nothing. Some new piece by Terry Riley I think the announcer said."

"Spare me," said Adelle.

"Have I ever *forced* you to listen to Terry Riley?"

"Yes. Often."

"I didn't think you had another set of keys," I noted, holding out my hand.

"Until I've got all my things out, I have every right to have a set of keys."

"I thought you had everything now you agreed you had any right to."

"I made a list of what I'd forgotten." She handed me her list.

I ran down the two columns, which were headed "Negotiable" and "Non-negotiable." The blender was non-negotiable. "The blender?" I protested. "You've *got* the food processor. It does everything a blender can do."

"The blender was a wedding present from my cousin in Tarrytown. There's no reason you should have it."

"No. I suppose not. But you'll have to wash it out."

"Fine." She stared at me defiantly, waiting for further objections, but none were forthcoming. She seemed disappointed. She once complained that my unwillingness to be combative about small things showed a lack of feeling.

For the next hour I tagged after her from room to room as she filled first one tote and then the other with all the negotiable and non-negotiable items. Vases vanished from tabletops, records from shelves, the Canadian codeine-laced aspirin from the medicine cabinet. By the time we'd reached the kitchen her second bag was nearly full.

"On second thought," she said, "I'll let you keep the carving board. There's really no room for it in the cupboard I've got now."

"Thanks."

"But I do want the blender."

"It's in the icebox."

She got the blender out of the refrigerator and sniffed at what was in it. "Yuck!"

"Try it, you'll like it."

"What in hell is it?"

"It's a kind of bean paste from the Pritikin Program Cookbook. Remember? You got it for me for my birthday two years ago."

"It smells *awful.*"

"It tastes better on a cracker than just plain. But I'm out of crackers."

"I'll let you keep the blender," Adelle conceded. "Since you've been so nice about everything else."

"I'm a basically nice guy."

She grimaced. Her eye lighted on the door to the basement. "I suppose I should have one last look down there."

"There's nothing on your list that would be down there," I said in what must have been a different tone of voice.

She looked at me strangely.

"Whatever is in the basement now is mine," I insisted. "That's my non-negotiable demand. Now give me those keys; you've got what you came for."

She gave me the keys, and another odd look, and then I helped her take the loaded totebags out to her car. When they were stowed in the backseat she offered her hand to be shaken.

"I must say," she said, "you seem a whole lot more . . . relaxed. Than last year, or even a month ago."

"I guess it's the Pritikin Program."

"Or not having me to contend with?"

"Honestly, Adelle, I never thought you were all that much trouble."

"You're still the world's coldest icicle—that hasn't changed."

"And you're still as pretty as the day we met. Age cannot wither."

"Go to hell," she said with a smile. She started her Datsun. "Go directly to hell. Do not pass Go. Do not collect $200."

She also still thought parroting catch-phrases counted as a sense of humor, but I didn't rub her nose in that. I just said "Bye now," and stood back from the curb.

Back in the house I tuned in on Amberwell. He'd left off chanting his mantra, and I could hear him, ever so faintly, crying. Somehow, though there was no surface resemblance, the sound he was making put me in mind of the Environments$_{TM}$ record, *Gentle Rain in a Pine Forest*.

Hush, poor Amberwell, I thought, as I scooped out his dinner from the blender. *Hush, poor bare forked radish, hush.*

February 6

After twice feigning he was incapable of writing, Amberwell has been persuaded to write, at my dictation, the following letter:

Dear Ann,

Who could have predicted that seeing a movie could change a man's life so completely as mine has changed—and in only a week's time! You won't easily believe what I have to tell you. I can scarcely believe it myself. Here's what's happened. I missed my flight on Sunday, the traffic was snarled on the way to the airport, and decided to take in the movie *Gandhi,* which has been getting such good reviews. Watching the movie, I was overcome with remorse for all the wrong and hurtful things I've done in the course of my business career. A Higher Spirit must have been looking on, for after the movie I was guided into the waiting arms of the good people who have helped me to understand how I can make restitution for the wrongs I've done. Some of my colleagues, who helped me commit those crimes and shared in ill-gotten profits, must suffer, but Justice must be done, I see that now. I shall write to the appropriate authorities in due course to give them the information they will need to begin an investigation, but I write to you first, my dear wife, so that you may prepare yourself to cooperate with the authorities, make my papers and bank statements available to them, etc. Do not attempt to stay the course of Justice. When they find, as they surely will, compelling proofs of my malfeasances, cooperate with them in making immediate restitution to those I've wronged. I am sorry I cannot be with you during the approaching period of travail, but my virtue is still a frail reed, and so I must continue under the guidance of my Spiritual Master. I will offer prayers for your enlightenment to Rama, avatar of the great Vishnu, and to his wife Sita, whose attendants are white elephants. May the light soon enter your life that has entered mine.

> With holy love,
> Alec Amberwell

P.S. I am leaving the Lincoln for you.
P.P.S. Go see *Gandhi* as soon as you can.

I put the letter into an envelope together with one of the Polaroids I'd taken on Friday. Then I drove to the airport parking lot, where Amberwell's limousine was parked in the same space I'd left it a week ago. I put the letter in the driver's seat, the keys beneath it out of sight. Then I phoned Amberwell's home and informed the maid that I was an airport security officer and that Mr. Amberwell's Lincoln appeared to have been deserted at the airport parking lot. I made her write down the precise directions for finding the car and then hung up.

The trouble with sending Christmas presents to faraway friends is that you can't be on hand to see them unwrapped.

Got home just in time to catch the start of *The Winds of War*.

February 7

The office was a madhouse today, but in the rush of more important matters I did not neglect to phone Amberwell's secretary and ask to have his decision anent Unitask's option to purchase some ten thousand depositary receipts. (It had been the ongoing negotiations over this matter, conducted mainly through his secretary, that had allowed me to pick up the odds and ends of information I'd needed in order to waylay Amberwell at the opportune moment of his intended departure.)

I was informed that Mr. Amberwell was not in.

"Oh," said I. "I understood that he was due back today. There's no one else who can handle this, is there? The option expires on Friday."

"It will be the first thing Mr. Amberwell deals with when he gets back," I was assured.

This evening, after episode 2 of *The Winds of War*, I began to help Amberwell form an inventory of those corporate crimes he's assisted in for which tangible evidence is likely to be still recoverable. He spilled the beans like a silo in orgasm. Half this fair continent would seem to be planted with Unitask's time bombs, and every filing cabinet to conceal a smoking gun. I began to suspect that Amberwell was inventing crimes simply to appease my hunger for righteousness, but it's hard to doubt his sincerity at the moment of truth. Besides, Amberwell doesn't have enough imagination to spin a web of lies. His lies are all denials: "No, we didn't do it. No, I didn't write that memo. No, I don't know." What he *can* do—the reason there is a head on his shoulders—is remember details. His mind is all retrieval system, and that, of course, makes him just the right executive for this position. By 2 AM the first dossier was ready for mailing: top copy to Mrs.

Amberwell, urging her to share its contents with the press; first carbon to J. M. Carnell, Chairman of the Board of the ship Amberwell's revelations will scuttle; second carbon to Elizabeth Golub, author of *Our Children and the Toxic Timebomb* (Grossman, 1980).

Now for a couple days I'd better coddle the goose who lays such golden eggs. I fear I may have activated an ulcer, for Amberwell's stools are vermilion.

February 8

Easing the tension doesn't seem to have helped. Amberwell is in a state of almost total physical and mental collapse. Running a high temperature, incontinent, and babbling (when he thinks he's alone).

What's needed now is someone able to play the role of nice-guy partner, as against my blue meany, someone who could come in and stroke Amberwell's psyche and win his confidence and lift his morale. Lacking that, the best I could manage was a story: at dinnertime, while I spooned lovely, fresh-baked custard into his slack mouth, I told Amberwell how I've been ordered by our Spiritual Leader to treat him with more consideration as a reward for his confession (which I mailed off this morning from the central P.O.).

A gleam—of intelligence? purpose? hope? who can say?—came into his right eye. (His left is swollen shut.) "Who . . . is . . . our—"

I pressed my hands together, Gandhi-style. "Her name is Kali-Ananda, Kali's Joy. She cannot come to you until your purification has been complete, but if you would like to venerate her picture, you can do that."

"Yes." Amberwell nodded. "Let me . . . venerate her picture."

Up in the bedroom I dug out the box of memorabilia from the back of the closet and sorted through the various 8-by-11 prints I'd made of Adelle back in the days when the torture chamber was only a darkroom. The one I was looking for showed her in ballet tights, in lotus position (the Iyengar book was hers originally), and smiling that caught-in-the-act smile a camera always induced from her. It wasn't at all hard to re-imagine this Adelle as Kali-Ananda.

Back in the torture chamber I taped this icon of our Spiritual Leader to the wall between the posters of Ganesh and Shiva.

"Hail, Kali-Ananda!" I declared.

"Hail, Kali-Ananda," Amberwell agreed.

Then, without a hint from me, anxious to comply as a newly housebroken dog whining beside the door to the street, Amberwell wrestled his legs into a lotus position, faced the photograph of Adelle, and began to chant his mantra.

Later I revealed to him, as to one being initiated into a solemn mystery, the last of the nursery rhyme's four stanzas:

> Why does the lamb love Mary so?
>   The eager children cry;
> Why, Mary loves the lamb, you know,
>   The teacher did reply.

Amberwell's reaction was to break down, quite helplessly, into tears. He's much more in touch with his feelings these days.

"Amberwell," I said softly, "why are you crying?"

He shook his head. "I don't know."

"There must be a reason."

"Please," he said. The tears were gone. "Don't hurt me anymore. Just kill me and be done with it. You'll have to some day, I understand that. It's obvious that you can never let me go free. And I've told you everything you need to shaft Unitask in court, anything more would just be trimming. So please don't hurt me anymore, *please.*"

"I will ask Kali-Ananda," I promised him. "She knows what is best for all her minions. I too once despaired, Mr. Amberwell, but now I rejoice to be her servant." I turned to Adelle's photo and made an obeisance. "So may you, Mr. Amberwell . . . in time. Now, hold your arms out."

Amberwell held out his arms, like a child accepting his pajamas, and I assisted him into his straitjacket.

February 9

Speaking more truly than she knew, Amberwell's secretary informs me that he has taken a leave of absence for reasons of personal health. Mr. Kramer has been assigned to deal with me in the matter of the option to purchase. Kramer was one of the four Unitask VIPs whom Amberwell's confession most deeply and provably implicate. Patience! I only mailed off Amberwell's manuscript yesterday. Unitask may not have an inkling yet of the tornado heading their way. Unless Mrs. Amberwell went to them, rather than to the police, with her husband's letter. Come to think of it, she must be cooperating in the story of her husband's "leave of absence," or there would already be headlines: TOP EXEC JOINS NUT CULT.

No matter. Even if Mrs. A. joins Unitask in a cover-up, there is still the copy that went to Elizabeth Golub. She is certain to avail herself of Amberwell's revelations. So there's no need to worry—only to wait.

At home, Amberwell is on the mend. His temperature's down to a mild 101°. He's re-established sovereignity over his bowels. His appetite is back. And he asked me to forget what he'd said yesterday. He was depressed and delirious. He does not want to die. He will be Kali-Ananda's servant in all she requires.

"Our Spiritual Leader will be happy to hear of your devotion," I assured him. "And tonight, after our hour of worship, I will tell you the story of her holy life. But first—" I handed him a plastic waterbucket and a sponge. "—you'd better get this place cleaned up. It's getting smelly in here."

Upstairs I phoned for a take-out delivery from the area's one Indian restaurant, then finished all the snowy parts of the jigsaw. Nothing left now but the dark pieces—pine trees and shadowed stone.

The delivery came just as episode 4 of *The Winds of War* was repeating its opening montage/synopsis. I nipped downstairs to retrieve the bucket and the sponge, buckled Amberwell into the chair (as a change of pace from the lotus-position-cum-straitjacket), and set him to chanting his mantra. Then back to the living room for two hours of video popcorn and beef vindaloo. Also, a tad too much Courvoisier, inspired by which I thought it would be amusing—and more verisimilar—if I were to appear before Amberwell in the spare dhoti that I'd bought with his incontinence in mind. To show him that we are *both* worshippers of Shiva, Ganesh, and Kali-Ananda.

He seemed duly impressed. I lighted a candle and a stick of incense, then fed Amberwell the remains of my curry dinner. I spoke to him, consolingly, of the life he might expect to lead someday on our ashram in Nepal, doing penitence for his sins as a Unitask executive and worshipping our Spiritual Leader.

Then I told him the story of her life: how she was born in the all-too-aptly-named town of Bitter Lake,

Michigan, attended the Bitter Lake schools, and drank the chlorinated waters of Bitter Lake, never suspecting that there were other chemicals than chlorine added to those waters, chemicals that were the cause of the cramps and headaches she'd suffered through her adolescent years and of the kidney disorder her younger brother died of when he was thirteen, chemicals that would, even ten years after she had moved away from Bitter Lake, be responsible for the miscarriage of her first pregnancy and the severe abnormalities of her only child, Jonathan, now living a vegetable life in a home for vegetable children not five miles from the Unitask Corp. facility that had produced the toluene wastes that Gurnsey Hauling had hauled to Bitter Lake and Axelrod Disposal Systems had there disposed of.

Gurnsey Hauling and Axelrod Disposal Systems were both wholly owned subsidiaries of Unitask, and much of Amberwell's confession detailed the means by which Unitask had divested itself of the embarrassment that Gurnsey and Axelrod had come to represent— and, at the same time, evaded any legal responsibility for their actions. That part of the story, of course, Amberwell already knew.

"There you have it, Mr. Amberwell," I said, as the candle guttered in its socket. "The story of the youth and young womanhood of our Spiritual Leader, and the reasons why she, and so many other concerned citizens, including myself, feel a grievance against Unitask Corporation, Gurnsey Hauling, and Axelrod Disposal Systems."

Is it a true story, you may be asking yourself. Was this nameless narrator's wife really one of the Bitter Lake disaster victims? Or is he just saying this to underscore Amberwell's guilt, to make at least one of Unitask's victims something more than a statistic?

Scout's honor, it's all true, all but the obvious lie that

my-not-yet-ex-wife has been the guiding light behind Amberwell's re-education. For, far from being the sternly avenging Kali-Ananda I'd painted to Amberwell's imagination, Adelle is one of your classic cheek-turning, placard-bearing liberals who think they've scored points against the Unitasks of the world if they can get Rachel Carson's face on a postage stamp. It had been this—her milky-mild *goodness*—more than even a steadily encroaching tendency to vegetarianism that had led to our mostly amicable breakup.

However, in one inessential respect Adelle *is* a fiction: her name is not Adelle, nor was she born by the shores of the infamous Bitter Lake, nor yet by those of Love Canal, but by a toxic waste dump of lesser notoriety. These and some few other small details and proper names have been changed in order to protect the innocent and baffle pursuit. So if you have been thinking of playing detective, forget it. There is no Nymphomania, no Aghora Panthis Meditation Center, no option to purchase ten thousand depository receipts. Anything that might look like a clue is, in fact, a red herring. Why, even Amberwell's name might be something else than Amberwell. Yet you wouldn't for all that, deny that he and his kind exist, would you? Or that it's possibly for anyone so resolved to step up behind his or her selected Amberwell, tap him on the shoulder, and say, "Come with me, sir. I am making a citizen's arrest."?

In fact, however, Amberwell's name *is* Amberwell, and he is, or was, an executive for Unitask. My tracks are well enough covered that in that crucial particular I can be candid and boast openly of my accomplishment. There he is. Behold the son of a bitch. Think what he's done, and ask yourself if you aren't really a little pleased that he got a bit of what he gave.

Stop me before I preach more.

February 10

Just as I tapped the last piece of the puzzle in place and Neuschwanstein stood complete, it came to me, the word I'd been looking for, the answer to Amberwell's riddle: imagination. That was what he lacked, the missing element of his mental makeup that allowed him to assist Unitask in creating its great national anti-lottery, where a winning ticket will buy you and your family a lifetime supply of dioxin right in your own backyard. Unitask's victims don't exist for Amberwell because they live in hick towns like Bitter Lake or Love Canal, while he, and the fifty or sixty human beings whose faces he can recognize and who may, on that account, be real to him, all live in the posher suburbs that Unitask has not yet got round to devastating (from the Latin, *devastare,* to lay waste).

That, from the carefully blinkered view of Big Business is the danger of imagination—i.e., of books and movies—that it gives names to that legion of victims who were otherwise only rolling freight. Names and faces, addresses, personal histories, inner lives, and voices that can rise off a printed page and say, "Don't kill us. O great Unitask. We're real, we're alive, we exist. If you prick us we bleed. If you tickle us we laugh. If you poison us we die."

The problem has always been getting someone like Amberwell to listen. And I appear to have solved that problem.

February 11

Such weather. As though winter meant to make up for all her mildness till now with one sockdolager blizzard. We'd had fair warning and didn't have to show. Notwithstanding which exemption I headed in to the office, made myself visible at two meetings, lunched with my boss, and then, at three PM, just as the snowfall had escalated from impressive to awesome, I taxied to the "Discrete, Sumptuous, Comfortable Chamber of Fantasy" of the "Notorious" Mademoiselle X. (I quote from her two-column ad in the back pages of a weekly tabloid paper.)

Mademoiselle appeared at the door of the Chamber of Fantasy attired in a black spandex body stocking and thigh-high boots with stiletto heels. She touched my chest with her riding crop. *"You* must be Mr. Amberwell."

I smiled sheepishly by way of confirmation. Then, realizing my smile would be invisible behind my Phantom of the Opera domino-cum-veil, I said, "I am he."

She made a sweeping gesture with her riding crop. *"Entrez, Monsieur, dans ma chambre du mal et du volupté."*

"Merci, Mademoiselle."

From my briefcase I took out the cassette recorder, and from its file folder the script I'd spent yesterday evening preparing.

Mademoiselle X's fee, five $20 bills, was paper-clipped to the script.

"Won't you make yourself more comfortable, Mr. Amberwell?"

"Thank you," I said, and removed my hat.

She unclipped the money, made a neat bundle of it, and slipped it becomingly into the top of her boots. "And you are certain you do not desire to do anything else while you are here, but only . . . ?"

"Just for you to record the script as it is written, Mademoiselle, that's all. Perhaps if you read it through once to yourself, to see that it presents no problems. Then when you're ready, so is my recorder."

Mademoiselle X gave me a discreet, ironic look, removed a cigarette from the box on the low glass table, and sat back on the sumptuous, comfortable goatskin-draped futon, script in hand, waiting, with eyebrows raised, for her cigarette to be lighted. Once the dignity of her profession had been accorded this due deference, she turned her attention to the script. Her silent reading was quite as dramatic as that which she consigned to tape. Her high forehead would crinkle into a threatening frown, her eyes widen with alarm, her lips curl into a smile of ridicule or complicity.

"This is very professional work, Mr. Amberwell," she said, when she had finished reading. "Usually in this situation I am able to offer useful hints or suggestions. But this is a finished piece of work. It's nicely paced, it builds well, and overall it's thoroughly nasty. I hope for your sake, Mr. Amberwell, this script represents no more than a . . . fantasy. You would surely come to regret taking actions so . . . irreversible in their nature."

I blushed all unseen. "Thank you for your compliments, Mademoiselle. Are you ready to record?"

She sighed. "Someday," she said, "the women of our profession will get residuals for this sort of thing. *D'accord,* Mr. Amberwell, I am ready."

"Oh, and Mademoiselle?"

"Yes, Mr. Amberwell?"

"Use an ordinary tone of voice, please. Nothing too theatrical. You should sound, ideally, like somebody's mother."

She leered. "Oh, Mr. Amberwell, you have been a very bad boy. You have torn your best clothes. You have skinned your knee. And I am afraid that for such behavior you must be severely punished. *Comme ça?*"

"Just so," I assured her. "Ready?"

She stubbed out the cigarette, cleared her throat, held up the script, and nodded.

I pushed RECORD.

It looks like I won't be getting home tonight, and maybe not tomorrow. The snow is coming down not in flakes but in truckloads. The train station was a madhouse. I was lucky to find a hotel room.

So, it's a choice between "The Dukes of Hazzard," a werewolf movie, and episode 6 of *The Winds of War*. Despite my lifelong affinity for werewolves and a growing world-war-weariness (was there ever a conclusion so foreordained?), I watched Wouk's magnum opus. And he's right, of course. You can't let the Hitlers of the world walk all over you. You've got to draw a line. Gandhi's nonviolence only works against an enemy with an operational conscience.

February 12

All the drama of the Great Blizzard of '83 is over, even for Amberwell. Fortunately I'd left him in his straitjacket, not in the stricter confines of the chair. Except for the fright (he must have thought himself abandoned), he's none the worse for wear. After a hosing down and a bite to eat and a few minutes off the earphones, he seemed almost his old self.

"I think it's time," I said, unfolding the metal chair and sitting down before Amberwell, who was in a kneeling position and shivering, as the beads of water from his cleansing trickled down his face and soaked through the canvas straitjacket, "for you and me to have a heart-to-heart talk about your conscience, Mr. Amberwell. How is it that you were able to go on doing exactly the same things that had already done so much harm even after the Bitter Lake trial had begun?"

"We felt that the standards the government had set were too exacting. In fact, the E.P.A.'s new rulings tend to confirm our—"

I tromped lightly on the more sensitive of Amberwell's big toes. "Not *we*, Mr. Amberwell. I've read the transcripts of the trial and I know Unitask's position. It's *you*, second person singular, that I want to hear from. People were coming down with kidney and liver problems (which can be acutely painful), because of the poisons leeching into their drinking water. Their hair was falling out. Their children were stillborn. Don't tell me it hasn't been *proven:* all that is just sophistry. Where there's a third-degree burn there's fire."

"What do you want me to say?" Amberwell asked sullenly, petulance overcoming fear.

"Not that you're sorry, because I don't suppose you were. Just the truth—what you actually felt and thought about the crimes you were committing."

"I never thought what I was doing was a crime."

"Do you think anything is a crime? Murder, for instance."

"Yes, of course."

"What about this—what I'm doing to you—is that a crime?"

Amberwell glowered but made no reply.

"Be honest, Mr. Amberwell. Otherwise I'll feed you more pepper. I'll push pins under your fingernails; we haven't done that yet. I'll drill your teeth like Lawrence Olivier drilled Dustin Hoffman's in *Marathon Man*. Do you think what I'm doing to you is a crime?"

He took a deep breath and made his eyes meet mine. "Certainly. And you do too, you can't deny it."

"My ethical sense is not the issue, Mr. Amberwell. *Why* is it a crime?"

"Because . . . if you were caught you'd be arrested and put in jail."

"But if I'm not caught, and not put in jail—as Unitask wasn't and probably won't be—then does it follow that this is not a crime?"

"I didn't say that."

"What if I were an agent of the government, Mr. Amberwell? Suppose the F.B.I. were running another ABSCAM operation and decided that the only way to get the goods on Unitask was to put one of their executives through the wringer."

"Our government wouldn't do that."

"No? Some would."

The suggestion sank in. "Then . . . are you . . ."

"An F.B.I. agent? Sure, why not, if it'll make you feel more at home."

"Oh my god, I should have known."

I had to laugh, and I could tell, from the furrowing of Amberwell's brow, that his faith in the Justice Department was restored.

"Let's approach this from a different angle, Mr. Amberwell. Have you ever read a book called *The Scarlet Letter?*"

He shook his head. "I don't read many books."

"Or *The Retreat?*"

He shook his head.

"How about *I, the Jury?*"

"That's by Spillane, isn't it? I read some of his stuff when I was a kid, so I might have read that one."

So much for literature.

"Well, let's consider just the word itself: guilt. Have you ever felt guilty for *anything* you've done Mr. Amberwell?"

"Certainly. I'm no saint."

"For instance."

"I've, uh, cheated on my wife from time to time."

"And that made you feel guilty? Troubled? Perplexed?"

"Sure, all of that."

"Not just worried you might get the clap?"

"That too, I guess." He licked his upper lip, trying to think what it was I wanted him to say. "Maybe . . . maybe I don't understand those terms the same way you do. I mean, they're like words you read in the newspaper more than the ones you use in everyday life. For me anyhow." He looked up at me with the eager-to-please but certain-to-fail look of a student being examined in a subject he's never studied. Fearing the alternative, he was desperate to keep our little Socratic dialogue afloat, but the effort to try and speak in my language was as frustrating as if he'd been required to converse in Sanskrit (which is a long-term possibility worth considering; there must be instruction cassettes available somewhere).

"They didn't have required courses in ethics when you were getting your M.B.A., did they, Mr. Amberwell?"

"No. I graduated a good while before Watergate."

"Did you ever wonder, in the course of the Bitter Lake trial, whether you'd have acted differently if you had had such a course?"

"No. And I don't think it would make that much difference. At least I don't see any difference in the younger guys coming in, who've had to take that sort of stuff. I figure it's like requiring courses in the history of music. It doesn't really relate to the real world."

"I don't know about that, Mr. Amberwell. Isn't *this* the real world?"

Amberwell did not at once agree to that proposition. But at last, with no prompting, but without looking up from the floor, he nodded his head.

"Are you beginning to understand why you're being tortured, Mr. Amberwell?"

"To . . . uh . . . set an example, I suppose."

"You suppose correctly. Now look up at my camera,

Mr. Amberwell. I want a good clear picture of the original condition of your face, before we start tattooing."

Amberwell looked up with abject terror. "No! No, you wouldn't—"

"Smile," I said, adjusting the focus for a close-up. "Then, while we're getting you ready to set an example for other executives in the chemical industry, I'll fill you in on the basic plot of *The Scarlet Letter.*"

It was at that moment of purely psychological strain that Amberwell achieved something like a primal scream. His back arched, his neck corded, his face became a mask of beet-red rage, and the sound he made as the flashcube popped was utterly inhuman, an elemental roar that filled the torture chamber to its acoustical brim, as a Berlioz finale fills a concert hall. A single time Amberwell screamed so, and then fell silent, his last hope spent.

"It seems to me, Mr. Amberwell, that your soul is not yet prepared to pay the price that Kali-Ananda requires."

"You [expletive deleted]," said Amberwell. "Why don't you stop playing your [expletive deleted] games, and get this the [expletive deleted] over with."

"Kali-Ananda would derive no satisfaction from your mere death, Mr. Amberwell. It's atonement she's after. Once your heart is fully in accord with hers, then you will *ask* to be allowed to serve her with your whole being. You will be a role model for other executives. And when you have been taken to our secret ashram and dedicated completely to the goddess's worship, people will point to you with amazement and whisper, 'Is *that* Amberwell?' You will be a living legend. But I cannot say these things so well as Kali-Ananda herself can say them. She has taped a message for you, Mr. Amberwell. I will let Kali-Ananda explain to you, in her own voice, the nature and extent of your guilt—and how, with her help and mine, you can begin to seek expiation."

Though Amberwell struggled, he has become so weak that I had little difficulty securing him in the chair. I saw to it that by no amount of neck-twisting or shaking of his head could he dislodge the earphones. Then I inserted in the player the cassette that Mademoiselle X had recorded and left Amberwell alone, with one burning candle, to make the acquaintance of Kali-Ananda, whose joy is her wrath, whose kiss is a scourge, whose retribution is like the lightning that rends the oak.

February 13

Sunday, and the newspaper seems to tell of nothing but the misdeeds of the world's ever-busy Amberwells:

Item: For ten years Ford has been manufacturing cars with a transmission defect that has caused "scores of deaths and injuries"—a defect that Ford "could have corrected for 3 cents a vehicle."

Item: Miss Rita Lavelle has been appointed to be Reagan's ritual scapegoat in the impending scandals at E.P.A. "I can defend every action I have taken," she is quoted as saying. (So can I, Miss Lavelle, so can I! I wish we might have a chance to defend our actions together someday in intimate surroundings.)

Item: All Mexico's police are criminals. Ditto in Richmond, California.

Item: The Governor of Tennessee's conviction for conspiracy, mail fraud, and extortion was overturned by an appeals court judge on the grounds of "faulty jury selection."

Item: By a 3 to 2 margin, the American Bar Association has decided that a lawyer is to be *prohibited* from exposing a crime he knows his client intends to commit, unless the crime intended is murder or bodily harm. (A statute certain to make the world of corporate crime even more "discreet, sumptuous, and comfortable" than it is now, but one that is patently unfair to torturers.)

While I renewed my sense of indignation at this ever-replenished source, Amberwell, downstairs, listened to Kali-Ananda's laments, her accusations and revilings, her promise of redemption to the sinner who would embrace his punishment. Then, when the tape had automatically rewound itself, he listened again.

At eleven, when *The Winds of War* was over, and Pearl Harbor had been beautifully blasted to bits, I brought Amberwell his dinner of broccoli stalks, potato skins, and shredded salt codfish soaked in vermouth. He ate on his knees, in his straitjacket, snarfling up the mess vacuum-cleaner style.

"A penny for your thoughts, Mr. Amberwell," I said, when his bowl had been licked clean down to the Purina Dog-Chow logo.

He regarded me dully, such a gaze as a retarded deaf-mute child might give to the talk show on view on his ward's TV.

"Now, Mr. Amberwell, don't be difficult." I donned my comic Gestapo accent: "You know ve haf vays of making you talk."

He took a deep breath and closed his eyes. "I wasn't thinking. My mind was blank."

"Come, come, Mr. Amberwell. There's no such thing as a blank mind. You've had a whole day to meditate on the counsels and instruction of our Spiritual Leader. Your mind must be quite *full.*"

"I was glad you turned the tape off for a while," he said hollowly. "Her voice is . . . But I guess that's your idea, to see if you can drive me crazy. And I guess you will if you keep at it."

"You begin to sound resigned to your lot, Mr. Amberwell. Kali-Ananda will be pleased."

"Yeah." He smiled a smile that was a votive of offering to Kali's black heart. "You give my love to Kali-Ananda. You do that."

This seemed the propitious moment. I unstoppered the bottle of chloroform, dampened a wad of surgical gauze, and held it to Amberwell's face. He succumbed to its anesthetic influence without struggle.

While he was unconscious, I abraded the skin of his forehead with one of those miniature graters Dr. Scholl markets for filing away at the calluses on your feet. I scraped at Amberwell's forehead till the skin was raw, but I tried not to draw blood. Then I affixed a compress soaked in salt water to the area thus sensitized and secured the compress in place with loops and loops of surgical gauze until Amberwell's head was properly mummified from chin to crown. Strangely, as Amberwell became more abstract, he became more pathetic too. I pitied him as a mummy as I never had as a man.

I have no idea whether the sensation of a salty compress on sandpapered skin is more or less painful than the aftermath of a tattoo—but neither would Amberwell. Surely he wouldn't be able to resist the power of the suggestion, but to be doubly sure I left on the floor beside his bandaged head a sketch of his hypothetical tattoo. It represented—crudely, I confess, for I've never been much of a draftsman—the goddess Kali, as she is described in my Britannica: "a naked black woman, four-armed, wearing a garland of heads of giants slain by her, and a string of skulls round her neck . . . with gaping mouth and protruding tongue." To which devout motif I added a further decorative surround of interlinked U's and C's, the corporate emblem of Unitask Corporation. It looked, quite literally, god-awful.

February 14

I greeted Amberwell, who was already wide awake, with a cheery "Happy Valentine's Day!" and he lunged and plunged about like a rodeo rider. Donald Duck lives again. Amazing that after more than two weeks of semi-starvation he should still have such reserves of strength.

"Now how are you going to eat your good breakfast if you're in such a state of frenzy?" I asked rhetorically.

Amberwell replied with his limited stock of curses. Even rage can't fire the man's imagination.

"Very well then, I'll just leave them here—" I placed the juiceless orange rinds on the floor beside the drawing of Kali. (It's remarkable, by the way, how much altogether edible food the average person disposes of as "garbage.") "—and tonight when you're calmer, we'll take the photos to send to the press."

I left Amberwell still fuming and clanking his chains and took the train into town through the dazzling, redesigned landscape that Friday's great blizzard had left behind.

That was this morning. Since when my scenario has just been through a major revision at the hands of chance or tragic fate—take your pick.

Briefly: When I got home, at about seven, I found a valentine chocolate box on the dining room table, together with a comic homemade card.

From Adelle, of course. Adelle always remembers Valentine's Day. I always forget. She had, as I should have foreseen, made herself a spare set of keys—not from any deep need to be sneaky, just because she can't accustom herself to the idea that she's been excluded from my life.

At first I didn't think to be alarmed. I made a mental note to get this further set of keys from her and helped myself to a nut cluster from the chocolate box. Then I turned on the stereo to find out what, if anything, Amberwell might be up to. The torture chamber was silent.

Something in that silence made me uneasy. I went downstairs and discovered—beyond the door that stood ajar—Adelle dead and Amberwell gone.

It may have been my specific prohibition of the cellar on her previous visit that had piqued her curiosity. (Her valentine was inscribed "To Bluebeard.") Or she may have heard Amberwell carrying on. She knew where I hung the key to the room, since it had served not only as a darkroom but as a storage vault for our choicer stealables when we'd gone off on holidays. Naturally enough, when she'd discovered Amberwell straitjacketed and wrapped in gauze, she had released him. (Conceivably, so mummified, she might have thought him to be me; we're of the same general stature.)

Amberwell, seeing the woman he recognized from her photograph as Kali-Ananda, *might* have said very little. Or, just as possibly, he'd pleaded to have his straitjacket removed. In either case, how could Adelle have acted otherwise than to release him? Probably she'd taken off the straitjacket first, whereupon, having been provided with the only weapon he required, Amberwell had strangled her. Then, with the other keys on the ring she'd brought into the room, he'd been able to free himself from the shackles about his feet and the belt that was chained to the bolt in the floor.

Once at liberty, he'd behaved with remarkable composure and—given what I must assume to be his purpose—well-considered purposefulness. He could not, having just murdered Adelle, call 911 for help. Instead, he helped himself—first to some food (most of a box of Wheaties and two quarts of milk), then to clothes from my closet, then to a suitcase into which he packed all of the paraphernalia from the torture chamber. Finally he'd taken the keys to Adelle's Datsun from her purse, together with her spare cash, and driven . . . where? To a hotel? To one of the banks where he's established a clandestine account? In the long term I'm quite sure I know what Amberwell intends.

I think the moral of the story is clear: I've converted Amberwell to the wrong religion.

February 21

Can it be only a week gone by? I feel . . . I don't know what I feel. Adelle would always be asking me that question: What are you *feeling*? And I would say I didn't know, or that I was feeling nothing in particular. And it's still the case. No, that's not quite true—I feel jittery. I've locked up the house and taken a hotel room around the corner from work. But apart from the nervousness of feeling hunted, I've been really quite self-possessed. There's been no overwhelming guilt or grief.

And that's not quite true either, for there was a day last week when I had to excuse myself from a staff meeting and go into the john and cry, and for a while I thought I might not be able to stop. But it wasn't the thought of Adelle's death that had undone me. It was remembering a scene from the end of *Gandhi*, when Gandhi, who's fasted himself almost to death, advises a vengeful Hindu, whose son has been slain by Moslems, that he can only cure the wound of that loss if he will adopt an orphaned Moslem child as his own, and raise him in the Moslem faith. I don't know why that should rack me up so, but it does. I could go off on another crying jag right now if I let myself.

Would I (I've been wondering) have killed Amberwell finally? I did make provision for that eventuality. (Fortunately, for I was able, thereby, to dispose of Adelle's corpse expeditiously.) But I like to think that in the end, when my satisfaction in acting as public avenger had palled, I would have simply driven the chloroformed Amberwell to some secluded spot— ideally one of Unitask's own dumping grounds—and left him there to wake up as a free man, leaving it to him whether to raise a public hue and cry for what had been done. Somehow I doubt he'd have done that. I also doubt he'd have been able, with or without the help of the authorities, to discover who had played such a nasty trick upon him, since I'd taken reasonable precautions to cover my tracks. Amberwell never saw me without my Phantom of the Opera mask.

In the event my precautions are all quite pointless. Amberwell has my entire *curriculum vitae*. He took my business papers, my passport, a family photo album, a stack of family letters, my Rolodex—everything but this manuscript, which had accompanied me to work in my attaché case.

Should I give some kind of warning—at least to my parents? They spend their summers at a lakeside cabin whose seclusion is half of its charm. I haven't done so from a dread of having to enter into explanations. In any case, what is the use of a warning so ill-defined? My hope, such as it is, must be that Amberwell's appetite for revenge will be limited to my sole self.

On the cue of my finishing the preparation of this manuscript, which will be entrusted to my attorney, to be opened only in the event of a prolonged and unexplained absence, I received a phone call here in my hotel room. After I answered the fourth ring—which I did with reluctance, having registered here under an assumed name—there was a longish pause, then a click, and then the voices of the Mother Goose Consort singing:

> One-ery, two-ery, tickery, seven,
> Hallibo, crackibo, ten and eleven,
> Spin, span, muskidan,
> Twiddle-um, twaddle-um, twenty-one.
> Eeerie, orie, ourie,
> You, are, out!

Violet Hunt (1866–1942)

THE PRAYER

Violet Hunt was a socially connected British author, journalist and biographer, who was a friend and correspondent of Henry James, H. G. Wells, and Ford Madox Ford, among others, and travelled in the social sphere of the finest writers of her day. She was a committed feminist. She published two collections of weird and supernatural stories, *Tales of the Uneasy* (1911), which is a rare book, and *More Tales of the Uneasy* (1925). Her fiction is characterized by a somewhat Jamesian manner and eye for social detail, and is worthy of serious attention and comparison to Edith Wharton's ghost stories. "The Prayer" is a straightforward story of the Christian supernatural, an uncommon form of horror practiced notably in the contemporary period by Russell Kirk, but without any theological allegory in Hunt's penetrating psychological portrayal of a bizarre marriage. The story resembles nothing so much as a Victorian children's story, with the ironic moral: be careful what you pray for—you might get it and be punished horribly. It is interesting to compare it to the children's stories of Lucy Clifford, a close friend of Hunt's (and James'). Also to Thomas Hardy's "Barbara, of the House of Grebe," which deals with similar thematic material.

I

> "It is but giving over of a game,
> That must be lost"
>
> —Philaster

"Come, Mrs. Arne—come, my dear, you must not give way like this! You can't stand it—you really can't! Let Miss Kate take you away—now do!" urged the nurse, with her most motherly of intonations.

"Yes, Alice, Mrs. Joyce is right. Come away—do come away—you are only making yourself ill. It is all over; you can do nothing! Oh, oh, do come away!" implored Mrs. Arne's sister, shivering with excitement and nervousness.

A few moments ago Dr. Graham had relinquished his hold on the pulse of Edward Arne with the hopeless movement of the eyebrows that meant—the end.

The nurse had made the little gesture of resignation that was possibly a matter of form with her. The young sister-in-law had hidden her face in her hands. The wife had screamed a scream that had turned them all hot and cold—and flung herself on the bed over her dead husband. There she lay; her cries were terrible, her sobs shook her whole body.

The three gazed at her pityingly, not knowing what to do next. The nurse, folding her hands, looked towards the doctor for directions, and the doctor drummed with his fingers on the bed-post. The young girl timidly stroked the shoulder that heaved and writhed under her touch.

"Go away! Go away!" her sister reiterated continually, in a voice hoarse with fatigue and passion.

"Leave her alone, Miss Kate," whispered the nurse at last; "she will work it off best herself, perhaps."

She turned down the lamp as if to draw a veil over the

scene. Mrs. Arne raised herself on her elbow, showing a face stained with tears and purple with emotion.

"What! Not gone?" she said harshly. "Go away, Kate, go away! It is my house. I don't want you, I want no one—I want to speak to my husband. Will you go away—all of you. Give me an hour, half-an-hour—five minutes!"

She stretched out her arms imploringly to the doctor.

"Well . . ." said he, almost to himself.

He signed to the two women to withdraw, and followed them out into the passage. "Go and get something to eat," he said peremptorily, "while you can. We shall have trouble with her presently. I'll wait in the dressing-room."

He glanced at the twisting figure on the bed, shrugged his shoulders, and passed into the adjoining room, without, however, closing the door of communication. Sitting down in an arm-chair drawn up to the fire, he stretched himself and closed his eyes. The professional aspects of the case of Edward Arne rose up before him in all its interesting forms of complication . . .

It was just this professional attitude that Mrs. Arne unconsciously resented both in the doctor and in the nurse. Through all their kindness she had realised and resented their scientific interest in her husband, for to them he had been no more than a curious and complicated case; and now that the blow had fallen, she regarded them both in the light of executioners. Her one desire, expressed with all the shameless sincerity of blind and thoughtless misery, was to be free of their hateful presence and alone—alone with her dead!

She was weary of the doctor's subdued manly tones —of the nurse's commonplace motherliness, too habitually adapted to the needs of all to be appreciated by the individual—of the childish consolation of the young sister, who had never loved, never been married, did not know what sorrow was! Their expressions of sympathy struck her like blows, the touch of their hands on her body, as they tried to raise her, stung her in every nerve.

With a sigh of relief she buried her head in the pillow, pressed her body more closely against that of her husband, and lay motionless.

Her sobs ceased.

The lamp went out with a gurgle. The fire leaped up, and died. She raised her head and stared about her helplessly, then sinking down again she put her lips to the ear of the dead man.

"Edward—dear Edward!" she whispered, "why have you left me? Darling, why have you left me? I can't stay behind—you know I can't. I am too young to be left. It is only a year since you married me. I never thought it was only for a year. 'Till death us do part!' Yes, I know that's in it, but nobody ever thinks of that! I never thought of living without you! I meant to die with you . . .

"No—no—I can't die—I must not—till my baby is born. You will never see it. Don't you want to see it? Don't you? Oh, Edward, speak! Say something, darling, one word—one little word! Edward! Edward! are you there? Answer me for God's sake, answer me!

"Darling, I am so tired of waiting. Oh, think, dearest. There is so little time. They only gave me half-an-hour. In half-an-hour they will come and take you away from me—take you where I can't come to you—with all my love I can't come to you! I know the place—I saw it once. A great lonely place full of graves, and little stunted trees dripping with dirty London rain . . . and gas-lamps flaring all round . . . but quite, quite dark where the grave is . . . a long grey stone just like the rest. How could you stay there?—all alone—all alone —without me?

"Do you remember, Edward, what we once said—that whichever of us died first should come back to watch over the other, in the spirit? I promised you, and you promised me. What children we were! Death is not what we thought. It comforted us to say that then.

"Now, it's nothing—nothing—worse than nothing! I don't want your spirit—I can't see it—or feel it—I want you, you, your eyes that looked at me, your mouth that kissed me—"

She raised his arms and clasped them round her neck, and lay there very still, murmuring, "Oh, hold me, hold me! Love me if you can. Am I hateful? This is me! These are your arms . . ."

The doctor in the next room moved in his chair. The noise awoke her from her dream of contentment, and she unwound the dead arm from her neck, and, holding it up by the wrist, considered it ruefully.

"Yes, I can put it round me, but I have to hold it there. It is quite cold—it doesn't care. Ah, my dear, you don't care! You are dead. I kiss you, but you don't kiss me. Edward! Edward! Oh, for heaven's sake kiss me once. Just once!

"No, no, that won't do—that's not enough! that's nothing! worse than nothing! I want you back, you, all you . . . What shall I do? . . . I often pray . . . Oh, if there be a God in heaven, and if He ever answered a prayer, let Him answer mine—my only prayer. I'll never ask another—and give you back to me! As you were—as I loved you—as I adored you! He must listen. He must! My God, my God, he's mine—he's my husband, he's my lover—give him back to me!"

"Left alone for half-an-hour or more with the corpse! It's not right!"

The muttered expression of the nurse's revolted sense of professional decency came from the head of the staircase, where she had been waiting for the last few minutes. The doctor joined her.

"Hush, Mrs. Joyce! I'll go to her now."

The door creaked on its hinges as he gently pushed it open and went in.

"What's that? What's that?" screamed Mrs. Arne. "Doctor! Doctor! Don't touch me! Either I am dead or he is alive!"

"Do you want to kill yourself, Mrs. Arne?" said Dr. Graham, with calculated sternness, coming forward; "come away!"

"Not dead! Not dead!" she murmured.

"He is dead, I assure you. Dead and cold an hour ago! Feel!" He took hold of her, as she lay face downwards, and in so doing he touched the dead man's cheek—it was not cold! Instinctively his finger sought a pulse.

"Stop! Wait!" he cried in his intense excitement. "My dear Mrs. Arne, control yourself!"

But Mrs. Arne had fainted, and fallen heavily off the bed on the other side. Her sister, hastily summoned; attended to her, while the man they had all given over for dead was, with faint gasps and sighs and reluctant moans, pulled, as it were, hustled and dragged back over the threshold of life.

II

"Why do you always wear black, Alice?" asked Esther Graham. "You are not in mourning that I know of."

She was Dr. Graham's only daughter and Mrs. Arne's only friend. She sat with Mrs. Arne in the dreary drawing-room of the house in Chelsea. She had come to tea. She was the only person who ever did come to tea there.

She was brusque, kind, and blunt, and had a talent

for making inappropriate remarks. Six years ago Mrs. Arne had been a widow for an hour! Her husband had succumbed to an apparently mortal illness, and for the space of an hour had lain dead. When suddenly and inexplicably he had revived from his trance, the shock, combined with six weeks' nursing, had nearly killed his wife. All this Esther had heard from her father. She herself had only come to know Mrs. Arne after her child was born, and all the tragic circumstances of her husband's illness put aside, and it was hoped forgotten. And when her idle question received no answer from the pale absent woman who sat opposite, with listless lack-lustre eyes fixed on the green and blue flames dancing in the fire, she hoped it had passed unnoticed. She waited for five minutes for Mrs. Arne to resume the conversation, then her natural impatience got the better of her.

"Do say something, Alice!" she implored.

"Esther, I beg your pardon!" said Mrs. Arne. "I was thinking."

"What were you thinking of?"

"I don't know."

"No, of course you don't. People who sit and stare into the fire never do think, really. They are only brooding and making themselves ill, and that is what you are doing. You mope, you take no interest in anything, you never go out—I am sure you have not been out of doors today?"

"No—yes—I believe not. It is so cold."

"You are sure to feel the cold if you sit in the house all day, and sure to get ill! Just look at yourself!"

Mrs. Arne rose and looked at herself in the Italian mirror over the chimney-piece. It reflected faithfully enough her even pallor, her dark hair and eyes, the sweeping length of her eyelashes, the sharp curves of her nostrils, and the delicate arch of her eyebrows, that formed a thin sharp black line, so clear as to seem almost unnatural.

"Yes, I do look ill," she said with conviction.

"No wonder. You choose to bury yourself alive."

"Sometimes I do feel as if I lived in a grave. I look up at the ceiling and fancy it is my coffin-lid."

"Don't please talk like that!" expostulated Miss Graham, pointing to Mrs. Arne's little girl. "If only for Dolly's sake, I think you should not give way to such morbid fancies. It isn't good for her to see you like this always."

"Oh, Esther," the other exclaimed, stung into something like vivacity, "don't reproach me! I hope I am a good mother to my child!"

"Yes, dear, you are a model mother—and model wife too. Father says the way you look after your husband is something wonderful, but don't you think for your own sake you might try to be a little gayer? You encourage these moods, don't you? What is it? Is it the house?"

She glanced around her—at the high ceiling, at the heavy damask *portières,* the tall cabinets of china, the dim oak panelling—it reminded her of a neglected museum. Her eye travelled into the farthest corners, where the faint filmy dusk was already gathering, lit only by the bewildering cross-lights of the glass panels of cabinet doors—to the tall narrow windows—then back again to the woman in her mourning dress, cowering by the fire. She said sharply—

"You should go out more."

"I do not like to—leave my husband."

"Oh, I know that he is delicate and all that, but still, does he never permit you to leave him? Does he never go out by himself?"

"Not often!"

"And you have no pets! It is very odd of you. I simply can't imagine a house without animals."

"We did have a dog once," answered Mrs. Arne plaintively, "but it howled so we had to give it away. It would not go near Edward . . . But please don't imagine that I am dull! I have my child." She laid her hand on the flaxen head at her knee.

Miss Graham rose, frowning.

"Ah, you are too bad!" she exclaimed. "You are like a widow exactly, with one child, stroking its orphan head and saying, 'Poor fatherless darling.'"

Voices were heard outside. Miss Graham stopped talking quite suddenly, and sought her veil and gloves on the mantelpiece.

"You need not go, Esther," said Mrs. Arne. "It is only my husband."

"Oh, but it is getting late," said the other, crumpling up her gloves in her muff, and shuffling her feet nervously.

"Come!" said her hostess, with a bitter smile, "put your gloves on properly—if you must go—but it is quite early still."

"Please don't go, Miss Graham," put in the child.

"I must. Go and meet your papa, like a good girl."

"I don't want to."

"You mustn't talk like that, Dolly," said the doctor's daughter absently, still looking towards the door. Mrs. Arne rose and fastened the clasps of the big fur-cloak for her friend. The wife's white, sad, oppressed face came very close to the girl's cheerful one, as she murmured in a low voice—

"You don't like my husband, Esther? I can't help noticing it. Why don't you?"

"Nonsense!" retorted the other, with the emphasis of one who is repelling an overtrue accusation. "I do, only—"

"Only what?"

"Well, dear, it is foolish of me, of course, but I am—a little afraid of him."

"Afraid of Edward!" said his wife slowly. "Why should you be?"

"Well, dear—you see—I—I suppose women can't help being a little afraid of their friends' husbands—they can spoil their friendships with their wives in a moment, if they choose to disapprove of them. I really must go! Good-bye, child; give me a kiss! Don't ring, Alice. Please don't! I can open the door for myself—"

"Why should you?" said Mrs. Arne. "Edward is in the hall; I heard him speaking to Foster."

"No; he has gone into his study. Good-bye, you apathetic creature!" She gave Mrs. Arne a brief kiss and dashed out of the room. The voices outside had ceased, and she had reasonable hopes of reaching the door without being intercepted by Mrs. Arne's husband. But he met her on the stairs. Mrs. Arne, listening intently from her seat by the fire, heard her exchange a few shy sentences with him, the sound of which died away as they went downstairs together. A few moments after, Edward Arne came into the room and dropped into the chair just vacated by his wife's visitor.

He crossed his legs and said nothing. Neither did she.

His nearness had the effect of making the woman look at once several years older. Where she was pale he was well-coloured; the network of little filmy wrinkles that, on a close inspection, covered her face, had no parallel on his smooth skin. He was handsome; soft, well-groomed flakes of auburn hair lay over his forehead, and his steely blue eyes shone equally, a contrast to the sombre fire of hers, and the masses of dark crinkly hair that shaded her brow. The deep lines of permanent discontent furrowed that brow as she sat with her chin propped on her hands, and her elbows resting on her knees. Neither spoke. When the hands of the clock over Mrs. Arne's head pointed to seven, the white-aproned figure of the nurse appeared in the doorway, and the little girl rose and kissed her mother very tenderly.

Mrs. Arne's forehead contracted. Looking uneasily at her husband, she said to the child tentatively, yet boldly, as one grasps the nettle, "Say good night to your father!"

The child obeyed, saying "Good night" indifferently in her father's direction.

"Kiss him!"

"No, please—please not."

Her mother looked down on her curiously, sadly . . .

"You are a naughty, spoilt child!" she said, but without conviction. "Excuse her, Edward."

He did not seem to have heard.

"Well, if you don't care—" said his wife bitterly. "Come, child!" She caught the little girl by the hand and left the room.

At the door she half turned and looked fixedly at her husband. It was a strange ambiguous gaze; in it passion and dislike were strangely combined. Then she shivered and closed the door softly after her.

The man in the arm-chair sat with no perceptible change of attitude, his unspeculative eyes fixed on the fire, his hands clasped idly in front of him. The pose was obviously habitual. The servant brought lights and closed the shutters, drew the curtains, and made up the fire noisily, without, however, eliciting any reproof from his master.

Edward Arne was an ideal master, as far as Foster was concerned. He kept cases of cigars, but never smoked them, although the supply had often to be renewed. He did not care what he ate or drank, although he kept as good a cellar as most gentlemen— Foster knew that. He never interfered, he counted for nothing, he gave no trouble. Foster had no intention of ever leaving such an easy place. True, his master was not cordial; he very seldom addressed him or seemed to know whether he was there, but then neither did he grumble if the fire in the study was allowed to go out, or interfere with Foster's liberty in any way. He had a better place of it than Annette, Mrs. Arne's maid, who would be called up in the middle of the night to bathe her mistress's forehead with eau-de-Cologne, or made to brush her long hair for hours together to soothe her. Naturally enough Foster and Annette compared notes as to their respective situations, and drew unflattering parallels between this capricious wife and model husband.

III

Miss Graham was not a demonstrative woman. On her return home she somewhat startled her father, as he sat by his study table, deeply interested in his diagnosis book, by the sudden violence of her embrace.

"Why this excitement?" he asked, smiling and turning round. He was a young-looking man for his age; his thin wiry figure and clear colour belied the evidence of his hair, tinged with grey, and the tired wrinkles that gave value to the acuteness and brilliancy of the eyes they surrounded.

"I don't know!" she replied, "only you are so nice and alive somehow. I always feel like this when I come back from seeing the Arnes."

"Then don't go to see the Arnes."

"I'm so fond of her, father, and she will never come here to me, as you know. Or else nothing would induce me to enter her tomb of a house, and talk to that walking funeral of a husband of hers. I managed to get away today without having to shake hands with him. I always try to avoid it. But, father, I do wish you would go and see Alice."

"Is she ill?"

"Well, not exactly ill, I suppose, but her eyes make me quite uncomfortable, and she says such odd things! I don't know if it is you or the clergyman she wants, but she is all wrong somehow! She never goes out except to church; she never pays a call, or has any one to call on her! Nobody ever asks the Arnes to dinner, and I'm sure I don't blame them—the sight of that man at one's table would spoil any party—and they never entertain. She is always alone. Day after day I go in and find her sitting over the fire, with that same brooding expression. I shouldn't be surprised in the least if she were to go mad some day. Father, what is it? What is the tragedy of the house? There is one, I am convinced. And yet, though I have been the intimate friend of that woman for years, I know no more about her than the man in the street."

"She keeps her skeleton safe in the cupboard," said Dr. Graham. "I respect her for that. And please don't talk nonsense about tragedies. Alice Arne is only morbid—the malady of the age. And she is a very religious woman."

"I wonder if she complains of her odious husband to Mr. Bligh. She is always going to his services."

"Odious?"

"Yes, odious!" Miss Graham shuddered. "I cannot stand him! I cannot bear the touch of his cold froggy hands, and the sight of his fishy eyes! That inane smile of his simply makes me shrivel up. Father, honestly, do you like him yourself?"

"My dear, I hardly know him! It is his wife I have known ever since she was a child, and I a boy at college. Her father was my tutor. I never knew her husband till six years ago, when she called me in to attend him in a very serious illness. I suppose she never speaks of it? No? A very odd affair. For the life of me I cannot tell how he managed to recover. You needn't tell people, for

it affects my reputation, but I didn't save him! Indeed I
have never been able to account for it. The man was
given over for dead!"

"He might as well be dead for all the good he is," said
Esther scornfully. "I have never heard him say more
than a couple of sentences in my life."

"Yet he was an exceedingly brilliant young man; one
of the best men of his year at Oxford—a good deal run
after—poor Alice was wild to marry him!"

"In love with that spiritless creature? He is like a
house with someone dead in it, and all the blinds
down!"

"Come, Esther, don't be morbid—not to say silly!
You are very hard on the poor man! What's wrong with
him? He is the ordinary, commonplace, cold-blooded
specimen of humanity, a little stupid, a little selfish—
people who have gone through a serious illness like that
are apt to be—but on the whole, a good husband, a
good father, a good citizen—"

"Yes, and his wife is afraid of him, and his child hates
him!" exclaimed Esther.

"Nonsense!" said Dr. Graham sharply. "The child is
spoilt. Only children are apt to be—and the mother
wants a change or a tonic of some kind. I'll go and talk
to her when I have time. Go along and dress. Have you
forgotten that George Graham is coming to dinner?"

After she had gone the doctor made a note on the
corner of his blotting-pad, "Mem.: to go and see Mrs.
Arne," and dismissed the subject of the memorandum
entirely from his mind.

George Graham was the doctor's nephew, a tall, weedy,
cumbrous young man, full of fads and fallacies, with a
gentle manner that somehow inspired confidence. He
was several years younger than Esther, who loved to
listen to his semi-scientific, semi-romantic stories of

things met with in the course of his profession. "Oh, I come across very queer things!" he would say mysteriously. "There's a queer little widow—!"

"Tell me about your little widow?" asked Esther that day after dinner, when, her father having gone back to his study, she and her cousin sat together as usual.

He laughed.

"You like to hear of my professional experiences? Well, she certainly interested me," he said thoughtfully. "She is an odd psychological study in her way. I wish I could come across her again."

"Where did you come across her, and what is her name?"

"I don't know her name, I don't want to; she is not a personage to me, only a case. I hardly know her face even. I have never seen it except in the twilight. But I gathered that she lived somewhere in Chelsea, for she came out on to the Embankment with only a kind of lacy thing over her head; she can't live far off, I fancy."

Esther became instantly attentive. "Go on," she said.

"It was three weeks ago," said George Graham. "I was coming along the Embankment about ten o'clock. I walked through that little grove, you know, just between Cheyne Walk and the river, and I heard in there someone sobbing very bitterly. I looked and saw a woman sitting on a seat, with her head in her hands, crying. I was most awfully sorry, of course, and I thought I could perhaps do something for her, get her a glass of water, or salts, or something. I took her for a woman of the people—it was quite dark, you know. So I asked her very politely if I could do anything for her, and then I noticed her hands—they were quite white and covered with diamonds."

"You were sorry you spoke, I suppose," said Esther.

"She raised her head and said—I believe she laughed —'Are you going to tell me to move on?'"

"She thought you were a policeman?"

"Probably—if she thought at all—but she was in a semi-dazed condition. I told her to wait till I came back, and dashed round the corner to the chemist's and bought a bottle of salts. She thanked me, and made a little effort to rise and go away. She seemed very weak. I told her I was a medical man, I started in and talked to her."

"And she to you?"

"Yes, quite straight. Don't you know that women always treat a doctor as if he were one step removed from their father confessor—not human—not in the same category as themselves? It is not complimentary to one as a man, but one hears a good deal one would not otherwise hear. She ended by telling me all about herself—in a veiled way, of course. It soothed her—relieved her—she seemed not to have had an outlet for years!"

"To a mere stranger!"

"To a doctor. And she did not know what she was saying half the time. She was hysterical, of course. Heavens! what nonsense she talked! She spoke of herself as a person somehow haunted, cursed by some malign fate, a victim of some fearful spiritual catastrophe, don't you know? I let her run on. She was convinced of the reality of a sort of 'doom' that she had fancied had befallen her. It was quite pathetic. Then it got rather chilly—she shivered—I suggested her going in. She shrank back; she said, 'If you only knew what a relief it is, how much less miserable I am out here! I can breathe; I can live—it is my only glimpse of the world that is alive—I live in a grave—oh, let me stay!' She seemed positively afraid to go home."

"Perhaps someone bullied her at home."

"I suppose so, but then—she had no husband. He died, she told me, years ago. She had adored him, she said—"

"Is she pretty?"

"Pretty! Well, I hardly noticed. Let me see! Oh, yes, I suppose she was pretty—no, now I think of it, she would be too worn and faded to be what you call pretty."

Esther smiled.

"Well, we sat there together for quite an hour, then the clock of Chelsea church struck eleven, and she got up and said 'Good-bye,' holding out her hand quite naturally, as if our meeting and conversation had been nothing out of the common. There was a sound like a dead leaf trailing across the walk and she was gone."

"Didn't you ask if you should see her again?"

"That would have been a mean advantage to take."

"You might have offered to see her home."

"I saw she did not mean me to."

"She was a lady, you say," pondered Esther. "How was she dressed?"

"Oh, all right, like a lady—in black—mourning, I suppose. She has dark crinkly hair, and her eyebrows are very thin and arched—I noticed that in the dusk."

"Does this photograph remind you of her?" asked Esther suddenly, taking him to the mantelpiece.

"Rather!"

"Alice! Oh, it couldn't be—she is not a widow, her husband is alive—has your friend any children?"

"Yes, one, she mentioned it."

"How old?"

"Six years old, I think she said. She talks of the 'responsibility of bringing up an orphan.'"

"George, what time is it?" Esther asked suddenly.

"About nine o'clock."

"Would you mind coming out with me?"

"I should like it. Where shall we go?"

"To St. Adhelm's! It is close by here. There is a special late service tonight, and Mrs. Arne is sure to be there."

"Oh, Esther—curiosity!"

"No, not mere curiosity. Don't you see if it is my Mrs.

Arne who talked to you like this, it is very serious? I have thought her ill for a long time; but as ill as that—"

At St. Adhelm's Church, Esther Graham pointed out a woman who was kneeling beside a pillar in an attitude of intense devotion and abandonment. She rose from her knees, and turned her rapt face up towards the pulpit whence the Reverend Ralph Bligh was holding his impassioned discourse. George Graham touched his cousin on the shoulder, and motioned to her to leave her place on the outermost rank of worshippers.

"That is the woman!" said he.

IV

"Mem.: to go and see Mrs. Arne." The doctor came across this note in his blotting-pad one day six weeks later. His daughter was out of town. He had heard nothing of the Arnes since her departure. He had promised to go and see her. He was a little conscience-stricken. Yet another week elapsed before he found time to call upon the daughter of his old tutor.

At the corner of Tite Street he met Mrs. Arne's husband, and stopped. A doctor's professional kindliness of manner is, or ought to be, independent of his personal likings and dislikings, and there was a pleasant cordiality about his greeting which should have provoked a corresponding fervour on the part of Edward Arne.

"How are you, Arne?" Graham said. "I was on my way to call on your wife."

"Ah—yes!" said Edward Arne, with the ascending inflection of polite acquiescence. A ray of blue from his eyes rested transitorily on the doctor's face, and in that short moment the latter noted its intolerable vacuity, and for the first time in his life he felt a sharp pang of sympathy for the wife of such a husband.

"I suppose you are off to your club?—er—good bye!" he wound up abruptly. With the best will in the world he somehow found it almost impossible to carry on a conversation with Edward Arne, who raised his hand to his hat-brim in token of salutation, smiled sweetly, and walked on.

"He really is extraordinarily good-looking," reflected the doctor, as he watched him down the street and safely over the crossing with a certain degree of solicitude for which he could not exactly account. "And yet one feels one's vitality ebbing out at the finger-ends as one talks to him. I shall begin to believe in Esther's absurd fancies about him soon. Ah, there's the little girl!" he exclaimed, as he turned into Cheyne Walk and caught sight of her with her nurse, making violent demonstrations to attract his attention. "She is alive, at any rate. How is your mother, Dolly?" he asked.

"Quite well, thank you," was the child's reply. She added, "She's crying. She sent me away because I looked at her. So I did. Her cheeks are quite red."

"Run away—run away and play!" said the doctor nervously. He ascended the steps of the house, and rang the bell very gently and neatly.

"Not at—" began Foster, with the intonation of polite falsehood, but stopped on seeing the doctor, who, with his daughter, was a privileged person. "Mrs. Arne will see you, Sir."

"Mrs. Arne is not alone?" he said interrogatively.

'Yes, Sir, quite alone. I have just taken tea in."

Dr. Graham's doubts were prompted by the low murmur as of a voice, or voices, which came to him through the open door of the room at the head of the stairs. He paused and listened while Foster stood by, merely remarking, "Mrs. Arne do talk to herself sometimes, Sir."

It was Mrs. Arne's voice—the doctor recognised it now. It was not the voice of a sane or healthy woman.

He at once mentally removed his visit from the category of a morning call, and prepared for a semi-professional inquiry.

"Don't announce me," he said to Foster, and quietly entered the back drawing-room, which was separated by a heavy tapestry *portière* from the room where Mrs. Arne sat, with an open book on the table before her, from which she had been apparently reading aloud. Her hands were now clasped tightly over her face, and when, presently, she removed them and began feverishly to turn page after page of her book, the crimson of her cheeks was seamed with white where her fingers had impressed themselves.

The doctor wondered if she saw him, for though her eyes were fixed in his direction, there was no apprehension in them. She went on reading, and it was the text, mingled with passionate interjection and fragmentary utterances, of the burial service that met his ears.

"'For as in Adam all die!' All die! It says all! For he must reign . . . The last enemy that shall be destroyed is Death. What shall they do if the dead rise not at all . . . I die daily! . . . Daily! No, no, better get it over . . . dead and buried . . . out of sight, out of mind . . . under a stone. Dead men don't come back . . . Go on! Get it over. I want to hear the earth rattle on the coffin, and then I shall know it is done. 'Flesh and blood cannot inherit!' Oh, what did I do? What have I done? Why did I wish it so fervently? Why did I pray for it so earnestly? God gave me my wish—"

"Alice! Alice!" groaned the doctor.

She looked up. "'When this corruptible shall have put on incorruption—' 'Dust to dust, ashes to ashes, earth to earth—' Yes, that is it. 'After death, though worms destroy this body—'"

She flung the book aside and sobbed.

"That is what I was afraid of. My God! My God! Down there—in the dark—for ever and ever and ever!

I could not bear to think of it! My Edward! And so I interfered . . . and prayed . . . and prayed till . . . Oh! I am punished. Flesh and blood could not inherit! I kept him there—I would not let him go . . . I kept him . . . I prayed . . . I denied him Christian burial . . . Oh, how could I know . . ."

"Good heavens, Alice!" said Graham, coming sensibly forward, "what does this mean? I have heard of schoolgirls going through the marriage service by themselves, but the burial service—"

He laid down his hat and went on severely, "What have you to do with such things? Your child is flourishing—your husband alive and here—"

"And who kept him here?" interrupted Alice Arne fiercely, accepting the fact of his appearance without comment.

"You did," he answered quickly, "with your care and tenderness. I believe the warmth of your body, as you lay beside him for that half-hour, maintained the vital heat during that extraordinary suspension of the heart's action, which made us all give him up for dead. You were his best doctor, and brought him back to us."

"Yes, it was I—it was I—you need not tell me it was I!"

"Come, be thankful!" he said cheerfully. "Put that book away, and give me some tea, I'm very cold."

"Oh, Dr. Graham, how thoughtless of me!" said Mrs. Arne, rallying at the slight imputation on her politeness he had purposely made. She tottered to the bell and rang it before he could anticipate her.

"Another cup," she said quite calmly to Foster, who answered it. Then she sat down quivering all over with the suddenness of the constraint put upon her.

"Yes, sit down and tell me all about it," said Dr. Graham good-humouredly, at the same time observing her with the closeness he gave to difficult cases.

"There is nothing to tell," she said simply, shaking

her head, and futilely altering the position of the tea-cups on the tray. "It all happened years ago. Nothing can be done now. Will you have sugar?"

He drank his tea and made conversation. He talked to her of some Dante lectures she was attending; of some details connected with her child's Kindergarten classes. These subjects did not interest her. There was a subject she wished to discuss, he could see that a question trembled on her tongue, and tried to lead up to it.

She introduced it herself, quite quietly, over a second cup. "Sugar, Dr. Graham? I forget. Dr. Graham, tell me, do you believe that prayers—wicked unreasonable prayers—are granted?"

He helped himself to another slice of bread and butter before answering.

"Well," he said slowly, "it seems hard to believe that every fool who has a voice to pray with, and a brain where to conceive idiotic requests with, should be permitted to interfere with the economy of the universe. As a rule, if people were long-sighted enough to see the result of their petitions, I fancy very few of us would venture to interfere."

Mrs. Arne groaned.

She was a good Churchwoman, Graham knew, and he did not wish to sap her faith in any way, so he said no more, but inwardly wondered if a too rigid interpretation of some of the religious dogmas of the Vicar of St. Adhelm's, her spiritual adviser, was not the clue to her distress. Then she put another question—

"Eh! What?" he said. "Do I believe in ghosts? I will believe you if you will tell me you have seen one."

"You know, Doctor," she went on, "I was always afraid of ghosts—of spirits—things unseen. I couldn't ever read about them. I could not bear the idea of someone in the room with me that I could not see. There was a text that always frightened me that hung up in my room: 'Thou, God, seest me!' It frightened me when I was a child, whether I had been doing wrong or not. But now," shuddering, "I think there are worse things than ghosts."

"Well, now, what sort of things?" he asked good-humouredly. "Astral bodies—?"

She leaned forward and laid her hot hand on his.

"Oh, Doctor, tell me, if a spirit—without the body we know it by—is terrible, what of a body"—her voice sank to a whisper, "a body—senseless—lonely—stranded on this earth—without a spirit?"

She was watching his face anxiously. He was divided between a morbid inclination to laugh and the feeling of intense discomfort provoked by this wretched scene. He longed to give the conversation a more cheerful turn, yet did not wish to offend her by changing it too abruptly.

"I have heard of people not being able to keep body and soul together," he replied at last, "but I am not aware that practically such a division of forces has ever been achieved. And if we could only accept the theory of the de-spiritualised body, what a number of antipathetic people now wandering about in the world it would account for!"

The piteous gaze of her eyes seemed to seek to ward off the blow of his misplaced jocularity. He left his seat and sat down on the couch beside her.

"Poor child! poor girl! you are ill, you are over-excited. What is it? Tell me," he asked her as tenderly as the father she had lost in early life might have done. Her head sank on his shoulder.

"Are you unhappy?" he asked her gently.

"Yes!"

"You are too much alone. Get your mother or your sister to come and stay with you."

"They won't come," she wailed. "They say the house is like a grave. Edward has made himself a study in the basement. It's an impossible room—but he has moved all his things in, and I can't—I won't go to him there . . ."

"You're wrong. For it's only a fad," said Graham, "he'll tire of it. And you must see more people somehow. It's a pity my daughter is away. Had you any visitors today?"

"Not a soul has crossed the threshold for eighteen days."

"We must change all that," said the doctor vaguely. "Meantime you must cheer up. Why, you have no need to think of ghosts and graves—no need to be melancholy—you have your husband and your child—"

"I have my child—yes."

The doctor took hold of Mrs. Arne by the shoulder and held her a little away from him. He thought he had found the cause of her trouble—a more commonplace one than he had supposed.

"I have known you, Alice, since you were a child," he said gravely. "Answer me! You love your husband, don't you?"

"Yes." It was as if she were answering futile prefatory questions in the witness-box. Yet he saw by the intense excitement in her eyes that he had come to the point she feared, and yet desired to bring forward.

"And he loves you?"

She was silent.

"Well, then, if you love each other, what more can you want? Why do you say you have only your child in that absurd way?"

She was still silent, and he gave her a little shake.

"Tell me, have you and he had any difference lately? Is there any—coldness—any—temporary estrangement between you?"

He was hardly prepared for the burst of foolish laughter that proceeded from the demure Mrs. Arne as she rose and confronted him, all the blood in her body seeming for the moment to rush to her usually pale cheeks.

"Coldness! Temporary estrangement! If that were all! Oh, is everyone blind but me? There is all the world between us!—all the difference between this world and the next!"

She sat down again beside the doctor and whispered in his ear, and her words were like a breath of hot wind from some Gehenna of the soul.

"Oh, Doctor, I have borne it for six years, and I must speak. No other woman could bear what I have borne, and yet be alive! And I loved him so; you don't know how I loved him! That was it—that was my crime—"

"Crime?" repeated the doctor,

"Yes, crime! It was impious, don't you see? But I have been punished. Oh, Doctor, you don't know what my life is! Listen! I must tell you. To live with a— At first before I guessed when I used to put my arms round him, and he merely submitted—and then it dawned on me what I was kissing! It is enough to turn a living woman into stone—for I am living, though sometimes I forget it. Yes, I am a live woman, though I live in a grave. Think what it is!—to wonder every night if you will be alive in the morning, to lie down every night in an open grave—to smell death in every corner—every room—to breathe death—to touch it . . ."

The *portière* in front of the door shook, a hoopstick parted it, a round white clad bundle supported on a pair of mottled red legs peeped in, pushed a hoop in front of her. The child made no noise. Mrs. Arne seemed to have heard her, however. She slewed round violently as she sat on the sofa beside Dr. Graham, leaving her hot hands clasped in his.

"You ask Dolly," she exclaimed. "She knows it, too—she feels it."

"No, no, Alice, this won't do!" the doctor adjured her very low. Then he raised his voice and ordered the child from the room. He had managed to lift Mrs. Arne's feet and laid her full length on the sofa by the time the maid appeared. She had fainted.

He pulled down her eyelids and satisfied himself as to certain facts he had up till now dimly apprehended. When Mrs. Arne's maid returned, he gave her mistress over to her care and proceeded to Edward Arne's new study in the basement.

"Morphial," he muttered to himself, as he stumbled and faltered through gaslit passages, where furtive servants eyed him and scuttled to their burrows.

"What is he burying himself down here for?" he thought. "Is it to get out of her way? They *are* a nervous pair of them!"

Arne was sunk in a large arm-chair drawn up before the fire. There was no other light, except a faint reflection from the gas-lamp in the road, striking down past the iron bars of the window that was sunk below the level of the street. The room was comfortless and empty, there was little furniture in it except a large bookcase at Arne's right hand and a table with a Tantalus on it standing some way off. There was a faded portrait in pastel of Alice Arne over the mantelpiece, and beside it, a poor pendant, a pen and ink sketch of the master of the house. They were quite discrepant, in size and medium, but they appeared to look at each other with the stolid attentiveness of newly married people.

"Seedy, Arne?" Graham said.

"Rather, today. Poke the fire for me, will you?"

"I've known you quite seven years," said the doctor cheerfully, "so I presume I can do that . . . There, now! . . . And I'll presume further—What have we got here?"

He took a small bottle smartly out of Edward Arne's fingers and raised his eyebrows. Edward Arne had rendered it up agreeably; he did not seem upset or annoyed.

"Morphia. It isn't a habit. I only got hold of the stuff yesterday—found it about the house. Alice was very jumpy all day, and communicated her nerves to me, I suppose. I've none as a rule, but do you know, Graham, I seem to be getting them—feel things a good deal more than I did, and want to talk about them."

"What, are you growing a soul?" said the doctor carelessly, lighting a cigarette.

"Heaven forbid!" Arne answered equably. "I've done very well without it all these years. But I'm fond of old Alice, you know, in my own way. When I was a young man, I was quite different. I took things hardly and got excited about them. Yes, excited. I was wild about Alice, wild! Yes, by Jove! though she has forgotten all about it."

"Not that, but still it's natural she should long for some little demonstration of affection now and then . . . and she'd be awfully distressed if she saw you fooling with a bottle of morphia! You know, Arne, after that narrow squeak you had of it six years ago, Alice and I have a good right to consider that your life belongs to us!"

Edward Arne settled in his chair and replied, rather fretfully—

"All very well, but you didn't manage to do the job thoroughly. You didn't turn me out lively enough to please Alice. She's annoyed because when I take her in my arms, I don't hold her tight enough. I'm too quiet, too languid! . . . Hang it all, Graham, I believe she'd like me to stand for Parliament! . . . Why can't she let me just go along my own way? Surely a man who's come through an illness like mine can be let off parlour tricks? All this worry—it culminated the other day when I said I wanted to colonise a room down here, and did, with a spurt that took it out of me horribly,—all this worry, I say, seeing her upset and so on, keeps me low, and so I feel as if I wanted to take drugs to soothe me."

"Soothe!" said Graham. This stuff is more than soothing if you take enough of it. I'll send you something more like what you want, and I'll take this away, by your leave."

"I really can't argue!" replied Arne . . . "If you see Alice, tell her you find me fairly comfortable and don't put her off this room. I really like it best. She can come and see me here, I keep a good fire, tell her . . . I feel as if I wanted to sleep . . ." he added brusquely.

"You have been indulging already," said Graham softly, Arne had begun to doze off. His cushion had sagged down, the doctor stooped to rearrange it, carelessly laying the little phial for the moment in a crease of the rug covering the man's knees.

Mrs. Arne in her mourning dress was crossing the hall as he came to the top of the basement steps and pushed open the swing door. She was giving some orders to Foster, the butler, who disappeared as the doctor advanced.

"You're about again," he said, "good girl!"

"Too silly of me," she said, "to be hysterical! After all these years! One should be able to keep one's own counsel. But it is over now, I promise I will never speak of it again."

"We frightened poor Dolly dreadfully. I had to order her out like a regiment of soldiers."

"Yes, I know, I'm going to her now!"

On his suggestion that she should look in on her husband first she looked askance.

"Down there!"

"Yes, that's his fancy. Let him be. He is a good deal depressed about himself and you. He notices a great deal more than you think. He isn't quite as apathetic as

you describe him to be . . . Come here!" He led her
into the unlit dining-room a little way. "You expect too
much, my dear. You do really! You make too many
demands on the vitality you saved."

"What did one save him for?" she asked fiercely. She
continued more quietly, "I know. I am going to be
different."

"Not you," said Graham fondly. He was very partial
to Alice Arne in spite of her silliness. "You'll worry
about Edward till the end of the chapter. I know you.
And"—he turned her round by the shoulder so that she
fronted the light in the hall—"you elusive thing, let me
have a good look at you . . . Hum! Your eyes, they're a
bit starey . . ."

He let her go again with a sigh of impotence. Something must be done . . . soon . . . he must think . . . He
got hold of his coat and began to get into it . . .

Mrs. Arne smiled, buttoned a button for him and
then opened the front door, like a good hostess, a very
little way. With a quick flirt of his hat he was gone, and
she heard the clap of his brougham door and the order
"Home."

"Been saying good-bye to that thief Graham?" said her
husband gently, when she entered his room, her pale
eyes staring a little, her thin hand busy at the front of
her dress . . .

"Thief? Why? One moment! Where's your switch?"

She found it and turned on a blaze of light from
which her husband seemed to shrink.

"Well, he carried off my drops. Afraid of my poison-
ing myself, I suppose?"

"Or acquiring the morphia habit," said his wife in a
dull level voice, "as I have."

She paused. He made no comment. Then, picking up
the little phial Dr. Graham had left in the crease of the
rug, she spoke—

"You are the thief, Edward, as it happens, this is mine."

"Is it? I found it knocking about: I didn't know it was yours. Well, will you give me some?"

"I will, if you like."

"Well, dear, decide. You know I am in your hands and Graham's. He was rubbing that into me today."

"Poor lamb!" she said derisively; "I'd not allow my doctor, or my wife either, to dictate to me whether I should put an end to myself, or not."

"Ah, but you've got a spirit, you see!" Arne yawned. "However, let me have a go at the stuff and then you put it on top of the wardrobe or a shelf, where I shall know it is, but never reach out to get it, I promise you."

"No, you wouldn't reach out a hand to keep yourself alive, let alone kill yourself," said she. "That is you all over, Edward."

"And don't you see that is why I did die," he said, with earnestness unexpected by her. "And then, unfortunately, you and Graham bustled up and wouldn't let Nature take its course . . . I rather wish you hadn't been so officious."

"And let you stay dead," said she carelessly. "But at the time I cared for you so much that I should have had to kill myself, or commit suttee like a Bengali widow. Ah, well!"

She reached out for a glass half-full of water that stood on the low ledge of a bookcase close by the arm of his chair . . . "Will this glass do? What's in it? Only water? How much morphia shall I give you? An overdose?"

"I don't care if you do, and that's fact."

"It was a joke, Edward," she said piteously.

"No joke to me. This fag end of life I've clawed hold of, doesn't interest me. And I'm bound to be interested in what I'm doing or I'm no good. I'm no earthly good now. I don't enjoy life, I've nothing to enjoy it with—in here—he struck his breast. "It's like a dull party one goes to by accident. All I want to do is to get into a cab and go home."

His wife stood over him with a half-full glass in one hand and the little bottle in the other. Her eyes dilated . . . her chest heaved . . .

"Edward!" she breathed. "Was it all so useless?"

"Was what useless? Yes, as I was telling you, I go as one in a dream—a bad, bad dream, like the dreams I used to have when I overworked at college. I was brilliant, Alice, brillant, do you hear? At some cost, I expect! Now I hate people—my fellow creatures. I've left them. They come and go, jostling me, and pushing me, on the pavements as I go along, avoiding them. Do you know where they should be, really, in relation to me?"

He rose a little in his seat—she stepped nervously aside, made as if to put down the bottle and the glass she was holding, then thought better of it and continued to extend them mechanically.

"They should be over my head. I've already left them and their petty nonsense of living. They mean nothing to me, no more than if they were ghosts walking. Or perhaps, it's I who am a ghost to them? . . . You don't understand it. It's because I suppose you have no imagination. You just know what you want and do your best to get it. You blurt out your blessed petition to your Deity and the idea that you're irrelevant never enters your head, soft, persistent, High Church thing that you are! . . ."

Alice Arne smiled, and balanced the objects she was holding. He motioned her to pour out the liquid from one to the other, but she took no heed; she was listening with all her ears. It was the nearest approach to the language of compliment, to anything in the way of loverlike personalities that she had heard fall from his lips since his illness. He went on, becoming as it were lukewarm to his subject—

"But the worst of it is that once break the cord that links you to humanity—it can't be mended. Man doesn't live by bread alone . . . or lives to disappoint you. What am I to you, without my own poor personality? . . . Don't stare so, Alice! I haven't talked so much or so intimately for ages, have I? Let me, try and have it out . . . Are you in any sort of hurry?"

"No, Edward."

"Pour that stuff out and have done . . . Well, Alice, it's a queer feeling, I tell you. One goes about with one's looks on the ground, like a man who eyes the bed he is going to lie down in, and longs for. Alice, the crust of the earth seems a barrier between me and my own place. I want to scratch the boardings with my nails and shriek something like this: "Let me get down to you all, there where I belong!" It's a horrible sensation, like a vampire reversed! . . ."

"Is that why you insisted on having this room in the basement?" she asked breathlessly.

"Yes, I can't bear being upstairs, somehow. Here, with these barred windows and stone-cold floors . . . I can see the people's feet walking above there in the street . . . one has some sort of illusion . . ."

"Oh!" She shivered and her eyes travelled like those of a caged creature round the bare room and fluttered when they rested on the sombre windows imperiously barred. She dropped her gaze to the stone flags that showed beyond the oasis of Turkey carpet on which Arne's chair stood . . . Then to the door, the door that she had closed on entering. It had heavy bolts, but they were not drawn against her, though by the look of her eyes it seemed she half imagined they were . . .

She made a step forward and moved her hands slightly. She looked down on them and what they held . . . then changed the relative positions of the two objects and held the bottle over the glass . . .

"Yes, come along!" her husband said. "Are you going to be all day giving it me?"

With a jerk, she poured the liquid out into a glass and handed it to him. She looked away—towards the door . . .

"Ah, your way of escape!" said he, following her eyes. Then he drank, painstakingly.

The empty bottle fell out of her hands. She wrung them, murmuring—

"Oh, if I had only known!"

"Known what? That I should go near to cursing you for bringing me back?"

He fixed his cold eyes on her, as the liquid passed slowly over his tongue . . .

"—Or that you would end by taking back the gift you gave?"

John W. Campbell (1910–1971)

WHO GOES THERE?

John W. Campbell was a revolutionary magazine editor in the science fiction and fantasy genre from 1937 to his death in 1971. His short-lived (1939–44) magazine, *Unknown*, had a profound influence on the development of horror fiction for decades. His entire body of fiction, written as a young man before he ceased writing as a job condition of becoming editor of *Astounding Stories*, was in the science fiction genre. His one exceptional piece of horror is the popular and influential novella, ''Who Goes There?'' the title story of one of the two later collections of his stories, and the source of the famous 1950s film, *The Thing*. ''Science fiction,'' says Leslie Fiedler, ''evokes a cataclysmic horror that threatens the entire earth . . . it is essentially terror fiction.'' To the extent that this is true, it gets at the intimate connections between science fiction and the horror genre in the twentieth century. Campbell, a technological optimist, did not characteristically write in this mode, and when he did, published his stories under a pseudonym originally. Further, writing in the genre that had been invented only in 1926 (when the first issue of *Amazing Stories* declared a new genre of literature, ''scientifiction''), for *Astounding*, the science fiction magazine that had published several major Lovecraft stories of cosmic horror and many stories by his circle, Campbell set out to write a science fiction story that would ''scare the pants off people,'' as he told me in conversation, but in a clear, unobtrusive style. He succeeded in creating not only an acknowledged classic of modern science fiction but one of the most influential horror stories of the century.

I

The place stank. A queer, mingled stench that only the ice-buried cabins of an Antarctic camp know, compounded of reeking human sweat, and the heavy, fish-oil stench of melted seal blubber. An overtone of liniment combatted the musty smell of sweat-and-snow drenched furs. The acrid odor of burnt cooking fat, and the animal, not-unpleasant smell of dogs, diluted by time, hung in the air.

Lingering odors of machine oil contrasted sharply with the taint of harness dressing and leather. Yet, somehow, through all that reek of human beings and their associates—dogs, machines, and cooking—came another taint. It was a queer, neck-ruffling thing, a faintest suggestion of an odor alien among the smells of industry and life. And it was a life-smell. But it came from the thing that lay bound with cord and tarpaulin on the table, dripping slowly, methodically onto the heavy planks, dank and gaunt under the unshielded glare of the electric light.

Blair, the little bald-pated biologist of the expedition, twitched nervously at the wrappings, exposing clear, dark ice beneath and then pulling the tarpaulin back into place restlessly. His little birdlike motions of suppressed eagerness danced his shadow across the fringe of dingy gray underwear hanging from the low ceiling, the equatorial fringe of stiff, graying hair around his naked skull a comical halo about the shadow's head.

Commander Garry brushed aside the lax legs of a

suit of underwear, and stepped toward the table. Slowly his eyes traced around the rings of men sardined into the Administration Building. His tall, stiff body straightened finally, and he nodded. "Thirty-seven. All here." His voice was low, yet carried the clear authority of the commander by nature, as well as by title.

"You know the outline of the story back of that find of the Secondary Pole Expedition. I have been conferring with Second-in-Command McReady, and Norris, as well as Blair and Dr. Copper. There is a difference of opinion, and because it involves the entire group, it is only just that the entire Expedition personnel act on it.

"I am going to ask McReady to give you the details of the story, because each of you has been too busy with his own work to follow closely the endeavors of the others. McReady?"

Moving from the smoke-blued background, McReady was a figure from some forgotten myth, a looming, bronze statue that held life, and walked. Six-feet-four inches he stood as he halted beside the table, and with a characteristic glance upward to assure himself of room under the low ceiling beams, straightened. His rough, clashingly orange windproof jacket he still had on, yet on his huge frame it did not seem misplaced. Even here, four feet beneath the drift-wind that droned across the antarctic waste above the ceiling, the cold of the frozen continent leaked in, and gave meaning to the harshness of the man. And he was bronze—his great red-bronze beard, the heavy hair that matched it. The gnarled, corded hands gripping, relaxing, gripping and relaxing on the table planks were bronze. Even the deep-sunken eyes beneath heavy brows were bronzed.

Age-resisting endurance of the metal spoke in the cragged heavy outlines of his face, and the mellow tones of the heavy voice. "Norris and Blair agree on one thing; that animal we found was not—terrestrial in origin. Norris fears there may be danger in that; Blair says there is none.

"But I'll go back to how, and why we found it. To all that was known before we came here, it appeared that this point was exactly over the South Magnetic Pole of Earth. The compass does point straight down here, as you all know. The more delicate instruments of the physicists, instruments especially designed for this expedition and its study of the magnetic pole, detected a secondary effect, a secondary, less powerful magnetic influence about 80 miles southwest of here.

"The Secondary Magnetic Expedition went out to investigate it. There is no need for details. We found it, but it was not the huge meteorite or magnetic mountain Norris had expected to find. Iron ore is magnetic, of course; iron more so—and certain special steels even more magnetic. From the surface indications, the secondary pole we found was small, so small that the magnetic effect it had was preposterous. No magnetic material conceivable could have that effect. Soundings through the ice indicated it was within one hundred feet of the glacier surface.

"I think you should know the structure of the place. There is a broad plateau, a level sweep that runs more than 150 miles due south from the Secondary station, Van Wall says. He didn't have time or fuel to fly farther, but it was running smoothly due south then. Right there, where that buried thing was, there is an ice-drowned mountain ridge, a granite wall of unshakable strength that has dammed back the ice creeping from the south.

"And four hundred miles due south is the South Polar Plateau. You have asked me at various times why it gets warmer here when the wind rises, and most of you know. As a meteorologist I'd have staked my word that no wind could blow at −70 degrees; that no more than a 5-mile wind could blow at −50; without causing warming due to friction with ground, snow and ice and the air itself.

"We camped there on the lip of that ice-drowned mountain range for twelve days. We dug our camp into the blue ice that formed the surface, and escaped most of it. But for twelve consecutive days the wind blew at 45 miles an hour. It went as high as 48, and fell to 41 at times. The temperature was −63 degrees. It rose to −60 and fell to −68. It was meteorologically impossible, and it went on uninterruptedly for twelve days and twelve nights.

"Somewhere to the south, the frozen air of the South Polar Plateau slides down from that 18,000 foot bowl, down a mountain pass, over a glacier, and starts north. There must be a funneling mountain chain that directs it, and sweeps it away for four hundred miles to hit that bald plateau where we found the secondary pole, and 350 miles farther north reaches the Antarctic Ocean.

"It's been frozen there since Antarctica froze twenty million years ago. There never has been a thaw there.

"Twenty million years ago Antarctica was beginning to freeze. We've investigated, though, and built speculations. What we believe happened was about like this.

"Something came down out of space, a ship. We saw it there in the blue ice, a thing like a submarine without a conning tower or directive vanes, 280 feet long and 45 feet in diameter at its thickest.

"Eh, Van Wall? Space? Yes, but I'll explain that better later." McReady's steady voice went on.

"It came down from space, driven and lifted by forces men haven't discovered yet, and somehow— perhaps something went wrong then—tangled with Earth's magnetic field. It came south here, out of control probably, circling the magnetic pole. That's a savage country there; but when Antarctica was still freezing, it must have been a thousand times more savage. There must have been blizzard snow, as well as drift, new snow falling as the continent glaciated. The swirl there must have been particularly bad, the wind hurling a solid blanket of white over the lip of that now-buried mountain.

"The ship struck solid granite head-on, and cracked up. Not every one of the passengers in it was killed, but the ship must have been ruined, her driving mechanism locked. It tangled with Earth's field, Norris believes. No thing made by intelligent beings can tangle with the dead immensity of a planet's natural forces and survive.

"One of its passengers stepped out. The wind we saw there never fell below 41, and the temperature never rose above −60. Then—the wind must have been stronger. And there was drift falling in a solid sheet. The *thing* was lost completely in ten paces." He paused for a moment, the deep, steady voice giving way to the drone of wind overhead and the uneasy, malicious gurgling in the pipe of the galley-stove.

Drift—adrift-wind was sweeping by overhead. Right now the snow picked up by the mumbling wind fled in level, blinding lines across the faces of the buried camp. If a man stepped out of the tunnels that connected each of the camp buildings beneath the surface, he'd be lost in ten paces. Out there, the slim, black finger of the radio mast lifted 300 feet into the air, and at its peak was the clear night sky. A sky of thin, whining wind rushing steadily from beyond to another beyond under the licking, curling mantle of the aurora. And off north, the horizon flamed with queer, angry colors of the midnight twilight. That was spring 300 feet above Antarctica.

At the surface—it was white death. Death of a needle-fingered cold driven before the wind, sucking heat from any warm thing. Cold—and white mist of endless, everlasting drift, the fine, line particles of licking snow that obscured all things.

Kinner, the little, scar-faced cook, winced. Five days ago he had stepped out to the surface to reach a cache of frozen beef. He had reached it, started back—and the drift-wind leapt out of the south. Cold, white death that streamed across the ground blinded him in twenty seconds. He stumbled on wildly in circles. It was half an hour before rope-guided men from below found him in the impenetrable murk.

It was easy for man—or *thing*—to get lost in ten paces. "And the drift-wind then was probably more impenetrable than we know." McReady's voice snapped Kinner's mind back. Back to welcome, dank warmth of the Ad Building. "The passenger of the ship wasn't prepared either, it appears. It froze within ten feet of the ship.

"We dug down to find the ship, and our tunnel hapnel happened to find the frozen—animal. Barclay's ice-ax struck its skull.

"When we saw what it was, Barclay went back to the tractor, started the fire up and when the steam pressure built, sent a call for Blair and Dr. Copper. Barclay himself was sick then. Stayed sick for three days, as a matter of fact.

"When Blair and Copper came, we cut out the animal in a block of ice, as you see, wrapped it and loaded it on the tractor for return here. We wanted to get into that ship.

"We reached the side and found the metal was something we didn't know. Our beryllium-bronze, non-magnetic tools wouldn't touch it. Barclay had some tool-steel on the tractor, and that wouldn't scratch it either. We made reasonable tests—even tried some acid from the batteries with no results.

"They must have had a passivating process to make

magnesium metal resist acid that way, and the alloy must have been at least 95% magnesium. But we had no way of guessing that, so when we spotted the barely opened lock door, we cut around it. There was clear, hard ice inside the lock, where we couldn't reach it. Through the little crack we could look in and see that only metal and tools were in there, so we decided to loosen the ice with a bomb.

"We had decanite bombs and thermite. Thermite is the ice-softener; decanite might have shattered valuable things, where the thermite's heat would just loosen the ice. Dr. Copper, Norris and I placed a 25-pound thermite bomb, wired it, and took the connector up the tunnel to the surface, where Blair had the steam tractor waiting. A hundred yards the other side of that granite wall we set off the thermite bomb.

"The magnesium metal of the ship caught of course. The glow of the bomb flared and died, then it began to flare again. We ran back to the tractor, and gradually the glare built up. From where we were we could see the whole ice-field illuminated from beneath with an unbearable light; the ship's shadow was a great, dark cone reaching off toward the north, where the twilight was just about gone. For a moment it lasted, and we counted three other shadow-things that might have been other—passengers—frozen there. Then the ice was crashing down and against the ship.

"That's why I told you about that place. The wind sweeping down from the Pole was at our backs. Steam and hydrogen flame were torn away in white ice-fog; the flaming heat under the ice there was yanked away toward the Antarctic Ocean before it touched us. Otherwise we wouldn't have come back, even with the shelter of that granite ridge that stopped the light.

"Somehow in the blinding inferno we could see great hunched things—black bulks. They shed even the furious incandescence of the magnesium for a time.

Those must have been the engines, we knew. Secrets going in blazing glory—secrets that might have given Man the planets. Mysterious things that could lift and hurl that ship—and had soaked in the force of the Earth's magnetic field. I saw Norris's mouth move, and ducked. I couldn't hear him.

"Insulation—something—gave way. All earth's field they'd soaked up twenty million years before broke loose. The aurora in the sky above licked down, and the whole plateau there was bathed in cold fire that blanketed vision. The ice-ax in my hand got red hot, and hissed on the ice. Metal buttons on my clothes burned into me. And a flash of electric blue seared upward from beyond the granite wall.

"Then the walls of ice crashed down on it. For an instant it squealed the way dry-ice does when it's pressed between metal.

"We were blind and groping in the dark for hours while our eyes recovered. We found every coil within a mile was fused rubbish, the dynamo and every radio set, the earphones and speakers. If we hadn't had the steam tractor, we wouldn't have gotten over to the Secondary Camp.

"Van Wall flew in from Big Magnet at sun-up, as you know. We came home as soon as possible. That is the history of—that." McReady's great bronze beard gestured toward the thing on the table.

II

Blair stirred uneasily, his little, bony fingers wriggling under the harsh light. Little brown freckles on his knuckles slid back and forth as the tendons under the skin twitched. He pulled aside a bit of the tarpaulin and looked impatiently at the dark ice-bound thing inside.

McReady's big body straightened somewhat. He'd

ridden the rocking, jarring steam tractor forty miles that day, pushing on to Big Magnet here. Even his calm will had been pressed by the anxiety to mix again with humans. It was lone and quiet out there in Secondary Camp, where a wolf-wind howled down from the Pole. Wolf-wind howling in his sleep—winds droning and the evil, unspeakable face of that monster leering up as he'd first seen it through clear, blue ice, with a bronze ice-ax buried in its skull.

The giant meteorologist spoke again. "The problem is this. Blair wants to examine the thing. Thaw it out and make micro slides of its tissues and so forth. Morris doesn't believe that is safe, and Blair does. Dr. Copper agrees pretty much with Blair. Norris is a physicist, of course, not a biologist. But he makes a point I think we should all hear. Blair has described the microscopic life-forms biologists find living, even in this cold and inhospitable place. They freeze every winter, and thaw every summer—for three months—and live.

"The point Norris makes is—they thaw, and live again. There must have been microscopic life associated with this creature. There is with every living thing we know. And Norris is afraid that we may release a plague—some germ disease unknown to Earth—if we thaw those microscopic things that have been frozen there for twenty million years.

"Blair admits that such micro life might retain the power of living. Such unorganized things as individual cells can retain life for unknown periods, when solidly frozen. The beast itself is as dead as those frozen mammoths they find in Siberia. Organized, highly developed life-forms can't stand that treatment.

"But micro-life could. Norris suggests that we may release some disease-form that man, never having met it before, will be utterly defenseless against.

"Blair's answer is that there may be such still-living

germs, but that Norris has the case reversed. They are utterly non-immune to man. Our life-chemistry probably—"

"Probably!" The little biologist's head lifted in a quick, birdlike motion. The halo of gray hair about his bald head ruffled as though angry. "Heh, one look—"

"I know," McReady acknowledged. "The thing is not Earthly. It does not seem likely that it can have a life-chemistry sufficiently like ours to make cross-infection remotely possible. I would say that there is no danger."

McReady looked toward Dr. Copper. The physician shook his head slowly. "None whatever," he asserted confidently. "Man cannot infect or be infected by germs that live in such comparatively close relatives as the snakes. And they are, I assure you," his clean-shaven face grimaced uneasily, "*much* nearer to us than—*that!*"

Vance Norris moved angrily. He was comparatively short in this gathering of big men, some five-feet-eight, and his stocky, powerful build tended to make him seem shorter. His black hair was crisp and hard, like short, steel wires, and his eyes were the gray of fractured steel. If McReady was a man of bronze, Norris was all steel. His movements, his thoughts, his whole bearing had the quick, hard impulse of a steel spring. His nerves were steel—hard, quick-acting—swift corroding.

He was decided on his point now, and he lashed out in its defense with a characteristic quick, clipped flow of words. "Different chemistry be damned. That thing may be dead—or, by God, it may not—but I don't like it. Damn it, Blair, let them see the monstrosity you are petting over there. Let them see the foul thing and decide for themselves whether they want that thing thawed out in this camp.

"Thawed out, by the way. That's got to be thawed out

in one of the shacks tonight, if it is thawed out. Somebody—who's watchman tonight? Magnetic—oh, Connant. Cosmic rays tonight. Well, you get to sit up with that twenty-millon-year-old mummy of his. Unwrap it, Blair. How the hell can they tell what they are buying, if they can't see it? It may have a different chemistry. I don't care what else it has, but I know it has something I don't want. If you can judge by the look on its face—it isn't human so maybe you can't—it was annoyed when it froze. Annoyed, in fact, is just about as close an approximation of the way it felt, as crazy, mad, insane hatred. Neither one touches the subject.

"How the hell can these birds tell what they are voting on? They haven't seen those three red eyes and that blue hair like crawling worms. Crawling—damn, it's crawling there in the ice right now!

"Nothing Earth ever spawned had the unutterable sublimation of devastating wrath that thing let loose in its face when it looked around its frozen desolation twenty million years ago. Mad? It was mad clear through—searing, blistering mad!

"Hell, I've had bad dreams ever since I looked at those three red eyes. Nightmares. Dreaming the thing thawed out and came to life—that it wasn't dead, or even wholly unconscious all those twenty million years, but just slowed, waiting—waiting. You'll dream too, while that damned thing that Earth wouldn't own is dripping, dripping in the Cosmos House tonight.

"And, Connant," Norris whipped toward the cosmic ray specialist, "won't you have fun sitting up all night in the quiet. Wind whining above—and that thing dripping—" He stopped for a moment, and looked around.

"I know. That's not science. But this is, it's psychology. You'll have nightmares for a year to come. Every night since I looked at that thing I've had 'em. That's why I hate it—sure I do—and don't want it around. Put it back where it came from and let it freeze for another twenty million years. I had some swell nightmares—that it wasn't made like we are—which is obvious—but of a different kind of flesh that it can really control. That it can change its shape, and look like a man—and wait to kill and eat—

"That's not a logical argument. I know it isn't. The thing isn't Earth-logic anyway.

"Maybe it has an alien body-chemistry, and maybe its bugs do have a different body-chemistry. A germ might not stand that, but, Blair and Copper, how about a virus? That's just an enzyme molecule, you've said. That wouldn't need anything but a protein molecule of any body to work on.

"And how are you so sure that, of the million varieties of microscopic life it may have, *none* of them are dangerous. How about diseases like hydrophobia—rabies—that attacks any warm-blooded creature, whatever its body chemistry may be? And parrot fever? Have you a body like a parrot, Blair? And plain rot—gangrene—necrosis if you want? *That* isn't choosy about body chemistry!"

Blair looked up from his puttering long enough to meet Norris's angry, gray eyes for an instant. "So far the only thing you have said this thing gave off that was catching was dreams. I'll go so far as to admit that." An impish, slightly malignant grin crossed the little man's seamed face. "I had some too. So. It's dream-infectious. No doubt an exceedingly dangerous malady.

"So far as your other things go, you have a baldly mistaken idea about viruses. In the first place, nobody has shown that the enzyme-molecule theory, and that alone, explains them. And in the second place, when you catch tobacco mosaic or wheat rust, let me know. A wheat plant is a lot nearer your body-chemistry than this otherworld creature is.

"And your rabies is limited, strictly limited. You can't get it from, nor give it to, a wheat plant or a fish—which is a collateral descendant of a common ancestor of yours. Which this, Norris, is not." Blair nodded pleasantly toward the tarpaulined bulk on the table.

"Well, thaw the damned thing in a tub of formalin if you must. I've suggested that—"

"And I've said there would be no sense in it. You can't compromise. Why did you and Commander Garry come down here to study magnetism? Why weren't you content to stay at home? There's magnetic force enough in New York. I could no more study the life this thing once had from a formalin-pickled sample than you could get the information you wanted back in New York. And—if this one is so treated, *never in all time to come can there be a duplicate!* The race it came from must have passed away in the twenty million years it lay frozen, so that even if it came from Mars then, we'd never find its like. And—the ship is gone.

"There's only one way to do this—and that is the best possible way. It must be thawed slowly, carefully, and not in formalin."

Commander Garry stood forward again, and Norris stepped back muttering angrily. "I think Blair is right, gentlemen. What do you say?"

Connant grunted. "It sounds right to us, I think— only perhaps he ought to stand watch over it while it's thawing." He grinned ruefully, brushing a stray lock of ripe-cherry hair back from his forehead. "Swell idea, in fact—if he sits up with his jolly little corpse."

Garry smiled slightly. A general chuckle of agreement rippled over the group. "I should think any ghost it may have had would have starved to death if it hung around here that long, Connant," Garry suggested. "And you look capable of taking care of it. 'Ironman' Connant ought to be able to take out any opposing players, still."

Connant shook himself uneasily. "I'm not worrying about ghosts. Let's see that thing. I—"

Eagerly Blair was stripping back the ropes. A single throw of the tarpaulin revealed the thing. The ice had melted somewhat in the heat of the room, and it was clear and blue as thick, good glass. It shone wet and sleek under the harsh light of the unshielded globe above.

The room stiffened abruptly. It was face-up there on the plain, greasy planks of the table. The broken haft of the bronze ice-ax was still buried in the queer skull. Three mad, hate-filled eyes blazed up with a living fire, bright as fresh-spilled blood, from a face ringed with a writhing, loathsome nest of worms, blue, mobile worms that crawled where hair should grow—

Van Wall, six feet and two hundred pounds of ice-nerved pilot, gave a queer, strangled gasp, and butted, stumbled his way out to the corridor. Half the company broke for the doors. The others stumbled away from the table.

McReady stood at one end of the table watching them, his great body planted solid on his powerful legs. Norris from the opposite end glowered at the thing with smouldering hate. Outside the door, Garry was talking with half a dozen of the men at once.

Blair had a tack hammer. The ice that cased the thing *schluffed* crisply under its steel claw as it peeled from the thing it had cased for twenty thousand thousand years—

III

"I know you don't like the thing, Connant, but it just has to be thawed out right. You say leave it as it is till we get back to civilization. All right, I'll admit your argument that we could do a better and more complete job there is sound. But—how are we going to get this across the Line? We have to take this through one temperate zone, the equatorial zone, and half way through the other temperate zone before we get it to New York. You don't want to sit with it one night, but you suggest, then, that I hang its corpse in the freezer with the beef?" Blair looked up from his cautious chipping, his bald freckled skull nodding triumphantly.

Kinner, the stocky, scar-faced cook, saved Connant the trouble of answering. "Hey, you listen, mister. You put that thing in the box with the meat, and by all the gods there ever were, I'll put you in to keep it company. You birds have brought everything movable in this camp in onto my mess tables here already, and I had to stand for that. But you go putting things like that in my meat box, or even my meat cache here, and you cook your own damn grub."

"But, Kinner, this is the only table in Big Magnet that's big enough to work on," Blair objected. "Everybody's explained that."

"Yeah, and everybody's brought everything in here. Clark brings his dogs every time there's a fight and sews them up on that table. Ralsen brings in his sledges. Hell, the only thing you haven't had on that table is the Boeing. And you'd 'a' had that in if you coulda figured a way to get it through the tunnels."

Commander Garry chuckled and grinned at Van Wall, the huge Chief Pilot. Van Wall's great blond beard twitched suspiciously as he nodded gravely to Kinner. "You're right, Kinner. The aviation department is the only one that treats you right."

"It does get crowded, Kinner," Garry acknowledged. "But I'm afraid we all find it that way at times. Not much privacy in an antarctic camp."

"Privacy? What the hell's that? You know, the thing that really made me weep, was when I saw Barclay marchin' through here chantin' 'The last lumber in the camp! The last lumber in the camp!' and carryin' it out to build that house on his tractor. Damn it, I missed that moon cut in the door he carried out more'n I missed the sun when it set. That wasn't just the last lumber Barclay was walkin' off with. He was carryin' off the last bit of privacy in this blasted place."

A grin rode even on Connant's heavy face as Kinner's perennial, good-natured grouch came up again. But it died away quickly as his dark, deep-set eyes turned again to the red-eyed thing Blair was chipping from its cocoon of ice. A big hand ruffed his shoulder-length hair, and tugged at a twisted lock that fell behind his ear in a familiar gesture. "I know that cosmic ray shack's going to be too crowded if I have to sit up with that thing," he growled. "Why can't you go on chipping the ice away from around it—you can do that without anybody butting in, I assure you—and then hang the thing up over the power-plant boiler? That's warm enough. It'll thaw out a chicken, even a whole side of beef, in a few hours."

"I know," Blair protested, dropping the tack hammer to gesture more effectively with his bony, freckled fingers, his small body tense with eagerness, "but this is too important to take any chances. There never was a find like this; there never can be again. It's the only chance men will ever have, and it has to be done exactly right.

"Look, you know how the fish we caught down near the Ross Sea would freeze almost as soon as we got them on deck, and come to life again if we thawed them gently? Low forms of life aren't killed by quick freezing and slow thawing. We have—"

"Hey, for the love of Heaven—you mean that damned thing will come to life!" Connant yelled. "You get the damned thing—Let me at it! That's going to be in so many pieces—"

"No! *No,* you fool—" Blair jumped in front of Connant to protect his precious find. "No. Just *low* forms of life. For Pete's sake let me finish. You can't thaw higher forms of life and have them come to. Wait a moment now—hold it! A fish can come to after freezing because it's so low a form of life that the individual cells of its body can revive, and that alone is enough to reestablish life. Any higher forms thawed out that way are dead. Though the individual cells revive, they die because there must be organization and cooperative effort to live. That cooperation cannot be reestablished. There is a sort of potential life in any uninjured, quick-frozen animal. But it can't—can't under any circumstances—become active life in higher animals. The higher animals are too complex, too delicate. This is an intelligent creature as high in its evolution as we are in ours. Perhaps higher. It is as dead as a frozen man would be."

"How do you know?" demanded Connant, hefting the ice-ax he had seized a moment before.

Commander Garry laid a restraining hand on his heavy shoulder. "Wait a minute, Connant. I want to get this straight. I agree that there is going to be no thawing of this thing if there is the remotest chance of its revival. I quite agree it is much too unpleasant to have alive, but I had no idea there was the remotest possibility."

Dr. Copper pulled his pipe from between his teeth and heaved his stocky, dark body from the bunk he had been sitting in. "Blair's being technical. That's dead. As dead as the mammoths they find frozen in Siberia. We have all sorts of proof that things don't live after being frozen—not even fish, generally speaking—and no proof that higher animal life can under any circumstances. What's the point, Blair?"

The little biologist shook himself. The little ruff of hair standing out around his bald pate waved in righteous anger. "The point is," he said in an injured tone, "that the individual cells might show the characteristics they had in life if it is properly thawed. A man's muscle cells live many hours after he has died. Just because they live, and a few things like hair and fingernail cells still live, you wouldn't accuse a corpse of being a Zombie, or something.

"Now if I thaw this right, I may have a chance to determine what sort of world it's native to. We don't, and can't know by any other means, whether it came from Earth or Mars or Venus or from beyond the stars.

"And just because it looks unlike men, you don't have to accuse it of being evil, or vicious or something. Maybe that expression on its face is its equivalent to a resignation to fate. White is the color of mourning to the Chinese. If men can have different customs, why can't a so-different race have different understandings of facial expressions?"

Connant laughed softly, mirthlessly. "Peaceful resignation! If that is the best it could do in the way of resignation, I should exceedingly dislike seeing it when it was looking mad. That face was never designed to express peace. It just didn't have any philosophical thoughts like peace in its make-up.

"I know it's your pet—but be sane about it. That thing grew up on evil, adolesced slowly roasting alive the local equivalent of kittens, and amused itself through maturity on new and ingenious torture."

"You haven't the slightest right to say that," snapped Blair. "How do you know the first thing about the meaning of a facial expression inherently inhuman? It may well have no human equivalent whatever. That is just a different development of Nature, another example of Nature's wonderful adaptability. Growing on another, perhaps harsher world, it has different form and features. But it is just as much a legitimate child of Nature as you are. You are displaying that childish human weakness of hating the different. On its own world it would probably class you as a fish-belly, white monstrosity with an insufficient number of eyes and a fungoid body pale and bloated with gas.

"Just because its nature is different, you haven't any right to say it's necessarily evil."

Norris burst out a single, explosive, "Haw!" He looked down at the thing. "Maybe that things from other worlds don't *have* to be evil just because they're different. But that thing *was!* Child of Nature, eh? Well, it was a hell of an evil Nature."

"Aw, will you mugs cut crabbing at each other and get the damned thing off my table?" Kinner growled. "And put a canvas over it. It looks indecent."

"Kinner's gone modest," jeered Connant.

Kinner slanted his eyes up to the big physicist. The scarred cheek twisted to join the line of his tight lips in a twisted grin. "All right, big boy, and what were you grousing about a minute ago? We can set the thing in a chair next to you tonight, if you want."

"I'm not afraid of its face," Connant snapped. "I don't like keeping a wake over its corpse particularly, but I'm going to do it."

Kinner's grin spread. "Uh-huh." He went off to the galley stove and shook down ashes vigorously, drowning the brittle chipping of the ice as Blair fell to work again.

IV

"Cluck," reported the cosmic ray counter, *"cluck-burrrp-cluck."*

Connant started and dropped his pencil.

"Damnation." The physicist looked toward the far corner, back at the Geiger counter on the table near that corner. And crawled under the desk at which he had been working to retrieve the pencil. He sat down at his work again, trying to make his writing more even. It tended to have jerks and quavers in it, in time with the abrupt proud-hen noises of the Geiger counter. The muted whoosh of the pressure lamp he was using for illumination, the mingled gargles and bugle calls of a dozen men sleeping down the corridor in Paradise House formed the background sounds for the irregular, clucking noises of the counter, the occasional rustle of falling coal in the copper-bellied stove. And a soft, steady *drip-drip-drip* from the thing in the corner.

Connant jerked a pack of cigarettes from his pocket, snapped it so that a cigarette protruded, and jabbed the cylinder into his mouth. The lighter failed to function, and he pawed angrily through the pile of papers in search of a match. He scratched the wheel of the lighter several times, dropped it with a curse and got up to pluck a hot coal from the stove with the coal-tongs.

The lighter functioned instantly when he tried it on returning to the desk. The counter ripped out a series of chuckling guffaws as a burst of cosmic rays struck through to it. Connant turned to glower at it, and tried to concentrate on the interpretation of data collected during the past week. The weekly summary—

He gave up and yielded to curiosity, or nervousness. He lifted the pressure lamp from the desk and carried it over to the table in the corner. Then he returned to the stove and picked up the coal tongs. The beast had been thawing for nearly eighteen hours now. He poked at it with an unconscious caution; the flesh was no longer hard as armor plate, but had assumed a rubbery texture. It looked like wet, blue rubber glistening under droplets of water like little round jewels in the glare of the gasoline pressure lantern. Connant felt an unreasoning desire to pour the contents of the lamp's reservoir over the thing in its box and drop the cigarette into it. The three red eyes glared up at him sightlessly, the ruby eyeballs reflecting murky, smoky rays of light.

He realized vaguely that he had been looking at them for a very long time, even vaguely understood that they were no longer sightless. But it did not seem of importance, of no more importance than the labored, slow motion of the tentacular things that sprouted from the base of the scrawny, slowly pulsing neck.

Connant picked up the pressure lamp and returned to his chair. He sat down, staring at the pages of mathematics before him. The clucking of the counter was strangely less disturbing, the rustle of the coals in the stove no longer distracting.

The creak of the floorboards behind him didn't interrupt his thoughts as he went about his weekly report in an automatic manner, filling in columns of data and making brief, summarizing notes.

The creak of the floorboards sounded nearer.

V

Blair came up from the nightmare-haunted depths of sleep abruptly. Connant's face floated vaguely above him; for a moment it seemed a continuance of the wild horror of the dream. But Connant's face was angry, and a little frightened. "Blair—Blair you damned log, wake up."

"Uh-eh?" the little biologist rubbed his eyes, his bony, freckled finger crooked to a mutilated child-fist. From surrounding bunks other faces lifted to stare down at them.

Connant straightened up. "Get up—and get a lift on. Your damned animal's escaped."

"Escaped—what!" Chief Pilot Van Wall's bull voice roared out with a volume that shook the walls. Down the communication tunnels other voices yelled suddenly. The dozen inhabitants of Paradise House tumbled in abruptly, Barclay, stocky and bulbous in long woolen underwear, carrying a fire extinguisher.

"What the hell's the matter?" Barclay demanded.

"Your damned beast got loose. I fell asleep about twenty minutes ago, and when I woke up, the thing was gone. Hey, Doc, the hell you say those things can't come to life. Blair's blasted potential life developed a hell of a lot of potential and walked out on us."

Copper stared blankly. "It wasn't—Earthly," he sighed suddenly. "I—I guess Earthly laws don't apply."

"Well, it applied for leave of absence and took it. We've got to find it and capture it somehow." Connant swore bitterly, his deep-set black eyes sullen and angry. "It's a wonder the hellish creature didn't eat me in my sleep."

Blair started back, his pale eyes suddenly fear-struck. "Maybe it di—er—uh—we'll have to find it."

"You find it. It's your pet. I've had all I want to do with it, sitting there for seven hours with the counter clucking every few seconds, and you birds in here singing night-music. It's a wonder I got to sleep. I'm going through to the Ad Building."

Commander Garry ducked through the doorway, pulling his belt tight. "You won't have to. Van's roar sounded like the Boeing taking off down wind. So it wasn't dead?"

"I didn't carry it off in my arms, I assure you," Connant snapped. "The last I saw, the split skull was oozing green goo, like a squashed caterpillar. Doc just said our laws don't work—it's unearthly. Well, it's an unearthly monster, with an unearthly disposition, judging by the face, wandering around with a split skull and brains oozing out."

Norris and McReady appeared in the doorway, a doorway filling with other shivering men. "Has anybody seen it coming over here?" Norris asked innocently. "About four feet tall—three red eyes—brains oozing— Hey, has anybody checked to make sure this isn't a cracked idea of humor? If it is, I think we'll unite in tying Blair's pet around Connant's neck like the Ancient Mariner's albatross."

"It's no humor," Connant shivered. "Lord, I wish it were. I'd rather wear—" He stopped. A wild, weird howl shrieked through the corridors. The men stiffened abruptly, and half turned.

"I think it's been located," Connant finished. His dark eyes shifted with a queer unease. He darted back to his bunk in Paradise House, to return almost immediately with a heavy .45 revolver and an ice-ax. He hefted both gently as he started for the corridor toward Dogtown. "It blundered down the wrong corridor— and landed among the huskies. Listen—the dogs have broken their chains—"

The half-terrorized howl of the dog pack changed to a wild hunting melee. The voices of the dogs thundered in the narrow corridors, and through them came a low rippling snarl of distilled hate. A shrill of pain, a dozen snarling yelps.

Connant broke for the door. Close behind him, McReady, then Barclay and Commander Garry came. Other men broke for the Ad Building, and weapons— the sledge house. Pomroy, in charge of Big Magnet's five cows, started down the corridor in the opposite direction—he had a six-foot-handled, long-tined pitchfork in mind.

Barclay slid to a halt, as McReady's giant bulk turned abruptly away from the tunnel leading to Dogtown, and vanished off at an angle. Uncertainly, the mechanician wavered a moment, the fire extinguisher in his hands, hesitating from one side to the other. Then he was racing after Connant's broad back. Whatever McReady had in mind, he could be trusted to make it work.

Connant stopped at the bend in the corridor. His breath hissed suddenly through his throat. "Great God—" The revolver exploded thunderously; three numbing, palpable waves of sound crashed through the confined corridors. Two more. The revolver dropped to the hard-packed snow of the trail, and Barclay saw the ice-ax shift into defensive position. Connant's powerful body blocked his vision, but beyond he heard something mewing, and, insanely, chuckling. The dogs were quieter; there was a deadly seriousness in their low snarls. Taloned feet scratched at hard-packed snow, broken chains were clinking and tangling.

Connant shifted abruptly, and Barclay could see what lay beyond. For a second he stood frozen, then his breath went out in a gusty curse. The Thing launched itself at Connant, the powerful arms of the man swung the ice-ax flatside first at what might have been a hand. It scrunched horribly, and the tattered flesh, ripped by a half-dozen savage huskies, leapt to its feet again. The red eyes blazed with an unearthly hatred, an unearthly, unkillable vitality.

Barclay turned the fire extinguisher on it; the blinding, blistering stream of chemical spray confused it, baffled it, together with the savage attacks of the huskies, not for long afraid of anything that did, or could live, held it at bay.

McReady wedged men out of his way and drove down the narrow corridor packed with men unable to reach the scene. There was a sure fore-planned drive to McReady's attack. One of the giant blow-torches used in warming the plane's engines was in his bronzed hands. It roared gustily as he turned the corner and opened the valve. The mad mewing hissed louder. The dogs scrambled back from the three-foot lance of blue-hot flame.

"Bar, get a power cable, run it in somehow. And a handle. We can electrocute this—monster, if I don't incinerate it." McReady spoke with an authority of planned action. Barclay turned down the long corridor to the power plant, but already before him Norris and Van Wall were racing down.

Barclay found the cable in the electrical cache in the tunnel wall. In a half minute he was hacking at it, walking back. Van Wall's voice rang out in warning shout of "Power!" as the emergency gasoline-powered dynamo thudded into action. Half a dozen other men were down there now; the coal, kindling were going into the firebox of the steam power plant. Norris, cursing in a low, deadly monotone, was working with quick, sure fingers on the other end of Barclay's cable, splicing a contacter into one of the power leads.

The dogs had fallen back when Barclay reached the corridor bend, fallen back before a furious monstrosity that glared from baleful red eyes, mewing in trapped hatred. The dogs were a semi-circle of red-dipped muzzles with a fringe of glistening white teeth, whining with a vicious eagerness that near matched the fury of the red eyes. McReady stood confidently alert at the corridor bend, the gustily muttering torch held loose and ready for action in his hands. He stepped aside without moving his eyes from the beast as Barclay came up. There was a slight, tight smile on his lean, bronzed face.

Norris's voice called down the corridor, and Barclay stepped forward. The cable was taped to the long handle of a snow-shovel, the two conductors split and held 18 inches apart by a scrap of lumber lashed at right angles across the far end of the handle. Bare copper conductors, charged with 220 volts, glinted in the light of pressure lamps. The Thing mewed and hated and dodged. McReady advanced to Barclay's side. The dogs beyond sensed the plan with the almost-telepathic intelligence of trained huskies. Their whining grew shriller, softer, their mincing steps carried them nearer.

Abruptly a huge night-black Alaskan leapt onto the trapped thing. It turned squalling, saber-clawed feet slashing.

Barclay leapt forward and jabbed. A weird, shrill scream rose and choked out. The smell of burnt flesh in the corridor intensified; greasy smoke curled up. The echoing pound of the gas-electric dynamo down the corridor became a slogging thud.

The red eyes clouded over in a stiffening, jerking travesty of a face. Armlike, leglike members quivered and jerked. The dogs leapt forward, and Barclay yanked back his shovel-handled weapon. The thing on the snow did not move as gleaming teeth ripped it open.

VI

Garry looked about the crowded room. Thirty-two men, some tensed nervously standing against the wall, some uneasily relaxed, some sitting, most perforce standing as intimate as sardines. Thirty-two, plus the five engaged in sewing up wounded dogs, made thirty-seven, the total personnel.

Garry started speaking. "All right, I guess we're here. Some of you—three or four at most—saw what happened. All of you have seen that thing on the table, and can get a general idea. Anyone hasn't, I'll lift——" His hand strayed to the tarpaulin bulking over the thing on the table. There was an acrid odor of singed flesh seeping out of it. The men stirred restlessly, hasty denials.

"It looks rather as though Charnauk isn't going to lead any more teams," Garry went on. "Blair wants to get at this thing, and make some more detailed examination. We want to know what happened, and make sure right now that this is permanently, totally dead. Right?"

Connant grinned. "Anybody that doesn't can sit up with it tonight."

"All right then, Blair, what can you say about it? What was it?" Garry turned to the little biologist.

"I wonder if we ever saw its natural form," Blair looked at the covered mass. "It may have been imitating the beings that built that ship—but I don't think it was. I think that was its true form. Those of us who were up near the bend saw the thing in action; the thing on the table is the result. When it got loose, apparently, it started looking around. Antartica still frozen as it was ages ago when the creature first saw it—and froze. From my observations while it was thawing out, and the bits of tissue I cut and hardened then, I think it was native to a hotter planet than Earth. It couldn't, in its natural form, stand the temperature. There is no lifeform on Earth that can live in Antartica during the winter, but the best compromise is the dog. It found the dogs, and somehow got near enough to Charnauk to get him. The others smelled it—heard it—I don't know—anyway they went wild, and broke chains, and attacked it before it was finished. The thing we found was part Charnauk, queerly only half-dead, part Charnauk half-digested by the jellylike protoplasm of that creature, and part the remains of the thing we originally found, sort of melted down to the basic protoplasm.

"When the dogs attacked it, it turned into the best fighting thing it could think of. Some otherworld beast apparently."

"Turned," snapped Garry. "How?"

"Every living thing is made up of jelly—protoplasm and minute, submicroscopic things called nuclei, which control the bulk, the protoplasm. This thing was just a modification of that same worldwide plan of Nature; cells made up of protoplasm, controlled by infinitely tinier nuclei. You physicists might compare it—an individual cell of any living thing—with an atom; the bulk of the atom, the space-filling part, is made up of the electron orbits, but the character of the thing is determined by the atomic nucleus.

"This isn't wildly beyond what we already know. It's just a modification we haven't seen before. It's as natural, as logical, as any other manifestation of life. It obeys exactly the same laws. The cells are made of protoplasm, their character determined by the nucleus.

"Only, in this creature, the cell-nuclei can control those cells *at will.* It digested Charnauk, and as it digested, studied every cell of his tissue, and shaped its own cells to imitate them exactly. Parts of it—parts that had time to finish changing—are dog-cells. But they don't have dog-cell nuclei." Blair lifted a fraction of the tarpaulin. A torn dog's leg, with stiff gray fur protruded. "That, for instance, isn't dog at all; it's imitation. Some parts I'm uncertain about; the nucleus was hiding itself, covering up with dog-cell imitation nucleus. In time, not even a microscope would have shown the difference."

"Suppose," asked Norris bitterly, "it had had lots of time?"

"Then it would have been a dog. The other dogs would have accepted it. I don't think anything would have distinguished it, not microscope, nor X ray, nor any other means. This is a member of a supremely intelligent race, a race that has learned the deepest secrets of biology, and turned them to its use."

"What was it planning to do?" Barclay looked at the humped tarpaulin.

Blair grinned unpleasantly. The wavering halo of thin hair round his bald pate wavered in a stir of air. "Take over the world, I imagine."

"Take over the world! Just it, all by itself?" Connant gasped. "Set itself up as a lone dictator?"

"No." Blair shook his head. The scalpel he had been fumbling in his bony fingers dropped; he bent to pick it up, so that his face was hidden as he spoke. "It would become the population of the world."

"Become—populate the world? Does it reproduce asexually?"

Blair shook his head and gulped. "It's—it doesn't have to. It weighed 85 pounds. Charnauk weighed about 90. It would have become Charnauk, and had 85 pounds left, to become—oh, Jack for instance, or Chinook. It can imitate anything—that is, become anything. If it had reached the Antarctic Sea, it would have become a seal, maybe two seals. They might have attacked a killer whale, and become either killers, or a herd of seals. Or maybe it would have caught an albatross, or a skua gull, and flown to South America."

Norris cursed softly. "And every time it digested something, and imitated it—"

"It would have had its original bulk left, to start again," Blair finished. "Nothing would kill it. It has no natural enemies, because it becomes whatever it wants to. If a killer whale attacked it, it would become a killer whale. If it was an albatross, and an eagle attacked it, it would become an eagle. Lord, it might become a female eagle. Go back—build a nest and lay eggs!"

"Are you sure that thing from hell is dead?" Dr. Copper asked softly.

"Yes, thank Heaven," the little biologist gasped. "After they drove the dogs off, I stood there poking Bar's electrocution thing into it for five minutes. It's dead and—cooked."

"Then we can only give thanks that this is Antarctica, where there is not one, single, solitary, living thing for it to imitate, except these animals in camp."

"Us," Blair giggled. "It can imitate us. Dogs can't make 400 miles to the sea; there's no food. There aren't any skua gulls to imitate at this season. There aren't any penguins this far inland. There's nothing that can reach the sea from this point—except us. We've got brains.

We can do it. Don't you see—*it's got to imitate us—it's got to be one of us—that's the only way it can fly an airplane—fly a plane for two hours, and rule—be—all Earth's inhabitants.* A world for the taking—*if it imitates us!*

"It didn't know yet. It hadn't had a chance to learn. It was rushed—hurried—took the thing nearest its own size. Look—I'm Pandora! I opened the box! And the only hope that can come out is—that nothing can come out. You didn't see me. I did it. I fixed it. I smashed every magneto. Not a plane can fly. Nothing can fly." Blair giggled and lay down on the floor crying.

Chief Pilot Van Wall made a dive for the door. His feet were fading echoes in the corridors as Dr. Copper bent unhurriedly over the little man on the floor. From his office at the end of the room he brought something, and injected a solution into Blair's arm. "He might come out of it when he wakes up," he sighed rising. McReady helped him lift the biologist onto a near-by bunk. "It all depends on whether we can convince him that thing is dead."

Van Wall ducked into the shack brushing his heavy blond beard absently. "I didn't think a biologist would do a thing like that up thoroughly. He missed the spares in the second cache. It's all right. I smashed them."

Commander Garry nodded. "I was wondering about the radio."

Dr. Copper snorted. "You don't think it can leak out on a radio wave, do you? You'd have five rescue attempts in the next three months if you stop the broadcasts. The thing to do is talk loud and not make a sound. Now I wonder—"

McReady looked speculatively at the doctor. "It might be like an infectious disease. Everything that drank any of its blood?"

Copper shook his head. "Blair missed something. Imitate it may, but it has, to a certain extent, its own body-chemistry, its own metabolism. If it didn't, it would become a dog—and be a dog and nothing more. It has to be an imitation dog. Therefore you can detect it by serum tests. And its chemistry, since it comes from another world, must be so wholly, radically different that a few cells, such as gained by drops of blood, would be treated as disease germs by the dog, or human body."

"Blood—would one of those imitations bleed?" Norris demanded.

"Surely. Nothing mystic about blood. Muscle is about 90% water; blood differs only in having a couple percent more water, and less connective tissue. They'd bleed all right," Copper assured him.

Blair sat up in his bunk suddenly. "Connant—where's Connant?"

The physicist moved over toward the little biologist. "Here I am. What do you want?"

"Are you?" giggled Blair. He lapsed back into the bunk contorted with silent laughter.

Connant looked at him blankly. "Huh? Am I what?"

"*Are* you there?" Blair burst into gales of laughter. "*Are* you Connant? The beast wanted to be *man*—not a dog—"

VII

Dr. Copper rose wearily from the bunk, and washed the hypodermic carefully. The little tinkles it made seemed loud in the packed room, now that Blair's gurgling laughter had finally quieted. Copper looked toward Garry and shook his head slowly. "Hopeless, I'm afraid. I don't think we can ever convince him the thing is dead now."

Norris laughed uncertainly. "I'm not sure you can convince me. Oh, damn you, McReady."

"McReady?" Commander Garry turned to look from Norris to McReady curiously.

"The nightmares," Norris explained. "He had a theory about the nightmares we had at the Secondary Station after finding that thing."

"And that was?" Garry looked at McReady levelly.

Norris answered for him, jerkily, uneasily. "That the creature wasn't dead, had a sort of enormously slowed existence, an existence that permitted it, nonetheless, to be vaguely aware of the passing of time, of our coming, after endless years. I had a dream it could imitate things."

"Well," Copper grunted, "it can."

"Don't be an ass," Norris snapped. "That's not what's bothering me. In the dream it could read minds, read thoughts and ideas and mannerisms."

"What's so bad about that? It seems to be worrying you more than the thought of the joy we're going to have with a madman in an antarctic camp." Copper nodded toward Blair's sleeping form.

McReady shook his great head slowly. "You know that Connant is Connant, because he not merely looks like Connant—which we're beginning to believe that beast might be able to do—but he thinks like Connant, moves himself around as Connant does. That takes more than merely a body that looks like him; that takes Connant's own mind, and thoughts and mannerisms. Therefore, though you know that the thing might make itself *look* like Connant, you aren't much bothered, because you know it has a mind from another world, a totally unhuman mind, that couldn't possibly react and think and talk like a man we know, and do it so well as to fool us for a moment. The idea of the creature imitating one of us is fascinating, but unreal, because it is too completely unhuman to deceive us. It doesn't have a human mind."

"As I said before," Norris repeated, looking steadily

at McReady, "you can say the damnedest things at the damnedest times. Will you be so good as to finish that thought—one way or the other?"

Kinner, the scar-faced expedition cook, had been standing near Connant. Suddenly he moved down the length of the crowded room toward his familiar galley. He shook the ashes from the galley stove noisily.

"It would do it no good," said Dr. Copper, softly as though thinking out loud, "to merely look like something it was trying to imitate; it would have to understand its feelings, its reactions. It *is* unhuman; it has powers of imitation beyond any conception of man. A good actor, by training himself, can imitate another man, another man's mannerisms, well enough to fool most people. Of course no actor could imitate so perfectly as to deceive men who had been living with the imitated one in the complete lack of privacy of an antarctic camp. That would take a superhuman skill."

"Oh, you've got the bug too?" Norris cursed softly.

Connant, standing alone at one end of the room, looked about him wildly, his face white. A gentle eddying of the men had crowded them slowly down toward the other end of the room, so that he stood quite alone. "My God, will you two Jeremiahs shut up?" Connant's voice shook. "What am I? Some kind of a microscopic specimen you're dissecting? Some unpleasant worm you're discussing in the third person?"

McReady looked up at him; his slowly twisting hands stopped for a moment. "Having a lovely time. Wish you were here. Signed: Everybody.

"Connant, if you think you're having a hell of a time, just move over on the other end for a while. You've got one thing we haven't; you know what the answer is. I'll tell you this, right now you're the most feared and respected man in Big Magnet."

"Lord, I wish you could see your eyes," Connant

gasped. "Stop staring, will you! What the hell are you going to do?"

"Have you any suggestions, Dr. Copper?" Commander Garry asked steadily. "The present situation is impossible."

"Oh, is it?" Connant snapped. "Come over here and look at that crowd. By Heaven, they look exactly like that gang of huskies around the corridor bend. Benning, will you stop hefting that damned ice-ax?"

The coppery blade rang on the floor as the aviation mechanic nervously dropped it. He bent over and picked it up instantly, hefting it slowly, turning it in his hands, his brown eyes moving jerkily about the room.

Copper sat down on the bunk beside Blair. The wood creaked noisily in the room. Far down a corridor, a dog yelped in pain, and the dog-drivers' tense voices floated softly back. "Microscopic examination," said the doctor thoughtfully, "would be useless, as Blair pointed out. Considerable time has passed. However, serum tests would be definitive."

"Serum tests? What do you mean exactly?" Commander Garry asked.

"If I had a rabbit that had been injected with human blood—a poison to rabbits, of course, as is the blood of any animal save that of another rabbit—and the injections continued in increasing doses for some time, the rabbit would be human-immune. If a small quantity of its blood were drawn off, allowed to separate in a test-tube, and to the clear serum, a bit of human blood were added, there would be a visible reaction, proving the blood was human. If cow, or dog blood were added—or any protein material other than that one thing, human blood—no reaction would take place. That would prove definitely."

"Can you suggest where I might catch a rabbit for you, Doc?" Norris asked. "That is, nearer than Australia; we don't want to waste time going that far."

"I know there aren't any rabbits in Antarctica." Copper nodded. "But that is simply the usual animal. Any animal except man will do. A dog for instance. But it will take several days, and due to the greater size of the animal, considerable blood. Two of us will have to contribute."

"Would I do?" Garry asked.

"That will make two," Copper nodded. "I'll get to work on it right away."

"What about Connant in the meantime," Kinner demanded. "I'm going out that door and head off for the Ross Sea before I cook for him."

"He may be human—" Copper started.

Connant burst out in a flood of curses. "Human! *May* be human, you damned sawbones! What in hell do you think I am?"

"A monster," Copper snapped sharply. "Now shut up and listen." Connant's face drained of color and he sat down heavily as the indictment was put in words. "Until we know—you know as well as we do that we have reason to question the fact, and only you know how that question is to be answered—we may reasonably be expected to lock you up. If you are—unhuman—you're a lot more dangerous than poor Blair there, and I'm going to see that he's locked up thoroughly. I expect that his next stage will be a violent desire to kill you, all the dogs, and probably all of us. When he wakes, he will be convinced we're all unhuman, and nothing on the planet will ever change his conviction. It would be kinder to let him die, but we can't do that, of course. He's going in one shack, and you can stay in Cosmos House with your cosmic ray apparatus. Which is about what you'd do anyway. I've got to fix up a couple of dogs."

Connant nodded bitterly. "I'm human. Hurry that test. Your eyes—Lord, I wish you could see your eyes staring—"

Commander Garry watched anxiously as Clark, the dog-handler, held the big brown Alaskan husky, while Copper began the injection treatment. The dog was not anxious to cooperate; the needle was painful, and already he'd experienced considerable needle work that morning. Five stitches held closed a slash that ran from his shoulder, across the ribs, halfway down his body. One long fang was broken off short; the missing part was to be found half buried in the shoulder bone of the monstrous thing on the table in the Ad Building.

"How long will that take?" Garry asked, pressing his arm gently. It was sore from the prick of the needle Dr. Copper had used to withdraw blood.

Copper shrugged. "I don't know, to be frank. I know the general method. I've used it on rabbits. But I haven't experimented with dogs. They're big, clumsy animals to work with; naturally rabbits are preferable, and serve ordinarily. In civilized places you can buy a stock of human-immune rabbits from suppliers, and not many investigators take the trouble to prepare their own."

"What do they want with them back there?" Clark asked.

"Criminology is one large field. *A* says he didn't murder *B*, but that the blood on his shirt came from killing a chicken. The State makes a test, then it's up to *A* to explain how it is the blood reacts on human-immune rabbits, but not on chicken-immunes."

"What are we going to do with Blair in the meantime?" Garry asked wearily. "It's all right to let him sleep where he is for a while, but when he wakes up——"

"Barclay and Benning are fitting some bolts on the door of Cosmos House," Copper replied grimly. "Connant's acting like a gentleman. I think perhaps the way the other men look at him makes him rather want privacy. Lord knows, heretofore we've all of us individually prayed for a little privacy."

Clark laughed brittly. "Not anymore, thank you. The more the merrier."

"Blair," Copper went on, "will also have to have privacy—and locks. He's going to have a pretty definite plan in mind when he wakes up. Ever hear the old story of how to stop hoof-and-mouth disease in cattle?"

Clark and Garry shook their heads silently.

"If there isn't any hoof-and-mouth disease, there won't be any hoof-and-mouth disease," Copper explained. "You get rid of it by killing every animal that exhibits it, and every animal that's been near the diseased animal. Blair's a biologist, and knows that story. He's afraid of this thing we loosed. The answer is probably pretty clear in his mind now. Kill everybody and everything in this camp before a skua gull or a wandering albatross coming in with the spring chances out this way and—catches the disease."

Clark's lips curled in a twisted grin. "Sounds logical to me. If things get too bad—maybe we'd better let Blair get loose. It would save us committing suicide. We might also make something of a vow that if things get bad, we see that that does happen."

Copper laughed softly. "The last man alive in Big Magnet—wouldn't be a man," he pointed out. "Somebody's got to kill those—creatures that don't desire to kill themselves, you know. We don't have enough thermite to do it all at once, and the decanite explosive wouldn't help much. I have an idea that even small pieces of one of those beings would be self-sufficient."

"If," said Garry thoughtfully, "they can modify their protoplasm at will, won't they simply modify themselves to birds and fly away? They can read all about birds, and imitate their structure without even meeting them. Or imitate, perhaps, birds of their home planet."

Copper shook his head, and helped Clark to free the dog. "Man studied birds for centuries, trying to learn how to make a machine to fly like them. He never did do the trick; his final success came when he broke away entirely and tried new methods. Knowing the general idea, and knowing the detailed structure of wing and bone and nerve-tissue is something far, far different. And as for otherworld birds, perhaps, in fact very probably, the atmospheric conditions here are so vastly different that their birds couldn't fly. Perhaps, even, the being came from a planet like Mars with such a thin atmosphere that there were no birds."

Barclay came into the building, trailing a length of airplane control cable. "It's finished, Doc. Cosmos House can't be opened from the inside. Now where do we put Blair?"

Copper looked toward Garry. "There wasn't any biology building. I don't know where we can isolate him."

"How about East Cache?" Garry said after a moment's thought. "Will Blair be able to look after himself—or need attention?"

"He'll be capable enough. We'll be the ones to watch out," Copper assured him grimly. "Take a stove, a couple of bags of coal, necessary supplies and a few tools to fix it up. Nobody's been out there since last fall, have they?"

Garry shook his head. "If he gets noisy—I thought that might be a good idea."

Barclay hefted the tools he was carrying and looked up at Garry. "If the muttering he's doing now is any sign, he's going to sing away the night hours. And we won't like his song."

"What's he saying?" Copper asked.

Barclay shook his head. "I didn't care to listen much. You can if you want to. But I gathered that the blasted idiot had all the dreams McReady had, and a few more. He slept beside the thing when we stopped on the trail coming in from Secondary Magnetic, remember. He dreamt the thing was alive, and dreamt more details. And—damn his soul—knew it wasn't all dream, or had reason to. He knew it had telepathic powers that were stirring vaguely, and that it could not only read minds, but project thoughts. They weren't dreams, you see. They were stray thoughts that thing was broadcasting, the way Blair's broadcasting his thoughts now—a sort of telepathic muttering in its sleep. That's why he knew so much about its powers. I guess you and I, Doc, weren't so sensitive—if you want to believe in telepathy."

"I have to," Copper sighed. "Dr. Rhine of Duke University has shown that it exists, shown that some are much more sensitive than others."

"Well, if you want to learn a lot of details, go listen in on Blair's broadcast. He's driven most of the boys out of the Ad Building; Kinner's rattling pans like coal going down a chute. When he can't rattle a pan, he shakes ashes.

"By the way, Commander, what are we going to do this spring, now the planes are out of it?"

Garry sighed. "I'm afraid our expedition is going to be a loss. We cannot divide our strength now."

"It won't be a loss—if we continue to live, and come out of this," Copper promised him. "The find we've made if we can get it under control, is important enough. The cosmic ray data, magnetic work, and atmospheric work won't be greatly hindered."

Garry laughed mirthlessly. "I was just thinking of the radio broadcasts. Telling half the world about the wonderful results of our exploration flights, trying to fool men like Byrd and Ellsworth back home there that we're doing something."

Copper nodded gravely. "They'll know something's wrong. But men like that have judgment enough to know we wouldn't do tricks without some sort of reason, and will wait for our return to judge us. I think it comes to this: men who know enough to recognize our deception will wait for our return. Men who haven't discretion and faith enough to wait will not have the experience to detect any fraud. We know enough of the conditions here to put through a good bluff."

"Just so they don't send 'rescue' expeditions," Garry prayed. "When—if—we're ever ready to come out, we'll have to send word to Captain Forsythe to bring a stock of magnetos with him when he comes down. But—never mind that."

"You mean if we don't come out?" asked Barclay. "I was wondering if a nice running account of an eruption or an earthquake via radio—with a swell windup by using a stick of decanite under the microphone— would help. Nothing, of course, will entirely keep people out. One of those swell, melodramatic 'last-man-alive-scenes' might make 'em go easy though."

Garry smiled with genuine humor. "Is everybody in camp trying to figure that out too?"

Copper laughed. "What do you think, Garry? We're confident we can win out. But not too easy about it, I guess."

Clark grinned up from the dog he was petting into calmness. "Confident, did you say, Doc?"

VIII

Blair moved restlessly around the small shack. His eyes jerked and quivered in vague, fleeting glances at the four men with him; Barclay, six feet tall and weighing over 190 pounds; McReady, a bronze giant of a man; Dr. Copper, short, squatly powerful; and Benning, five-feet-ten of wiry strength.

Blair was huddled up against the far wall of the East Cache cabin, his gear piled in the middle of the floor beside the heating stove, forming an island between him and the four men. His bony hands clenched and fluttered, terrified. His pale eyes wavered uneasily as his bald, freckled head darted about in birdlike motion.

"I don't want anybody coming here. I'll cook my own food," he snapped nervously. "Kinner may be human now, but I don't believe it. I'm going to get out of here, but I'm not going to eat any food you send me. I want cans. Sealed cans."

"O.K., Blair, we'll bring 'em tonight," Barclay promised. "You've got coal, and the fire's started. I'll make a last—" Barclay started forward.

Blair instantly scurried to the farthest corner. "Get out! Keep away from me, you monster!" the little biologist shrieked, and tried to claw his way through the wall of the shack. "Keep away from me—keep away—I won't be absorbed—I won't be—"

Barclay relaxed and moved back. Dr. Copper shook his head. "Leave him alone, Bar. It's easier for him to fix the thing himself. We'll have to fix the door, I think—"

The four men let themselves out. Efficiently, Benning and Barclay fell to work. There were no locks in Antarctica; there wasn't enough privacy to make them needed. But powerful screws had been driven in each side of the doorframe, and the spare aviation control cable, immensely strong, woven steel wire, was rapidly caught between them and drawn taut. Barclay went to work with a drill and a keyhole saw. Presently he had a trap cut in the door through which goods could be passed without unlashing the entrance. Three powerful hinges from a stock-crate, two hasps and a pair of three-inch cotterpins made it proof against opening from the other side.

Blair moved about restlessly inside. He was dragging something over to the door with panting gasps, and muttering frantic curses. Barclay opened the hatch and glanced in, Dr. Copper peering over his shoulder. Blair had moved the heavy bunk against the door. It could not be opened without his cooperation now.

"Don't know but what the poor man's right at that." McReady sighed. "If he gets loose, it is his avowed intention to kill each and all of us as quickly as possible, which is something we don't agree with. But we've something on our side of that door that is worse than a homicidal maniac. If one or the other has to get loose, I think I'll come up and undo these lashings here."

Barclay grinned. "You let me know, and I'll show you how to get these off fast. Let's go back."

The sun was painting the northern horizon in multi-colored rainbows still, though it was two hours below the horizon. The field of drift swept off to the north, sparkling under its flaming colors in a million reflected glories. Low mounds of rounded white on the northern horizon showed the Magnet Range was barely awash above the sweeping drift. Little eddies of wind-lifted snow swirled away from their skis as they set out toward the main encampment two miles away. The spidery finger of the broadcast radiator lifted a gaunt black needle against the white of the Antarctic continent. The snow under their skis was like fine sand, hard and gritty.

"Spring," said Benning bitterly, "is come. Ain't we got fun! And I've been looking forward to getting away from this blasted hole in the ice."

"I wouldn't try it now, if I were you." Barclay grunted. "Guys that set out from here in the next few days are going to be marvelously unpopular."

"How is your dog getting along, Dr. Copper?" McReady asked. "Any results yet?"

"In thirty hours? I wish there were. I gave him an

injection of my blood today. But I imagine another five days will be needed. I don't know certainly enough to stop sooner."

"I've been wondering—if Connant were—changed, would he have warned us so soon after the animal escaped? Wouldn't he have waited long enough for it to have a real chance to fix itself? Until we woke up naturally?" McReady asked slowly.

"The thing is selfish. You didn't think it looked as though it were possessed of a store of the higher justices, did you?" Dr. Copper pointed out. "Every part of it is all of it, every part of it is all for itself, I imagine. If Connant were changed, to save his skin, he'd have to—but Connant's feelings aren't changed; they're imitated perfectly, or they're his own. Naturally, the imitation, imitating perfectly Connant's feelings, would do exactly what Connant would do."

"Say, couldn't Norris or Vane give Connant some kind of a test? If the thing is brighter than men, it might know more physics than Connant should, and they'd catch it out," Barclay suggested.

Copper shook his head wearily. "Not if it reads minds. You can't plan a trap for it. Vane suggested that last night. He hoped it would answer some of the questions of physics he'd like to know answers to."

"This expedition-of-four idea is going to make life happy." Benning looked at his companions. "Each of us with an eye on the other to make sure he doesn't do something—peculiar. Man, aren't we going to be a trusting bunch! Each man eyeing his neighbors with the grandest exhibition of faith and trust—I'm beginning to know what Connant meant by 'I wish you could see your eyes.' Every now and then we all have it, I guess. One of you looks around with a sort of 'I-wonder-if-the-other-*three*-are' look. Incidentally, I'm not excepting myself."

"So far as we know, the animal is dead, with a slight question as to Connant. No other is suspected," McReady stated slowly. "The 'always-four' order is merely a precautionary measure."

"I'm waiting for Garry to make it four-in-a-bunk," Barclay sighed. "I thought I didn't have any privacy before, but since that order—"

IX

None watched more tensely than Connant. A little sterile glass test-tube, half-filled with straw-colored fluid. One—two—three—four—five drops of the clear solution Dr. Copper had prepared from the drops of blood from Connant's arm. The tube was shaken carefully, then set in a beaker of clear, warm water. The thermometer read blood heat, a little thermostat clicked noisily, and the electric hotplate began to glow as the lights flickered slightly. Then—little white flecks of precipitation were forming, snowing down in the clear straw-colored fluid. "Lord," said Connant. He dropped heavily into a bunk, crying like a baby. "Six days—" Connant sobbed, "six days in there— wondering if that damned test would lie—"

Garry moved over silently, and slipped his arm across the physicist's back.

"It couldn't lie," Dr. Copper said. "The dog was human-immune—and the serum reacted."

"He's—all right?" Norris gasped. "Then—the animal is dead—dead forever?"

"He is human," Copper spoke definitely, "and the animal is dead."

Kinner burst out laughing, laughing hysterically. McReady turned toward him and slapped his face with a methodical one-two, one-two action. The cook laughed, gulped, cried a moment, and sat up rubbing his cheeks, mumbling his thanks vaguely. "I was scared. Lord, I was scared—"

Norris laughed brittly. "You think we weren't, you ape? You think maybe Connant wasn't?"

The Ad Building stirred with a sudden rejuvenation. Voices laughed, the men clustering around Connant spoke with unnecessarily loud voices, jittery, nervous voices relievedly friendly again. Somebody called out a suggestion, and a dozen started for their skis. Blair, Blair might recover— Dr. Copper fussed with his test-tubes in nervous relief, trying solutions. The party of relief for Blair's shack started out the door, skis clapping noisily. Down the corridor, the dogs set up a quick yelping howl as the air of excited relief reached them.

Dr. Copper fussed with his tubes. McReady noticed him first, sitting on the edge of the bunk, with two precipitin-whitened test-tubes of straw-colored fluid, his face whiter than the stuff in the tubes, silent tears slipping down from horror-widened eyes.

McReady felt a cold knife of fear pierce through his heart and freeze in his breast. Dr. Copper looked up. "Garry," he called hoarsely. "Garry, for God's sake, come here."

Commander Garry walked toward him sharply. Silence clapped down on the Ad Building. Connant looked up, rose stiffly from his seat.

"Garry—tissue from the monster—precipitates too. It proves nothing. Nothing but—but the dog was monster-immune too. That *one of the two contributing blood—one of us two,* you and I, Garry—*one of us is a monster.*"

X

"Bar, call back those men before they tell Blair," McReady said quietly. Barclay went to the door; faintly his shouts came back to the tensely silent men in the room. Then he was back.

"They're coming," he said. "I didn't tell them why. Just that Dr. Copper said not to go."

"McReady," Garry sighed, "you're in command now. May God help you. I cannot."

The bronzed giant nodded slowly, his deep eyes on Commander Garry.

"I may be the one," Garry added. "I know I'm not, but I cannot prove it to you in any way. Dr. Copper's test has broken down. The fact that he showed it was useless, when it was to the advantage of the monster to have that uselessness not known, would seem to prove he was human."

Copper rocked back and forth slowly on the bunk. "I know I'm human. I can't prove it either. One of us two is a liar, for that test cannot lie, and it says one of us is. I gave proof that the test was wrong, which seems to prove I'm human, and now Garry has given that argument which proves me human—which he, as the monster, should not do. Round and round and round and round and—"

Dr. Copper's head, then his neck and shoulders began circling slowly in time to the words. Suddenly he was lying back on the bunk, roaring with laughter. "It doesn't have to prove *one* of us is a monster! It doesn't have to prove that at all! Ho-ho. If we're *all* monsters it works the same—we're all monsters—all of us— Connant and Garry and I—and all of you."

"McReady," Van Wall, the blond-bearded Chief Pilot, called softly, "you were on the way to an M.D. when you took up meteorology, weren't you? Can you make some kind of test?"

McReady went over to Copper slowly, took the hypodermic from his hand, and washed it carefully in 95% alcohol. Garry sat on the bunk-edge with wooden face, watching Copper and McReady expressionlessly. "What Copper said is possible." McReady sighed. "Van, will you help here? Thanks." The filled needle jabbed into Copper's thigh. The man's laughter did not stop, but slowly faded into sobs, then sound sleep as the morphia took hold.

McReady turned again. The men who had started for Blair stood at the far end of the room, skis dripping snow, their faces as white as their skis. Connant had a lighted cigarette in each hand; one he was puffing absently, and staring at the floor. The heat of the one in his left hand attracted him and he stared at it and the one in the other hand stupidly for a moment. He dropped one and crushed it under his heel slowly.

"Dr. Copper," McReady repeated, "could be right. I know I'm human—but of course can't prove it. I'll repeat the test for my own information. Any of you others who wish to may do the same."

Two minutes later, McReady held a test-tube with white precipitin settling slowly from straw-colored serum. "It reacts to human blood too, so they aren't both monsters."

"I didn't think they were," Van Wall sighed. "That wouldn't suit the monster either; we could have destroyed them if we knew. Why hasn't the monster destroyed us, do you suppose? It seems to be loose."

McReady snorted. Then laughed softly. "Elementary, my dear Watson. The monster wants to have life-forms available. It cannot animate a dead body, apparently. It is just waiting—waiting until the best opportunities come. We who remain human, it is holding in reserve."

Kinner shuddered violently. "Hey. Hey, Mac. Mac,

would I know if I was a monster? Would I know if the monster had already got me? Oh Lord, I may be a monster already."

"You'd know," McReady answered.

"But we wouldn't," Norris laughed shortly, half-hysterically.

McReady looked at the vial of serum remaining. "There's one thing this damned stuff is good for, at that," he said thoughtfully. "Clark, will you and Van help me? The rest of the gang better stick together here. Keep an eye on each other," he said bitterly. "See that you don't get into mischief, shall we say?"

McReady started down the tunnel toward Dog Town with Clark and Van Wall behind him. "You need more serum?" Clark asked.

McReady shook his head. "Tests. There's four cows and a bull, and nearly seventy dogs down there. This stuff reacts only to human blood and—monsters."

XI

McReady came back to the Ad Building and went silently to the washstand. Clark and Van Wall joined him a moment later. Clark's lips had developed a tic, jerking into sudden, unexpected sneers.

"What did you do?" Connant exploded suddenly. "More immunizing?"

Clark snickered, and stopped with a hiccough. "Immunizing. Haw! Immune all right."

"That monster," said Van Wall steadily, "is quite logical. Our immune dog was quite all right, and we drew a little more serum for the tests. But we won't make anymore."

"Can't—can't you use one man's blood on another dog—" Norris began.

"There aren't," said McReady softly, "any more dogs. Nor cattle, I might add."

"No more dogs?" Benning sat down slowly.

"They're very nasty when they start changing," Van Wall said precisely. "But slow. That electrocution iron you made up, Barclay, is very fast. There is only one dog left—our immune. The monster left that for us, so we could play with our little test. The rest—" He shrugged and dried his hands.

"The cattle—" gulped Kinner.

"Also. Reacted very nicely. They look funny as hell when they start melting. The beast hasn't any quick escape, when it's tied in dog chains, or halters, and it had to be to imitate."

Kinner stood up slowly. His eyes darted around the room, and came to rest horribly quivering on a tin bucket in the galley. Slowly, step by step, he retreated toward the door, his mouth opening and closing silently, like a fish out of water.

"The milk—" he gasped. "I milked 'em an hour ago—" His voice broke into a scream as he dived through the door. He was out on the ice-cap without windproof or heavy clothing.

Van Wall looked after him for a moment thoughtfully. "He's probably hopelessly mad," he said at length, "but he might be a monster escaping. He hasn't skis. Take a blow-torch—in case."

The physical motion of the chase helped them; something that needed doing. Three of the other men were quietly being sick. Norris was lying flat on his back, his face greenish, looking steadily at the bottom of the bunk above him.

"Mac, how long have the—cows been not-cows—"

McReady shrugged his shoulders hopelessly. He went over to the milk bucket, and with his little tube of serum went to work on it. The milk clouded it, making certainty difficult. Finally he dropped the test-tube in the stand, and shook his head. "It tests negatively. Which means either they were cows then, or that, being perfect imitations, they gave perfectly good milk."

Copper stirred restlessly in his sleep and gave a gurgling cross between a snore and a laugh. Silent eyes fastened on him. "Would morphia—a monster—" somebody started to ask.

"Lord knows." McReady shrugged. "It affects every Earthly animal I know of."

Connant suddenly raised his head. "Mac! The dogs must have swallowed pieces of the monster, and the pieces destroyed them! The dogs were where the monster resided. I was locked up. Doesn't that prove—"

Van Wall shook his head. "Sorry. Proves nothing about what you are, only proves what you didn't do."

"It doesn't do that." McReady sighed. "We are helpless because we don't know enough, and so jittery we don't think straight. Locked up! Ever watch a white corpuscle of the blood go through the wall of a blood vessel? No? It sticks out a pseudopod. And there it is—on the far side of the wall."

"Oh," said Van Wall unhappily. "The cattle tried to melt down, didn't they? They could have melted down—become just a thread of stuff and leaked under a door to re-collect on the other side. Ropes—no—no, that wouldn't do it. They couldn't live in a sealed tank or—"

"If," said McReady, "you shoot it through the heart, and it doesn't die, it's a monster. That's the best test I can think of, offhand."

"No dogs," said Garry quietly, "and no cattle. It has to imitate men now. And locking up doesn't do any good. Your test might work, Mac, but I'm afraid it would be hard on the men."

XII

Clark looked up from the galley stove as Van Wall, Barclay, McReady, and Benning came in, brushing the drift from their clothes. The other men jammed into the Ad Building continued studiously to do as they were doing, playing chess, poker, reading. Ralsen was fixing a sledge on the table; Vane and Norris had their heads together over magnetic data, while Harvey read tables in a low voice.

Dr. Copper snored softly on the bunk. Garry was working with Dutton over a sheaf of radio messages on the corner of Dutton's bunk and a small fraction of the radio table. Connant was using most of the table for cosmic ray sheets.

Quite plainly through the corridor, despite two closed doors, they could hear Kinner's voice. Clark banged a kettle onto the galley stove and beckoned McReady silently. The meteorologist went over to him.

"I don't mind the cooking so damn much," Clark said nervously, "but isn't there some way to stop that bird? We all agreed that it would be safe to move him into Cosmos House."

"Kinner?" McReady nodded toward the door. "I'm afraid not. I can dope him, I suppose, but we don't have an unlimited supply of morphia, and he's not in danger of losing his mind. Just hysterical."

"Well, we're in danger of losing ours. You've been out for an hour and a half. That's been going on steadily ever since, and it was going for two hours before. There's a limit, you know."

Garry wandered over slowly, apologetically. For an instant, McReady caught the feral spark of fear—horror—in Clark's eyes, and knew at the same instant it was in his own. Garry—Garry or Copper—was certainly a monster.

"If you could stop that, I think it would be a sound policy, Mac," Garry spoke quietly. "There are—tensions enough in this room. We agreed that it would be safe for Kinner in there, because everyone else in camp is under constant eyeing." Garry shivered slightly. "And try, try in God's name, to find some test that will work."

McReady sighed. "Watched or unwatched, everyone's tense. Blair's jammed the trap so it won't open now. Says he's got food enough, and keeps screaming 'Go away, go away—you're monsters. I won't be absorbed. I won't. I'll tell men when they come. Go away.' So—we went away."

"There's no other test?" Garry pleaded.

McReady shrugged his shoulders. "Copper was perfectly right. The serum test could be absolutely definitive if it hadn't been—contaminated. But that's the only dog left, and he's fixed now."

"Chemicals? Chemical tests?"

McReady shook his head. "Our chemistry isn't that good. I tried the microscope you know."

Garry nodded. "Monster-dog and real dog were identical. But—you've got to go on. What are we going to do after dinner?"

Van Wall had joined them quietly. "Rotation sleeping. Half the crowd sleep; half stay awake. I wonder how many of us are monsters? All the dogs were. We thought we were safe, but somehow it got Copper—or you." Van Wall's eyes flashed uneasily. "It may have gotten every one of you—all of you but myself may be wondering, looking. No, that's not possible. You'd just spring then, I'd be helpless. We humans must somehow have the greater numbers now. But—" he stopped.

McReady laughed shortly. "You're doing what Norris complained of in me. Leaving it hanging. 'But if one more is changed—that may shift the balance of power.

It doesn't fight. I don't think it ever fights. It must be a peaceable thing, in its own—inimitable—way. It never had to, because it always gained its end otherwise."

Van Wall's mouth twisted in a sickly grin. "You're suggesting then, that perhaps it already *has* the greater numbers, but is just waiting—waiting, all of them—all of you, for all I know—waiting till I, the last human drop my wariness in sleep. Mac, did you notice their eyes, all looking at us."

Garry sighed. "You haven't been sitting here for four straight hours, while all their eyes silently weighed the information that one of us two, Copper or I, is a monster certainly—perhaps both of us."

Clark repeated his request. "Will you stop that bird's noise? He's driving me nuts. Make him tone down, anyway."

"Still praying?" McReady asked.

"Still praying." Clark groaned. "He hasn't stopped for a second. I don't mind his praying if it relieves him, but he yells, he sings psalms and hymns and shouts prayers. He thinks God can't hear well way down here."

"Maybe he can't," Barclay grunted. "Or he'd have done something about this thing loosed from hell."

"Somebody's going to try that test you mentioned, if you don't stop him," Clark stated grimly. "I think a cleaver in the head would be as positive a test as a bullet in the heart."

"Go ahead with the food. I'll see what I can do. There may be something in the cabinets." McReady moved wearily toward the corner Copper had used as his dispensary. Three tall cabinets of rough boards, two locked, were the repositories of the camp's medical supplies. Twelve years ago, McReady had graduated, had started for an internship, and been diverted to meteorology. Copper was a picked man, a man who knew his profession thoroughly and modernly. More than half the drugs available were totally unfamiliar to

McReady; many of the others he had forgotten. There was no huge medical library here, no series of journals available to learn the things he had forgotten, the elementary, simple things to Copper, things that did not merit inclusion in the small library he had been forced to content himself with. Books are heavy, and every ounce of supplies had been freighted in by air.

McReady picked a barbiturate hopefully. Barclay and Van Wall went with him. One man never went anywhere alone in Big Magnet.

Ralsen had his sledge put away, and the physicists had moved off the table, the poker game broken up, when they got back. Clark was putting out the food. The click of spoons and the muffled sounds of eating were the only sign of life in the room. There were no words spoken as the three returned; simply all eyes focused on them questioningly while the jaws moved methodically.

McReady stiffened suddenly. Kinner was screeching out a hymn in a hoarse, cracked voice. He looked wearily at Van Wall with a twisted grin and shook his head. "Uh-uh."

Van Wall cursed bitterly, and sat down at the table. "We'll just plumb have to take that till his voice wears out. He can't yell like that forever."

"He's got a brass throat and a cast-iron larynx," Norris declared savagely. "Then we could be hopeful, and suggest he's one of our friends. In that case he could go on renewing his throat till doomsday."

Silence clamped down. For twenty minutes they ate without a word. Then Connant jumped up with an angry violence. "You sit as still as a bunch of graven images. You don't say a word, but oh, Lord, what expressive eyes you've got. They roll around like a bunch of glass marbles spilling down a table. They wink and blink and stare—and whisper things. Can you guys look somewhere else for a change, please?

"Listen, Mac, you're in charge here. Let's run movies for the rest of the night. We've been saving those reels to make 'em last. Last for what? Who is it's going to see those last reels, eh? Let's see 'em while we can, and look at something other than each other."

"Sound idea, Connant. I, for one, am quite willing to change this in any way I can."

"Turn the sound up loud, Dutton. Maybe you can drown out the hymns," Clark suggested.

"But don't," Norris said softly, "don't turn off the lights altogether."

"The lights will be out." McReady shook his head. "We'll show all the cartoon movies we have. You won't mind seeing the old cartoons will you?"

"Goody, goody—a moom-pitcher show. I'm just in the mood." McReady turned to look at the speaker, a lean, lanky New Englander, by the name of Caldwell. Caldwell was stuffing his pipe slowly, a sour eye cocked up to McReady.

The bronze giant was forced to laugh. "O.K., Bart, you win. Maybe we aren't quite in the mood for Popeye and trick ducks, but it's something."

"Let's play Classifications," Caldwell suggested slowly. "Or maybe you call it Guggenheim. You draw lines on a piece of paper, and put down classes of things— like animals, you know. One for 'H' and one for 'U' and so on. Like 'Human' and 'Unknown' for instance. I think that would be a hell of a lot better game. Classification, I sort of figure, is what we need right now a lot more than movies. Maybe somebody's got a pencil that he can draw lines with, draw lines between the 'U' animals and the 'H' animals for instance."

"McReady's trying to find that kind of a pencil," Van Wall answered quietly, "but, we've got three kinds of animals here, you know. One that begins with 'M.' We don't want any more."

"Mad ones, you mean. Uh-huh. Clark, I'll help you

with those pots so we can get our little peep-show going." Caldwell got up slowly.

Dutton and Barclay and Benning, in charge of the projector and sound mechanism arrangements, went about their job silently, while the Ad Building was cleared and the dishes and pans disposed of. McReady drifted over toward Van Wall slowly, and leaned back in the bunk beside him. "I've been wondering, Van," he said with a wry grin, "whether or not to report my ideas in advance. I forgot the 'U animal' as Caldwell named it, could read minds. I've a vague idea of something that might work. It's too vague to bother with, though. Go ahead with your show, while I try to figure out the logic of the thing. I'll take this bunk."

Van Wall glanced up, and nodded. The movie screen would be practically on a line with this bunk, hence making the pictures least distracting here, because least intelligible. "Perhaps you should tell us what you have in mind. As it is, only the unknowns know what you plan. You might be—unknown before you got it into operation."

"Won't take long, if I get it figured out right. But I don't want any more all-but-the-test-dog-monsters things. We better move Copper into this bunk directly above me. He won't be watching the screen either." McReady nodded toward Copper's gently snoring bulk. Garry helped them lift and move the doctor.

McReady leaned back against the bunk, and sank into a trance, almost, of concentration, trying to calculate chances, operations, methods. He was scarcely aware as the others distributed themselves silently, and the screen lit up. Vaguely Kinner's hectic, shouted prayers and his rasping hymn-singing annoyed him till the sound accompaniment started. The lights were turned out, but the large, light-colored areas of the screen reflected enough light for ready visibility. It made men's eyes sparkle as they moved restlessly.

Kinner was still praying, shouting, his voice a raucous accompaniment to the mechanical sound. Dutton stepped up the amplification.

So long had the voice been going on, that only vaguely at first was McReady aware that something seemed missing. Lying as he was, just across the narrow room from the corridor leading to Cosmos House, Kinner's voice had reached him fairly clearly, despite the sound accompaniment of the pictures. It struck him abruptly that it had stopped.

"Dutton, cut that sound," McReady called as he sat up abruptly. The pictures flickered a moment, soundless and strangely futile in the sudden, deep silence. The rising wind on the surface above bubbled melancholy tears of sound down the stove pipes. "Kinner's stopped," McReady said softly.

"For God's sake start that sound then; he may have stopped to listen," Norris snapped.

McReady rose and went down the corridor. Barclay and Van Wall left their places at the far end of the room to follow him. The flickers bulged and twisted on the back of Barclay's gray underwear as he crossed the still-functioning beam of the projector. Dutton snapped on the lights, and the pictures vanished.

Norris stood at the door as McReady had asked. Garry sat down quietly in the bunk nearest the door, forcing Clark to make room for him. Most of the others had stayed exactly where they were. Only Connant walked slowly up and down the room, in steady, unvarying rhythm.

"If you're going to do that, Connant," Clark spat, "we can get along without you altogether, whether you're human or not. Will you stop that damned rhythm?"

"Sorry." The physicist sat down in a bunk, and watched his toes thoughtfully. It was almost five minutes, five ages, while the wind made the only sound, before McReady appeared at the door.

"We," he announced, "haven't got enough grief here already. Somebody's tried to help us out. Kinner has a knife in his throat, which was why he stopped singing, probably. We've got monsters, madmen and murderers. Any more 'M's' you can think of, Caldwell? If there are, we'll probably have 'em before long."

XIII

"Is Blair loose?" someone asked.

"Blair is not loose. Or he flew in. If there's any doubt about where our gentle helper came from—this may clear it up." Van Wall held a foot-long, thin-bladed knife in a cloth. The wooden handle was half-burnt, charred with the peculiar pattern of the top of the galley stove.

Clark stared at it. "I did that this afternoon. I forgot the damn thing and left it on the stove."

Van Wall nodded. "I smelled it, if you remember. I knew the knife came from the galley."

"I wonder," said Benning looking around at the party warily, "how many more monsters have we? If somebody could slip out of his place, go back of the screen to the galley and then down to the Cosmos House and back—he did come back didn't he? Yes—everybody's here. Well, if one of the gang could do all that—"

"Maybe a monster did it," Garry suggested quietly. "There's that possibility."

"The monster, as you pointed out today, has only men left to imitate. Would he decrease his—supply, shall we say?" Van Wall pointed out. "No, we just have a plain, ordinary louse, a murderer to deal with.

Ordinarily we'd call him an 'inhuman murderer' I suppose, but we have to distinguish now. We have inhuman murderers, and now we have human murderers. Or one at least."

"There's one less human," Norris said softly. "Maybe the monsters have the balance of power now."

"Never mind that." McReady sighed and turned to Barclay. "Bar, will you get your electric gadget? I'm going to make certain—"

Barclay turned down the corridor to get the pronged electrocuter, while McReady and Van Wall went back toward Cosmos House. Barclay followed them in some thirty seconds.

The corridor to Cosmos House twisted, as did nearly all corridors in Big Magnet, and Norris stood at the entrance again. But they heard, rather muffled, McReady's sudden shout. There was a savage flurry of blows, dull *ch-thunk, shluff* sounds. "Bar—Bar—" And a curious, savage mewing scream, silenced before even quick-moving Norris had reached the bend.

Kinner—or what had been Kinner—lay on the floor, cut half in two by the great knife McReady had had. The meteorologist stood against the wall, the knife dripping red in his hand. Van Wall was stirring vaguely on the floor, moaning, his hand half-consciously rubbing at his jaw. Barclay, an unutterably savage gleam in his eyes, was methodically leaning on the pronged weapon in his hand, jabbing—jabbing, jabbing.

Kinner's arms had developed a queer, scaly fur, and the flesh had twisted. The fingers had shortened, the hand rounded, the finger nails become three-inch long things of dull red horn, keened to steel-hard, razor-sharp talons.

McReady raised his head, looked at the knife in his hand and dropped it. "Well, whoever did it can speak up now. He was an inhuman murderer at that—in that he murdered an inhuman. I swear by all that's holy,

Kinner was a lifeless corpse on the floor here when we arrived. But when It found we were going to jab It with the power—It changed."

Norris stared unsteadily. "Oh, Lord, those things can act. Ye gods—sitting in here for hours, mouthing prayers to a God it hated! Shouting hymns in a cracked voice—hymns about a Church it never knew. Driving us mad with its ceaseless howling—

"Well. Speak up, whoever did it. You didn't know it, but you did the camp a favor. And I want to know how in blazes you got out of the room without anyone seeing you. It might help in guarding ourselves."

"His screaming—his singing. Even the sound projector couldn't drown it." Clark shivered. "It was a monster."

"Oh," said Van Wall in sudden comprehension. "You *were* sitting right next to the door, weren't you? And almost behind the projection screen already."

Clark nodded dumbly. "He—it's quiet now. It's a dead—Mac, your test's no damn good. It was dead anyway, monster or man, it was dead."

McReady chuckled softly. "Boys, meet Clark, the only one we know is human! Meet Clark, the one who proves he's human by trying to commit murder—and failing. Will the rest of you please refrain from trying to prove you're human for a while? I think we may have another test."

"A test!" Connant snapped joyfully, then his face sagged in disappointment. "I suppose it's another either-way-you-want-it."

"No," said McReady steadily. "Look sharp and be careful. Come into the Ad Building. Barclay, bring your electrocuter. And somebody—Dutton—stand with Barclay to make sure he does it. Watch every neighbor, for by the hell these monsters came from, I've got something, and they know it. They're going to get dangerous!"

The group tensed abruptly. An air of crushing menace entered into every man's body, sharply they looked at each other. More keenly than ever before—*is that man next to me an inhuman monster?*

"What is it?" Garry asked, as they stood again in the main room. "How long will it take?"

"I don't know, exactly," said McReady, his voice brittle with angry determination. "But I *know* it will work, and no two ways about it. It depends on a basic quality of the *monsters,* not on us. 'Kinner' just convinced me." He stood heavy and solid in bronzed immobility, completely sure of himself again at last.

"This," said Barclay, hefting the wooden-handled weapon tipped with its two sharp-pointed, charged conductors, "is going to be rather necessary, I take it. Is the power plant assured?"

Dutton nodded sharply. "The automatic stoker bin is full. The gas power plant is on stand-by. Van Wall and I set it for the movie operation—and we've checked it over rather carefully several times, you know. Anything those wires touch, dies," he assured them grimly. *"I* know that."

Dr. Copper stirred vaguely in his bunk, rubbed his eyes with fumbling hand. He sat up slowly, blinked his eyes blurred with sleep and drugs, widened with an unutterable horror of drug-ridden nightmares. "Garry," he mumbled, "Garry—listen. Selfish—from hell they came, and hellish shellfish—I mean self— Do I? What do I mean?" He sank back in his bunk, and snored softly.

McReady looked at him thoughtfully. "We'll know presently." He nodded slowly. "But selfish is what you mean, all right. You may have thought of that, half-sleeping, dreaming there. I didn't stop to think what dreams you might be having. But that's all right. Selfish is the word. They must be, you see." He turned to the men in the cabin, tense, silent men staring with wolfish eyes each at his neighbor. "Selfish, and as Dr. Copper said—*every part is a whole*. Every piece is self-sufficient, an animal in itself.

"That, and one other thing, tell the story. There's nothing mysterious about blood; it's just as normal a body tissue as a piece of muscle, or a piece of liver. But it hasn't so much connective tissue, though it has millions, billions of life-cells."

McReady's great bronze beard ruffled in a grim smile. "This is satisfying, in a way. I'm pretty sure we humans still outnumber you—others. Others standing here. And we have what you, your otherworld race, evidently doesn't. Not an imitated, but a bred-in-the-bone instinct, a driving, unquenchable fire that's genuine. We'll fight, fight with a ferocity you may attempt to imitate, but you'll never equal! We're human. We're real. You're imitations, false to the core of your every cell.

"All right. It's a showdown now. *You* know. You, with your mind-reading. You've lifted the idea from my brain. You can't do a thing about it.

"Standing here—

"Let it pass. Blood is tissue. They have to bleed; if they don't bleed when cut, then by Heaven, they're phoney from hell! If they bleed—then that blood, separated from them, is an individual—*a newly formed individual in its own right, just as they—split, all of them from one original—are individuals!*

"Get it, Van? See the answer, Bar?"

Van Wall laughed very softly. "The blood—the blood will not obey. It's a new individual, with all the desire to protect its own life that the original—the main mass from which it was split—has. The *blood* will live—and try to crawl away from a hot needle, say!"

McReady picked up the scalpel from the table. From the cabinet, he took a rack of test-tubes, a tiny alcohol lamp, and a length of platinum wire set in a little glass rod. A smile of grim satisfaction rode his lips. For a moment he glanced up at those around him. Barclay and Dutton moved toward him slowly, the wooden-handled electric instrument alert.

"Dutton," said McReady, "suppose you stand over by the splice there where you've connected that in. Just make sure no—thing pulls it loose."

Dutton moved away. "Now, Van, suppose you be first on this."

White-faced, Van Wall stepped forward. With a delicate precision, McReady cut a vein in the base of his thumb. Van Wall winced slightly, then held steady as a half inch of bright blood collected in the tube. McReady put the tube in the rack, gave Van Wall a bit of alum, and indicated the iodine bottle.

Van Wall stood motionlessly watching. McReady heated the platinum wire in the alcohol lamp flame, then dipped it into the tube. It hissed softly. Five times he repeated the test. "Human, I'd say." McReady sighed, and straightened. "As yet, my theory hasn't been actually proven—but I have hopes. I have hopes.

"Don't, by the way, get too interested in this. We have with us some unwelcome ones, no doubt. Van, will you relieve Barclay at the switch? Thanks. O.K., Barclay, and may I say I hope you stay with us? You're a damned good guy."

Barclay grinned uncertainly; winced under the keen edge of the scalpel. Presently, smiling widely, he retrieved his long-handled weapon.

"Mr. Samuel Dutt—*Bar!*"

The tensity was released in that second. Whatever of hell the monsters may have had within them, the men in that instant matched it. Barclay had no chance to move his weapon, as a score of men poured down on the thing that had seemed Dutton. It mewed, and spat, and tried to grow fangs—and was a hundred broken, torn pieces. Without knives, or any weapon save the brute-given strength of a staff of picked men, the thing was crushed, rent.

Slowly they picked themselves up, their eyes smouldering, very quiet in their motions. A curious wrinkling of their lips betrayed a species of nervousness.

Barclay went over with the electric weapon. Things smouldered and stank. The caustic acid Van Wall dropped on each spilled drop of blood gave off tickling, cough-provoking fumes.

McReady grinned, his deep-set eyes alight and dancing. "Maybe," he said softly, "I underrated man's abilities when I said nothing human could have the ferocity in the eyes of that thing we found. I wish we could have the opportunity to treat in a more befitting manner these things. Something with boiling oil, or melted lead in it, or maybe slow roasting in the power boiler. When I think what a man Dutton was—

"Never mind. My theory is confirmed by—by one who knew? Well, Van Wall and Barclay are proven. I think, then, that I'll try to show you what I already know. That I, too, am human." McReady switched the scalpel in absolute alcohol, burned it off the metal blade, and cut the base of his thumb expertly.

Twenty seconds later he looked up from the desk at the waiting men. There were more grins out there now, friendly grins, yet withal, something else in the eyes.

"Connant," McReady laughed softly, "was right. The huskies watching that thing in the corridor bend had nothing on you. Wonder why we think only the wolf blood has the right to ferocity? Maybe on spontaneous viciousness a wolf takes tops, but after these seven days—abandon all hope, ye wolves who enter here!

"Maybe we can save time. Connant, would you step for—"

Again Barclay was too slow. There were more grins, less tensity still, when Barclay and Van Wall finished their work.

Garry spoke in a low, bitter voice. "Connant was one of the finest men we had here—and five minutes ago I'd have sworn he was a man. Those damnable things are more than imitation." Garry shuddered and sat back in his bunk.

And thirty seconds later, Garry's blood shrank from the hot platinum wire, and struggled to escape the tube, struggled as frantically as a suddenly feral, red-eyed, dissolving imitation of Garry struggled to dodge the snake-tongue weapon Barclay advanced at him, white-faced and sweating. The Thing in the test-tube screamed with a tiny, tinny voice as McReady dropped it into the glowing coal of the galley stove.

XIV

"The last of it?" Dr. Copper looked down from his bunk with bloodshot, saddened eyes. "Fourteen of them—"

McReady nodded shortly. "In some ways—if only we could have permanently prevented their spreading —I'd like to have even the imitations back. Commander Garry—Connant—Dutton—Clark—"

"Where are they taking those things?" Copper nodded to the stretcher Barclay and Norris were carrying out.

"Outside. Outside on the ice, where they've got fifteen smashed crates, half a ton of coal, and presently will add ten gallons of kerosene. We've dumped acid on every spilled drop, every torn fragment. We're going to incinerate those."

"Sounds like a good plan." Copper nodded wearily. "I wonder, you haven't said whether Blair—"

McReady started. "We forgot him? We had so much else! I wonder—do you suppose we can cure him now?"

"If—" began Dr. Copper, and stopped meaningly.

McReady started a second time. "Even a madman. It imitated Kinner and his praying hysteria—" McReady turned toward Van Wall at the long table. "Van, we've got to make an expedition to Blair's shack."

Van looked up sharply, the frown of worry faded for an instant in surprised remembrance. Then he rose, nodded. "Barclay better go along. He applied the lashings, and may figure how to get in without frightening Blair too much."

Three quarters of an hour, through −37° cold, while the aurora curtain bellied overhead. The twilight was nearly twelve hours long, flaming in the north on snow like white, crystalline sand under their skis. A five-mile wind piled it in drift-lines pointing off to the northwest. Three quarters of an hour to reach the snow-buried shack. No smoke came from the little shack, and the men hastened.

"Blair!" Barclay roared into the wind when he was still a hundred yards away. "Blair!"

"Shut up," said McReady softly. "And hurry. He may be trying a lone hike. If we have to go after him—no planes, the tractors disabled—"

"Would a monster have the stamina a man has?"

"A broken leg wouldn't stop it for more than a minute," McReady pointed out.

Barclay gasped suddenly and pointed aloft. Dim in the twilit sky, a winged thing circled in curves of indescribable grace and ease. Great white wings tipped gently, and the bird swept over them in silent curiosity. "Albatross—" Barclay said softly. "First of the season, and wandering way inland for some reason. If a monster's loose—"

Norris bent down on the ice, and tore hurriedly at his heavy, windproof clothing. He straightened, his coat flapping open, a grim blue-metaled weapon in his hand. It roared a challenge to the white silence of Antarctica.

The thing in the air screamed hoarsely. Its great wings worked frantically as a dozen feathers floated down from its tail. Norris fired again. The bird was moving swiftly now, but in an almost straight line of retreat. It screamed again, more feathers dropped, and with beating wings it soared behind a ridge of pressure ice, to vanish.

Norris hurried after the others. "It won't come back," he panted.

Barclay cautioned him to silence, pointing. A curiously, fiercely blue light beat out from the cracks of the shack's door. A very low, soft humming sounded inside, a low, soft humming and a clink and click of tools, the very sounds somehow bearing a message of frantic haste.

McReady's face paled. "Lord help us if that thing has—" He grabbed Barclay's shoulder, and made snipping motions with his fingers, pointing toward the lacing of control-cables that held the door.

Barclay drew the wirecutters from his pocket, and kneeled soundlessly at the door. The snap and twang of cut wires made an unbearable racket in the utter quiet of the Antarctic hush. There was only that strange, sweetly soft hum from within the shack, and the queerly, hectically clipped clicking and rattling of tools to drown their noises.

McReady peered through a crack in the door. His breath sucked in huskily and his great fingers clamped cruelly on Barclay's shoulder. The meteorologist backed down. "It isn't," he explained very softly, "Blair. It's kneeling on something on the bunk—something that keeps lifting. Whatever it's working on is a thing like a knapsack—and it lifts."

"All at once," Barclay said grimly. "No. Norris, hang back, and get that iron of yours out. It may have—weapons."

Together, Barclay's powerful body and McReady's

giant strength struck the door. Inside, the bunk jammed against the door screeched madly and crackled into kindling. The door flung down from broken hinges, the patched lumber of the doorpost dropping inward.

Like a blue rubber ball, a Thing bounced up. One of its four tentacle-like arms looped out like a striking snake. In a seven-tentacled hand a six-inch pencil of winking, shining metal glinted and swung upward to face them. Its line-thin lips twitched back from snake-fangs in a grin of hate, red eyes blazing.

Norris's revolver thundered in the confined space. The hate-washed face twitched in agony, the looping tentacle snatched back. The silvery thing in its hand a smashed ruin of metal, the seven-tentacled hand became a mass of mangled flesh oozing greenish-yellow ichor. The revolver thundered three times more. Dark holes drilled each of the three eyes before Norris hurled the empty weapon against its face.

The Thing screamed in feral hate, a lashing tentacle wiping at blinded eyes. For a moment it crawled on the floor, savage tentacles lashing out, the body twitching. Then it staggered up again, blinded eyes working, boiling hideously, the crushed flesh sloughing away in sodden gobbets.

Barclay lurched to his feet and dove forward with an ice-ax. The flat of the weighty thing crushed against the side of the head. Again the unkillable monster went down. The tentacles lashed out, and suddenly Barclay fell to his feet in the grip of a living, livid rope. The thing dissolved as he held it, a white-hot band that ate into the flesh of his hands like living fire. Frantically he tore the stuff from him, held his hands where they could not be reached. The blind Thing felt and ripped at the tough, heavy, windproof cloth, seeking flesh—flesh it could convert—

The huge blowtorch McReady had brought coughed solemnly. Abruptly it rumbled disapproval throatily.

Then it laughed gurglingly, and thrust out a blue-white, three-foot tongue. The Thing on the floor shrieked, flailed out blindly with tentacles that writhed and withered in the bubbling wrath of the blowtorch. It crawled and turned on the floor, it shrieked and hobbled madly, but always McReady held the blowtorch on the face, the dead eyes burning and bubbling uselessly. Frantically the Thing crawled and howled.

A tentacle sprouted a savage talon—and crisped in the flame. Steadily McReady moved with a planned, grim campaign. Helpless, maddened, the Thing retreated from the grunting torch, the caressing, licking tongue. For a moment it rebelled, squalling in inhuman hatred at the touch of the icy snow. Then it fell back before the charring breath of the torch, the stench of its flesh bathing it. Hopelessly it retreated—on and on across the Antarctic snow. The bitter wind swept over it, twisting the torch-tongue; vainly it flopped, a trail of oily, stinking smoke bubbling away from it—

McReady walked back toward the shack silently. Barclay met him at the door. "No more?" the giant meteorologist asked grimly.

Barclay shook his head. "No more. It didn't split?"

"It had other things to think about," McReady assured him. "When I left it, it was a glowing coal. What was it doing?"

Norris laughed shortly. "Wise boys, we are. Smash magnetos, so planes won't work. Rip the boiler tubing out of the tractors. And leave that Thing alone for a week in this shack. Alone and undisturbed."

McReady looked in at the shack more carefully. The air, despite the ripped door, was hot and humid. On a table at the far end of the room rested a thing of coiled wires and small magnets, glass tubing and radio tubes. At the center a block of rough stone rested. From the center of the block came the light that flooded the place, the fiercely blue light bluer than the glare of an electric arc, and from it came the sweetly soft hum. Off to one side was another mechanism of crystal glass, blown with an incredible neatness and delicacy, metal plates and a queer, shimmery sphere of insubstantiality.

"What is that?" McReady moved nearer.

Norris grunted. "Leave it for investigation. But I can guess pretty well. That's atomic power. That stuff to the left—that's a neat little thing for doing what men have been trying to do with 100-ton cyclotrons and so forth. It separates neutrons from heavy water, which he was getting from the surrounding ice."

"Where did he get all—oh. Of course. A monster couldn't be locked in—or out. He's been through the apparatus caches." McReady stared at the apparatus. "Lord, what minds that race must have—"

"The shimmery sphere—I think it's a sphere of pure force. Neutrons can pass through any matter, and he wanted a supply reservoir of neutrons. Just project neutrons against silica—calcium—beryllium—almost anything, and the atomic energy is released. That thing is the atomic generator."

McReady plucked a thermometer from his coat. "It's 120° in here, despite the open door. Our clothes have kept the heat out to an extent, but I'm sweating now."

Norris nodded. "The light's cold. I found that. But it gives off heat to warm the place through that coil. He had all the power in the world. He could keep it warm and pleasant, as his race thought of warmth and pleasantness. Did you notice the light, the color of it?"

McReady nodded. "Beyond the stars is the answer. From beyond the stars. From a hotter planet that circled a brighter, bluer sun they came."

McReady glanced out the door toward the blasted, smoke-stained trail that flopped and wandered blindly off across the drift. "There won't be any more coming. I guess. Sheer accident it landed here, and that was twenty million years ago. What did it do all that for?" He nodded toward the apparatus.

Barclay laughed softly. "Did you notice what it was working on when we came? Look." He pointed toward the ceiling of the shack.

Like a knapsack made of flattened coffee-tins, with dangling cloth straps and leather belts, the mechanism clung to the ceiling. A tiny, glaring heart of supernal flame burned in it, yet burned through the ceiling's wood without scorching it. Barclay walked over to it, grasped two of the dangling straps in his hands, and pulled it down with an effort. He strapped it about his body. A slight jump carried him in a weirdly slow arc across the room.

"Anti-gravity," said McReady softly.

"Anti-gravity." Norris nodded. "Yes, we had 'em stopped, with no planes, and no birds. The birds hadn't come—but it had coffee-tins and radio parts, and glass and the machine shop at night. And a week—a whole week—all to itself. America in a single jump—with anti-gravity powered by the atomic energy of matter.

"We had 'em stopped. Another half hour—it was just tightening these straps on the device so it could wear it—and we'd have stayed in Antarctica, and shot down any moving thing that came from the rest of the world."

"The albatross—" McReady said softly. "Do you suppose—"

"With this thing almost finished? With that death weapon it held in its hand?

"No, by the grace of God, who evidently does hear very well, even down here, and the margin of half an hour, we keep our world, and the planets of the system too. Anti-gravity, you know, and atomic power. Because They came from another sun, a star beyond the stars. *They* came from a world with a bluer sun."

Theodore Sturgeon (1918–1985)

. . . AND MY FEAR IS GREAT

Theodore Sturgeon was one of the finest and most influential science fiction and fantasy writers of the mid-twentieth century. He once claimed never to have written a story in the horror genre, but many of his stories, and one of his novels, the stunning *Some of Your Blood* (1961), are central to the development of genre horror between the 1930s and the 1980s. His early fantasy stories published in *Unknown* and *Weird Tales* were a seminal influence on Ray Bradbury's early work—Bradbury wrote an introduction to Sturgeon's first story collection, *Without Sorcery* (1949)—and were centrally in the horror mode, if not the genre. Many of his science fiction stories, for instance, the classic "Killdozer" (1944), concerning the possession of a discarded World War II bulldozer by an alien life-form—certainly an ancestor of Matheson's "Duel"—also used the horror mode to striking effect. The Penguin *Encyclopedia* describes him as a writer "whose frequent excursions into dark fantasy sought, with lambent lyrical prose, a unified vision of beauty and horror." His story "It" (1940) is the ancestor of many images of crawling horrors later the province of 1950s comics, particularly "the heap." Sturgeon's literary and emotional range was wide, and he was particularly known as an experimenter in prose style, especially in his use of poetic meter in prose. The long quotation from William Butler Yeats in the present story is a clue to the metric underpinnings of Sturgeon's own prose here.

". . . and my fear is great" is certainly a story of the supernatural and the fantastic and certainly dramatizes material on the edge of repression, but is most comparable to Hardy's "Barbara, of the House of Grebe" in the present collection in its use of horrific moments and investigation of evil.

He hefted one corner of the box high enough for him to get his knuckle on the buzzer, then let it sag. He stood waiting, wheezing. The door opened.

"Oh! You *didn't* carry it up five flights!"

"No, huh?" he grunted, and pushed inside. He set the groceries down on the sink top in the kitchenette and looked at her. She was sixty something and could have walked upright under his armpit with her shoes on.

"That old elevator . . ." she said. "Wait. Here's something."

He wiped sweat out of his eyes and sensed her approach. He put out his hand for the coin but it wasn't a coin. It was a glass. He looked at it, mildly startled. He wished it were beer. He tasted it, then gulped it down. Lemonade.

"Slow-ly, slow-ly," she said, too late. "You'll get heat cramps. What's your name?" Her voice seemed to come from a distance. She seemed, in an odd way, to stand at a distance as well. She was small as a tower is small on the horizon.

"Don," he grunted.

"Well, Donny," she said, "sit down and rest."

He had said, "Don," not "Donny." When he was in rompers he was "Donny." He turned to the door. "I got to go."

"Wait a bit."

He stopped without turning.

"That's a beautiful watch for a boy like you."

"I like it."

"May I see it?"

Breath whistled briefly in his nostrils. She had her fingers lightly on the heel of his hand before he could express any more annoyance than that.

Grudgingly, he raised his arm and let her look.

"Beautiful. Where did you get it?"

He looked at her, surlily. "In a store."

Blandly she asked, "Did you buy it?"

He snatched his hand away. He swiped nervously, twice, with a hooked index finger at his upper lip. His eyes were slits. "What's it to you?"

"Well, did you?"

"Look, lady. I brought your groceries and I got my lemonade. It's all right about the watch, see? Don't worry about the watch. I got to go now."

"You stole it."

"Whaddaya—crazy? I didn't steal no watch."

"You stole that one."

"I'm gettin' outa here." He reached for the knob.

"Not until you tell me about the watch."

He uttered a syllable and turned the knob. The door stayed closed. He twisted, pulled, pushed, twisted again. Then he whirled, his back thudding against the door. His gangly limbs seemed to compact. His elbows came out, his head down. His teeth bared like an animal's. "Hey, what is this?"

She stood, small and chunky and straight, and said in her faraway voice, "Are you going to tell me?" Her eyes were a milky blue, slightly protruding, and unreadable.

"You lemme out, hear?"

She shook her head.

"You better lemme out," he growled. He took two steps toward her. "Open that door."

"You needn't be frightened. I won't hurt you."

"Somebuddy's goin' to get hurt," he said.

"Not—another—step," she said without raising her voice.

He released an ugly bark of nervous laughter and took the other step. His feet came forward and upward and his back slammed down on the floor. For a moment he lay still, then his eyelids moved slowly up and down and up again while for a moment he gave himself over to the purest astonishment. He moved his head forward so that he could see the woman. She had not moved.

He sat up, clenching his jaw against pain, and scuttled backward to the door. He helped himself rise with the doorpost, never taking his eyes off her. "Jesus, I slipped."

"Don't curse in this house," she said—just as mild, just as firm.

"I'll say what I damn please!"

Wham! His shoulders hit the floor again. His eyes were closed, his lips drawn back. He lifted one shoulder and arched his spine. One long agonized wheeze escaped through his teeth like an extrusion.

"You see, you didn't slip," said the woman. "Poor child. Let me help you."

She put her strong, small hand on his left biceps and another between his shoulder blades. She would have led him to a chair but he pulled away.

"I'm awright," he said. He said it again, as if unconvinced, and, "What'd you . . . do?"

"Sit down," she said solicitously. He cowered where he was. "Sit down," she said again, no more sharply, but there was a difference.

He went to the chair. He sidled along the wall, watching her, and he did not go very fast, but he went. He sank down into it. It was a very low chair. His long legs doubled and his knees thrust up sharply. He looked like a squashed grasshopper. He panted.

"About the watch," she prompted him.

He panted twice as fast for three breaths and whimpered, "I don't want no trouble, lady, just lemme go, huh?"

She pointed at his wrist.

"Awright, you want the watch?" Hysterically he stripped it off and dangled it toward her. "Okay? Take it." His eyes were round and frightened and wary. When she made no move he put the watch on her ancient gateleg table. He put his palms on the seat of the chair and his feet walked two paces doorward, though he did not rise, but swiveled around, keeping his face to her, eager, terrified.

"Where did you get it?"

He whimpered, wordless. He cast one quick, hungry look at the door, tensed his muscles, met her gaze again, and slumped. "You gonna turn me in?"

"Of course not!" she said with more force than she had used so far.

"You're goin' to, all the same."

She simply shook her head, and waited.

He turned, finally, picked up the watch, snapped the flexible gold band. "I swiped it—off Eckhart," he whispered.

"Who?"

"Eckhart on Summit Av-noo. He lives behind the store. It was just laying there, on the counter. I put a box of groceries on it and snagged it out from under. You gonna tell?"

"Well, Donny! Don't you feel better, now you've confessed?"

He looked up at her through his eyebrows, hesitated. "Yeah."

"Is that the truth, Donny?"

"Uh-huh." Then, meeting those calm, imponderable eyes, he said, "Well, no. I dunno, lady. I dunno. You got me all mixed up. Can I go now?"

"What about the watch?"

"I don't want it no more."

"I want you to take it back where you got it."

"What?" He recoiled, primarily because in shock he had raised his voice and the sound of it frightened him. "Je—shucks, lady, you want him to put me in the can?"

"My name is Miss Phoebe, not 'lady.' No, Donny, I think you'll do it. Just a moment."

She sat at a shaky escritoire and wrote for a moment, while he watched. Presently, "Here," she said. She handed him the sheet. He looked at her and then at the paper.

Dear Mr. Eckhart,

Inside the clasp of this watch your name and address is stamped. Would you be good enough to see that it gets to its rightful owner?

Yours very truly,
(Miss) Phoebe Watkins

She took it out of his hand, folded it. She put the watch in an envelope, folded that neatly into a square, dropped it in a second envelope with the note, sealed it and handed it to Don.

"You—you're givin' it right back to me!"

"Am I?"

He lowered his eyes, pinched the top edge of the envelope, pulled it through his fingers to crease the top edge sharply. "I know. You're gonna phone him. You're gonna get me picked up."

"You would be no good to me in the reformatory, Donny."

He looked quickly at her eyes, one, then the other. "I'm gonna be some good to you?"

"Tomorrow at four, I want you to come to tea," she said abruptly.

"To what?"

"To tea. That means wash your face and hands, put on a tie and don't be late."

Wash your face and hands. Nobody had dared to order him around like that for years. And yet, instead of resentment, something sharp and choking rose up in his throat. It was not anger. It was something which, when swallowed, made his eyes wet. He frowned and blinked hard.

"You'd better go," she said, before he could accept or refuse, "before the stores close." She didn't even say which stores.

He rose. He pulled his shoulder blades together and his back cracked audibly. He winced, shambled to the door and stood waiting—not touching it, head down, patient—like a farm horse before a closed gate.

"What is it, Donny?"

"Ain'tcha gonna unlock it?"

"It was never locked."

For a long moment he stood frozen, his back to her, his eyes down. Then he put a slow hand to the knob, turned it. The door opened. He went out, almost but not quite pausing at the threshold, almost but not quite turning to look back. He closed the door quietly and was gone.

She put her groceries away.

He did not come at four o'clock.

He came at four minutes before the hour, and he was breathing hard.

"Come in, Donny!" She held the door for him. He looked over his shoulder, down the corridor, at the elevator gates and the big window where feathery trees and the wide sky showed, and then he came into the room. He stood just inside, watching her as she moved to the kitchenette. He looked around the room, looking for policemen, perhaps, for bars on the windows.

There was nothing in the room but its old-not-antique furniture, the bowlegged occasional chair with the new upholstery which surely looked as old as it had before it was redone; there was the gateleg table, now bearing a silver tea-service with a bit of brass showing at the shoulder of the hot-water pot, and a sugar bowl with delicate tongs which did not match the rest of the set. There was the thin rug with its nap quite swept off, and the dustless books; there was the low chair where he had sat before with its tasseled antimacassars on back and arms.

"Make yourself at home," said her quiet voice, barely competing, but competing easily with the susurrus of steam that rose from the kettle.

He moved a little further in and stopped awkwardly. His Adam's apple loomed mightily over the straining button of his collar. His tie was blue and red, and he wore a horrendous sports jacket, much too small, with a violent yellow-and-gray tweed weave. His trousers were the color of baked earth, and had as much crease as his shoes had shine, and their soles had more polish than the uppers. But he'd scrubbed his face almost raw, and his hair was raked back so hard that his forehead gleamed like scoured porcelain.

When she faced him he stood his ground and said abruptly, before she could tell him to sit down, "I din' wanna come."

"Didn't you?"

"Well, I did, but I wasn' gonna."

"Why did you come, then?"

"I wuz scared not to."

She crossed the room with a large platter of little sandwiches. There were cheese and Spam and egg salad and liverwurst. They were not delicacies; they were food. She put it down next to a small store-bought chocolate cake and two bowls of olives, one ripe, one green, neither stuffed.

She said, "You had nothing to be afraid of."

"No, huh?" He wet his lips, took a deep breath. The rehearsed antagonism blurted out. "You done something to me yesterday I don't know what it was. How I know I ain't gonna drop dead if I don't show up or somep'n like that?"

"I did nothing to you, child!"

"Somebuddy sure as h— sure did."

"You did it to yourself."

"What?"

She looked at him. "Angry people don't live very long, Donny, did you know? But sometimes—" Her eyes fell to her hand on the table, and his followed. With one small age-mottled finger she traced around the table's edge, from the far side around one end. "—Sometimes it takes a long time to hurt them. But the hurt can come short and quickly, like *this!*" and she drew her finger straight across from side to side.

Don looked at the table as if something were written on it in a strange language. "Awright, but you made it do that."

"Come and sit down," she said.

But he hadn't finished. "I took the watch back."

"I knew you would."

"Well, okay then. Thass what I come to tell you. That's what you wanted me for, isn't it?"

"I asked you to *tea*. I didn't want to bully you and I didn't want to discuss that silly watch—that matter is closed. It was closed yesterday. Now *do* come and sit down."

"Oh," he said. "I get it. You mean sit down *or else.*"

She fixed her eyes on his and looked at him without speaking and without any expression at all until his gaze dropped. "Donny, go and open the door."

He backed away, felt behind him for the knob. He paused there, tense. When she nodded he opened it.

"You're free to go whenever you like. But before you

do, I want you to understand that there are a lot of people I could have tea with. I haven't asked anyone but you. I haven't asked the grocery boy or the thief or any of the other people you seem to be sometimes. Just *you.*"

He pulled the door to and stood yanking at his bony knuckles. "I don't know about none of that," he said confusedly. He glanced down between his ribs and his elbow at the doorknob. "I just din' want you to think you hadda put on no feedbag to fin' out did I take the watch back."

"I could have telephoned to Mr. Eckhart."

"Well, din't you?"

"Certainly not. There was no need. Was there?"

He came and sat down.

"Sugar?"

"Huh? Yeah—yeah."

"Lemon, or cream?"

"You mean I can have whichever?"

"Of course."

"Then both."

"Both? I think perhaps the cream would curdle."

"In lemon ice cream it don't."

She gave him cream. He drank seven cups of tea, ate all the sandwiches and most of the cake. He ate quickly, not quite glancing over his shoulder to drive away enemies who might snatch the food. He ate with a hunger that was not of hours or days, but the hunger of years. Miss Phoebe patiently passed and refilled and stoked and served until he was done. He loosened his belt, spread out his long legs, wiped his mouth with one sleeve and his brow with the other, closed his eyes and sighed.

"Donny," she said when his jaws had stopped moving, "have you ever been to a bawdy house?"

The boy literally and immediately fell out of his chair. In this atmosphere of doilies and rectitude he could not have been more jolted by a batted ball on his mountainous Adam's apple. He floundered on the carpet, bumped the table, slopped her tea, and crawled back into his seat with his face flaming.

"No," he said, in a strangled voice.

She began then to talk to him quite calmly about social ills of many kinds. She laid out the grub and smut and greed and struggle of his own neighborhood streets as neatly and as competently as she had laid the tea table.

She spoke without any particular emphasis of the bawdy house she had personally closed up, after three reports to the police had no effect. (She had called the desk sergeant, stated her name and intentions, and had asked to be met at the house in twenty minutes. When the police got there she had the girls lined up and two-thirds of their case histories already written.) She spoke of playgrounds and civil defense of pool-rooms, dope pushers, candy stores with beer taps in the soda fountains, and the visiting nurse service.

Don listened, fairly humming with reaction. He had seen all the things she mentioned, good and bad. Some he had not understood, some he had not thought about, some he wouldn't dream of discussing in mixed company. He knew vaguely that things were better than they had been twenty, fifty, a hundred years ago, but he had never before been face to face with one of those who integrate, correlate, extrapolate this progress, who dirty their hands on this person or that in order to work for people.

Sometimes, he bit the insides of his cheeks to keep from laughing at her bluntness and efficiency—he wished he could have seen that desk sergeant's *face!*— or to keep from sniggering self-consciously at the way unmentionables rolled off her precise tongue. Sometimes he was puzzled and lost in the complexities of the organizations with which she was so familiar. And sometimes he was slackjawed with fear for her, thinking of the retribution she must surely be in the way of, breaking up rackets like that. But then his own aching back would remind him that she had ways of taking care of herself, and a childlike awe would rise in him.

There was no direct instruction in anything she said. It was purely description. And yet, he began to feel that in this complex lay duties for him to perform. Exactly what they might be did not emerge. It was simply that he felt, as never before, a functioning part, rather than an excrescence, of his own environment.

He was never to remember all the details of that extraordinary communion, nor the one which immediately followed; for somehow she had stopped speaking and there was a long quiet between them. His mind was so busy with itself that there seemed no break in this milling and chewing of masses of previously unregarded ideas.

For a time she had been talking, for a time she did not talk, and in it all he was completely submerged. At length she said, "Donny, tell me something ugly."

"What do you mean ugly?" The question and its answer had flowed through him almost without contact; had she not insisted, he would have lapsed into his busy silence.

"Donny, something that you know about that you've done. Anything at all. Something you've seen."

It was easy to turn from introspection to deep recalls. "Went to one of those summer camps that there paper runs for kids. I wus about seven, I guess."

"Donny," she said, after what may have been a long time, "go on."

"Wasps," he said, negotiating the divided sibilant with some difficulty. "The ones that make paper nests." Suddenly he turned quite pale. "They stung me, it was on the big porch. The nurse, she came out an' hugged me and went away and came back with a bottle, ammonia it was, and put it on where I was stung." He coughed. "Stuff stunk, but it felt fine. Then a counsellor, a big kid from up the street, he came with a long stick. There was a ol' rag tied on the end, it had kerosene on it. He lit it up with a match, it burned all yellow and smoky. He put it up high by them paper nests. The wasps, they come out howlin', they flew right into the fire. When they stopped comin' he pushed at the nest and down it come.

"He gone on to the next one, and down the line, twelve, fifteen of them. Every time he come to a new one the wasps they flew into the fire. You could see the wings go, not like burning, not like melting, sort of *fzzz!* they gone. They fall. They fall all over the floor, they wiggle around, some run like ants, some with they legs burned off they just go around in one place like a phonograph.

"Kids come from all over, watching bugeyed, runnin' around the porch, stampin' on them wasps with their wings gone, they can't sting nobody. Stamp on 'em and squeal and run away an' run back and stamp some more. I'm back near the door, I'm bawlin'. The nurse is squeezin' me, watchin' the wasps, wipin' the ammonia on me any old place, she's not watchin' what she's doin'.

"An' all the time the fire goes an' goes, the wasps fly at it, never once a dumb damn wasp goes to see who's at the other end of the stick. An' I'm there with the nurse, bawlin'. *Why am I bawlin'?"* It came out a deep, basic demand.

"You must have been stung quite badly," said Miss Phoebe. She was leaning forward, her strange unlovely eyes fixed on him. Her lower lip was wet.

"Nah! Three times, four . . ." He struggled hard to fit rich sensation to a poverty of words. "It was me, see. I guess if I got stung every wasp done it should get killed. Maybe burned even. But them wasps in the nest-es, they din't sting nobody, an' here they are all . . . all *brave,* that's what, brave, comin' and fallin' and comin' and fallin' and gettin' squashed. Why? Fer *me,* thass why! Me, it was me, I hadda go an' holler because I got stung an' make all that happen." He screwed his eyes tight shut and breathed as if he had been running. Abruptly his eyes opened very wide and he pressed himself upward in his chair, stretching his long bony neck as if he sat in rising water up to his chin. "What am I talkin' about, wasps? We wasn't talkin' about no wasps. How'd we get talkin' like this?"

She said, "It's all part of the same thing." She waited for him to quiet down. He seemed to, at last. "I asked you to tell me something ugly, and you did. Did it make you feel better?"

He looked at her strangely. *Wasn't there something—oh, yes. Yesterday, about the watch. She made him tell and then asked if he didn't feel better. Was she getting back to that damn watch? I guess not,* he thought, and for some reason felt very ashamed. "Yeah, I feel some better." He looked into himself, found that what he had just said was true, and started in surprise. "Why should that be?" he asked, and it was the first time in his whole life he had asked such a question.

"There's two of us carrying it now," she explained.

He thought, and then protested, "There was twenty people there."

"Not one of them knew why you were crying."

Understanding flashed in him, bloomed almost to revelation. "God damn," he said softly.

This time she made no comment. Instead she said, "You learned something about bravery that day, didn't you?"

"Not until . . . now."

She shrugged. "That doesn't matter. As long as you understand, it doesn't matter how long it takes. Now, if all that happened just to make you understand something about bravery, it isn't an ugly thing at all, is it?"

He did not answer, but his very silence was a response.

"Perhaps one day you will fly into the fire and burn your wings and die, because it's all you can do to save something dear to you," she said softly. She let him think about that for a moment and then said, "Perhaps you will be a flame yourself, and see the brave ones fly at you and lose their wings and die. Either way, you'd know a little better what you were doing, because of the wasps, wouldn't you?"

He nodded.

"The playgrounds," she said, "the medicines, the air-raid watching, the boys' clubs, everything we were discussing . . . each single one of them kills something to do its work, and sometimes what is killed is very brave. It isn't easy to know good from evil."

"You know," he blurted.

"Ah," she said, "but there's a reason for that. You'd better go now, Donny."

Everything she had said flew to him as she spoke it, rested lightly on him, soaked in while he waited, and in time found a response. This was no exception. When he understood what she had said he jumped up, guiltily covering the thoughtful and receptive self with self-consciousness like a towel snatched up to cover nakedness.

"Yeah I got to, what time is it?" he muttered. "Well," he said, "yeah. I guess I should." He looked about him as if he had forgotten some indefinable thing, turned and gave her a vacillating smile and went to the door. He opened it and turned. Silently and with great difficulty his mouth moved. He pressed the lips together.

"Good-by, Donny."

"Yeah. Take it easy," he said.

As he spoke he saw himself in the full-length mirror fixed to the closet door. His eyes widened. It was himself he saw there—no doubt of that. But there was no sharp-cut, seam-strained sports jacket, no dull and tattered shoes, no slicked-down hair, smooth in front and down-pointing shag at the nape. In the reflection, he was dressed in a dark suit. The coat matched the trousers. The tie was a solid color, maroon, and was held by a clasp so low down that it could barely be seen in the V of the jacket. The shoes gleamed, not like enamel but like the sheen of a new black-iron frying pan.

He gasped and blinked, and in that second the reflection told him only that he was what he was, flashy and clumsy and very much out of place here. He turned one long scared glance on Miss Phoebe and bolted through the door.

Don quit his job at the market. He quit jobs often, and usually needed no reason, but he had one this time. The idea of delivering another package to Miss Phoebe made him sweat, and the sweat was copious and cold. He did not know if it was fear or awe or shame, because he did not investigate the revulsion. He acknowledged it and acted upon it and otherwise locked the broad category labeled "Miss Phoebe" in the most guarded passages of his mind.

He was, unquestionably, haunted. Although he refused to acknowledge its source, he could not escape what can only be described as a sense of function. When he sharked around the pool halls to pick up some change—he carried ordinary seaman's papers, so could get a forty-cent bed at the Seaman's Institute—he was of the nonproductive froth on the brackish edges of a backwater, and he knew it acutely.

When he worked as helper in a dockside shop,

refurbishing outdated streetcars to be shipped to South America, his hand was unavoidably a link in a chain of vision and enterprise starting with an idea and ending with a peasant who, at this very moment, walked, but who would inevitably ride. Between that idea and that shambling peasant were months and miles and dollars, but the process passed through Don's hands every time they lifted a wrench, and he would watch them with mingled wonder and resentment.

He was a piece of nerve tissue becoming aware of the proximity of a ganglion, and dimly conscious of the existence, somewhere, of a brain. His resentment stemmed from a nagging sense of loss. In ignorance he had possessed a kind of freedom—he'd have called it loneliness while he had it—which in retrospect filled him with nostalgia. He carried his inescapable sense of *belonging* like a bundle of thorns, light but most irritating. It was with him in drunkenness and the fights, the movies and the statistical shoutings of the baseball season. He never slept, but was among those who slept. He could not laugh without the realization that he was among the laughers. He no longer moved in a static universe, or rested while the world went by, for his every action had too obvious a reaction. Unbidden, his mind made analogies to remind him of this invert-unwanted duality.

The street, he found, pressed upward to his feet with a force equal to his weight. A new job and he approached one another with an equal magnetism, and he lost it or claimed it not by his effort or lack of it, but by an intricate resultant compounded of all the forces working with him matched against those opposed.

On going to bed he would remove one shoe, and wake from a reverie ten minutes later to find with annoyance that he had sat motionless all that time to contemplate the weight of the shoe versus the upward force of the hand that held it. No birth is painless, and the stirrings of departure from a reactive existence are most troubling, since habit opposes it and there is no equipment to define the motivating ambition.

His own perceptions began to plague him. There had been a time when he was capable of tuning out that which did not concern him. But whatever it was that was growing within him extended its implacable sense of kinship to more areas than those of human endeavor. *Why,* he would ask himself insistently, *is the wet end of a towel darker than the dry end? What do spiders do with their silk when they climb up a single strand? What makes the brows of so many big executives tilt downward from the center?*

He was not a reader, and though he liked to talk, his wharf-rat survival instinct inhibited him from talking "different" talk, which is what his "different" questions would be, for one does not expose oneself to the sharp teeth of raillery.

He found an all-night cafe where the talk was as different as the talkers could make it; where girls who were unsure of their difference walked about with cropped hair and made their voices boom, and seedy little polyglots surreptitiously ate catsup and sugar with their single interminable cup of coffee; where a lost man could exchange his broken compass for a broken oar.

He went there night after night, sitting alone and listening, held by the fact that many of these minds were genuinely questing. Armed with his strange understanding of opposites, he readily recognized those on one side or the other of forces which most naturally oppose one another, but since he could admire neither phrasing nor intensity for their own sakes, he could only wonder at the misery of these children perched so lonesomely on their dialectical seesaws, mourning the fact that they did not get off the ground while refusing to let anyone get on the other end.

Once he listened raptly to a man with a bleeding ear who seemed to understand the things he felt, but instead of believing many things, this man believed in nothing. Don went away, sad, wondering if there were anyone anywhere who cared importantly that when you yawn, an Italian will ask you if you're hungry while a Swede will think you need sleep; or that only six parallel cuts on a half-loaf of bread will always get you seven slices.

So for many months he worked steadily so that his hands could drain off tensions and let him think. When he had worked through every combination and permutation of which he was capable, he could cast back and discover that all his thoughts had stemmed from Miss Phoebe. His awe and fear of her ceased to exist when he decided to go back, not to see her, but to get more material.

A measure of awe returned, however, when he phoned. He heard her lift the receiver, but she did not say "Hello." She said, "Why, Don! How are you?"

He swallowed hard and said, "Good, Miss Phoebe."

"Four o'clock tomorrow," she said, and hung up.

He put the receiver back carefully and stood looking at the telephone. He worked the tip of the finger-stop under his thumbnail and stood for a long time in the booth, carefully cleaning away the thin parenthesis of oily grime which had defied his brush that morning. When it was gone, so was his fright, but it took a long time. *I've forgotten it all right,* he thought, *but oh, my aching back!*

Belatedly he thought, *Why, she called me Don, not Donny.*

He went back to the cafe that night, feeling a fine new sense of insulation. He had so much to look forward to that searches could wait. And like many a searcher before him, he found what he was looking for as soon as he stopped looking. It was a face that could not have drawn him more if it had been luminous, or leaf-green. It was a face with strong and definite lines, with good pads of laughter-muscles under the cheekbones, and eye-sockets shaped to catch and hold laughter early and long. Her hair was long and seemed black, but its highlights were not blue but red. She sat with six other people around a large table, her eyes open and sleeping, her mouth lax and miserable.

He made no attempt to attract her attention, or to join the group. He simply watched her until she left, which was some three or four hours later. He followed her and so did another man. When she turned up the steps of a brownstone a few blocks away the man followed her, and was halfway up the steps when she was at the top, fumbling for a key. When Don stopped, looking up, the man saw him and whirled. He blocked Don's view of the girl. To Don he was not a person at all, but something in the way.

Don made an impatient, get-out-of-the-way gesture with his head, and only then realized that the man was at bay, terrified, caught red-handed. His eyes were round and he drooled. Don stood, looking upward, quite astonished, as the man sidled down, glaring, panting, and suddenly leaped past him and pelted off down the street.

Don looked from the shadowed, dwindling figure to the lighted doorway. The girl had both hands on the side of the outer, open doorway and was staring down at him with bright unbelief in her face. "Oh, dear God," she said.

Don saw that she was frightened, so he said, "It's all right." He stayed where he was.

She glanced down the street where the man had gone and found it empty. Slowly, she came toward Don and stopped on the third step above him. "Are you an angel?" she asked. In her voice was a childlike eagerness and the shadow of the laughter that her face was made for.

Don made a small, abashed sound. "Me? Not me."

She looked down the street and shuddered. "I thought I didn't care anymore *what* happened," she said, as if she were not speaking to him at all. Then she looked at him. "Anyway, thanks. Thanks. I don't know what he might've . . . if you . . ."

Don writhed under her clear, sincere eyes. "I didn't do nothing." He backed off a pace. "What do you mean, am I a angel?"

"Didn't you ever hear about a guardian angel?"

He had, but he couldn't find it in himself to pursue such a line of talk. He had never met anyone who talked like this. "Who was that guy?"

"He's crazy. They had him locked up for a long time, he hurt a little girl once. He gets like that once in a while."

"Well, you want to watch out," he said.

She nodded gravely. "I guess I care after all," she said. "I'll watch out."

"Well, take it easy," he said.

She looked quickly at his face. His words had far more dismissal in them than he had intended, and he suddenly felt miserable. She turned and slowly climbed the steps. He began to move away because he could think of nothing else to do. He looked back over his shoulder and saw her in the doorway, facing him. He thought she was going to call out, and stopped. She went inside without speaking again, and he suddenly felt very foolish. He went home and thought about her all night and all the next day. He wondered what her name was.

When he pressed the buzzer, Miss Phoebe did not come to the door immediately. He stood there wondering if he should buzz again or go away or what. Then the door opened. "Come in, Don."

He stepped inside, and though he thought he had forgotten about the strange mirror, he found himself looking for it even before he saw Miss Phoebe's face. It was still there, and in it he saw himself as before, with the dark suit, the quiet tie, the dull, clean-buffed shoes. He saw it with an odd sense of disappointment, for it had given him such a wondrous shock before, but now reflected only what a normal mirror would, since he was wearing such a suit and tie and shoes, but wait— the figure in the reflection carried something and he did not. A paper parcel . . . a wrapped bunch of flowers; not a florist's elaboration, but tissue-wrapped jonquils from a subway peddler. He blinked, and the reflection was now quite accurate again.

All this took place in something over three seconds. He now became aware of a change in the room, *it's—oh, the light.* It had been almost glary with its jewel-clean windows and scrubbed white woodwork, but now it was filled with mellow orange light. Part of this was sunlight struggling through the inexpensive blinds, which were drawn all the way down. Part was something else he did not see until he stepped fully into the room and into the range of light from the near corner. He gasped and stared, and, furiously, he felt tears rush into his eyes so that the light wavered and ran.

"Happy birthday, Don," said Miss Phoebe severely.

Don said, "Aw." He blinked hard and looked at the little round cake with its eighteen five-and-dime candles. "Aw."

"Blow them out quickly," she said. "They run."

He bent over the cake.

"Every one, mind," she said. "In one breath."

He blew. All the candles went out but one. He had no air left in his lungs, and he looked at the candle in purple panic. In a childlike way, he could not bring himself to break the rules she had set up. His mouth yawped open and closed like that of a beached fish. He puffed his cheeks out by pushing his tongue up and forward, leaned very close to the candle, and released the air in his mouth with a tiny explosive pop. The candle went out.

"Splendid. Open the blinds for me like a good boy."

He did as he was asked without resentment. As she plucked the little sugar candleholders out of the cake, he said, "How'd you know it was my birthday?"

"Here's the knife. You must cut it first, you know."

He came forward. "It's real pretty. I never had no birthday cake before."

"I'm glad you like it. Hurry now. The tea's just right."

He busied himself, serving and handing and receiving and setting down, moving chairs, taking sugar. He was too happy to speak.

"Now then," she said when they were settled. "Tell me what you've been up to."

He assumed she knew, but if she wanted him to say, why, he would. "I'm a typewriter mechanic now," he said. "I like it fine. I work nights in big offices and nobody bothers me none. How've you been?"

She did not answer him directly, but her serene expression said that nothing bad could ever happen to her. "And is that all? Just work and sleep?"

"I been thinkin'," he said. He looked at her curiously. "I thought a lot about what you said." She did not respond. "I mean about everything working on everything else, an' the wasps and all." Again she was silent, but now there was response in it.

He said, "I was all mixed up for a long time. Part of the time I was mad. I mean, like you're working for a boss who won't let up on you, thinks he owns you just because you work there. Used to be I thought about whatever I wanted to, I could stop thinkin' like turnin' a light off."

"Very apt," she remarked. "It was exactly that."

He waited while this was absorbed. "After I was here I couldn't turn off the light; the switch was busted. The more I worked on things, the more mixed up they got." In a moment he added, "For a while."

"What things?" she asked.

"Hard to say," he answered honestly. "I never had nobody to tell me much, but I had some things pretty straight. It's wrong to swipe stuff. It's right to do what they tell you. It's right to go to church."

"It's right to worship," she interjected. "If you can worship in a church, that's the best place to do it. If you can worship better in another place, then that's where you should go instead."

"*That's* what I mean!" he barked, pointing a bony finger like a revolver. "You say something like that, so sure and easy, an' all the—the fences go down. Everything's all in the right box, see, an' you come along and shake everything together. You don't back off from nothing. You say what you want about anything, an' you let me say anything I want to you. Everything I ever thought was right or wrong could be wrong or right. Like those wasps dyin' because of me, and you say they maybe died *for* me, so's I could learn something. Like you sayin' I could be a wasp or a fire, an' still know what was what . . . I'll get mixed up again if I go on talkin' about it."

"I think not," she said, and he felt very pleased. She said, "It's in the nature of things to be 'shaken all together,' as you put it. A bird brings death to a worm and a wildcat brings death to the bird. Can we say that what struck the worm and the bird was evil, when the wildcat's kittens took so much good from it? Or if the murder of the worm is good, can we call the wildcat evil?"

"There isn't no . . . no *altogether* good or bad, huh."

"Now, that is a very wrong thing to say," she said with soft-voiced asperity.

"You gone an' done it again!" he exclaimed.

She did not smile with him. "There is an absolute good and an absolute evil. They cannot be confused with right and wrong, or building and destroying as we know them, because, like the cat and the worm, those things depend on whose side you take. Don, I'm going to show you something very strange and wonderful."

She went to her little desk and got pencil and paper. She drew a circle, and within it she sketched in an S-shaped line. One side of this line she filled in with quick short strokes of her pencil:

"This," she said, as Don pored over it, "is the most ancient symbol known to man. It's called 'yin and yang.' 'Yin' is the Chinese term for darkness and earth. 'Yang' means light and sky. Together they form the complete circle—the universe, the cosmos—everything. Nothing under heaven can be altogether one of these things or the other. The symbol means light and dark. It means birth and death. It is everything which holds together and draws down, with everything that pours out and disperses. It is male and female, hope and history, love and hate. It's—everything there is or could be. It's why you can't say the murder of a worm by a bird is good or evil."

"This here yin an' yang's in everything we do, huh."

"Yes."

"It's God an' the Devil then."

"Good and *evil."* She placed her hand over the entire symbol. "God is all of it."

"Well, all right!" he exclaimed. "So it's like I said. There ain't a 'altogether good' and a 'altogether bad.' Miss Phoebe, how you know you're right when you bust up some pusher's business or close a joint?"

"There's a very good way of knowing, Don. I'm very glad you asked me that question." She all but beamed at him—she, who hardly ever even smiled. "Now listen carefully. I am going to tell you something which it took me many years to find out. I am going to tell you because I do not see why the young shouldn't use it.

"Good and evil are active forces—almost like living things. I said that nothing under heaven can be completely one of these things or the other, and it's true. But, Don—good and evil come to us from *somewhere.* They reach this cosmos as living forces, constantly replenished—from *somewhere.* It follows that there is a Source of good and a Source of evil . . . or call them light and dark, or birth and death if you like."

She put her finger on the symbol. "Human beings, at least with their conscious wills, try to live here, in the yang part. Many find themselves on the dark side, some cross and recross the borderline. Some set a course for themselves and drive it straight and true, and never understand that the border itself turns and twists and will have them in one side and then the other.

"In any case, these forces are in balance, and they must remain so. But as they are living, vital forces, there must be those who willingly and purposefully work with them."

With his thumbnail he flicked the paper. "From this, everything's so even-steven you'd never know who you're working for."

"Not true, Don. There are ways of knowing."

He opened his lips and closed them, turned away, shaking his head.

"You may ask me, Don," she said.

"Well, okay. You're one of 'em. Right?"

"Perhaps so."

"Perhaps *nothing*. You knocked me flat on my noggin twice in a row an' never touched me. You're—you're somethin' special, that's for sure. You even knew about my birthday. You know who's callin' when the phone rings."

"There are advantages."

"All right then, here's what I'm gettin' to, and I don't want you to get mad at me. What I want to know is, why ain't you rich?"

"What do you mean by *rich?*"

He kicked the table leg gently. "Junk," he said. He waved at the windows. "Everybody's got venetian blinds now. Look there, cracks in the ceiling 'n you'll get a rent rise if you complain, long as it ain't leakin'. You know, if I could do the things you do, I'd have me a big house an' a car. I'd have flunkies to wash dishes an' all like that."

"I wouldn't be rich if I had all those things, Don."

He looked at her guardedly. He knew she was capable of a preachment, though he had been lucky so far. "Miss Phoebe," he said respectfully, "You ain't goin' to tell me the—uh—inner riches is better'n a fishtail Cadillac."

"I'll ask *you*," she said patiently. "Would you want a big house and servants and all those things?"

"Well, *sure!*"

"Why?"

"Why? Well, because, because—well, that's the way to live, that's all."

"Why is it the way to live?"

"Well, anyone can see why."

"Don, answer the question! Why is that the way to live?"

"Well," he said. He made a circular gesture and put his hand down limply. He wet his lips. "Well, because you'd have what you wanted." He looked at her hopefully and realized he'd have to try again. "You could make anyone do what you wanted."

"Ah," she said. "Why would you want to do that?"

"So you wouldn't have to do your own work."

"Aside from personal comfort—why would you want to be able to tell other people what to do?"

"You tell me," he said with some warmth.

"The answers are in you if you'll only look, Don. Tell me: Why?"

He considered. "I guess it'd make me feel good."

"Feel good?"

"The boss. The Man. You know. I say jump, they jump."

"Power?"

"Yeah, that's it, power."

"Then you want riches so you'll have a sense of power."

"You're in."

"And you wonder why I don't want riches. Don, I've *got* power. Moreover, it was given me and it's mine. I needn't buy it for the rest of my life."

"Well, now . . ." he breathed.

"You can't imagine power in any other terms than cars and swimming pools, can you?"

"Yes I can," he said instantly. Then he grinned and added, "But not yet."

"I think that's more true than you know," she said, giving him her sparse smile. "You'll come to understand it."

They sat in companionable silence. He picked up a crumb of cake icing and looked at it. "Real good cake," he murmured, and ate it. Almost without change of inflection, he said, "I got a real ugly one to tell you."

She waited, in the responsive silence he was coming to know so well.

"Met a girl last night."

He was not looking at her and so did not see her eyes click open, round and moist. He hooked his heel in the chair rung and put his fist on the raised knee, thumb up. He lowered his head until the thumb fitted into the hollow at the bridge of his nose. Resting his head precariously there, rolling it slightly from time to time as if he perversely enjoyed the pressure and the ache, he began to speak. And if Miss Phoebe found surprising the leaps from power to birthday cake to a girl to what happened in the sewer, she said nothing.

"Big sewer outlet down under the docks at Twenty-seventh," he said. "Wuz about nine or ten, playing there. Kid called Renzo. We were inside the pipe; it was about five feet high, and knee-deep in storm water. Saw somethin' bobbin' in the water, got close enough to look. It was the hind feet off a dead rat, a great big one, and *real* dead. Renzo, he was over by the outlet tryin' to see if he could get up on a towboat out there, and I thought it might be fine if I could throw the rat on his back on account he didn't have no shirt on. I took hold of the rat's feet and pulled, but that rat, he had his head stuck in a side-pipe somehow, an' I guess he swole some too. I guess I said something and Renzo he come over, so there was nothin' for it then but haul the rat out anyway. I got a good hold and yanked, an' something popped an' up he came. I pulled 'im right out of his skin. There he was wet an' red an' bare an' smellin' a good deal. Renzo, he lets out a big holler, laughin', I can still hear it in that echoey pipe. I'm standin' there like a goofball, starin' at this rat. Renzo says, 'Hit'm quick, Doc, or he'll never start breathin'!" I just barely got the idea when the legs come off the rat an' it fell in the water with me still holdin' the feet."

It was very quiet for a while. Don rocked his head, digging his thumb into the bridge of his nose. "Renzo and me we had a big fight after. He tol' everybody I had a baby in the sewer. He tol' 'em I's a firstclass stork. They all started to call me Stork, I hadda fight five of 'em in two days before they cut it out.

"Kid stuff," he said suddenly, too loudly, and sat upright, wide-eyed, startled at the sound. "I know it was kid stuff, I can forget it. But it won't . . . it won't forget."

Miss Phoebe stirred, but said nothing.

Don said, "Girls. I never had nothing much to do with girls, kidded 'em some if there was somebody with me started it, and like that. Never by myself. I tell you how it is, it's—" He was quiet for a long moment. His lips moved as if he were speaking silently, words after words until he found the words he wanted. He went on in precisely the same tone, like an interrupted tape recorder.

"—Like this, I get so I like a girl a whole lot, I want to get close to her, I think about her like any fellow does. So before I can think much about it, let alone *do* anything, zing! I'm standin' in that stinkin' sewer, Renzo's yellin' 'Hit'm quick, Doc,' an' all the rest of it." He blew sharply from his nostrils. "The better a girl smells," he said hoarsely, "the worse it is. So I think about girls, I think about rats, I think about babies, it's Renzo and me and that echo. Laughin'," he mumbled, "him laughin'.

"I met a girl last night," he said clearly, "I don't want ever to think about like that. I walked away. I don't know what her name is. I want to see her some more. I'm afraid. So that's why."

After a while he said, "That's why I told you."

And later, "You were a big help before, the wasps."

As he spoke he realized that there was no point in hurrying her; she had heard him the first time and would wait until she was ready. He picked up another piece of icing, crushed it, tossed the pieces back on the plate.

"You never asked me," said Miss Phoebe, "about the power I have, and how it came to me."

"Din't think you'd say. I wouldn't, if I had it. This girl was—"

"Study," said Miss Phoebe. "More of it than you realize. Training and discipline and, I suppose, a certain natural talent which," she said, fixing him sternly with her eyes as he was about to interrupt, "I am sure you also have. To a rather amazing degree. I have come a long way, a long hard way, and it isn't so many years ago that I first began to feel this power . . . I like to think of you with it, young and strong and . . . and good, growing greater, year by year. Don, would you like the power? Would you work hard and patiently for it?"

He was very quiet. Suddenly he looked up at her. "What?"

She said—and for once the control showed—"I thought you might want to answer a question like that."

He scratched his head and grinned. "Gee, I'm sorry, Miss Phoebe, but for that one second I was thinkin' about . . . something else, I guess. Now," he said brightly, "what was it you wanted to know?"

"What was this matter you found so captivating?" she asked heavily. "I must say I'm not used to talking to myself, Don."

"Ah, don't jump salty, Miss Phoebe," he said contritely. "I'll pay attention, honest. It's just that I—you din't say *one* word about what I told you. I guess I was tryin' to figure it out by myself if you wasn't goin' to help."

"Perhaps you didn't wait long enough."

"Oh." He looked at her and his eyes widened. *"Oh!* I never thought of that. Hey, go ahead, will you?" He drew his knees together and clasped them, turned to face her fully.

She nodded with a slightly injured satisfaction. "I asked you, Don, if you'd like the kind of power I have, for yourself."

"Me?" he demanded, incredulously.

"You. And I also asked you if you would work hard and patiently to get it. Would you?"

"Would I! Look, you don't really think, I mean, I'm just a—"

"We'll see," she said.

She glanced out the window. Dusk was not far away. The curtains hung limp and straight in the still air. She rose and went to the windows, drew the blinds down. The severe velour drapes were on cranes. She swung them over the windows. They were not cut full enough to cover completely, each window admitted a four-inch slit of light. But that side of the building was in shadow, and she turned back to find Don blinking in deep obscurity. She went back to her chair.

"Come closer," she said. "No, not that way—facing me. That's it. Your back to the window. Now, I'm going to cover my face. That's because otherwise the light would be on it; I don't want you to look at me or at anything but what you find inside yourself." She took a dark silk scarf from the small drawer in the end of the gateleg table. "Put your hands out. Palms down. So." She dropped the scarf over her face and hair, and felt for his hands. She slipped hers under his, palms upward, and leaned forward until she could grasp his wrists. "Hold mine that way too. Good. Be absolutely quiet."

He was.

She said, "There's something the matter. You're all tightened up. And you're not close enough. Don't move! I mean, in your mind . . . ah, I see. You'll have your questions answered. Just trust me." A moment later she said, "That's *much* better. There's something on your mind, though, a little something. Say it, whatever it is."

"I was thinkin', this is a trapeze grip, like in the circus."

"So it is! Well, it's a good contact. Now, don't think of anything at all. If you want to speak, well, do; but nothing will be accomplished until you no longer feel like talking.

"There is a school of discipline called Yoga," she said quietly. "For years I have studied and practiced it. It's a lifetime's work in itself, and still it's only the first part of what I've done. It has to do with the harmony of the body and the mind, and the complete control of both. My breathing will sound strange to you. Don't be frightened, it's perfectly all right."

His hands lay heavily in hers. He opened his eyes and looked at her but there was nothing to see, just the black mass of her silk-shrouded head and shoulders in the dim light. Her breathing deepened. As he became more and more aware of other silences, her breathing became more and more central in his attention. He began to wonder where she was putting it all; an inhalation couldn't possibly continue for so long, like the distant hiss of escaping steam. And when it dwindled, the silence was almost too complete, for too long; no one could hold such a deep breath for as long as that! And when at last the breath began to come out again, it seemed as if the slow hiss went on longer even than the inhalation. If he had wondered where she was putting it, he now wondered where she was getting it.

And at last he realized that the breathing was not deep at all, but shallow in the extreme; it was just that the silence was deeper and her control greater than he had imagined. His hands—

"It tingles. Like electric," he said aloud.

His voice did not disturb her in the least. She made no answer in any area. The silence deepened, the darkness deepened, the tingling continued and grew . . . not grew; it spread. When he first felt it, it had lived in a spot on each wrist, where it contacted hers. Now it uncoiled, sending a thin line of sensation up into his forearms and down into his hands. He followed its growth, fascinated. Around the center of each palm the tingling drew a circle, and sent a fine twig of feeling growing into his fingers, and at the same time he could feel it negotiating the turn of his elbows.

He thought it had stopped growing, and then realized that it had simply checked its twig-like creeping, and was broadening; the line in his arms and fingers was becoming a band, a bar of feeling. It crossed his mind that if this bothered him at all he could pull his hands away and break the contact, and that if he did that Miss Phoebe would not resent it in any way. And, since he knew he was free to do it, knew it without question, he was not tempted. He sat quietly, wonder-struck, tasting the experience.

With a small silent explosion there were the tingling, hair-thin lines of sensation falling like distant fireworks through his chest and abdomen, infusing his loins and thighs and the calves of his legs. At the same time more of them crept upward through his neck and head, flared into and around his ears, settled and boiled and shimmered through his lobes and cheeks, curled and clasped the roots of his eyelids. And again there was the feeling of the lines broadening, fusing one with the other as they swelled. Distantly he recognized their ultimate; they would grow inward and outward until they were a complete thing, bounded exactly by everything he was, every hair, every contour, every thought and function.

He opened his eyes, and the growth was not affected.

The dark mass of Miss Phoebe's head was where it had been, friendly and near and reassuring. He half-smiled, and the sparkling delicate little lines of feeling on his lips yielded to the smile, played in it like infinitesimal dolphins, gave happy news of it to all the other threads, and they all sang to his half-smile and gave him joy. He closed his eyes comfortably, and cheerful filaments reached for one another between his upper and lower lashes.

An uncountable time passed. Time now was like no time he knew of, drilling as it always had through event after event, predictable and dictatorial to rust, springtime, and the scissoring hands of clocks. This was a new thing, not a suspension, for it was too alive for that. It was different, that's all, different the way this feeling was, and now the lines and bands and bars were fused and grown, and he was filled . . . he was, himself, of a piece with what had once been the tingling of a spot on his wrist.

It was a feeling, still a feeling, but it was a substance too, Don-sized, Don-shaped. A color . . . no, it wasn't a color, but if it had been a color it was beginning to glow and change. It was glowing as steel glows in the soaking-pits, a color impossible to call black because it is red inside; and now you can see the red; and now the red has orange in it, and now in the orange is yellow, and when white shows in the yellow you may no longer look, but still the radiation beats through you, intensifying . . . not a color, no; this thing had no color and no light, but if it had been a color, this would have been its spectral growth.

And this was the structure, this the unnamable *something* which now found itself alive and joyous. It was from such a peak that the living thing rose as if from sleep, became conscious of its own balance and strength, and leaped heavenward with a single cry like all the satisfying, terminal resolving chords of all music, all uttered in a wingbeat of time.

Then it was over not because it was finished, like music or a meal, but because it was perfect—like foam or a flower caught in the infrangible amber of memory. Don left the experience without surfeit, without tension, without exhaustion. He sat peacefully with his hands in Miss Phoebe's, not dazzled, not numb, replenished in some luxurious volume within him which kept what it gained for all of life, and which had an infinite capacity. But for the cloth over her face and the odd fact that their hands were dripping with perspiration, they might just that second have begun. It may even have been that second.

Miss Phoebe disengaged her hands and plucked away the cloth. She was smiling—really smiling, and Don understood why she so seldom smiled, if this were the expression she used for such experiences.

He answered the smile, and said nothing, because about perfect things nothing can be said. He went and dried his hands and then pulled back the drapes and raised the blinds while she straightened the chairs.

"The ancients," said Miss Phoebe, "recognized four elements: earth, air, fire and water. This power can do anything those four elements can do." She put down the clean cups, and went to get her crumb brush. "To start with," she added.

He placed the remark where it would soak in, and picked up a piece of icing from the cake plate. This time he ate it. "Why is a wet towel darker than a dry one?"

"I—why, I hadn't thought," she said. "It is, now that you mention it. I'm sure I don't know why, though."

"Well, maybe you know this," he said. "Why I been worrying about it so much?"

"Worrying?"

"You know what I mean. That and why most motors

that use heat for power got to have a cooling system,
and why do paper towels tear where they ain't
perf'rated, and a zillion things like that. I never used
to."

"Perhaps it's . . . yes, I know. Of *course!*" she said
happily. "You're getting a—call it a kinship with
things. A sense of interrelationship."

"Is that good?"

"I think it is. It means I was right in feeling that you
have a natural talent for what I'm going to teach you."

"It takes up a lot of my time," he grumbled.

"It's good to be alive all the time," she said. She
poured. "Don, do you know what a revelation is?"

"I heard of it."

"It's a sudden glimpse of the real truth. You had one
about the wasps."

"I had it awful late."

"That doesn't matter. You had it, that's the important thing. You had one with the rat, too."

"I did?"

"With the wasps you had a revelation of sacrifice and
courage. With the rat—well, you know yourself what
effect it has had on you."

"I'm the only one I know has no girl," he said.

"That is exactly it."

"Don't tell me it's s'posed to be that way!"

"For you, I—I'd say so."

"Miss Phoebe, I don't think I know what you're
talkin' about."

She looked at her teacup. "I've never been married."

"Me too," he said somberly. "Wait, is that what
you—"

"Why do people get married?"

"Kids."

"Oh, that isn't all."

He said, with his mouth full, "They wanna be

together, I guess. Team up, like. One pays the bills, the other runs the joint."

"That's about it. Sharing. They want to share. You know the things they share."

"I heard," he said shortly.

She leaned forward. "Do you think they can share anything like what we've had this afternoon?"

"That I never heard," he said pensively.

"I don't wonder. Don, your revelation with the rat is as basic a picture of what is called 'original sin' as anything I have ever heard."

"Original sin," he said thoughtfully. "That's about Adam an'—no, wait. I remember. Everybody's supposed to be sinful to start with because it takes a sin to get'm started."

"Once in a while," she said, "it seems as if you know so few words because you don't need them. That was beautifully put. Don, I think that awful thing that happened to you in the sewer was a blessing. I think it's a good thing, not a bad one. It might be bad for someone else, but not for you. It's kept you as you are, so far. I don't think you should try to forget it. It's a warning and a defense. It's a weapon against the 'yin' forces. You are a very special person, Don. You were made for better things than—than others."

"About the wasps," he said. "As soon as you started to talk I begun to feel better. About this, I don't feel better." He looked up to the point where the wall met the ceiling and seemed to be listening to his own last phrase. He nodded definitely. "I don't feel better. I feel worse."

She touched his arm. It was the only time she had made such a gesture. "You're strong and growing and you're just eighteen." Her voice was very kind. "It would be a strange thing indeed if a young man your age didn't have his problems and struggles and tempta—I mean, battles. I'm sorry I can't resolve it for you, Don. I wish I could. But I know what's right. Don't I, Don, don't I?"

"Every time," he said glumly. "But I . . ." His gaze became abstracted.

She watched him anxiously. "Don't think about her," she whispered. "Don't. You don't have to. Don, do you know that what we did this afternoon was only the very beginning, like the first day of kindergarten?"

His eyes came back to her, bright.

"Yeah, huh. Hey, Miss Phoebe, how about that."

"When would you like to do some more?"

"Now?"

"Bless you, no! We both have things to do. And besides, you have to think. You know it takes time to think."

"Yeah, okay. When?"

"A week."

"Don't worry about me, I'll be here. Hey, I'm gonna be late for work."

He went to the door. "Take it easy," he said.

He went out and closed the door but before the latch clicked he pushed it open again. He crossed the room to her.

He said, "Hey, thanks for the birthday cake. It was . . ." His mouth moved as he searched. "It was a good birthday cake." He took her hand and shook it heartily. Then he was gone.

Miss Phoebe was just as pink as the birthday cake. To the closed door she murmured, "Take it easy."

Don was in a subway station two nights later, waiting for an express. The dirty concrete shaft is atypical and mysterious at half-past four in the morning. The platforms are unlittered and deserted, and there is a complete absence of the shattering roar and babble and bustle for which these urban entrails are built. An approaching train can be heard starting and running and stopping sometimes ten or twelve minutes before it pulls in, and a single set of footfalls on the mezzanine above will outlast it. The few passengers waiting seem always to huddle together near one of the wooden benches, and there seems to be a kind of inverse square law in operation, for the closer they approach one another the greater the casual unnoticing manners they affect, though they will all turn to watch someone walking toward them from two hundred feet away. And when angry voices bark out, the effect is more shocking than it would be in a cathedral.

A tattered man slept uneasily on the bench. Two women buzz-buzzed ceaselessly at the other end. A black-browed man in gray tweed strode the platform, glowering, looking as if he were expected to decide on the recall of the Ambassador to the Court of St. James by morning.

Don happened to be looking at the tattered man, and the way the old brown hat was pulled down over the face (it could have been a headless corpse, and no one would have been the wiser) when the body shuddered and stirred. A strip of stubbled skin emerged between the hat and the collar, and developed a mouth into which was stuffed a soggy collection of leaf-mold which may have been a cigar butt yesterday. The man's hand came up and fumbled around for the thing. The jaws worked, the lips smacked distastefully. The hand pushed the hat brim up only enough to expose a red eye, which glared at the butt. The hat fell again, and the hand pitched the butt away.

At this point the black-browed man hove to, straddle-legged in front of the bench. He opened his coat and hooked his thumbs in the armholes of his waistcoat. He tilted his head back, half-closed his eyes, and sighted through the cleft on his chin at the huddled creature on the bench. "You!" he grated, and everyone swung around to stare at him. He thumped the sleeping man's ankle with the side of his foot. "You!" Everyone looked at the bench.

The tattered man said "Whuh-wuh-wuh-wuh," and smacked his lips. Suddenly he was bolt upright, staring.

"You!" barked the black-browed man. He pointed to the butt. "Pick that up!"

The tattered man looked at him and down at the butt. His hand strayed to his mouth, felt blindly on and around it. He looked down again at the butt and dull recognition began to filter into his face. "Oh, sure, boss, sure," he whined. He cringed low, beginning to stoop down off the bench but afraid to stop talking, afraid to turn his gaze away from the danger point. "I don't make no trouble for anybody, mister, not me, honest I don't," he wheedled. "A feller gets down on his luck, you know how it is, but I never make trouble, mister . . ."

"Pick it up!"

"Oh sure, sure, right away, boss."

That was when Don, to his amazement, felt himself approaching the black-browed man. He tapped him on the shoulder.

"Mister," he said. He prayed that his tight voice would not break. "Mister, make *me* pick it up, huh?"

"What?"

Don waved at the tattered man. "A two-year-old kid could push him around. So what are you proving, you're a big man or something? Make *me* pick up the butt, you're such a big man."

"Get away from me," said the black-browed man. He took two quick paces backward. "I know what you are, you're one of those subway hoodlums."

Don caught a movement from the corner of his eye. The tattered man had one knee on the platform, and was leaning forward to pick up the butt. "Get away from that," he snapped, and kicked the butt onto the local tracks.

"Sure, boss, sure, I don't want no . . ."

"Get away from me, both of you," said the black-browed man. He was preparing for flight. Don suddenly realized that he was afraid—afraid that he and the tattered man might join forces, or perhaps even that they had set the whole thing up in advance. He laughed. The black-browed man backed into a pillar. And just then a train roared in, settling the matter.

Something touched Don between the shoulder blades and he leaped as if it had been an icepick. But it was one of the women. "I just had to tell you, that was very brave. You're a fine young man," she said. She sniffed in the direction of the distant tweed-clad figure and marched to the train. It was a local. Don watched it go, and smiled. He felt good.

"Mister, you like to save my life, you did. I don't want no trouble, you unnerstan', I never do. Feller gets down on his luck once in a wh—"

"Shaddup!" said Don. He turned away and froze. Then he went back to the man and snatched off the old hat. The man cringed.

"I know who you are. You just got back from the can. You got sent up for attackin' a girl."

"I ain't done a *thing,*" whispered the man. "Gimme back my hat, please, mister?"

Don looked down at him. He should walk away, he ought to leave this hulk to rot, but his questing mind was against him. He threw the hat on the man's lap and wiped his fingers on the side of his jacket. "I saw you stayin' out of trouble three nights ago on Mulberry Street. Followin' a girl into a house there."

"It was you chased me," said the man. "Oh God." He tucked himself up on the bench in a uterine position and began to weep.

"Cut that out," Don snarled. "I ain't hit you. If I

wanted I coulda thrown you in front of that train, right?"

"Yeah, instead you saved me f'm that killer," said the man brokenly. "Y'r a prince, mister. Y'r a real prince, that's what you are."

"You goin' to stay away from that girl?"

"Your girl? Look, I'll never even walk past her house no more. I'll kill anybody looks at her."

"Never mind that. Just *you* stay away from her."

The express roared in. Don rose and so did the man. Don shoved him back to the bench. "Take the next one."

"Yeah, sure, anything you say. Just you say the word."

Don thought, *I'll ask him what it is that makes it worth the risk, chance getting sent up for life just for a thing like that.* Then, *No,* he thought. *I think I know why.*

He got on the train.

He sat down and stared dully ahead. *A man will give up anything, his freedom, his life even, for a sense of power. How much am I giving up? How should I know?*

He looked at the advertisements. "Kulkies are better." "The better skin cream." He wondered if anyone ever wanted to know what these things were better *than.* "For that richer, creamier, safer lather." "Try Miss Phoebe for that better, more powerful power."

He wondered, and wondered . . .

Summer dusk, all the offices closed, the traffic gone, no one and nothing in a hurry for a little while. Don put his back against a board fence where he could see the entrance, and took out a toothpick. She might be going out, she might be coming home, she might be home and not go out, she might be out and not come home. He'd stick around.

He never even got the toothpick wet.

She stood at the top of the steps, looking across at

him. He simply looked back. There were many things he might have done. Rushed across. Waved. Done a time-step. Looked away. Run. Fallen down.

But he did nothing, and the single fact that filled his perceptions at that moment was that as long as she stood there with russet gleaming in her black hair, with her sad, sad cups-for-laughter eyes turned to him, with the thin summer cloak whipping up and falling to her clean straight body, why there was nothing he could do.

She came straight across to him. He broke the toothpick and dropped it, and waited. She crossed the sidewalk and stopped in front of him, looking at his eyes, his mouth, his eyes. "You don't even remember me."

"I remember you all right."

She leaned closer. The whites of her eyes showed under her pupils when she did that, like the high crescent moon in the tropics that floats startlingly on its back. These two crescents were twice as startling. "I don't think you do."

"Over there." With his chin he indicated her steps. "The other night."

It was then, at last, that she smiled, and the eyes held what they were made for. "I saw him again."

"He try anything?"

She laughed. "He *ran!* He was afraid of me. I don't think anybody was ever afraid of me."

"I am."

"Oh, that's the silliest—" She stopped, and again leaned toward him. "You mean it, don't you?"

He nodded.

"Don't ever be afraid of me," she said gravely, "not *ever*. What did you do to that man?"

"Nothin'. Talked to him."

"You didn't hurt him?"

He nodded.

"I'm glad," she said. "He's sick and he's ugly and he's bad, too, I guess, but I think he's been hurt enough. What's your name?"

"Don."

She counted on her fingers. "Don is a Spanish grandee. Don is putting on clothes. Don is the sun coming up in the morning. Don is . . . is the opposite of up. You're a whole lot of things, Don." Her eyes widened. "You laughed!"

"Was that wrong?"

"Oh, *no!* But I didn't know you ever laughed.

"I watched you for three hours the other night and *you* didn't laugh. You didn't even talk."

"I would've talked if I'd known you were there. Where were you?"

"That all-night joint. I followed you."

He looked at his shoeshine. With his other foot, he carefully stepped on it.

"Why did you follow me? Were you going to talk to me?"

"No!" he said. "No, by God, I wasn't. I wouldn'ta."

"Then why did you follow me?"

"I liked looking at you. I liked seeing you walk." He glanced across at the brownstone steps. "I didn't want anything to happen to you, all alone like that."

"Oh, I didn't care."

"That's what you said that night."

The shadow that crossed her face crossed swiftly, and she laughed. "It's all right now."

"Yeah, but what was it?"

"Oh," she said. Her head moved in an impatient gesture, but she smiled at the sky. "There was nothing and nobody. I left school. Daddy was mad at me. Kids from school acted sorry for me. Other kids, the ones you saw, they made me tired. I was tired because they were the same way all the time about the same things all the time, and I was tired because they kept me up so late."

"What did you leave school for?"

"I found out what it was for."

"It's for learning stuff."

"It isn't," she said positively. "It's for learning how to learn. And I know that already. I can learn anything. Why did you come here today?"

"I wanted to see you. Where were you going when you came out?"

"Here," she said, tapping her foot. "I saw you from the window. I was waiting for you. I was waiting for you yesterday too. What's the matter?"

He grunted.

"Tell me, tell me!"

"I never had a girl talk to me like you do."

"Don't you like the way I talk?" she asked anxiously.

"Oh for Pete's sake it ain't that!" he exploded. Then he half-smiled at her. "It's just I had a crazy idea. I had the idea you always talk like this. I mean, to anybody."

"I don't, I don't!" she breathed. "Honestly, you've got to believe that. Only you. I've always talked to you like this."

"What do you mean always?"

"Well, everybody's got somebody to talk to, all their life. You know what they like to talk about and when they like to say nothing, when you can be just silly and when they'd rather be serious and important. The only thing you don't know is their face. For that you wait. And then one day you see the face, and then you have it all."

"You ain't talkin' about *me!*"

"Yes I am."

"Look," he said. He had to speak between heartbeats. He had never felt like this in his whole life before. "You could be—takin' a—*awful* chance."

She shook her head happily.

"Did you ever think maybe everybody ain't like that?"

"It doesn't matter. I am."

His face pinched up. "Suppose I just walked away now and never saw you again."

"You wouldn't."

"But suppose."

"Why then I—I'd've had this. Talking to you."

"Hey, you're crying!"

"Well," she said, "there you were, walking away."

"You'd've called me back though."

She turned on him so quickly a tear flew clear off her face and fell sparkling to the back of his hand. Her eyes blazed. "Never that!" she said between her teeth. "I want you to stay, but if you want to go, you go, that's all. All *I* want to do is make you want to stay. I've managed so far . . ."

"How many minutes?" he teased.

"Minutes? Years," she said seriously.

"The—somebody you talked to, you kind of made him up, huh?"

"I suppose."

"How could he ever walk away?"

"Easiest thing in the world," she said. "Somebody like that, they're somebody to live up to. It isn't always easy. You've been very patient," she said. She reached out and touched his cheek.

He snatched her wrist and held it, hard. "You know what I think," he said in a rough whisper, because it was all he had. "I think you're out of your goddam head."

She stood very straight with her eyes closed. She was trembling.

"What's your name, anyway?"

"Joyce."

"I love you too, Joyce. Come on, I want you to meet a friend of mine. It's a long ride on the subway and I'll tell you all about it."

He tried hard but he couldn't tell her all of it. For some of it there were no words at all. For some of it there were no words he could use. She was attentive and puzzled. He bought flowers from a cart, just a few—red and yellow rosebuds.

"Why flowers?"

He remembered the mirror. That was one of the things he hadn't been able to talk about. "It's just what you do," he said, "bring flowers."

"I bet she loves you."

"Whaddaya mean, she's pushin' sixty!"

"All the same," said Joyce, "if she does she's not going to like me."

They went up in the elevator. In the elevator he kissed her.

"What's the matter, Don?"

"If you want to crawl around an' whimper like a puppy-dog," he whispered, "if you feel useful as a busted broom-handle and worth about two wet sneezes in a hailstorm—this is a sense of power?"

"I don't understand."

"Never mind."

In the corridor he stopped. He rubbed a smudge off her nose with his thumb. "She's sorta funny," he said. "Just give her a little time. She's quite a gal. She looks like Sunday school and talks the same way but she knows the score. Joyce, she's the best friend I ever had."

"All right all right all *right!* I'll be good."

He kissed where the smudge had been.

"Come on."

One of Miss Phoebe's envelopes was stuck to the door by its flap. On it was his name.

They looked at one another and then he took the envelope down and got the note from it.

Don:
I am not at home. Please phone me this evening.

P.W.

"Don, I'm *sorry!*"

"I shoulda phoned. I wanted to surprise her."

"Surprise her? She knew you were coming."

"She didn't know you were coming. Damn it anyway."

"Oh it's all right," she said. She took his hand. "There'll be other times. Come on. What'll you do with those?"

"The flowers? I dunno. Want 'em?"

"They're hers," said Joyce.

He gave her a puzzled look. "I got a lot of things to get used to. What do you mean when you say somethin' that way?"

"Almost exactly what I say."

He put the flowers against the door and they went away.

The phone rang four times before Miss Phoebe picked it up.

"It is far too late," she said frigidly, "for telephone calls. You should have called earlier, Don. However, it's just as well. I want you to know that I am *very* displeased with you. I have given you certain privileges, young man, but among them is not that of calling on me unexpectedly."

"Miss—"

"Don't interrupt. In addition, I have never indicated to you that you were free to—"

"But Miss Ph—"

"—to bring to my home any casual acquaintance you happen to have scraped up in heaven knows where—"

"Miss *Phoebe!* Please! I'm in *jail.*"

"—and invade my—you are *what?*"

"Jail, Miss Phoebe, I got arrested."

"Where are you now?"

"County. But you don't need—"

"I'm coming right down," said Miss Phoebe.

"No, Miss Phoebe, I didn't call you for that. You go back to b—"

Miss Phoebe hung up.

Miss Phoebe strode into the County Jail with grim familiarity, and before her, red tape disappeared like confetti in a blast furnace. Twelve minutes after she arrived she had Don out of his cell and into a private room, his crisp new jail-record card before her, and was regarding him with a strange expression of wooden ferocity.

"Sit there," she said, as the door clicked shut behind an awed and reverberating policeman.

Don sat. He was rumpled and sleepy, angry and hurt, but he smiled when he said, "I never thought you'd come. I never expected that, Miss Phoebe."

She did not respond. Instead she said coldly, "Indeed? Well, young man, the matters I have to discuss will not wait." She sat down opposite him and picked up the card.

"Miss Phoebe," he said, "could you be wrong about what you said about me and girls . . . that original sin business, and all? I'm all mixed up, Miss Phoebe. I'm all mixed up!" In his face was a desperate appeal.

"Be quiet," she said sternly. She was studying the card. "This," she said, putting the card down on the table with a dry snap, "tells a great deal, but says nothing. Public nuisance, indecent exposure, suspicion of rape, impairing the morals of a minor, resisting an officer, and destruction of city property. Would you care to explain this—this catalogue to me?"

"What you mean, tell you what happened?"

"That is what I mean."

"Miss Phoebe, where is she? What they done with her?"

"With whom? You mean the girl? I do not know; moreover, it doesn't concern me and it should no longer concern you. Didn't she get you into this?"

"I got her into it. Look, could you find out, Miss Phoebe?"

"I do not know what I will do. You'd better explain to me what happened."

Again the look of appeal, while she waited glacially. He scratched his head hard with both hands at once. "Well, we went to your house."

"I am aware of that."

"Well, you wasn't home so we went out. She said take her father's car. I got a license; it was all right. So we went an' got the car and rode around. Well, we went to a place an' she showed me how to dance some. We went somewheres else an' ate. Then we parked over by the lake. Then, well, a cop come over and poked around an' made some trouble an' I got mad an' next thing you know here we are."

"I asked you," said Miss Phoebe evenly, "what happened?"

"Aw-w." It was a long-drawn sound, an admixture of shame and irritation. "We were in the car an' this cop came pussyfootin' up. He had a big flashlight *this* long. I seen him comin'. When he got to the car we was all right. I mean, I had my arm around Joyce, but that's all."

"What *had* you been doing?"

"Talkin', that's all, just talkin', and . . ."

"And what?"

"Miss Phoebe," he blurted, "I always been able to say anything to you I wanted, about anything. Listen, I *got* to tell you about this. That thing that happened, the way it is with me and girls because of the rat, well, it just wasn't there with Joyce, it was nothin', it was like it never happened. Look, you and me, we had that thing with the hands; it was . . . I can't say it, you know how good it was. Well, with Joyce it was somepin' different. It was like I could fly. I never felt like that before. Miss Phoebe, I had too much these last few days, I don't know what goes on . . . you was right, you was always right, but this I had with Joyce, that was right too, and they can't both be right." He reached across the table, not quite far enough to touch her. The reaching was in his eyes and his voice.

Miss Phoebe stiffened a spine already straight as a bowstring. "I have asked you a simple question and all you can do is gibber at me. *What happened in that car?*"

Slowly he came back to the room, the hard chair, the bright light, Miss Phoebe's implacable face. "That cop," he said. "He claimed he seen us. Said he was goin' to run us in, I said what for, he said carryin' on like that in a public place. There was a lot of argument. Next thing you know he told Joyce to open her dress, he said when it was the way he seen it before he'd let me know. Joyce she begun to cry an' I tol' her not to do it, an' the cop said if I was goin' to act like that he would run us in for *sure*. You know, I got the idea if she'd done it he'da left us alone after?

"So I got real mad, I climbed out of the car, I tol' him we ain't done nothin', he pushes me one side, he shines the light in on Joyce. She squinchin' down in the seat, cryin', he says, 'Come on, you, you know what to do.' I hit the flashlight. I on'y meant to get the light off her, but I guess I hit it kind of hard. It came up and clonked him in the teeth. Busted the flashlight too. That's the city property I destroyed. He started to cuss and I tol' him not to. He hit me and opened the car door an' shoved me in. He got in the back an' took out his gun and tol' me to drive to the station house." He shrugged. "So I had to. That's all."

"It is not all. You have not told me what you did before the policeman came."

He looked at her, startled. "Why, I—we—" His face flamed, "I love her," he said, with difficulty, as if he spoke words in a new and troublesome tongue. "I mean I . . . do, that's all."

"What did you do?"

"I kissed her."

"What else did you do?"

"I—" He brought up one hand, made a vague circular gesture, dropped the hand. He met her gaze. "Like when you love somebody, that's all."

"Are you going to tell me exactly what you did, or are you not?"

"Miss Phoebe . . ." he whispered, "I ain't never seen you look like that."

"I want the whole filthy story," she said. She leaned forward so far that her chin was only a couple of inches from the tabletop. Her protruding, milky eyes seemed to whirl, then it was as if a curtain over them had been twitched aside, and they blazed.

Don stood up. "Miss Phoebe," he said. "Miss Phoebe . . ." It was the voice of terror itself.

Then a strange thing happened. It may have been the mere fact of his rising, of being able, for a moment, to stand over her, look down on her. "Miss Phoebe," he said, "there—ain't—no—filthy—story."

She got up and without another word marched to the door. As she opened it the boy raised his fists. His wrists and forearms corded and writhed. His head went back, his lungs filled, and with all his strength he shouted the filthiest word he knew. It had one syllable, it was sibilant and explosive, it was immensely satisfying.

Miss Phoebe stopped, barely in balance between one pace and the next, momentarily paralyzed. It was like the breaking of the drive-coil on a motion picture projector.

"They locked her up," said Don hoarsely. "They took her away with two floozies an' a ole woman with DT's. She ain't never goin' to see me again. Her ole man'll kill me if he ever sets eyes on me. You were all I had left. Get the hell out of here . . ."

She reached the door as it was opened from the other side by a policeman, who said, "What's goin' on here?"

"Incorrigible," Miss Phoebe spat, and went out. They took Don back to his cell.

The courtroom was dark and its pew-like seats were almost empty. Outside it was raining, and the statue of Justice had a broken nose. Don sat with his head in his hands, not caring about the case then being heard, not caring about his own, not caring about people or things or feelings. For five days he had not cared about the whitewashed cell he had shared with the bicycle thief; the two prunes and weak coffee for breakfast, the blare of the radio in the inner court; the day in, day out screaming of the man on the third tier who hoarsely yelled, "I din't do it I din't do it I din't do . . ."

His name was called and he was led or shoved—he didn't care which—before the bench. A man took his hand and put it on a book held by another man who said something rapidly. "I do," said Don. And then Joyce was there, led up by a tired kindly old fellow with eyes like hers and an unhappy mouth. Don looked at her once and was sure she wasn't even trying to recognize his existence. If she had left her hands at her sides, she was close enough for him to have touched one of them secretly, for they stood side by side, facing the judge. But she kept her hands in front of her and stood with her eyes closed, with her whole face closed, her lashes down on her cheeks like little barred gates.

The cop, the lousy cop was there too, and he reeled off things about Don and things about Joyce that were things they hadn't done, couldn't have done, wouldn't do . . . he cared about that for a moment, but as he listened it seemed very clear that what the cop was saying was about two other people who knew a lot about flesh and nothing about love; and after that he stopped caring again.

When the cop was finished, the kindly tired man came forward and said that he would press no charges against this young man if he promised he would not see his daughter again until she was twenty-one. The judge pushed down his glasses and looked over them at Don. "Will you make that promise?"

Don looked at the tired man, who turned away. He looked at Joyce, whose eyes were closed. "Sure," he told the judge.

There was some talk about respecting the laws of society which were there to protect innocence, and how things would be pretty bad if Don ever appeared before that bench again, and next thing he knew he was being led through the corridors back to the jail, where they returned the wallet and fountain pen they had taken away from him, made him sign a book, unlocked three sets of doors and turned him loose. He stood in the rain and saw, half a block away, Joyce and her father getting into a cab.

About two hours later one of the jail guards came out and saw him. "Hey, boy. You like it here?"

Don pulled the wet hair out of his eyes and looked at
the man, and turned and walked off without saying
anything.

"Well, hello!"

"Now you get away from me, girl. You're just going to
get me in trouble and I don't want no trouble."

"I won't make any trouble for you, really I won't.
Don't you want to talk to me?"

"Look, you know me, you heard about me. Hey, you
been sick?"

"No."

"You look like you been sick. I was sick a whole lot.
Fellow down on his luck, everything happens. Here
comes the old lady from the delicatessen. She'll see us."

"That's all right."

"She'll see you, she knows you, she'll see you talkin'
to me. I don't want no trouble."

"There won't be any trouble. Please don't be afraid.
I'm not afraid of you."

"I ain't scared of you either but one night that young
fellow of yours, that tall skinny one, he said he'll throw
me under a train if I talk to you."

"I have no fellow."

"Yes you have, that tall skin—"

"Not anymore. Not anymore . . . talk to me for a
while. Please talk to me."

"You sure? You sure he ain't . . . you ain't . . ."

"I'm sure. He's gone, he doesn't write, he doesn't
care."

"You been sick."

"No, no, no, no!—I want to tell you something: if
ever you eat your heart out over something, hoping and
wishing for it, dreaming and wanting it, doing everything you can to make yourself fit for it, and then that
something comes along, know what to do?"

"I do' wan' no trouble . . . yea, grab it!"

"No. *Run!* Close your eyes and turn your back and run away. Because wanting something you've never had hurts, sometimes, but not as much as having it and then losing it."

"I never had *nothing.*"

"You did so. And you were locked up for years."

"I didn't have it, girl. I used it. It wasn't mine."

"You didn't lose it, then—ah, I *see!*"

"If a cop comes along he'll pinch me just because I'm talkin' to you. I'm just a bum, I'm down on my luck, we can't stand out here like this."

"Over there, then. Coffee."

"I ain't got but four cents."

"Come on. I have enough."

"What'sa matter with you, you want to talk to a bum like me!"

"Come on, come on . . . listen, listen to this:

" *'It is late last night the dog was speaking of you; the snipe was speaking of you in her deep marsh. It is you are the lonely bird throughout the woods; and that you may be without a mate until you find me.*

" *'You promised me and you said a lie to me, that you would be before me where the sheep are flocked. I gave a whistle and three hundred cries to you; and I found nothing there but fleeting lamb.*

" *'You promised me a thing that was hard for you, a ship of gold under a silver mast; twelve towns and a market in all of them, and a fine white court by the side of the sea.*

" *'You promised me a thing that is not possible; that you would give me gloves of the skin of a fish; that you would give me shoes of the skin of a bird, and a suit of the dearest silk in Ireland.*

" *'My mother said to me not to be talking with you,*

to-day or to-morrow or on Sunday. It was a bad time she took for telling me that, it was shutting the door after the house was robbed . . .

" '*You have taken the east from me, you have taken the west from me, you have taken what is before me and what is behind me; you have taken the moon, you have taken the sun from me, and my fear is great you have taken God from me.*"

". . . That's something I remembered. I remember, I remember everything."

"That's a lonesome thing to remember."

"Yes . . . and no one knows who she was. A man called Yeats heard this Irish girl lamenting, and took it down."

"I don't know, I seen you around, I never saw you like this, you been sick."

"Drink your coffee and we'll have another cup."

Dear Miss Phoebe:

Well dont fall over with surprise to get a letter from me I am not much at letter writing to any body and I never thot I would wind up writing to you.

I know you was mad at me and I guess I was mad at you too. Why I am writing this is I am trying to figure out what it was all about. I know why I was mad I was mad because you said there was something dirty about what I did. Mentioning no names. I did not do nothing dirty and so thats why I was mad.

But all I know about you Miss Phoebe is you was mad I dont know why. I never done nothing to you I was ascared to in the first place and anyway I thot you was my friend. I thot anytime there was something on my mind I could not figure it out, all I had to do was to tell you. This one time I was in more trouble then I ever had in my entire. All you did you got mad at me.

Now if you want to stay mad at me thats your busnis but I wish you would tell me why. I wish we was freinds again but okay if you dont want to.

Well write to me if you feel like it at the Seamans Institute thats where I am picking up my mail these days I took a ride on a tank ship and was sick most of the time but thats life.

I am going to get a new fountain pen this one wont spell right (joke). So take it easy yours truly Don.

Don came out of the Seaman's Institute and stood looking at the square. A breeze lifted and dropped, carrying smells of fish and gasoline, spices, sea-salt, and a slight chill. Don buttoned up his pea-jacket and pushed his hands down into the pockets. Miss Phoebe's letter was there, straight markings on inexpensive, efficient paper, the envelope torn almost in two because of the way he had opened it. He could see it in his mind's eye without effort.

My Dear Don:

Your letter came as something of a surprise to me. I thought you might write, but not that you would claim unawareness of the reasons for my feelings toward you.

You will remember that I spent a good deal of time and energy in acquainting you with the nature of Good and the nature of Evil. I went even further and familiarized you with a kind of union between souls which, without me, would have been impossible to you. And I feel I made quite clear to you the fact that a certain state of grace is necessary to the achievement of these higher levels of being.

Far from attempting to prove to me that you were a worthy pupil of the teachings I might have given you, you plunged immediately into actions which indicate that there is a complete confusion in your mind as to Good and Evil. You have grossly defiled yourself, almost as if you insisted upon being unfit. You engaged in foul and carnal practices which make a mockery of the pure meetings of the higher selves which once were possible to you.

You should understand that the Sources of the power I once offered you are ancient and sacred and not to be taken lightly. Your complete lack of reverence for these antique matters is to me the most unforgivable part of your inexcusable conduct. The Great Thinkers who developed these powers in ancient times surely meant a better end for them than that they be given to young animals.

Perhaps one day you will become capable of understanding the meaning of reverence, obedience, and honor to ancient mysteries. At that time I would be interested to hear from you again.

> Yours very truly,
> (Miss) Phoebe Watkins

Don growled deep in his throat. Subsequent readings would serve to stew all the juices from the letter; one reading was sufficient for him to realize that in the note was no affection and no forgiveness. He remembered the birthday cake with a pang. He remembered the painful hot lump in his throat when she had ordered him to wash his face; she had *cared* whether he washed his face or not.

He went slowly down to the street. He looked older;

he felt older. He had used his seaman's papers for something else besides entree to a clean and inexpensive dormitory. Twice he had thought he was near that strange, blazing loss of self he had experienced with Miss Phoebe, just in staring at the living might of the sea. Once, lying on his back on deck in a clear moonless night, he had been sure of it. There had been a sensation of having been *chosen* for something, of having been fingertip-close to some simple huge fact, some great normal coalescence of time and distance, a fusion and balance, like yin and yang, in all things. But it had escaped him, and now it was of little assistance to him to know that his sole authority in such things considered him as disqualified.

"Foul an' carnal practices," he said under his breath. *Miss Phoebe,* he thought, *I bet I could tell you a thing or two about 'reverence, obedience an' honor to ancient mysteries.* In a flash of deep understanding, he saw that those who hold themselves aloof from the flesh are incapable of comprehending this single fact about those who do not: only he who is free to take it is truly conscious of what he does when he leaves it alone.

Someone was in his way. He stepped aside and the man was still in the way. He snapped out of his introspection and brought his sight back to earth, clothed in an angry scowl.

For a moment he did not recognize the man. He was still tattered, but he was clean and straight, and his eyes were clear. It was obvious that he felt the impact of Don's scowl, he retreated a short pace, and with the step were the beginnings of old reflexes; to cringe, to flee. But then he held hard, and Don had to stop.

"Y'own the sidewalk?" Don demanded. "Oh—it's you."

"I got to talk to you," the man said in a strained voice.

"I got nothin' to talk to you about," said Don. "Get back underground where you belong. Go root for cigar butts in the subway."

"It's about Joyce," said the man.

Don reached and gathered together the lapels of the man's old jacket. "I told you once to stay away from her. That means don't even talk about her."

"Get your hands off me," said the man evenly.

Don grunted in surprise, and let him go.

The man said, "I had somepin' to tell you, but now you can go to hell."

Don laughed. "What do you know! What are you—full of hash or somethin'?"

The man tugged at the lapels and moved to pass Don. Don caught his arm. "Wait. What did you want to tell me?"

The man looked into his face. "Remember you said you was going to kill me, I get near her?"

"I remember."

"I seen her this morning. I seen her yesterday an' four nights last week."

"The hell you did!"

"You got to get that through your head 'fore I tell you anything."

Don shook his head slowly. "This beats anything I ever seen. What happened to you?"

As if he had not heard, the man said, "I found out what ship you was on. I watched the papers. I figured you'd go to the Institoot for mail. I been waitin' three hours."

Don grabbed the thin biceps. "Hey. Is somethin' wrong with Joyce?"

"You give a damn?"

"Listen," said Don, "I can still break your damn neck."

The man simply shrugged.

Baffled, Don said, between his teeth, "Talk. You said you wanted to talk—go ahead."

"Why ain't you wrote to her?"

"What's that to you?"

"It's a whole lot to her."

"You seem to know a hell of a lot."

"I told you I see her all the time," the man pointed out.

"She must talk a lot."

"To me," said the man, closing his eyes, "a whole lot."

"She wouldn't want to hear from me," Don said. Then he barked, "What are you tryin' to tell me? You and her—what are *you* to her? You're not messin' with her, comin' braggin' to me about it?"

The man put a hand on Don's chest and pushed him away. There was disgust on his face, and a strange dignity. "Cut it out," he said. "Look, I don't like you. I don't like doin' what I'm doin' but I got to. Joyce, she's been half crazy, see. I don't know why she started to talk to me. Maybe she just didn't care anymore, maybe she felt so bad she wanted to dive in a swamp an' I was the nearest thing to it. She been talkin' to me, she . . . smiles when she sees me. She'll eat with me, even."

"You shoulda stayed away from her," Don mumbled uncertainly.

"Yeah, maybe. And suppose I did, what would she do? If she didn't have me to talk to, maybe it would be someone else. Maybe someone else wouldn't . . . be as . . . leave her . . ."

"You mean, take care of her," said Don softly.

"Well, if you want to call it that. Take up her time, anyway, she can't get into any other trouble." He looked at Don beseechingly. "I ain't never laid a hand on her. You believe that?"

Don said, "Yeah, I believe that."

"You going to see her?"

Don shook his head.

The man said in a breathy, shrill voice, "I oughta punch you in the mouth!"

"Shaddup," said Don miserably. "What you want me to see her for?"

Suddenly there were tears in the weak blue eyes. But the voice was still steady. "I ain't got nothin'. I'll never have nothin'. This is all I can do, make you go back. Why won't you go back?"

"She wouldn't want to see me," said Don, "after what I done."

"You better go see her," whispered the man. "She thinks she ain't fit to live, gettin' you in jail and all. She thinks it was her fault. She thinks you feel the same way. She even . . . she even thinks that's right. You dirty rotten no-good lousy—" he cried. He suddenly raised his fists and hit his own temples with them, and made a bleating sound. He ran off toward the waterfront.

Don watched him go, stunned to the marrow. Then he turned blindly and started across the street. There was a screeching of brakes, a flurry of movement, and he found himself standing with one hand on the front fender of a taxi.

"Where the hell you think you're goin'?"

Stupidly, Don said, "What?"

"What's the matter with you?" roared the cabby.

Don fumbled his way back to the rear door. "A lot, a whole lot," he said as he got in. "Take me to 37 Mulberry Street," he said.

It was three days later, in the evening, when he went to see Miss Phoebe.

"Well!" she said when she opened to his ring.

"Can I come in?"

She did not move. "You received my letter?"

"Sure."

"You understood . . ."

"I got the idea."

"There were—ah—certain conditions."

"Yeah," said Don. "I got to be capable of understandin' the meaning of reverence, obedience, an' honor to certain ancient mysteries."

"Have you just memorized it, or do you feel you really are capable?"

"Try me."

"Very well." She moved aside.

He came in, shoving a blue knitted cap into his side pocket. He shucked out of the pea jacket. He was wearing blue slacks and a black sweater with a white shirt and blue tie. He was as different from the scrubbed schoolboy neatness of his previous visit as he was from the ill-fit flashiness of his first one. "How've you been?"

"Well, thank you," she answered coolly. "Sit down."

They sat facing one another. Don was watchful, Miss Phoebe wary.

"You've . . . grown," said Miss Phoebe. It was made not so much as a statement, but as an admission.

"I did a lot," said Don. "Thought a lot. You're so right about people in the world that work for—call it yin an' yang—an' know what they're doin', why they're doin' it. All you got to do is look around you. Read the papers."

She nodded. "Do you have any difficulty in determining which side these people are on?"

"No more."

"If that's true," she said, "it's wonderful." She cleared her throat. "You've seen that—that girl again."

"I couldn't lie."

"Are you willing to admit that beastliness is no substitute for the true meeting of minds?"

"Absolutely."

"Well!" she said. "This *is* progress!" She leaned forward suddenly. "Oh, Don, that wasn't for you. Not you! You are destined for great things, my boy. You have no idea."

"I think I have."

"And you're willing to accept my teaching?"

"Just as much as you'll teach me."

"I'll make tea," she said, almost gaily. She rose and as she passed him she squeezed his shoulder. He grinned.

When she was in the kitchenette he said, "Fellow in my neighborhood just got back from a long stretch for hurting a little girl."

"Oh?" she said. "What is his name?"

"I don't know."

"Find out," she said. "They have to be watched."

"Why?"

"Animals," she said, "wild animals. They have to be caught and caged, to protect society."

He nodded. The gesture was his own, out of her range. He said, "I ate already. Don't go to no trouble."

"Very well. Just some cookies." She emerged with the tea service. "It's good to have you back. I'm rather surprised. I'd nearly given you up."

He smiled. "Never do that."

She poured boiling water from the kettle into the teapot and brought it out. "You're almost like a different person."

"How come?"

"Oh, you—you're much more self-assured." She looked at him searchingly. "More complete. I think the word for it is 'integrated.' Actually, I can't seem to . . .to . . . Don, you're not hiding anything from me, are you?"

"Me? Why, how could I do that?"

She seemed troubled. "I don't know." She gave him a

quick glance, almost spoke, then shook her head
slightly.

"What's the matter? I do something wrong?"

"No, oh no."

They were quiet until the tea was steeped and
poured.

"Miss Phoebe . . ."

"What is it?"

"Just what did you think went on in that car before
we got arrested?"

"Isn't that rather obvious?"

"Well," he said, with a quick smile, "to me, yeah. I
was there."

"You can be cleansed," she said confidently.

"Can I now! Miss Phoebe, I just want to get this clear
in my mind. I think you got the wrong idea, and I'd like
to straighten you out. I didn't go the whole way with
that girl."

"You didn't?"

He shook his head.

"Oh," she said. "The policeman got there in time
after all."

He put down his teacup very carefully. "We had lots
of time. What I'm telling you is we just didn't."

"Oh," she said. "Oh!"

"What's the matter, Miss Phoebe?"

"Nothing," she said, tensely. "Nothing. This
. . . puts a different complexion on things."

"I sort of thought you'd be glad."

"But of course!" She whirled on him. "You are telling
me the truth, Don?"

"You can get in an' out of County," he reminded her.
"There's records of her medical examination there that
proves it, you don't believe me."

"Oh," she said, "oh dear." Suddenly her face cleared.
"Perhaps I've underestimated you. What you're telling
me is that you . . . you didn't *want* to, is that it? But

you said that the old memory of the rat left you when you were with her. Why didn't you—*why?"*

"Hey—easy, take it easy! You want to know why, it was because it wasn't the time. What we had would last, it would keep. We din't have to grab."

"You . . . really felt that way about her?"

He nodded.

"I had no idea," she said in a stunned whisper. "And afterward . . . did you . . . do you still . . ."

"You can find out, can't you? You know ways to find out what I'm thinking."

"I can't," she cried. "I can't! Something has happened to you. I can't get in, it's as if there were a steel plate between us!"

"I'm sorry," he said with grave cheerfulness.

She closed her eyes and made some huge internal effort. When she looked up, she seemed quite composed. "You are willing to work with me?"

"I want to."

"Very well. I don't know what has happened and I must find out, even if I have to use . . . drastic measures."

"Anything you say, Miss Phoebe."

"Lie down over there."

"Oh that? I'm longer than it is!" He went to the little sofa and maneuvered himself so that at least his shoulder blades and head were horizontal. "Like so?"

"That will do. Make yourself just as comfortable as you can." She threw a tablecloth over the lampshade and turned out the light in the kitchenette. Then she drew up a chair near his head, out of his visual range. She sat down.

It got very quiet in the room. "You're sleepy, you're so sleepy," she said softly. "You're sl—"

"No I ain't," he said briskly.

"Please," she said, "fall in with this. Just let your mind go blank and listen to me."

"Okay."

She droned on and on. His eyes half-closed, opened, then closed all the way. He began to breathe more slowly, more deeply.

". . . And sleep, sleep, but hear my voice, hear what I am saying, can you hear me?"

"Yes," he said heavily.

"Lie there and sleep, and sleep, but answer me truthfully, tell me only the truth, the truth, answer me, whom do you love?"

"Joyce."

"You told me you restrained yourself the night you were arrested. Is this true?"

"Yes."

Miss Phoebe's eyes narrowed. She wet her lips, wrung her hands.

"The union you had with me, that flight of soul, was that important to you?"

"Yes."

"Would you like to do more of it?"

"Yes."

"Don't you realize that it is a greater, more intimate thing than any union of the flesh?"

"Yes."

"Am I not the only one with whom you can do it?"

"No."

Miss Phoebe bit her lip. "Tell the truth, the truth," she said raggedly. "Who else?"

"Joyce."

"Have you ever done it with Joyce?"

"Not yet."

"Are you sure you can?"

"I'm sure."

Miss Phoebe got up and went into the kitchenette. She put her forehead against the cool tiles of the wall beside the refrigerator. She put her fingertips on her cheeks, and her hands contracted suddenly, digging her fingers in, drawing her flesh downward until her scalding, tightshut eyes were dragged open from underneath. She uttered an almost soundless whimper.

After a moment she straightened up, squared her shoulders and went noiselessly back to her chair. Don slumbered peacefully.

"Don, go on sleeping. Can you hear me?"

"Yes."

"I want you to go down deeper and deeper and deeper, down and down to a place where there is nothing at all, anywhere, anywhere, except my voice, and everything I say is true. Go down, down, deep, deep . . ." On and on she went, until at last she reached down and gently rolled back one of his eyelids. She peered at the eye, nodded with satisfaction.

"Stay down there, Don, stay there."

She crouched in the chair and thought, hard. She knew of the difficulty of hypnotically commanding a subject to do anything repugnant to him. She also knew, however, that it is a comparatively simple matter to convince a subject that a certain person is a pillow, and then fix the command that a knife must be thrust into that pillow.

She pieced and fitted, and at last, "Don, can you hear me?"

His voice was a bare whisper, slurred, "Yes . . ."

"The forces of evil have done a terrible thing to Joyce, Don. When you see her again she will look as before. She will speak and act as before. But she is different. The real Joyce has been taken away. A substitute has been put in her place. The substitute is dangerous. You will know, when you see her. You will not trust her. You will not touch her. You will share nothing with her. You will put her aside and have nothing to do with her.

"But the real Joyce is alive and well, although she was changed. I saved her. When she was replaced by the substitute, I took the real Joyce and made her a part of me. So now when you talk to Miss Phoebe you are talking to Joyce, when you touch Miss Phoebe you are touching Joyce, when you kiss and hold and love Miss Phoebe you will be loving Joyce. Only through Miss Phoebe can you know Joyce, and they are one and the same. And you will never call Joyce by name again. Do you understand?"

"Miss . . . Phoebe is . . . Joyce now . . ."

"That's right."

Miss Phoebe was breathing hard. Her mouth was wet.

"You will remember none of this deep sleep, except what I have told you. Don," she whispered, "my dear, my dear . . ."

Presently she rose and threw the cloth off the lamp-shade. She felt the teapot; it was still quite hot. She emptied the hot-water pot and filled it again from the kettle. She sat down at the tea table, covered her eyes, and for a moment the only sound in the room was her deep, slow, controlled breathing as she oxygenated her lungs.

She sat up, refreshed, and poured tea. "Don! Don! Wake up, Don!"

He opened his eyes and stared unseeingly at the ceiling. Then he raised his head, sat up, shook himself.

"Goodness!" said Miss Phoebe. "You're getting positively absentminded. I like to be answered when I speak to you."

"Whuh? Hm?" He shook himself again and rose. "Sorry, Miss Phoebe. Guess I sorta . . . did you ask me something?"

"The tea, the tea," she said with pleasant impatience. "I've just poured."

"Oh," he said. "Good."

"Don," she said, "we're going to accomplish so *very* much."

"We sure are. And we'll do it a hell of a lot faster with your help."

"I beg—*what?*"

"Joyce and me," he said patiently. "The things you can do, that planting a reflection in a mirror the way you want it, and knowing who's at the door and on the phone and all . . . we can sure use those things."

"I—I'm afraid I don't . . ."

"Oh God, Miss Phoebe, don't! I hate to see you cut yourself up like this!"

"You were faking."

"You mean just now, the hypnosis routine? No I wasn't. You had me under all right. It's just that it won't stick with me. Everything worked but the commands."

"That's—impossible!"

"No it ain't. Not if I had a deeper command to remember 'em—and disregard 'em."

"Why didn't I think of that?" she said tautly. *"She* did it!"

He nodded.

"She's evil, Don, can't you see? I was only trying to save—"

"I know what you were tryin' to save," he interrupted, not unkindly. "You're in real good shape for a woman your age, Miss Phoebe. This power of yours, it keeps you going. Keeps your glands going. With you, that's a problem. With us, now, it'll be a blessing. Pity you never thought of that."

"Foul," she said, "how perfectly foul . . ."

"No it ain't!" he rapped. "Look, maybe we'll all get a chance to work together after all, and if we do, you'll get an idea what kind of chick Joyce is. I hope that happens. But mind you, if it don't, we'll get along. We'll do all you can do, in time."

"I'd *never* cooperate with evil!"

"You went and got yourself a little mixed up about that, Miss Phoebe. You told me yourself about yin an' yang, how some folks set a course straight an' true an' never realize the boundary can twist around underneath them. You asked me just tonight was I sure which was which, an' I said yes. It's real simple. When you see somebody with power who is usin' it for what yang stands for—good, an' light, an' all like that, you'll find he ain't usin' it for himself."

"I wasn't using it for myself!"

"No, huh?" He chuckled. "Who was it I was goin' to kiss an' hold just like it was Joyce?"

She moaned and covered her face. "I just wanted to keep you pure," she said indistinctly.

"Now that's a thing you got to get straightened out on. That's a big thing. Look here." He rose and went to the long bookcase. Through her fingers, she watched him. "Suppose this here's all the time that has passed since there was anything like a human being on earth." He moved his hand from one end of the top shelf to the other. "Maybe way back at the beginning they was no more 'n smart monkeys, but all the same they had whatever it is makes us human beings. These forces you talk about, they were operatin' then just like now. An' the cavemen an' the savages an' all, hundreds an' hundreds of years, they kept developing until we got humans like us.

"All right. You talk about ancient mysteries, your Yoga an' all. An' this tieup with virgins. Look, I'm going to show you somepin. You an' all your studyin' and copyin' the ancient secrets, you know how ancient they were? I'll show you." He put out his big hand and put three fingers side by side on the "modern" end of the shelf.

"Those three fingers covers it—down to about fourteen thousand years before Christ. Well, maybe the thing did work better without sex. But only by throwin' sex into study instead of where it was meant to go. Now you want to free yourself from sex in your thinkin', there's a much better way than that. You do it like Joyce an' me. We're a bigger unit together than you ever could be by yourself. An' we're not likely to get pushed around by our glands, like you. No offense, Miss Phoebe . . . so there's your *really* ancient mystery. Male an' female together; there's a power for you. Why you s'pose people in love get to fly so high, get to feel like gods?" He swept his hand the full length of the shelf. "A *real* ancient one."

"Wh-where did you learn all this?" she whispered.

"Joyce. Joyce and me, we figured it out. Look, she's not just any chick. She quit school because she learns too fast. She gets everything right now, this minute, as soon as she sees it. All her life everyone around her seems to be draggin' their feet. An' besides, she's like a kid. I don't mean childish, I don't mean simple, I mean like she believes in something even when there's no evidence around for it, she keeps on believing until the evidence comes along. There must be a word for that."

"Faith," said Miss Phoebe faintly.

He came and sat down near her. "Don't take it so hard, Miss Phoebe," he said feelingly. "It's just that you got to stand aside for a later model. If anybody's going to do Yang work in a world like this, they got to get rid of a lot of deadwood. I don't mean you're deadwood. I mean a lot of your ideas are. Like that fellow was in jail about the little girl, you say *watch 'im!* one false move an' back in the cage he goes. And all that guy wanted all his life was just to have a couple people around him who give a damn, 'scuse me, Miss Phoebe. He never had that, so he took what he could get from whoever was weaker'n him, and that was only girls. You should see him now, he's goin' to be our best man."

"You're a child. You can't undertake work like this. You don't know the powers you're playing with."

"Right. We're goin' to make mistakes. An' that's where you come in. Are you on?"

"I—don't quite—"

"We want your help," he said, and bluntly added, "but if you can't help, don't hinder."

"You'd want to work with me after I . . . Joyce, Joyce will hate me!"

"Joyce ain't afraid of you." Her face crumpled. He patted her clumsily on the shoulder. "Come on, what do you say?"

She sniffled, then turned red-rimmed, protruding eyes up to him. "If you want me. I'd have to . . . I'd like to talk to Joyce."

"Okay. JOYCE!"

Miss Phoebe started. "She—she's not—*oh!*" she cried as the doorknob turned. She said, "It's locked."

He grinned. "No it ain't."

Joyce came in. She went straight to Don, her eyes on his face, searching, and did not look around her until her hand was in his. Then she looked down at Miss Phoebe.

"This here, this is Joyce," Don said.

Joyce and Miss Phoebe held each other's eyes for a long moment, tense at first, gradually softening. At last Miss Phoebe made a tremulous smile.

"I'd better make some tea," she said, gathering her feet under her.

"I'll help," said Joyce. She turned her face to the tea tray, which lifted into the air and floated to the kitchenette. She smiled at Miss Phoebe. "You tell me what to do."

Elizabeth Engstrom (b. 1951)

WHEN DARKNESS LOVES US

Elizabeth Engstrom entered the horror field with little fanfare in the 1980s with the publication of her book of two novellas, *When Darkness Loves Us* (1985), containing an introduction by Theodore Sturgeon, who was one of her teachers and literary mentors. Since then, she has written two horror novels, *Black Ambrosia* (1988) and *Lizzie Borden* (1990), in the process gaining a reputation among connoisseurs and an award nomination from the newly founded Horror Writers of America. Her reputation is still growing. Elizabeth Engstrom seems destined to become a central figure in the field. "When Darkness Loves Us" is a deeply disturbing tale that moves subtly, then with more force into the fantastic and grotesque to expose monstrous psychological abnormality. Its rural setting is reminiscent of many of Shirley Jackson's works, and its concerns link it closely to the horror fiction by women from the late nineteenth century to the present. It is interesting to compare it, for instance, to Violet Hunt's "The Prayer." There is no more direct or powerful examination of the darkness in relationships in the entire body of contemporary horror literature than this novella.

Part One

1

Sally Ann Hixson, full with the blush of spring and gleeful playfulness as only sixteen-year-olds know it, hid around the side of the huge tree at the edge of the woods as the great tractor drove past her. She saw her husband, torso bare, riding the roaring monster, his smooth muscles gliding under sweat-slick skin tanned a deep brown. She didn't want him to see her . . . not yet.

She plopped down into the long grass, feeling the rough bark of the big tree against her back as she gazed into the woods. This had been her favorite place to play when she was little. She could just barely see her parents' house on the hill about a mile off. Her mother had noticed her restlessness as soon as the major canning was done and sent her away to run, to play, to spy on her new husband as he worked with her father in the fields.

This summer, they would build their house on the other hill, and they could raise their family to be good country folk, just like their fathers and their fathers before them. She stretched her legs into a sunbeam, feeling them warm under her new jeans. She had a wild impulse to cast off her clothes and run naked through the grass. She thought of Michael then, and their delicious lovemaking the night before. She was not able to give of herself very freely while in her parents' house, but some nights Michael took her by the hand and led her out to the hill where their house would soon be built, high up on the knoll, and with the moon watching and the cicadas playing the romantic background music, they would make love, uninhibited, wonderful love. They explored each other's bodies and released sensations unfamiliar to either of them, with joy and togetherness in discovering the full potentials of their sexuality.

The idea made her tingle, then blush, and she crossed her legs, thinking of the times her thoughts strayed to such matters when she was with her mother. It was worse then, because she was sure lovemaking was not like that for her parents, and sometimes she had to excuse herself and go into the bathroom until she could stop grinning.

She picked up a long strand of grass and put it between her teeth as she peeked around the tree and watched her man, handsome and tousled, drive the machine over the next hill. She glanced around one more time to make sure her pest of a little sister wasn't lurking somewhere in the shadows. She jumped up and followed the edge of the woods until she could see the flatbed truck where her father waited. Michael would stop there and have a glass of iced water that she had put in a thermos jug for him that morning. She saw him turn to look behind him, so she dodged back into the woods . . . and saw the stone steps that led down into the ground.

It was so familiar. She used to play here when she was small, but she hadn't come here in years. There were two brand-new doors with shiny hinges mounted to the concrete, and she knew that it was going to be sealed against children and mishaps forever. What used to be the attraction here so long ago? She remembered the darkness and a tunnel, and she stepped down to the first step, then the second one, looking into a black hole that had no end.

It was cool, but not cold, and she took the sweatshirt that was tied around her waist and slipped it over her shoulders. She continued down into the eerie darkness and tried to remember the story about this place. A hiding place for runaway slaves, maybe. She continued her descent. The steps were sturdy, stone set in concrete. She felt her way along with her hand, the rough rock cool to the touch. The steps were narrow, set at an easy angle, and as she glanced back to reassure herself of the warm spring day above, she noticed that the entrance to the stairs would be out of sight before she reached the bottom. Yet down she went.

At the bottom there was a hole in the side of the wall, and memories, just out of reach, began to form themselves in her mind. She wondered if any of the old playthings were still in the tunnel. She crouched down to enter. Once inside, she straightened up—the tunnel was quite large. The small amount of light afforded by the entry provided very little visibility, but she made her way slowly along the tunnel, until the toe of her tennis shoe struck something that went ringing into the darkness. It was a baby spoon. The light glinted off the surface, just enough for her to find it. She picked it up, suddenly remembering the nursery rhymes and the frightening pleasure of having tea parties in such a forbidden place.

She rubbed the spoon between her fingers: tiny, smooth, and round, with a handle that doubled back upon itself, big enough for her finger. Then she remembered Jackie, killed in Vietnam. They were inseparable, always knew they'd eventually marry, and she had cried when he went off to the army. But now Jackie was gone and Michael was up there, and she had better go surprise him before she missed her chance. With one more thought of Jackie and a prayer for his soul, she moved back through the tunnel to the hole in the wall and the stairs, back to the sun and the springtime.

She heard Michael's voice above the roar of the idling tractor just as she came through the hole in the wall, caught the last words of his sentence. Angry that he had found her before she could surprise him, she had started running up the stairs when the doors above slammed shut, cutting off all light, and the sound of a padlock's shank driving home pierced her heart. She stood stock-still. The walls instantly closed in around her, and the air disappeared. She managed one scream, drowned by the earth-vibrating essence of the great engine above. She gasped, stumbled up one more step, then fell to her knees, fighting for breath, trying desperately to repress the horror of being locked in the darkness, while Michael's last words reverberated in her mind: ". . . before one of my kids falls down there."

Chest heaving, she tried to crawl up the stairs, fingers clawing—capable only of breathless moans rather than the strong screams she was trying desperately to utter in a vain attempt to bring father and husband to her rescue. She convulsed in fear, fingers stiffening, back arching. A muscular spasm turned her onto her back, the stone steps dug into her spine, and the darkness moved in and took over her mind.

2

The awakening was slow, starting with the pain in her lower back, then in her fingers, followed by the throbbing in her head. Slowly she opened her eyes. Darkness. She felt her eyes with her fingers to see if they were open or if she was dreaming. She felt the cold stone steps beneath her. Then she remembered. She looked around, but could see absolutely nothing. On her hands and knees, she mounted the steps until her head touched the heavy wooden doors, and she remembered the shiny new hinges and the solid, heavy wood that wouldn't rot as the seasons changed.

It must be night, she thought, or surely I could see a crack of daylight somewhere. She felt alone, isolated, abandoned. Tears leaked out the corners of her eyes as she focused all her panic and shot it to her husband, hoping that somewhere there was a God who would transmit the message to him, so he could sense her surroundings and come rescue her and take her home to their warm, soft bed.

She pushed on the door with her shoulders, and it didn't give at all. She lost hope of wiggling the hinges loose. Cold and afraid, she huddled on the first steps, knowing that soon Michael and her dad would be coming for her. It was the only possible place she could be. After she had been missing for a night, they would come looking for her here. And here she would be, brave (not really) and okay (barely) and so very glad to see them. She fought the claustrophobic feeling and tried to relax. She was desperately tired and uncomfortable. She put her head on her arms and slept.

When she awoke, it was still pitch-dark and she had to go to the bathroom. She couldn't be embarrassed by the foul smells of her own excretions when her husband came to rescue her, so she had to find some place to go. Slowly, with aching muscles, she moved crablike down the stairs, visualizing in her mind's eye the hole in the wall and the tunnel thereafter. She crouched, feeling the circumference of the hole so she wouldn't hit her head, and slipped through to the big tunnel.

She remembered that it ran wide and true to where she had picked up the spoon, and she took brave steps in the darkness. She remembered Jackie, talking to her when they were out walking in the countryside on dark moonless nights. "You'll never stumble if you walk boldly and pick your feet up high." It worked then, and it worked now. She walked through the darkness and the fear, until she sensed by the echoes around her that the tunnel took a turn to the right. In the corner she relieved herself.

Nothing could be worse than waiting at the top of the steps, so she decided to explore the tunnel just a little farther and exercise the kinks out of her legs. The tunnel wound around until she was certain she must be directly under the stairs; then it straightened again. Her breathing echoed off the walls in eerie rasps. She walked still farther, and the air turned cooler. It smelled different. Water. Suddenly overcome with thirst, she walked boldly and entered a large cavern. The change in acoustics was immediate. She felt small and lost after the intimacy of the tunnel. Pebbles crunched underfoot.

She picked up a handful of loose stones and began tossing them around her to get a bearing on the dimensions of the cavern. It was huge. A path seemed to continue right through it, water on both sides. Slowly she stepped off the right side of the path, taking baby steps down into the darkness until her tennis shoe splashed in water. She lifted a cupped handful to her nose, then tasted it. Delicious. Eagerly, with both feet in the water, she drank her fill.

Wouldn't Dad be surprised, she thought, to know of this underwater lake on his property. The water tasted like the cave smelled—mossy—but it seemed pure, and it did the trick. She splashed some on her face, stood up, and dried her hands on her sweatshirt.

Feeling far more comfortable, she picked up another handful of pebbles and started throwing them. On this side of the path was a small pond, but the lake on the other side seemed endless. She threw a rock as far as she could, and still it plopped into the water. She threw another to the side, and it splashed. She threw another and there was no sound. Her heart froze. Maybe it had landed on a moss island. She threw one more in roughly the same direction and heard it land with a plop, and she visualized the concentric circles of black ripples edging out toward her.

She walked along the path, humming away the discomfort, spraying pebbles in wide sweeping arcs. The sound was friendly. Pebbles gone, she continued walking until she could feel the cavern narrowing back into a tunnel, and it was then that she heard the splash behind her. A small splash, as if one of the pebbles had been held up from its fate, suspended, until it finally fell. She stopped, midstep, and listened. The darkness pressed in upon her, and she could hear her blood rush through her veins. Silence. She had resumed her walk, stepping quietly, when another splash came, closer behind her, and her mind again was seized with unparalleled terror. She froze. A third noise, a sucking sound coming from the water just inches away from her feet, made her start. Moans of panic churning up unbidden, she ran blindly, until she stumbled and collided at a turn with the wall of the tunnel. She wildly felt her way around the turn and continued running the length of it until the cave with its lake and resident monster were far behind her.

She stopped for breath, the tunnel becoming a close friend. She was sure of the walls around her, and there were only two directions to be concerned with. Still her heart pounded. She leaned against the wall of the tunnel in despair. The darkness was terrifying. She could dimly see some kind of tracers in front of her eyes as she passed her hand in front of her face, but could not make out even the shapes of her fingers. Her eyes ached from trying. The tears were a long time coming, beginning first with shuddering whimpers, then great, racking, soul-filled sobs. The hopelessness of the situation was overwhelming. There was no point in going on, and she could not go back past the creature in the lake. Just the thought of going back made her want to vomit. She would stay right there until she starved to death. Exhausted by the scare, the run, and the cry, eventually she slept.

She dreamed of Michael. They were running together through the waist-high grass, laughing. He tripped her, and holding her so she would not fall too hard, he came down on top of her, his face so close, and he moved as if to kiss her. Instead, he said, *"You're going to rot down there, aren't you?"*

She awoke with a piercing scream that echoed back to her again and again and again, so that even after she had stopped, she had to put her hands to her ears to keep out the terrible noise. She sat straight up, looking ahead at the darkness. "Oh, God." Her soul wrenched inside of her. "NO!" she shouted. "I WON'T rot down here! I WILL SURVIVE!" The loud sound of her voice set her heart pounding again, and she started to think clearly. The decision to survive created bravery in her, and she wanted to make a plan. She knew now that she would survive until she was rescued.

Shelter. That was a laugh. No problem. Because it was a bit warm, she rolled up her jeans to just below the knee. She certainly wasn't going to freeze. She stood and tied the sweatshirt again around her waist. Food. Now that was a problem. And she was definitely hungry. Water. If there was one lake, there must be another. Or a stream. She would continue down these tunnels until she found what she needed and then found a way out of here. She couldn't wait to be discovered. Where there was water, there was most likely food. Fish! Probably the monster in the lake was nothing more than a couple of fish, their long-undisturbed life in the lake interrupted by the stones. Maybe she could catch a fish to eat.

She thought back to her science books, to pale, sickly fish with bulging blind eyes and horrendous teeth that lived so deep in the ocean that no light penetrated their lair, and she shuddered. So much for the fish. She'd have to eat them raw anyway. No good. Moss, maybe. Seaweed was supposed to be good for you; maybe moss was just as good. Maybe also, there was a way out of here. She got up and started down the tunnel, thinking as she went, trying to ignore the gnawing in her belly that would soon, very soon, have to be satisfied.

She walked on, wondering how long she'd been there,

wondering how long it would be until she heard Michael's booming voice. She would keep track of time with marks on the cave wall, but that was pretty silly, because she wouldn't be able to see them. By the number of times she slept? No good. By her menstrual periods? Nonsense. She would never be here a whole month, and besides that, she hadn't had a period in the two months she and Michael had been married.

No matter how bravely she told herself that things were going to be all right, now she had two doubts nagging the back of her mind.

She walked until her legs were leaden; then she sat and slept and walked some more. There must be miles and miles of tunnel in here. She crossed two streams, both of which had water seeping from one wall, crossing the floor of the tunnel, and leaking out the other side. Barely enough to drink—she would put her lips to the wall and suck up what moisture was needed to keep the dangerous thirst away. She knew, too, that if she didn't find something to eat soon, she would no longer have the energy to look. Her jeans were a little baggy on her already slim frame, and her steps were slower and not always in a straight line.

Sleeping when tired, she made her way through the endless tunnel with its twistings and turnings, her hands raw from catching herself after stumbling over the uneven flooring as her steps began to drag. After countless naps, with weak legs, bleeding and blistered, she tripped over a rise in the tunnel floor and lay there, her will almost gone, overcome by thirst and hunger, so tired, wanting that final sleep that would bring peace.

In half consciousness, her brain fevered and delirious, she cried out "Michael!" and her voice reverberated off the walls of a large cavern. Then she heard water dripping.

She crawled painfully toward the sound and found a

pool of water, cold and delicious. She lay on her stomach and drank from her hands until she was full. It was in the half sleep that followed that Jackie came to her and brought her food. She heard his voice, and looked up. He stood over her, his face illuminated in the darkness by a glow, a radiance. "Eat these, Sally Ann. They're good for you." She picked one up. It was a fat slug, slippery on one side and rough on the other side, about the size of her thumb.

"I can't eat this."

"You can. It's good for you. You have to. Pop the whole thing in your mouth like a cherry tomato and bite once, then swallow. It's easy. Here. Try." Too tired to feel revulsion, she put the slug into her mouth and chomped down hard. She felt it burst, squirting down her throat and she swallowed quickly, followed by a handful of cold water. Yuck. It tasted awful. He encouraged her to eat more, and she did. She finished all those he had brought her and, stomach full, slept where she lay.

3

"Jackie?"

"Hmmm?"

"Are you a ghost?"

"I don't know."

The question had burned in her mind since she had first seen him the day he'd saved her. Fearing the worst—that she was mad—she had promised herself not to ask the question until he had been with her for a while.

"Well, how did you come to be here? And why can I see you when I can't even see my hands in front of my face?"

"I don't know that either, Sally Ann. All I know is

that I was in Vietnam, and we were carrying wounded back to the camp. There was a yell and some sniper fire. I got hit in the chest . . . and the next thing I knew was that you were dying and I had to find some food for you to eat. I can see you, too, you know. It is pretty strange."

"The Vietnam war ended more than five years ago, Jackie. You were killed there."

This bit of news seemed no surprise to him. They sat in the main cavern with their backs up against the wall, comfortable on a mattress of soft dry moss that Sally had gathered for their bed. Her pregnancy was confirmed—there was no other explanation for the growing bulge in her belly—and she had stopped wearing her jeans long ago.

It had taken her a long time to recover, but Jackie helped nurse her back to health. His devotion to her, and the baby she carried, helped her accept the fact that unless Michael found his way to her, she was stuck for the time being. The resiliency of youth healed her body and her mind. She adapted to her new surroundings as best she could, and as time went on, she pined less and less for her family.

Jackie urged her on, and together they explored the immediate regions of their homestead, discovered many large tunnels and smaller tributaries. One led to a swift-running stream, and it was here that Sally made her toilet. Another entered a monstrous cavern like a hollowed-out mountain, with sheer drops of hundreds or more feet, as she estimated by dropping rocks from their ledges.

A smaller cavern revealed what seemed to be thousands of skeletons. The final resting place, Sally Ann speculated, of all those slaves trying to escape. How long did they search for a way out before they sat down together and starved to death? What a terrible way to die. Lost, sightless, terrified. Their remains were a fortunate discovery, however, for from these bones Jackie and Sally fashioned plenty of useful tools—bowls, knives, awls, and supports. It also reaffirmed her will to survive.

This same cavern yielded mushrooms of many flavors. Sally found the mushroom patch by stepping on the spongy fungi as she walked carefully around, searching the area. Just as she found the mushrooms, Jackie discovered a tough razorlike lichen growing around the walls. Sally had begun the dangerous habit of tasting everything that smelled okay. She couldn't help herself. Sometimes the cravings were just too intense. The mushrooms didn't hurt her, and when she soaked the lichen, it too became palatable.

It was strange how she could see Jackie as he worked; he seemed so old, so smart. The only time her eyes hurt her now was when she was exploring a new region, straining vainly to see where she was stepping. Sometimes she just closed them and wandered. It made no difference. She could see Jackie and nothing else, eyes open or closed.

She still became frightened, especially when Jackie went away. He went off on exploration trips of his own at times, mostly when he sensed she needed to be alone. The fear was not of the caverns, though, nor of monsters (even though the lake creature continued to haunt her dreams) or bogeymen. The fear seeped in when she was reflecting on her past life—Michael, her mother, father, and sister. The fear told her that she would be here until she died, that her child and its father would never meet. When the fear came, and she started to pant with the physical effect, and her eyes bulged in the darkness, looking from side to side trying to find a way out, Jackie would come back and sit with her, and soon the calm would descend. They became very close.

There was always plenty of food. Sally had merely to pick the slugs from the walls, wash them in the pond, and eat. There was also a kind of kelp that grew on the edges of the rocks in the water and on the sides of the tunnel where the water ran down, and now and then a fish would float up, and she would ravenously eat it, bones and all.

The water level fluctuated, dramatically at times. Sometimes when they went to sleep the water would be low, but when they awoke, it would reach almost to their bed. Now and then they would find things floating in it: Apples sometimes showed up, even a cabbage once; frequently there were walnuts and an occasional dead rodent, all of which added up to an adequate diet.

Their bed was comfortable; they were dry, clean, warm, fed, and together. And it was at times like this that they philosophized about their predicament—she being both grateful and angry.

Sally Ann was a fairly responsible sort of a girl, level-headed and born with an instinct to roll with the punches. That's how she felt about their situation. They had to make the best of it. What concerned her most, though, was the birth of her child. What to name him? How to keep from losing him in the dark? Jackie seemed convinced it was to be a son, and Sally Ann had taken a liking to the name Clinton. It was a solid name, and had enough hard sounds to make it easily understood when she had to call to him in the darkness.

Jackie's undying cheerfulness helped chase away what blues came and went: He was totally unwilling to look at the negative side of things or talk of despair. They lay close together at sleep time and chased away the bad dreams. He even cut her hair. A tortuous process. Her blond hair was thin, and she had always worn it quite long, but in the time they spent in the underworld it had grown much too long to be manageable. It was always getting in her way and washing it was quite out of the question. She lay with her neck on her jeans, her head on a boulder; with a sharp rock, Jackie sawed away at her hair, wearing it through more than cutting it. The end result felt uneven and strange, but more comfortable.

The baby grew rapidly, and in the last days, it was too dangerous to be awkwardly stumbling around in the darkness. She confined herself to her moss mattress and contemplated Michael.

Again and again she would lapse into despair until Jackie came to lift her spirits. He told her how he had delivered babies for women in Nam, said he was experienced, that there was nothing to it, and though she didn't believe him, he talked to her in his calm, low voice until she was convinced there was nothing to fear.

But when the time came, when the pains racked her whole body, and her water broke, and she began to cry and scream and writhe on her bed, she wished for Dr. Stirling and his warm, confident hands. But Jackie was there, and he talked to her—rubbed her back between contractions and spoke of the coming baby and what a joy it would be. She thought of how happy it would make Michael to know that he had a baby, and she gritted her teeth and bore the pain and finally bore the baby. It emerged screaming and choking, and the reverberations in the cavern were joyous to hear.

She lifted the baby, warm and slippery, to her belly, and her hands moved over it to reassure herself that it was real, that it was whole and had all its parts. She discovered that it was indeed a son. Jackie brought her water in a skull bowl, and with the baby at her breast, they tied the umbilical cord with her shoelaces and severed it with a sharpened bone. He helped her deliver the afterbirth, which he put away to eat later, then cleaned up around them. He brought the fresh moss that had been stockpiled for the occasion, then lay down beside mother and son, and enshrouded in darkness, they all slept.

4

"I'm cold, Mommy."

"Well then, silly, come out of the water and I'll dry you off."

Tall as his mother's shoulder, Clint came dripping out of the pond and stood shivering by her side. She rubbed him briskly with a handful of soft dry moss to help restore circulation, then pulled him down to her lap. They sat together, rocking back and forth, naked, she appreciating the coolness of his body as he appreciated the warmth of hers. They were very close, too close at times, she thought, but she constantly had to reevaluate her standards. In such an abnormal situation, she had to trust her judgment. His mouth automatically groped for her breast, and he gently sucked on it as they sat together. Her milk had dried up long ago, but this closeness was very important.

His little body was hard, muscular, compact, with just a little potbelly protruding, and though he was small, he was strong. She often wondered about his physical development without the sun. He seemed healthy, and he certainly was happy. A joy to her, even though she had never seen his face.

"Tell me again about sun and sky." When he was a baby, Sally Ann had told him stories about his father and the place where she had lived above ground, and he never tired of hearing about the sun and the sky, the plants, meadows, fruits, and delicious things of nature.

"Morning time is when the sun comes up in the sky and makes everything bright and you can see for miles. There are woods by where my parents live, and acres and acres of wheat fields. Your daddy works in those fields and his skin is tanned and brown. He eats sweet jam that I made for him before I came here to have you."

"What's 'see' again?"

"It's another sense, honey. Like feeling or tasting or smelling. Listen. Hear that water drip? Well, if you go put your hand under it you can feel the drop, and if you could see it, it would look like a tiny jewel, a little precious piece of sunlight captured in the water. Someday you will see it. Someday your daddy will come down here and find us and take us back up to the farm and you'll be able to run in the sunlight."

"I wish he'd come soon, Mommy."

"Me too, honey." Her heart went out to this perfect child who didn't understand what seeing was, who didn't know the wonders of life and nature.

Sally Ann gathered up their things and started back to the main cavern which had been their home since Clint was born. Born to the darkness, he was naturally oriented, and ran ahead of her, totally unafraid, at peace with the elements of his underworld life. She walked along slowly. She knew that she was planting a few seeds of dissatisfaction when she talked to him of the aboveground world, that he longed to see the magic things that she talked of, but how else was she to explain life to him? And she did believe that one day they would be discovered and taken back.

He was a very independent boy, and he had thoughts of his own about the world above. Sally Ann could tell he doubted that everything she talked about existed. She could hardly blame him. How could he believe in the sun when he had never even used his eyes? When she stopped to think about it, as she did now, it saddened her. She wanted all the experiences of life to be his: to run and play in the meadow, to hear the birds, to see the stars. I guess it's a little like believing in God, she thought. One has to believe, and then belief becomes strengthened. If one disbelieves, then disbelief is strengthened. And turning your back, once you know the truth, leads to evil.

She showed him her tennis shoes in an attempt to pique his curiosity, but he wasn't interested. And there wasn't anything she could do but accept it, was there?

When Clint was far enough ahead of her, she called to Jackie and he joined her on her walk. Clint couldn't see or hear Jackie, so he reserved his visiting time for Sally alone, after Clint was asleep. Many times they discussed for hours the best way to help Clint understand. Sally was confident that he was growing up to be a normal boy. He delighted in finding new kinds of life in the caves, some of which they gratefully added to their diet—like the crayfish that blindly lived in the fast-running streams—and some of which provided hours of entertainment for Clint—like the dim-witted puff-fish that would let him pick them up and transport them from one pond to another and back again. He played war games with them, playfully pitting one against the other, with food as the supreme reward. They seemed, in their cold, reptilian way, to be almost affectionate to him. But then, he was always kind to them.

Clint was crossing the swift stream on the stepping-stones when he first discovered the crayfish. He was chewing one of a handful of slugs, when one slipped out between his fingers just at the edge of the stream and he heard it splash into the water. The water began boiling with activity, and unafraid as he was, he reached in and pulled out a crayfish as long as his arm.

Jackie said that as long as it ate what you ate, it should be okay for you to eat it. So they shelled it and discovered that it was delicious. Sally Ann couldn't quite get over her fear of putting her hand right into the black water, though Clint teased her about it, but she was grateful that he would bring her those delectable treats now and then.

Yes, he was a joy to her, but in her times alone she wondered many things. What would happen to him if she died? Was she glorifying the outside world to him so that he would never rest until he saw it? Was there a way out of here? She and Jackie had searched the tunnels and caverns for years, looking for a way out, and nothing had come of it yet. She knew that the stairs were securely locked and guarded by a beast in the lake, so they avoided that direction. Maybe, though, Clint would have the hunger, the burning desire to go to the magic place she had described for him, and through some mercy from heaven, he would be shown the way out. God knows a boy shouldn't live his life in tunnels and caves.

"Why so silent?" Jackie had been walking alongside her, respecting her contemplative mood.

"What is the purpose of all this, Jackie? Are we doing something here for someone's benefit? What possible part in God's plan are we fulfilling? I want my son out of here. We've been here for years, Jackie. YEARS! Clint is probably eight years old now, and he's never even SEEN, for God's sake. And Michael. What must he have thought, that his young wife had run away? And my parents. And my sister. Jackie. I've got to get out of here with my child, NOW!"

Jackie looked at her sadly. "I've a feeling, Sally Ann, that all this IS for a higher purpose."

"I can't accept that. Clint and I are going to find our way out of here—NOW!" Suddenly she was filled with a sense of purpose, of immediacy. The drive had taken hold of her with a single-mindedness that demanded attention. She knew, deep in her soul, that Clint was old enough now to be a help, not a hindrance, and if they were ever going to do it, now was the time.

She ran back to the main cavern and found Clint. She grabbed his shoulders with both hands and put her face up next to his.

"Clint. We've got to get out of here. We've got to get up to the sunshine and the grass and the fresh air, and see your daddy. We can stay here forever, and we probably will, if we don't make the commitment— right NOW—to get out of here. Now I'm going to pack up some moss and some water and some food, and we're going to keep going until we find a way out of these caves. Okay? Are you ready?"

"We've never looked the other way." Sally knew he meant the way of the monster in the lake. She had never returned that way, had never gone back, had never tried the stairs again. She had chosen to stay in the caves rather than risk what might be in that lake. But now she wasn't so sure.

"Then that's the way we'll start. Get ready."

They didn't speak again until they each had bundles tied to their backs and had entered the tunnel forbidden to Clint all his life. Then he said, "Why now, all of a sudden? You were happy here until now. Don't you want to be down here with me anymore?"

"Of course I want to be with you, honey. There are just better things for you than an old cave. I want to see your face. I want to see how much you look like your daddy."

"You always told me Daddy would rescue us. He hasn't, though, has he? And now you want to go find him. Why? We live here. This is our home. We're happy here. Don't you want to be with me anymore?"

Sally stopped and reached out for him, but he avoided her touch. She was astonished at his bitterness.

"Clint . . ."

"Don't! You don't want me anymore. You just want to go chasing a dream. There is no 'up there.' There is no 'daddy.' There's nothing but you and me and that's not good enough for you. You're a liar and I don't want YOU anymore, either!" He ran off into the darkness.

"Clint!" She screamed after him. There was no

response. She kept screaming as if the echoes were her only friends.

5

Filled with a stifling terror that had built upon itself over the years, Sally Ann felt her way along the side of the tunnel toward the opening she had first come through so long ago. Still sobbing and aching for her runaway son, she had but one thing in mind—to show him the truth. How could he not believe her? When she stopped to rest there was only silence around her. She heard nothing of her son but did not worry. Clint was far more capable of navigating the winding tunnels than she. She also resisted the temptation of calling Jackie. This was a situation she would have to deal with on her own.

For the first time, doubts began to fill her mind. Maybe it was all a lie. Maybe Jackie was a lie, too. Maybe this was all a dream, a nightmare; maybe there was nothing, really, except her and the darkness. No caves, no tunnels, no Clint, no Michael, no God. Maybe she was the product of the imagination of some madman who was dreaming. Maybe she was the central character of a novel, and the imagery of the writer was strong enough to flash her into existence. How else could she explain Jackie? Was he just the product of her need? How could he be real?

"There is only one way to find out. I will prove to Clint and I will prove to myself that there is something else—something better for us than the darkness, than these damned tunnels. I will get out of here and come back for Clint." She spoke loudly, boldly, as much to calm herself as in the hope that Clint could hear her.

She continued through the tunnel, reliving the journey from the tunnel entrance to the main cavern. She walked with her eyes closed, hoping her feet would remember the way and not let her mind guide her down the wrong tunnel, take the wrong turn at a fork, sabotage her freedom. When she was tired she slept, and when she was hungry she ate until all she had brought with her was gone. Still she walked, the ache within her abdomen a constant companion, the pain of a mother falsely accused of being dishonest with her child.

The old tennis shoes were finally rotting away, and she discarded the soles and the few strings that still held them together and continued barefoot. She soaked her cut and bleeding feet at the first stream she crossed. There she found more food, and rested until she was able to continue.

Limping, stumbling, and near the end of her endurance, she sensed a wall in front of her, and made her way to it. It was made of bricks! The first manmade substance she had known since leaving the stairs. Clint would have to believe her now! She felt her way along the wall and finally, hands pulling on her hair, sank to her knees. It was a dead end. The wall was solid.

She rested awhile, then scavenged the tunnel floor on all fours until she found a pointed rock. Chipping away at the old mortar proved to be a tremendous task, but she kept at it consistently, resting when she was too tired to go on, and taking trips back to the stream for fresh food and water. There was no sound except her own raspy breathing, no word from Clint. She knew that she was quite lost in the underground maze, that her bearings were so far off she might never again find either the Home Cavern or the stairs. This wall was her only hope. There must be something behind it.

She worked at the cement, chipping an inch at a time, until she had loosened one whole brick. With bleeding fingers she worked the brick loose from its slot and pulled it out. Half fearing what she would find, she reached her hand in the hole and felt . . . more bricks.

A double wall. Her soul wilted. Would she never get used to disappointment? She summoned courage and patience and kept going. Eventually she had worked an opening that was five bricks wide and seven bricks high. She began scraping at the mortar of the inner wall.

The second wall of bricks was not as solid, and by putting her foot in the opening and bracing her back, she could make the whole structure give a bit as she pushed.

She worked one brick until it became loose. She pushed it with her hand, then her foot, until it gave way and fell in. Holding her breath, she listened. Nothing. Then a splash, way, way below, and the nauseating stench of mold, must, and rotting stuff wafted through the hole.

It was an old well, and where there was a well, there was access from above. Overcoming her sickness, she doubled her efforts to push out the inner wall. With one brick gone, the wall crumbled fairly easily. Soon she had an opening big enough to crawl through.

The effort was exhausting. She sat back and rested while her mind raced ahead. Here is a way out for all of us! She thought of Jackie, and called him. Instantly, he was there. He looked in the hole, and pulled his head back in revulsion. "This place is diseased. You can't crawl up there. The well has been closed up for years. I'm sure the top has been sealed."

"I can do it. I've got to get Clint out of here."

"You *can't* do it. Look at you. You're skin and bones and half dead. Do you know how you'd get up there, with no rope? And once you got to the top, then what? How are you going to open the lid? Forget it, Sally Ann."

"I *can* do it and I *will* do it and I don't need you telling me I can't. Now you can help me or you can go away."

"I won't help you kill yourself. How fast have you been losing your teeth?" Her hand went to her mouth, to the sore gums and the holes she tried not to think about. "Come on, we can find our way back to the Home Cavern."

"And do what? Rot? Have you ever thought what will happen to Clint after I get old and die? No, Jackie, this is our only way out."

"What's the difference, Sally Ann? You can die here, or you can die in that hole."

She took his arm and looked into his eyes. He looked so sad. "Jackie, we can get out of here. All of us . . ."

"Not me, Sally Ann. I can't go. I don't know why, but when you don't need me anymore, I think I'm going away."

"Well, I certainly don't need you now!" She was instantly sorry she had said that, and had time only to see the hurt flash through Jackie's eyes before he faded away. "Jackie? Come back. I do need you . . . Jackie!" But he was gone. She curled up in the corner by her pile of bricks and cried herself to sleep.

6

She took her time preparing for the journey. A plan was carefully followed and executed. She was determined to succeed. She began by eating all she could find. Each time she ate, she stuffed herself until repelled by the thought of another bite. She licked salt from the wall until tears came to her eyes, ignoring the stinging in her mouth, then drank her fill from the fresh water in the stream. She even fearlessly fished for crayfish, and ate them eagerly. She continually called out for Clint to come join her, but there was never a reply. She didn't venture out farther than the stream for fear of losing her way back to the well, but her voice carried, and was so loud to her ears that she was certain he heard her. Each time the echoes rang hollowly back to her, the ache in her stomach rang with them.

She slept on a bed of moss that her body heat eventually made dry enough to be pliable. She shredded it, braided it back together, and wove a bag that she could sling over her shoulder to carry supplies, but she couldn't make a rope strong enough to be of any use. She braided another bundle of moss to weave a kind of shirt, since her clothes were long gone and the air from the well was decidedly cool. She made a snug-fitting pair of booties and wound some more moss around her elbows and hands.

Finally, she took a deep breath and stood. She was ready. She grabbed a handful of pebbles and put her head through the wall. She threw a pebble to the opposite wall and found it to be only about three feet away. She threw a stone straight up, but could not tell by the sound whether it was bouncing off the lid or off the side. The stones fell a long way before they splashed. She pulled her head out of the opening and gave one last shout to Clint. "I'm going into the well now, Clint. I'll bring your dad back."

Feet first, she entered the hole and felt for the other side. The sharp bricks bruised and cut her ribs before her feet found a purchase on the opposite wall. She walked her toes down until she could slide her torso through the opening and rest her back just below the hole. Slowly, moving her feet sideways, then inching her back around, she revolved around the inside of the well so as to miss the opening on her climb up the shaft. Already she knew she was in for an endurance test the likes of which she had never encountered. Her straining back muscles screamed, and she rested, willing herself to relax, placing the weight on her straightened legs and her toes.

With her arms straight out to her sides, the weight of her whole body was on her toes and her back. She was able to give her back some relief by raising herself up on her hands a little. The rough surface of the well wall helped. She was afraid her shoulders or elbows might give way, though, so this was only a momentary respite.

Up and up, through the vertical tunnel that had no ending and no beginning, she focused her mind on freedom and light and laughter in the sunshine and willed her bruised and torn back to go just one more inch, then one more, and another after that. She ate from her store and rested often, afraid of falling asleep, afraid of not falling asleep. Eventually she had blackout periods where she lost consciousness, and she was sure it was her mind insisting on the sleep she was denying it. Each time she awakened, her knees were locked tight and secure, but it was still startling, and her heart pounded.

Except for the loosened chunks of mortar and dirt splashing in the water far below, the only sound in the well was her echoed breathing. Now and then she heard a soft scuttling noise, but she refused to let her mind dwell on what might be making such a sound. She finally removed the moss shirt she had made when the moss became imbedded in the lacerations on her back. This exertion was enough to make her pant for breath and stay still until the dizziness left her. She put what was left of the bloody moss into her bag and continued her ascent after her head had cleared.

Feeling faint and frail, she stopped and considered going back to the tunnel, but she wasn't sure how far she had come, nor was she sure how far she had to go. The blackness was absolute. Going down would be as bad as going up, she reasoned, so she might as well make for the top. Giving up would be the same either way. Archaeologists would either find her bones wedged in the well shaft like a prop, or they would find them at the bottom. She felt the rough brick biting into her shoulders as she continued, and whispered a little prayer that thundered in the silence. Time for a rest. Just a little sleep. She knew she was in danger of hallucinating from lack of sleep and that her mind wasn't functioning clearly, so she wedged herself in very tightly and planned to rest there for a while. Sleep came quickly.

When she awoke, there were insects crawling over her legs. She screamed and brushed at her legs with her shoulder bag. "Oh, God! Get them off of me!" Cockroaches. They were two inches long, attracted by the smell of the rotting slugs in her bag and the blood and raw flesh of her feet and back. At her violent movements they scurried away—to wait. She suppressed the bile rising in her throat, and knew that if she allowed herself to be surprised like that again, she would be likely to fall. Then the venomous little beasts could feast.

She began again her torturous climb. Below her she could hear scrapings, but dared not think about their significance. She had to concentrate. As she moved upward inch by agonizing inch, she felt close to losing all. This was a foolish venture, and now she would die and it would all be for nothing.

"Mommy?"

"Oh, Jesus." More of a groan than words, she cursed the obsession that kept Clint foremost in her mind. She was surely hallucinating.

"Mommy, are you up there?"

"Clint!" The cry came from the depths of her soul. "Clint. I'm going to get us out of here." As she spoke, her voice reverberated around the walls of her circular cell, but she noticed a new dimension in the echoes, a flat sound from above. She was near the top! "Clint! I'm almost out! I'll come back and bring your daddy to get you out. Stay there."

The small voice came from far below. Much farther than she believed she could have come.

"Mommy, come back. Don't leave me here alone. You don't need to go, Mommy. The darkness loves us."

Darkness? How could he talk of darkness? Pieces of thoughts, concepts swirled through her fevered brain. How could he talk of darkness when he knew nothing else? There is only darkness when there is light to compare it with. Does he believe, then? Exhausted, she could talk no longer. "Wait there for me, Clint."

She rested for a while before continuing. Knowing she was near the top gave her added strength, but even when the spirit is renewed, the flesh needs sustenance. She knew from the odor that the food in her bag was no longer edible. She ripped the moss armband from her elbow and chewed on it. She managed to swallow a couple of mouthfuls before continuing. She also knew she was losing a fair amount of blood. It mixed with her sweat and trickled down her back. She couldn't quit now. Her baby depended on her.

She persevered, eyes closed, up the wall which was growing continually warmer. She kept going until she heard her breath echo off the lid; then she raised her hands and felt it. Wooden. Old. Cracked in the middle and split along one side. She braced her poor toes against the far wall and pushed with one arm. The bricks ripped freshly into the skin on her shoulders, but the wood gave a little bit. Encouraged, and blinded to the pain by the relief she saw in store, she heaved with all she had. One leg slipped off the wall, and for one precious moment, one heart-stopping second, she hung suspended, held only by one toe and one shoulder. Holding her breath, she inched her other leg up to join the first one, the muscles groaning and stiff, and soon she again had both feet on the wall. The blood rushed through her veins with a maddening roar. She rested.

Try again, she encouraged herself. She found one crack with the tips of her fingers and felt its length, looking for an opening large enough to accommodate her hand. Almost, but not quite. The second crack was a little bit wider, and by sacrificing the skin from her knuckles, she could get her fingers all the way through. She pulled, then pushed, and felt, then heard, the old wood splinter. Carefully, so she would not lose her precarious balance, she wiggled the board back and forth until it came loose, and she dropped it to the water below.

The opening was now about four inches wide and a foot and a half long. She inched her way up and reached through the hole; she felt nothing. She loosened the next board and it came away more easily; now a full half of the opening was uncovered. The remaining half of the cover was loose, and she wrestled with it, afraid it would fall on her on its way past. Successful, she heard it bounce and scrape its way to the bottom, for a final splash. The opening was now clear. So why wasn't there fresh air to breathe?

Part Two

1

Michael strode up the porch steps and into the kitchen, the screen door slamming behind him. He kissed his wife on the side of the neck, then pulled a cold beer from the refrigerator and sat at the kitchen table before opening it. She was a lovely girl, Maggie. A little plumper than the day they had married, but her face was just as pleasant and her disposition just as cheerful. She had passed that precious quality on to their children, too, both in their natural demeanor and in their attitudes. He loved her very much.

Maggie dried her hands on her apron, poured herself a glass of fresh lemonade, and sat at the table with him. The kids were not yet home from school, and these midafternoon talks with just the two of them at the kitchen table had become a daily ritual, one they both enjoyed. She looked at him closely. The years were wearing on him well. The lines etched deeply in his skin gave his face character. Tanned and rough, with a generous sprinkling of gray in his hair, he was more handsome now than ever before. Put a suit on him and he'd look the picture of a successful executive. She smiled. He was a farmer, though, and she liked that.

"I went to see your mom today," he said.

"How is she?" Michael had always felt closer to Maggie's parents than she had, and he visited Cora often since her husband had died of a stroke two years ago in the fields.

"She's good. She sent her love to you and the kids. She also sent some peaches she put up last season. They're in the truck."

Michael wished Maggie would pay more attention to her mother but didn't press the issue. He knew the problem. He sipped his beer.

Maggie stared into her glass. "I thought I'd drive her into town tomorrow. Maybe we could go shopping or something." Michael worked hard to suppress his surprise and pleasure. He didn't want to overdo it, but to have his wife and her mother together on a social basis was more than he could have wished for. It was, in fact, an answer to his prayers.

"I think that's a fine idea. Why don't you pick up some more yarn and knit me another of those sweaters? The winter is coming, and I've worn holes in the elbows of my favorite."

"What color would you like?"

"I don't know. Do you think red would make me sexy?"

She laughed and got up. "You don't need no help." She shooed him out of the kitchen and went back to fixing dinner.

2

"Momma? Sit down here a minute, would you, please? I've got something on my mind that I think needs put to rest." Maggie was in her mother's kitchen for the first time in a year. The table was piled high with their purchases from town, including some new red wool for Michael's sweater and a bolt of Pendleton blue plaid for the kids' winter clothes. She knew Michael would laugh when he saw she'd bought a whole bolt of it, like he did when she bought a whole bolt of red and white checkered cloth from the Sears, Roebuck catalog. But it had made a tablecloth, kitchen draperies, several aprons, towels, and dresses for the girls. He had liked the effect, even though it was all the same. Economy, she had told him, and he'd given her a kiss.

Cora sat across the table from her, a pot of steeping tea between them. She moved the packages aside and looked at her daughter.

"Yes, I believe it's time whatever is between us was laid to rest, Maggie." She poured the tea and waited.

"Momma, I've prayed long and hard about this, and I think I'm at fault. I'm feeling guilty, and have been laying it on you and Papa. Ever since Michael and I . . ."

"Hush, child. There's no reason to go over all that again."

"I can't hush, Momma. I've got to talk this out, and I've got to do it now, in order to cleanse myself and be rid of this feeling."

Cora sipped her tea and listened. Maggie always was a strong-willed girl. She waited.

"I guess I always thought it was wrong when Michael and me started loving one another, so soon after Sally Ann died. And then we went against Papa's wishes and yours and went ahead and lived together before she could be pronounced dead, and that bothered me a tremendous lot. That's why we went off and got married without you and Papa there. I was pregnant with Justin, and I was angry that we had to sneak around with our love for so long out of respect for Sally Ann's memory. When she just up and took off. Or whatever.

"But you have to know, Momma, it was all my doing. Michael loves you as well as he loved his own folks, and he was against getting married without your blessings. But, Momma . . ." The tears began to spill over her eyelids. "I was so tired of having to deal with Sally Ann. I had to deal with her all my life, because she was older, and slimmer, and prettier, and she married Michael, and I was always so jealous. And then Michael loved me when she took off, and she didn't deserve him and I did, but still I had to live in her shadow for seven long years. It was hard, Momma, and it went against my grain, and I always felt you and Papa were disappointed in me for not respecting Sally Ann's memory like you taught me to." The tears were coming faster, and the sobs broke from her chest.

"I'm a good wife, Momma. And a good mother. Our kids are bright and nice and Michael and I love each other so much . . . and I love you too, Momma, and I want us to be friends."

She looked up and saw silent tears on Cora's face. Neither spoke for a long time. Maggie felt the knot in the pit of her stomach ease up for the first time in all these years, and love for her mother and sorrow for the missed chances in their relationship coursed through her. The pent-up flood of tears broke and she put her forehead on her arms and cried. Cora came around and sat beside her.

"Maggie. I know you're a good wife and mother. I've got eyes. So did your papa. And we could see the way you and Michael looked at each other. There are no more perfect grandchildren in the whole world than the ones you've given us. What happened with your sister is over and done with now. Only God knows her fate, and it was God that brought you and Michael together right here under our roof. We've always loved you, and always prayed that you'd come back to us. God bless you, child. You've lived with a burden that wasn't necessarily yours to bear. Come now. Drink your tea."

Maggie looked up and smiled at her mother. And soon they were both laughing. Laughing with a joy of togetherness that they had never known.

3

Life sure is good, Michael thought to himself as he loaded the last of the calves on the back of the truck. He jumped in the cab, started the engine, and with a final wave to Maggie, set off to the city, where the calves would bring a nice price on the auction block. He always enjoyed this yearly three-day trip away from the farm. It gave him some time to think, to miss the family, to see some new sights, to get a taste of the other side of life. It always renewed his appreciation for what he had.

As he turned onto the main highway, his thoughts automatically went to Sally Ann. His first trip to market was one week after she had left, and she was the topic of conversation all the way in and all the way home with his father-in-law. He never seemed to be able to drive this way without trying to figure out why she had left, or where she had gone. It was so long ago, but still the mystery remained. He couldn't bear to consider that she had been killed, or kidnapped. He preferred, no matter how much it hurt, to think she had left him and was living a happy and comfortable life.

Oh, Sally Ann, how I loved you. I hope you are well. With that, he turned his thoughts to the load of beef on the back of his truck.

Maggie watched the truck disappear down the highway and returned to the kitchen where tubs of plump blueberries were to capture her attention for the rest of the day. She got the recipe file from the shelf and pulled cards for jam, jelly, and Michael's favorite compote. She called to Justin to get out of bed and help her bring in the cases of jars from the barn, then rousted the twins to wash their hands, then wash the blueberries. Time they learned how to get their hands all purple, too.

She was holding the door for Justin as he brought in the last case of jars when the phone rang.

"Maggie?"

"Hello, Momma."

"Maggie, has Michael left for market yet?"

"About a half hour ago, why?"

"Well, there's a noise going on over here that's starting to concern me and I was hoping I could catch him before he left. I'd like to find out what's wrong. I sure hope it isn't the water heater again, but I'm afraid it is, and it's been going on for a couple of days now."

"Justin and I can come over before we start the blueberries, Momma."

"No . . . I hate to bother you."

"No bother, Momma. We'll be right over."

Maggie hung up and wished she hadn't volunteered. Most likely it wasn't anything they could do anything about anyway, but it might set her mother's mind at ease.

"C'mon, Justin. We're going over to Grandma's for a few minutes." The girls squealed with delight. "You two keep washing those blueberries. We won't be gone but a couple of minutes." They returned to their task with sullen faces.

Cora met them in the drive, and the three went behind the house to the water-heater shed.

"Now listen."

A faint tapping broke the stillness, erratic but high-pitched, metal on metal.

"The sound's comin' from over there," Justin said. They all turned to where he pointed, and saw nothing but the neighboring field and the old well cover that stuck up about two feet from the ground. Justin walked toward the well cover, but the sound had stopped.

"It was louder yesterday," Cora said. "I just can't for the life of me figure what it might be."

Justin stopped in front of the old well. "What's this, Grandma?"

"Just an old well, Justin. It went dry years ago and your Grandpa put that cover on it to keep you young'uns from falling in and killing yourselves. There isn't anything down there."

He walked over to it and knocked on the domed iron lid. It rang solid. A moment later, the tapping began, furiously.

"It *is* coming from here! Listen!" They all heard it.

Justin examined the bolts that held the lid on. "I'm going to get the crowbar and get this lid off here, Momma. There's something in there that wants out."

The two women looked at each other.

An hour later, the last bolt broke. Cora stepped back out of the way while Maggie went to help her son slide the heavy lid off the well. A putrid odor assaulted them as the top grated open. They stopped, caught their breaths, and gave a final heave, and the lid slid off the opening and one edge fell to the ground.

"Good God!" Justin's hand covered his mouth. Maggie screamed and backed away. A moan escaped Sally Ann's black and swollen lips as she tried to shield her blind, jerking eyes with a forearm that had lost its muscular control. "Momma, help me!" Justin shouted. Maggie shook her head, eyes riveted on the apparition from the well, and backed farther away. "Grandma?" Cora moved in quickly and, fighting the reaction from the terrible smell, grabbed the thin brittle wrist and stilled its flailing about.

"Grab her ankles, Justin, and we'll ease her out of there." Sally Ann had wedged herself into a niche four inches high by three inches deep, between the cover and the top lip of the well. Working carefully, pulling gently, one leg at a time, the hips, then the shoulders were eased out. They set her down on the grass and Cora sent Justin for a bucket of cool water.

It was the body of a little girl, but it was as light as a paper bag. Breasts were sunken into the ribs, and the toes were worn down, leaving raw wounds on her feet. Strands of blond hair remained, but most of the head was bald and raw, and her shoulder bones were laid bare where the flesh had been scraped off. Eyes were sunk deep into their sockets and as Cora washed away the blood and grime from her face, the girl became semiconscious and started sucking the cloth. "Easy, girl. Not too much to drink at first." She removed the cloth, and immediately the girl tried to speak.

The swollen tongue wagged through toothless gums as clicking noises came gagging from deep in her throat. Cora turned to Justin who was gaping at the sight. "Justin, get your mother and cover up this hole, then help me get this poor thing into the house."

Maggie stepped forward. "No!"

Cora turned and looked up at her, a puzzled frown asking the question.

"She's come back to haunt me, Momma. It's Sally Ann, back from the grave!"

Cora looked down at the frail creature and she caught her breath. "Great Mother of God," she breathed quietly. She scooped the girl up in her arms and carried her into the cool house, the bent baby spoon still dangling from one finger.

4

After a brief knock on the door, Cora entered the room. "Are you awake?"

"Yes."

"I brought you some breakfast."

"I'm not very hungry."

"If you don't eat, girl, you won't be able to keep up your strength." Cora set the tray down on the dresser. "Here. At least have some toast."

Sally Ann sat up in bed and took the plate of wheat toast from her mother. "Thanks."

"And after you eat, I'll take another look at those toes. You should be up and walking about now. That'll bring back your appetite."

"I want to see Michael."

Cora sighed. She drew up a chair from the desk and sat down. "I guess it's time we talked the truth to each other, Sally Ann. Michael doesn't know you're here."

"Well, tell him. I'm well enough to see him now."

"It isn't that simple. You see, when you disappeared, Michael mourned you for a long, long time. We all did. We didn't know if you'd run off or been kidnapped or what. But there was never any word, and so we finally had to get over it and get on with living our lives. I know your Papa prayed for you every day of his life. And Michael . . . well, he had to get on with his life, too. Once you were declared dead, he remarried. So now he has a family, and we don't want anything to interfere with his happiness."

"Any *thing?* You mean me! But if he waited so long, he can't have much of a family yet. Oh, Momma, the only thing that kept me going down there was thinking of Michael. I've really got to see him. I've got something to tell him."

"You've been gone a long time, Sally Ann. Michael and Maggie have four children . . ."

"Maggie? *Maggie?* Michael married Maggie?" Sally threw the covers off her legs and started to get up. "You've no right to keep me here. I want to see my husband."

Cora pushed her back to bed with one hand. Still so frail, she thought. "He's not your husband any longer, Sally Ann. He and Maggie have four children; did you hear me?"

Sally stopped struggling against her mother and lay her head back on the pillow. She closed her eyes, feeling faint from the exertion. She couldn't possibly have heard what she thought she heard.

"You've been gone twenty years, Sally Ann."

The room started spinning. She heard a voice from far off saying "Clinton! Wait for me, Clint." It was her own voice, but her head seemed stuffed with cotton. She felt a cool cloth on her forehead, and she waited until the buzzing in her ears died away. Twenty years. Twenty years of her life wasted in an underground hole. She was now thirty-six years old. And scarred and ugly and Michael was lost to her forever. Tears leaked out of the corners of her eyes and she reached for her mother's hand.

5

Cora was cleaning up the luncheon dishes in the kitchen while Sally Ann did her daily exercises on the living-room floor. Her body had healed well, and though the scarred skin was pulled taut over her back, the muscles were starting to come back. She had gained weight and walked with barely a trace of a limp. Her eyes had stopped that incessant jerking, and her sight was returning rapidly.

"Momma?"

"Yes, dear?"

The problem, as she viewed herself in the mirror, was the face. Her parchment skin showed blue veins as it clung to her bones. Over her sunken cheeks were patches of scaly skin that itched and turned red and white when she scratched them. Her head was still bald and scarred, even though the hair was growing back in spots. A scarf hid most of that. Her lips and what teeth were left were black as tar. She looked like a living skull.

She thought constantly of Clint—she missed him almost more than she could bear—but there were things she needed to do before she could go back to him. He would be all right. He was in his element, he was twenty years old, and—the darkness loved him.

"I want to go to town."

"I think that's a very good idea if you're feeling up to it."

"I want to see the dentist."

Cora stood in the doorway and dried her hands on a dish towel. Sally Ann looked up at her and said, "Don't worry. I'll use a fake name."

Pain crossed Cora's face, and she turned and went back to the kitchen. It is so unfair, Sally thought. She was supposed to pick up the pieces of her life. But where was she to start, when her own family wouldn't even support her? Well, at least the situation was clear.

Cora walked to the bedroom and returned with a simple housedress that might fit Sally's slim frame.

"Here. Try this on and I'll call Dr. Green for an appointment."

The trip to town was traumatic for both of them. Cora didn't like lying to the doctor, and there wasn't much he could do about Sally Ann's teeth anyway. He filled two cavities, gave her a prescription for vitamins and calcium, and tried to get her to come back for dentures. Sally Ann knew he was trying to be kind, and he was more than curious about her appearance. She thanked him and they were on their way.

She bought a new pair of jeans, tennis shoes, socks, several T-shirts, and a jacket. Clothes felt so binding. She also bought a child's sweater, size ten, light blue and soft. Cora asked no questions. The worst of the trip was the way everyone stared. Cora introduced her as a friend from the city who had come to recuperate in the good country air, and people were nice, but they still stared. They stared at her face, her teeth, at the way she walked, and they kept their distance. By the time Cora and Sally got home, both were exhausted.

The next day, the inevitable happened. After two months, Michael finally came over, to ask about Cora's friend visiting from the city. He had heard from someone at church, and was hoping to get some information about a man he was working with on a land deal. Cora told him her friend was resting, and she was, but she was listening from the bedroom.

Michael's voice. Deeper now, but just as she remembered it. Could it hurt him all that much to see her? All these years of thinking of him, dreaming of him, wondering how he was faring. What did he look like? What had twenty years done to his face? To his body? Their voices were a murmur now; she assumed they had walked into the kitchen to talk, in order not to disturb Cora's resting friend.

Then he laughed. A hearty, resonant laugh, and her chest constricted with brutal force. What has he to laugh about? When was the last time I laughed? Oh, God, I want to laugh with him. Touch him. She got up from bed and put on her jeans and a T-shirt. She wrapped a scarf about her head quickly and put the tennis shoes over the bandages on her feet. She looked in the mirror and her heart fell. I can never let him see me like this. She opened the door a crack and peeked out.

He was standing by the front door, ready to leave, when he saw the door open. "I believe your friend is awake, Mom. Do you think she'd mind talking to me for a minute?"

Cora paled as she saw the door ajar. "Well, no, I suppose not, Michael. Let me ask her." She walked over to the door, knocked, and went in. *"What do you think you are doing?"* she hissed.

"Why no, I'd be delighted," Sally Ann said loudly and pushed past her mother and out the door. She walked directly to Michael who winced as he saw her, then quickly recovered with a smile.

"How do you do? I'm Michael Hixson. I understand you're visiting from the city, and I thought you might know of a man by the name of Ralph Lederer. I'm thinking of buying a piece of property that he owns next to my farm and wondered if you had any word of his reputation."

He didn't recognize her. She was lost for words. She was ready for his hurt, his anger, his denial, his love, his passing out and falling on the floor, but she was *not* ready for this! What to do? Should she say, hello, Michael, I'm Sally Ann and we have a son who is living in underground caverns like a bat? Should she throw her arms around him and kiss him and make him forget all about Maggie? Should she embarrass him and say, Michael, don't you even recognize your own wife when you see her? Should she sink to the floor and hug his knees and say how long she'd been dreaming of this moment?

She stared at him, then looked at her feet. "I don't know, Mr. Hixson. The name is not familiar."

"Well, okay. I appreciate your time. You look a little pale. Maybe I shouldn't have disturbed your rest."

"No, it's quite all right. Please excuse me." She returned to her room, shut the door, then leaned heavily against it.

After Michael left, Cora came into the room quietly and sat on the edge of the bed. Sally Ann was strangely quiet. The experiences Sally had gone through had prepared her in some ways for things Cora couldn't even dream about. "How about some lunch?"

Sally kept her gaze steady on the ceiling. "That would be nice, Momma."

6

Clint sat on the moss mattress and picked at it while he thought. He missed his mother. His eyes were swollen from crying, and his grief had given way to anger.

"I don't care." The sound of his voice in the Home Cavern was hollow, but comforting. He knew she had made it; he had stayed by the hole in the wall and listened. He heard other voices, and the hole was invaded by a powerful monster, a presence that pierced his brain and knocked him back into the tunnel. It hurt his head. It was like a dream he had when he slept, where images danced around and said silly things and "looked" a funny way. He still didn't understand "look," but that's what his mommy said. He lay there, frightened, until he heard the grating of the lid again and the monster was gone.

There really was an "up there." He had known it all along. He pretended he didn't believe, because he didn't want her to go. He didn't want to go. He liked it here. There were things to play with and it was comfortable. Up there was strange, and he didn't much like the stories she told.

"Why would she go there? What's up there that she needs? We have everything here. Why would she want to leave *me?*" Tears of anger again seeped out of his eyes, and he reached down to stroke himself, his only comfort. "I'd like to punish her when she gets back. Oh, yes." The pleasure was intense. "I'd like to hurt her like she hurt me." Faster. "I'll hit her and pinch her and knock her down." He thought he would burst. *"And she'll beg me."* His orgasm was violent, his whole body stiffened with the release.

Afterward, he felt happy and free. He went for a swim.

Every so often, he returned to the hole in the wall by the square rocks. She was never there. He felt lonely, he missed her, but he never really felt alone. The air of the tunnels, the familiar feel of the rocks under his feet, the cold ponds and their inhabitants were his companions. When he felt sad, or angry, he would think he had chased her away. Then he would stroke himself and feel better again. It gave him intense pleasure until he learned that cutting the fish was better. That was even more intense. He tortured them while they were still alive, and they flopped and writhed and slowly died.

He took all these fish and bundled them up in moss and carried them past the tunnel that led to the square rock wall to a different cavern, a cavern with a little pond on one side and a huge lake on the other side. He dumped them in the lake, far away from where the stench would bother him. These fish were dirty; he could not eat them.

But mostly, he waited. He sat in the dark, blind eyes staring into nothingness, thinking about his mother, choosing not to think about the light and the world above. He thought she would be back soon, and they would live forever in the caves. Together.

7

Sally diligently worked her body until it was fit. She swam in the old swimming hole she and Jackie used to frequent when they were children. She couldn't comprehend that she was now middle-aged, that Clint was twenty years old, that her life was thoroughly destroyed. She took long walks through the woods and the fields. The aged and worn boards that covered the stairs to the tunnel were still there, the lock and hinges rusted solid. She would sit with her back to the big trees and stare at the cover, thinking about time, about life, about fairness.

She'd seen Michael's children, too. Justin, about thirteen years old, strong, tall, looking much like his father. The twins, eleven years old, with thick red hair like Maggie's, turned-up noses and freckles; Ellen and Elsie. And Mary. Different from the rest. No more than four, she was small, thin, with hands and feet too big for her size and very, very shy. The children would swim in the pond as she watched, quietly hidden in the woods. She didn't want to frighten them, and she didn't want to have to answer any questions.

Cora was a good woman. They talked sometimes far into the night. But she could never understand. Sally Ann hadn't told her about Clint, because this was not his world. He didn't believe in it, and who was she to keep telling him that there was something better? She had survived with the dream that back with her family she would be happy again. She wanted a normal life for him. She wanted him to be surrounded by love and family and all the things she wanted for herself. But maybe none of that was to be for them. There was no happiness up here.

Her body was healed. She was gaining weight. Now she had some decisions to make.

Her mother encouraged her to get out and socialize, but the thought was frightening. She had nothing to say to anyone. Except Michael. She had plenty to say to him, and Maggie as well. But she wouldn't. There was no point. She sighed.

On the way back to the house, she saw Michael and Maggie's home on the hill where once her dream house was to have stood. The sun was going down and lights were on. It looked so homey, so comfortable. As if they had a will of their own, her feet took her closer to the house. She saw the barn off to the side. Michael kept it all painted up nice. The tractor looked fairly new; the grounds were neat, the trees tall and picturesque. Close enough now to see through the window, Sally Ann kept the big tree in the front yard between her and the kitchen window. When she reached it, she leaned against it and tried to talk sense into herself. "What are you hoping to accomplish by spying on them?" Her conscience would not let her alone.

The temptation however, ruled her actions, and she peered around the tree and into the kitchen. There was Maggie. Fat as always. She didn't want to see any more, but she couldn't help herself. She stood next to the tree, eyes riveted on the warm little scene inside, and she was fantasizing that she was the one in there, making dinner for the babies and loving them all. She was so caught up that she didn't hear Michael come up behind her until he spoke.

"Hello?"

Her face burned a bright red, and she was grateful for the fading light. "Oh, hello. I was, uh, just admiring your house."

He looked at her carefully. "You're Cora's friend, aren't you?"

"Yes. I was just out walking."

"It's getting late. I think you should be getting back." His face softened. "Can I give you a lift?"

"Oh, well . . ." She smiled. "If it wouldn't be too much of an inconvenience. I am rather tired."

"Not at all. Why don't you come in and meet my wife while I get the keys to the truck."

Sally Ann smiled inwardly. She felt devilish. She followed him to the door.

"Maggie? Honey, come meet a friend of your mom's. She was out walking and got a little too tired, so I'm going to give her a lift back." He turned to Sally. "I'll be back in a minute." He disappeared down the hall.

Maggie walked warily into the living room. Her tone was venomous. *"What in the hell are you doing here?"*

Sally Ann smiled. "Well, hello, Maggie. It's been a long time, hasn't it? You're looking well."

"Don't play cutsie with me, Sally Ann. If you tell Michael who you are, I'll finish ruining your ugly face."

Sally took a step toward her sister. "Maggie, I don't want to hurt anybody. I just want to make a life for myself."

"Then go make it somewhere else. You can't do it here, and you can't do it with us!" Maggie almost spit those last words, then turned on her heel and went back to the kitchen. Sally Ann sat down, put her face in her hands, and started to cry.

She felt Michael's hand on her shoulder. "Are you all right, Mrs. . . . Mrs. . . . uh, I don't even know your name—I'm sorry."

"SALLY ANN HIXSON!" she wanted to scream in his face. She looked up at the concern in his face and started to cry harder. "Can't . . ."

"Mrs. Cant? Maggie? Would you fetch a glass of water for Mrs. Cant, please?"

Sally Ann took the proffered glass of water and drank it down without looking at Maggie. She didn't need to see the hate that was written all over her face; she could feel it emanating from her whole being. "Thank you very much. I'm feeling better now. Maybe we'd better go."

She went straight to her room, past her mother sitting silently in the living room. The next morning she was gone.

8

"Clint? Clint. It's Mommy. I'm back." Sally Ann raced through the tunnel, holding tight to the wrist of the wailing child she was half dragging behind her. "Get up and walk or I'll leave you here!" The child cried louder, trying desperately to keep up, hiccuping fear. "Clint!"

Her sense of navigation came back in a rush. She knew exactly where she was going. The tunnels were her old friends. The smell, the roughness beneath her shoes, the blessed darkness, all meant she was home. And at home she would find peace.

She felt empathy for the child trailing behind her. The initial blindness was an awesome, frightening thing. They ran through the first tunnel that wound around, then approached the huge cavern with Monster Lake. She tried to hush up the girl before they entered, and succeeded in lowering her screams to a whimper. Sally tried to suppress the terrible constriction she felt in her stomach as they entered the cave. They crossed the path between the lakes as quickly and quietly as possible. As soon as they were back into the comfortable tunnels, they took off running again.

"Jackie?" But even as she called, she knew Jackie was gone forever. "Clint! Come see what Mommy has brought you." Out of breath, they slowed to a walk, and passed an auxiliary tunnel that had a dank and terrible smell to it. The well was at the end of this tunnel. She stopped and put her face up to Mary's. "Smell that?

You must never, never go near this place. The whole underworld is yours to play in, but you must return to the Home Cavern as soon as you get near that smell."

"I don't want to play here. Please. I'm scared. I want to go home."

"This is home for you now, Mary."

After an exhausted sleep, Mary was slightly more docile, and she followed Sally Ann as long as they kept contact with their hands. How flexible the young are, Sally thought. How adaptable. The sleep felt wonderful. She awoke refreshed and invigorated. Ready for a new day. It was so good to have your sleeping and eating regulated by the body rather than by the sun. She laughed and skipped along the main tunnel, teaching Mary how to quench her thirst by sucking the dripping water from the side of the tunnel.

Eventually, they reached Home Cavern, and Clint was there.

They hugged each other and cried together and she felt all over his whole body to make sure he was all right. Thin, perhaps, but that is the way of the underworld.

"I brought you some surprises, Clint. Some jam." She took the small jar out of her bag and handed it to him. She laughed at his puzzlement, took it back and opened it for him. He stuck his finger in and licked it.

"Ick. What's that taste?"

"Sugar, honey. You're supposed to like it."

"I don't like nothing from there."

"How about this?" and she handed him the sweater. "Here, I'll help you put it on."

"I don't much like this either." He kept running his hands over the soft wool. "What's making those noises?"

"That's your new sister, Mary. She's come to live with us and be your playmate."

"She doesn't sound so good."

"I was afraid like that when I first got here. Be nice to her. She'll learn the ways of our life soon."

Clint walked over to Mary. "Wanna swim?"

"I want to go home," she sniffed.

"She's dumb, Mommy."

"Give her time, honey."

While Mary slept, Sally Ann and Clint talked. He wasn't interested in hearing much about the time she'd spent "in the sun," but she did tell him that some people would probably come into the tunnels to look for them. "Can we find a place to hide for a while, Clint?"

"Sure. I've found some places that nobody else could find."

Sally sensed a change in Clint. He seemed older. Distant. Maybe it was because she knew that he was twenty years old, instead of thinking he was only about eight. Maybe being on his own for a couple of months had matured him.

After sleep they started. They dumped the jam into the lake and filled the jar with food. That went into her bag along with the extra T-shirts she had brought and some moss. Mary was a problem, but Sally Ann had expected it and was prepared. Clint tried to emulate her patience, but it was hard for him. He was so swift in the tunnels.

Clint led them down a series of side tunnels that were barely big enough to crawl through in some places. Up and down they went, following his lead.

Finally, one tunnel came to a dead end at a lake and they had to swim underwater to find the opening on the other side. This was nearly an impossible task for Mary, but the fact that she was so small and light helped a lot; they virtually held her breath for her and pulled her under and through the tunnel entrance.

The other side was a perfect space. It was dry and warm, with a deep swimming hole in the middle, and a brisk stream running down one side. The new Home Cavern.

Sally set up housekeeping, making beds, preparing a toilet, continually keeping her ears open for invaders. They came, but she never heard them.

Part Three

1

Sally Ann and Mary sat on the side of the swimming hole, their feet dangling in the water. The children were playing loudly in the pool, splashing and laughing. Clint was throwing them high into the air and they begged for turns over and over again. He was a good father.

"I'm going to go away for a while, Mary. I have some unfinished business to take care of."

Mary grabbed her hand. "Are you going up there? Can I go and take the boys? Can Clint go? Can we all go with you, Sally? Oh, please?"

"You know Clint and the children can never leave this place, Mary. And your place is here with them. This is your home now. I'll be back. I won't be gone long."

"I wish you wouldn't go."

"I know, dear. I'll be back before you miss me. Time passes quickly down here."

Clint had nothing to say when she told him. His silence spoke of his disapproval. She packed some gear and left without further discussion.

The door at the top of the stairs was open, as she expected. She knew Michael would leave it that way in case any of them cared to return. She spent two days at the bottom of the stairs, getting used to the light, then ventured up. It was hot.

How do I look now, she wondered. She skirted the woods and made her way to her mother's house. Strengthening her resolve, she knocked on the kitchen door. Her mother looked dully out at her.

"You've come back."

"Yes. Momma."

"Well, come in and clean up."

Not exactly a rousing welcome, but about what she had expected. After all, she had kidnapped Michael's youngest daughter and given her a life in the caverns. Not an act to endear her to the family.

After she showered, she put on the clean housedress her mother had laid out. She examined herself in the mirror. Her face looked about the same. A few more lines around the mouth and eyes, maybe. Somehow she didn't feel nearly as monstrous as she had the last time she was here. The smell of bacon frying came through from the kitchen. She joined her mother, wordlessly set the table, then sat down and waited.

"How's Mary?"

"She's fine. She's happy, Momma."

Her mother turned with fury in her eyes. "Don't you dare talk of happiness to me. You. Living under the earth like a worm. Destroying all that Michael and Maggie had by taking their little girl like you did. You're Satan himself."

Sally Ann endured her mother's venom. She knew it had to come out sooner or later, and was glad Cora could get it off her chest so soon. She stood up and put her arms around her mother as she stood at the stove. She felt the silent sobs shake her frail frame. Her mother had grown old. Very old.

"Oh, Sally Ann, why have you come back again? Just when a hurt has healed, you come back to pick it open again. Why do you do that?"

"I've come to see Michael."

"I guess I knew that the moment I saw you at the door. Well, there's the phone. Get it over with."

The number was written on a list Cora kept on the wall. Sally dialed the number slowly, praying that Maggie wouldn't answer the phone. She did.

"Hello?"

"Hello, Maggie. This is Sally Ann. May I speak to Michael, please?"

The phone bounced on the floor, and Sally Ann visualized Maggie's open-mouthed shock. The idea gave her distinct pleasure.

"Hello? Hello, who's this?" Michael asked.

"Hello, Michael. This is Sally Ann. Would you come to breakfast at Mother's this morning?"

"Oh, my God . . ." The phone went dead.

Sally smiled, slowly hanging up the phone. "He'll be right over, Momma." Cora left the room. Sally heard the bedroom door close.

Michael pulled up to the front door in a cloud of dust, got out of the truck, and walked up the front steps. He paused for a deep breath, then opened the screen door and came in. "Sally Ann?"

"In the kitchen, Michael."

He came in and sat down at the kitchen table. He was visibly trying to keep himself under control. "Where's Mary, Sally Ann?"

She turned to look at him and he took in the black teeth, the scaly, thin skin, the ragged hair, and the arms so thin they were like little sticks. All his anger disappeared.

"I came back to tell you that you have three grandchildren." His mouth fell open and he stared at her. "Three beautiful children, Michael. They play in the water and laugh and love. And they don't believe in you."

A new type of anger held him to his seat. The thought of three children in caves. What kind of a monster was this woman? Then he thought of Mary. Sweet Mary. Like a flower. She survived down there? But . . . who was the father? He laughed. "You're insane, Sally. There's no children. There's just you and your twisted ways. I knew Mary. She was too fragile. She could never have survived down there."

"You're wrong, Michael, *I* survived. And your *son* survived." Shock froze his face.

"My son?"

"Yes. *Our* son. And now he and Mary have three children. I'm sorry I don't have pictures of them for you."

He jumped up and grabbed her skull and started to squeeze. He could feel her thin, brittle bones, and he just wanted to pop her head like a melon. "You monster! I'll kill you for this!" His rage was born of fear, and didn't last. His hands slipped from her head to rest on her shoulders, and he started to cry. She put a comforting hand on his face.

"It's not so bad, Michael. They're really very happy. It's a whole different type of existence down there, but it's not a bad life."

"We looked for you," he sobbed. "We searched for weeks. There are so damned many tunnels down there. We all got sick. We couldn't believe that anybody could live down there. Oh, Sally Ann." He sank to the floor and hugged her legs. "My soul ached to think you have been down there all those years. All those years I had given you up for dead. I locked you down there that day and didn't know it. And I've lived with that guilt ever since."

She stroked his hair. "It's okay, Michael. I thought it wasn't, but it is now. Everything is all right. Our son is a good man, and he's a good father to the boys and a good husband to Mary."

"When Mary was missing and Maggie told me it was you staying here with Mom, I didn't believe her. I hit her. She makes me so angry sometimes. But I had to believe her when your Mom said the same thing, and the lock was broken off the door to the stairs. Our life hasn't been the same since." Sally Ann smiled slowly above his head. "How could you . . . ? How did you raise a child down there?"

"One has to do what one has to do, Michael. His name is Clinton."

"My God. Will you take me to see them?"

"Of course, Michael. You won't be able to really see them, it's too dark. But I'll take you to them, if you like."

Cora paled when Sally told her what had happened. "You can't take Michael down there!"

"I can and I will. Besides, he wants to go. He wants to see his son."

Cora looked at her in horror, then turned to her closet. She put on a jacket and scarf. "Where are you going, Momma?"

"To church."

2

Sally Ann laughed when she saw what Michael brought with him. A whole backpack, with sleeping bag, food, fresh clothes, and flashlights. "No flashlights," she said.

"I can't go down there without a flashlight."

"If you take a light, you go alone." He saw the resolve in her grotesque face. Reluctantly, he left them behind.

They descended. She breathed the familiar air of the main tunnel. Refreshing. She urged Michael to walk faster, but he was unaccustomed to walking in the dark so their progress was stumbling and slow. "At this rate, it will take us a month to get to them." He didn't think that was very funny, but Sally laughed. He was amazed at her ability to navigate.

When they reached Monster Lake, Sally told him of the beast that lived in the waters to the left of the path. They rested near the entrance, and when Sally made a meal of the slugs they found on the floor, Michael found this practice so revolting that he quite lost his appetite. She laughed at this, too. "You'll be eating them soon enough." He didn't believe that a monster lived in the lake and told her so. "Take a swim in there, then, if you don't believe." The thought of swimming in total darkness made his flesh crawl.

He found his backpack cumbersome, and Sally was quickly losing patience with his slow pace. In fact, she was not as thrilled to be with him as she had imagined she would be. He was foreign here. This was not his element. He didn't belong. Well, she would take him to see his children and grandchildren, and then he could go back.

They tiptoed through Monster Cavern, then resumed their normal slow pace. Sally found the temptation to leave him when he was sleeping deliciously irresistible. He would wake up and find himself alone. The panic in his voice as he shouted for her was comforting. Then she would return to him and he was so glad to have her back. At last she was needed. Clint had needed her, but that was different. This was Michael, the man she had needed for a long, long time. And now he needed her. Not for companionship, but for basic survival. She loved it.

They stopped frequently and slept. She convinced him that there were tunnels too small to take the pack into, so he agreed to leave it, taking with him only his essentials—sandwiches. Along the way she told him stories of Clint and his growing up and what a delight he was. He shared with her stories of his children.

Justin, he said, was in the air force, thinking about making a career of it. The twins had been modeling and making television ads for some time. He spoke of his marriage to Maggie, how it had come about, how her father had died, the relationship between Cora and Maggie. She encouraged him to talk; it made her realize how little she missed that world. In fact, she was glad she was back where she was comfortable.

As they passed the tunnel with the dank smell, she told him of her grueling trip up the well shaft, adding bits here and there about how much she had missed him. He was horrified. She was glad.

They reached the first Home Cavern and she showed him where she had given birth, where for twenty years they had had their home. He was beginning to have an appreciation for her strength, her courage. She could feel it, and he made little comments alluding to the fact that he had no idea . . . Of course he had no idea. What a fool he was. She impressed upon him the number of smaller tunnels, some dead ends, some leading to huge caverns with hundred-foot drop-offs, the dangers of wandering without knowing where you were going. He insisted he would stick close to her.

She felt a growing surge of power in this relationship. The tables had indeed turned and she was enjoying every minute of it. She toyed with the idea of just leaving him and letting him find for himself the overpowering fear. Let him discover his own inner strength, she told herself with contempt. It takes no balls to ride a tractor. Was this the man she had pined for during more than thirty years in the underworld? This was her God, this weak man who carried peanut-butter sandwiches with him and whined when she wasn't by his side when he awoke? She must have been insane.

They continued through tunnels barely large enough for Michael's muscular body, up and down shafts, eating when hungry, resting when tired. They finally reached the lake, and the underwater doorway to Home Cavern.

At the large lake, they camped. Michael didn't know that his children and grandchildren were so close, just on the other side of the wall. No sounds escaped the underwater entrance. Suddenly she didn't want Michael to see them. She wanted to keep him under her control. She realized that he might want to take her babies back with him, and that was out of the question. She prayed Clint or Mary or one of the boys wouldn't come out this way while they were there.

"Tell me, Michael. Does Maggie know you're with me?"

"Oh, yes. She didn't like it, but then she doesn't like much anymore. I didn't tell her about Clinton. I told her you were taking me to see Mary."

"I see." Sally Ann grinned in the darkness. A plan was taking form in her mind.

3

After sleeping three or four times, Michael was anxious to get under way. Sally Ann delayed their departure as long as she dared, then led him down a tunnel, far away from the Home Cavern where the children played. She remembered from long ago another cavern, much like the one Michael expected, and she took him there. It took them a long time. She doubled back down different tunnels, and frequently he would ask, "Didn't we come this way?" and she would laugh at him and call him foolish. She enjoyed the power she held over him. It was time he learned something.

Finally, they stopped just outside the cavern. Sally Ann talked to Michael in a low voice, as if the others could hear. "Michael. They're not used to anybody else, you know. Clinton doesn't even believe in you, so he won't let the boys believe in you, either. Mary has been here a long time, and she's not sure who to believe, so don't expect a major welcome. This is their territory, you know, and you're an intruder. They may even ignore you, or tell you to go away. But they're flexible. They'll get used to you."

How well he knew what an intruder he was. She had made him feel very uncomfortable since the beginning of this damned journey, and he was now sorry he had ever agreed to come. He was totally at her mercy, and he didn't like that at all. She seemed a little crazed. "I'll be all right. Let's go."

They turned the corner and Sally Ann went dancing into the cavern. "Clinton! We're home! Mary? Boys? Come see the surprise I've brought." Silence reverberated in the huge room.

"There's no one here, Sally."

"Oh, they're probably just busy. Or maybe they're hiding. They'll come back soon."

They sat down to wait. Sally fidgeted, as her mind raced. They didn't wait long. "Here they are, Michael." She got up and ran to the back of the cavern. "Hello, Clint. And Mary. How are you? I told you I wouldn't be gone long. Come say hello to your daddy." Michael was silent at the entrance to the cavern.

"There's nobody here, Sally."

"Nonsense, Michael. Here they are, right here. Clint, shake hands with your dad. Mary, where are the boys? Oh, here they are. Hello, fellas. My, you've grown, just in the short time I've been away. Michael, meet little Jimmy and Jerry and this is Jonah. Aren't they sweet?" She worked hard to keep up the chatter in the empty cavern.

"Sally, stop it!" His voice echoed in the cavern.

"Why, Michael? What's the matter?"

His breath stuck in his throat. She was insane. She talked such a good story that she had duped him into coming into this hellhole, and now he was stuck down here with a madwoman. He turned and darted down the tunnel.

"Michael, wait!" She could hardly suppress the giggles that seemed to have overtaken her. Whatever had gotten into her to do such a thing to him? She followed him out, her tennis shoes silent on the tunnel floor. "Michael," she called out musically to him. "You'll never make it out of here aloooone." She heard his footsteps echoing in the distance. She skipped along gaily behind him. She would be sure he wouldn't get lost. But a good scare never hurt anyone, either.

She was surprised at the way he circumvented her roundabout path. He seemed to know where he was going and didn't get lost in the maze of tunnels and tributaries. He crawled through the smaller tunnels with amazing speed, and this gave her great amusement. All the way back she teased and tantalized him with bits and pieces of her thoughts. Always out of reach, her voice echoed around him. He remained steadfastly silent.

When he stopped to sleep, she would sneak around him and wake him with great peals of echoing laughter, eerie in the pressing darkness. The low curses he muttered to himself tickled her even more. What had gotten into her that she would act this way? No matter. He was close to the stairs now. They passed the well tunnel and she hollered ahead to him, "Michael. Cockroaches almost ate me in there while I was coming to you. Doesn't that make you hungry, Michael? Have some slugs, Michael," and her insane giggles echoed through the night.

When he'd had enough, he stopped short and hid quietly in a turn of the tunnel. When she skipped past him, he reached out and grabbed her. "Sally Ann. Am I

on the right way out of here?" She laughed. "Tell me."
He shook her until she felt her eyes rattle in her head.

"Oh, Michael. Don't be a spoilsport. Of course
you're on the right way. I wouldn't let my little baby,
the love of my life, get lost in these dark, dirty tunnels,
now, would I?" He threw her to the side and continued
on, weak from hunger, heartsick and tired. He entered
Monster Cavern. She followed, making monster noises,
taunting him, wearing him down.

"Come here, Sally Ann." His voice was calm, quiet.

"No. You'll hurt me. You'll feed me to the monster."

"Don't be a petulant child. Come here. I want to talk
to you." He was sitting on a rock at the edge of the lake.
She heard him pick up a handful of pebbles and start
throwing them into the water. They landed with little
plops. "Sally Ann, I want you to come back with me.
They have places for people who need help readjusting
to a new environment. I'll pay for it, and you'll like it
there. There's no reason for you to stay down here
and . . ."

"And ROT?" She shouted in his ear, surprising him.
He stood up quickly, and his foot slipped on the rock.
Arms waving wildly, he couldn't regain his balance, and
he fell backward into the water. Sally Ann sobered
immediately and went to his aid, but she heard splashing and slapping sounds in the water and the old fear
once again took over her mind. She crouched on the
path and whimpered.

"Sally Ann . . ." he gasped. "Oh, God! Sally, help
me. Something's caught my leg. Sally! Oh, please."
There was silence while he ducked under the water. He
surfaced with a splash. *"Sally!"* One last scream, then
he was gone. The surface of the water continued to
agitate, and the waves lapped at her shoes as she stood
in the middle of the path, horrified. Then all was silent.

"Michael?" she called out softly. Silence. "Michael,
don't play any games with me. Come out of there." She

backed up, toward the entrance to the cave. "Michael?" A little louder, a little braver. "Oh, God, *Michael!*" She turned and ran.

4

Clint didn't need to be told what had happened. He read it in her face, in her body, as they felt each other in greeting. He knew that an era was dead, that he no longer needed to view the other world as a threat. It was over; she was his now, like Mary, like the boys. He felt her loss. It was, after all, what had sustained her all this time. She would get over it. She was a survivor. Like him.

The angry meanness that had consumed him soon after his mother had gone vanished with her return. He lay on his bed of moss, the only one awake, and contemplated his growing empire. Mary was pregnant again, but it wasn't soon enough. He told her she had to have a girl.

He would build something here far superior to anything up there. He and his mother. She would help him.

She needed some time, he knew, to let the wound heal. Then they would go up there, together, and get what they needed. Two more girls should be enough. Young ones.

He turned over on his side and snuggled up to Mary's back. His hand felt the smooth swell of her baby. Yes. He smiled to himself. This baby girl and two more.

Frederik Pohl (b. 1919)

WE PURCHASED PEOPLE

Frederik Pohl is one of the great living science fiction writers and editors, winner of many awards for his novels and stories, including both the Hugo and Nebula Awards several times. Kingsley Amis, in his study of the literature of science fiction, *New Maps of Hell*, called him the best living science fiction writer. He edited *Galaxy* magazine for more than a decade and has held various senior editorial positions in book publishing, but has always returned to writing. He has written no category horror. This piece however, whose ending may be compared to the finale of Mark Twain's *Puddin'head Wilson* for horrific effect, is a pure example of the style, tropes, and conventions of science fiction being used to create a devastating and horrid impact. Furthermore, this compressed and intense social allegory is not merely a tricky plotted story, but a work that uses horror to awaken the sensitivities of the reader to good and evil, humane feeling, social injustice. Pohl is a moralist, like Twain, like Vonnegut, and in spite of his utopian strain, his major mode has been satire, sometimes quite dark. It is also a fascinating transformation of Robert Silverberg's "Passengers," showing how writers in a genre (in this case, science fiction) make the tropes evolve.

On the third of March the purchased person named Wayne Golden took part in trade talks in Washington as the representative of the dominant race of the Groombridge star. What he had to offer was the license of the basic patents on a device to convert nuclear power plant waste products into fuel cells. It was a good item, with a ready market. Since half of Idaho was already bubbling with radioactive wastes, the Americans were anxious to buy, and he sold for a credit of $100 million. On the following day he flew to Spain. He was allowed to sleep all the way, stretched out across two seats in the first-class section of the Concorde, with the fastenings of a safety belt gouging into his side. On the fifth of the month he used up part of the trade credit in the purchase of fifteen Picasso oils-on-canvas, the videotape of a flamenco performance and a fifteenth-century harpsichord, gilt with carved legs. He arranged for them to be preserved, crated, and shipped in bond to Orlando, Florida, after which the items would be launched from Cape Kennedy on a voyage through space that would take more than twelve thousand years. The Groombridgians were not in a hurry and thought big. The Saturn Five booster rocket cost $11 million in itself. It did not matter. There was plenty of money left in the Groombridge credit balance. On the fifteenth of the month Golden returned to the United States, made a close connection at Logan Airport in Boston, and arrived early at his home kennel in Chicago. He was then given eighty-five minutes of freedom.

I knew exactly what to do with my eighty-five minutes. I always know. See, when you're working for the people who own you you don't have any choice about what you do, but up to a point you can think pretty much whatever you like. That thing you get in your head only controls you. It doesn't change you, or anyway I don't think it does. (Would I know if I were changed?)

My owners never lie to me. Never. I don't think they know what a lie is. If I ever needed anything to prove that they weren't human, that would be plenty, even if I didn't know they lived 86 zillion miles away, near some star that I can't even see. They don't tell me much, but they don't lie.

Not ever lying, that makes you wonder what they're like. I don't mean physically. I looked that up in the library once, when I had a couple of hours of free time. I don't remember where, maybe in Paris at the Bibliothèque Nationale, anyway I couldn't read what the language in the books said. But I saw the photographs and the holograms. I remember the physical appearance of my owners, all right. Jesus. The Altairians look kind of like spiders, and the Sirians are a little bit like crabs. But those folks from the Groombridge star, boy, they're something else. I felt bad about it for a long time, knowing I'd been sold to something that looked as much like a cluster of maggots on an open wound as anything else I'd ever seen. On the other hand, they're all those miles away, and all I ever have to do with them is receive their fast-radio commands and do what they tell me. No touching or anything. So what does it matter what they look like?

But what kind of freaky creature is it that never says anything that is not objectively the truth, never changes its mind, never makes a promise that it doesn't keep? They aren't machines, I know, but maybe they think I'm kind of a machine. You wouldn't bother to lie to a machine, would you? You wouldn't make it any promises. You wouldn't do it any favors, either, and they never do me any. They don't tell me that I can have eighty-five minutes off because I've done something they like, or because they want to sweeten me up because they want something from me. Everything considered, that's silly. What could they want? It isn't as if I had any choice. Ever. So they don't lie, or threaten, or bribe, or reward.

But for some reason they sometimes give me minutes or hours or days off, and this time I had eighty-five minutes. I started using it right away, the way I always do. The first thing was to check at the kennel location desk to see where Carolyn was. The locator clerk—he isn't owned, he works for a salary and treats us like shit—knows me by now. "Oh, hell, Wayne boy," he said with that imitation sympathy and lying friendliness that makes me want to kill him, "you just missed the lady friend. Saw her, let's see, Wednesday, was it? But she's gone." "Where to?" I asked him. He pushed around the cards on the locator board for a while, he knows I don't have very much time ever so he uses it up for me, and said: "Nope, not on my board at all. Say, I wonder. Was she with that bunch that went to Peking? Or was that the other little fat broad with the big boobs?" I didn't stop to kill him. If she wasn't on the board she wasn't in eighty-five-minute transportation range, so my eighty-five minutes—seventy-nine minutes—wasn't going to get me near her.

I went to the men's room, jerked off quickly, and went out into the miserable biting March Chicago wind to use up my seventy-nine minutes. Seventy-one minutes. There's a nice Mexican kind of restaurant near the kennel, a couple of blocks away past Ohio. They know me there. They don't care who I am. Maybe the brass plate in my head doesn't bother them because they think it's great that the people from the other stars are doing such nice things for the world, or maybe it's because I tip big. (What else do I have to do with the money I get?) I stuck my head in, whistled at Terry, the bartender, and said: "The usual. I'll be back in ten minutes." Then I walked up to Michigan and bought a clean shirt and changed into it, leaving the smelly old one. Sixty-six minutes. In the drugstore on the corner I picked up a couple of porno paperbacks and stuck them in my pockets, bought some cigarettes, leaned over and kissed the hand of the cashier, who was slim and fair-complexioned and smelled good, left her startled behind me, and got back to the restaurant just as Alicia, the waitress, was putting the gazpacho and the two bottles of beer on my table. Fifty-nine minutes. I settled down to enjoy my time. I smoked, and I ate, and I drank the beer, smoking between bites, drinking between puffs. You really look forward to something like that when you're working and not your own boss. I don't mean they don't let us eat when we're working. Of course they do, but we don't have any choice about what we eat or where we eat it. Pump fuel into the machine, keep it running. So I finished the guacamole and sent Alicia back for more of it when she brought the chocolate cake and American coffee, and ate the cake and the guacamole in alternate forkfuls. Eighteen minutes.

If I had had a little more time I would have jerked off again, but I didn't, so I paid the bill, tipped everybody, and left the restaurant. I got to the block where the kennel was with maybe two minutes to spare. Along the curb a slim woman in a fur jacket and pants suit was walking her Scottie away from me. I went up behind her and said, "I'll give you fifty dollars for a kiss." She turned around. She was all of sixty years old, but not bad, really, so I kissed her and gave her the fifty dollars. Zero minutes, and I just made it into the kennel when I felt the tingling in my forehead, and my owners took over again.

In the next seven days of March Wayne Golden visited Karachi, Srinagar, and Butte, Montana, on the business of the Groombridgians. He completed thirty-two assigned tasks. Quite unexpectedly he was then given 1,000 minutes of freedom.

That time I was in, I think it was, Pocatello, Idaho, or some place like that. I had to send a TWX to the faggy locator clerk in Chicago to ask about Carolyn. He took his time answering, as I knew he would. I walked around a little bit, waiting to hear. Everybody was very cheerful, smiling as they walked around through the dusty, sprinkly snow that was coming down, even smiling at me as though they didn't care that I was purchased, as they could plainly see from the golden oval of metal across my forehead that my owners use to tell me what to do. Then the message came back from Chicago: "Sorry, Wayne baby, but Carolyn isn't on my board. If you find her, give her one for me."

Well. All right. I have plenty of spending money, so I checked into a hotel. The bellboy brought me a fifth of Scotch and plenty of ice, fast, because he knew why I was in a hurry and that I would tip for speed. When I asked about hookers he offered anything I liked. I told him white, slim, beautiful asses. That's what I first noticed about Carolyn. It's special for me. The little girl I did in New Brunswick, what was her name—Rachel —she was only nine years old, but she had an ass on her you wouldn't believe.

I showered and put on clean clothes. The owners don't really give you enough time for that sort of thing. A lot of the time I smell. A lot of times I've almost wet my pants because they didn't let me go when I needed to. Once or twice I just couldn't help myself, held out as long as I could and, boy, you feel lousy when that happens. The worst was when I was covering some kind of a symposium in Russia, a place with a name like Akademgorodok. It was supposed to be on nuclear explosion processes. I don't know anything about that kind of stuff, and anyway I was a little mixed up because I thought that was one of the things the star people had done for us, worked out some way the different countries didn't have to have nuclear weapons and bombs and wars and so on anymore. But that wasn't what they meant. It was explosions at the nucleus of the galaxy they meant. Astronomical stuff. Just when a fellow named Eysenck was talking about how the FG prominence and the EMK prominence, whatever they were, were really part of an expanding pulse sphere, whatever that is, I crapped my pants. I knew I was going to. I'd tried to tell the Groombridge people about it. They wouldn't listen. Then the session redactor came down the aisle and shouted in my ear, as though my owners were deaf or stupid, that they would have to get me out of there, please, for reasons concerning the comfort and hygiene of the other participants. I thought they would be angry, because that meant they were going to miss some of this conference that they were interested in. They didn't do anything to me, though. I mean, as if there was anything they *could* do to me that would be any worse, or any different, from what they do to me all the time, and always will.

When I was all clean and in an open-necked shirt and chinos, I turned on the TV and poured a mild drink. I didn't want to be still drunk when my thousand minutes were up. There was a special program on all the networks, something celebrating a treaty between the United Nations and a couple of the star people, Sirians and Capellans it seemed to be. Everybody was very happy about it, because it seemed that now the Earth had bought some agricultural and chemical information, and pretty soon there would be more food than we could eat. How much we owed to the star people, the Secretary General of the UN was saying, in Brazilian-accented English. We could look forward to their wise guidance to help Earth survive its multitudinous crises and problems, and we should all be very happy.

But I wasn't happy, not even with a glass of John Begg and the hooker on her way up, because what I really wanted was Carolyn.

Carolyn was a purchased person, like me. I had seen her a couple of dozen times, all in all. Not usually when either of us was on freedom. Almost never when both of us were. It was sort of like falling in love by postcard, except that now and then we were physically close, even touching. And once or twice we had been briefly not only together, but out from under control. We had had about eight minutes once in Bucharest, after coming back from the big hydropower plant at the Iron Gate. That was the record, so far. Outside of that it was just that we passed, able to see each other but not to do anything about it, in the course of our duties. Or that one of us was free and found the other. When that happened the one of us that was free could talk, and even touch the other one, in any way that didn't interfere with what the other was doing. The one that was working couldn't do anything active, but could hear, or feel. We were both totally careful to avoid interfering with actual work. I don't know what would have happened if we had interfered. Maybe nothing? We didn't want to take that chance, though sometimes it was a temptation I could almost not resist. There was a time when I was free and I found Carolyn, working but not doing anything active, just standing there, at TWA Gate 51 at the St. Louis airport. She was waiting for someone to arrive. I really wanted to kiss her. I talked to her. I patted her, you know, holding my trenchcoat over my arm so that the people passing by wouldn't notice anything much. I told her things I wanted her to hear. But what I wanted was to kiss her, and I was afraid to. Kissing her on the mouth would have meant putting my head in front of her eyes. I didn't think I wanted to chance that. It might have meant she wouldn't see the person she was there to see.

Who turned out to be a Ghanaian police officer arriving to discuss the sale of some political prisoners to the Groombridgians. I was there when he came down the ramp, but I couldn't stay to see if she would by any chance be free after completing the negotiations with him, because then my own time ran out.

But I had had three hours that time, being right near her. It felt very sad and very strange, and I wouldn't have given it up for anything in the world. I knew she could hear and feel everything, even if she couldn't respond. Even when the owners are running you, there's a little personal part of you that stays alive. I talked to that part of her. I told her how much I wished we could kiss, and go to bed, and be with each other. Oh, hell. I even told her I loved her and wanted to marry her, although we both know perfectly well there's not ever going to be any chance of that ever. We don't get pensioned off or retired; we're *owned*.

Anyway, I stayed there with her as long as I could. I paid for it later. Balls that felt as though I'd been stomped, the insides of my undershorts wet and chilly. And there wasn't any way in the world for me to do anything about it, not even by masturbating, until my next free time. That turned out to be three weeks later. In Switzerland, for God's sake. Out of season. With nobody in the hotel except the waiters and bellboys and a couple of old ladies who looked at the gold oval in my forehead as though it smelled bad.

It is a terrible but cherished thing to love without hope.

I pretended there was hope, always. Every bit of freedom I got, I tried to find her. They keep pretty careful tabs on us, all two or three hundred thousand of us purchased persons, working for whichever crazy bunch of creepy crawlers or gassy ghosts happens to have bought us to be their remote-access facilities on the planet they themselves cannot ever visit. Carolyn and I were owned by the same bunch, which had its good side and its bad side. The good side was that there was a chance that someday we would be free for quite a long while at the same time. It happened. I don't know why. Shifts change on the Groombridge planet, or they have a holiday or something. But every once in a while there would be a whole day, maybe a week, when none of the Groombridge people would be doing anything at all, and all of us would be free at once.

The bad side was that they hardly ever needed to have more than one of us in one place. So Carolyn and I didn't run into each other a lot. And the times when I was free for a pretty good period it took most of that to find her, and by the time I did she was like a half a world away. No way of getting there and back in time for duty. I did so much want to fuck her, but we had never made it that far and maybe never would. I never even got a chance to ask her what she had been sentenced for in the first place. I really didn't know her at all, except enough to love her.

When the bellboy turned up with my girl I was comfortably buzzed, with my feet up and the Rangers on the TV. She didn't look like a hooker, particularly. She was wearing hip-huggers cut below the navel, bigger breasted than I cared about but with that beautiful curve of waist and back into hips that I like. Her name was Nikki. The bellboy took my money, took five for himself, passed the rest to her, and disappeared, grinning. What's so funny about it? He knew what I was, because the plate in my head told him, but he had to think it was funny.

"Do you want me to take my clothes off?" She had a pretty, breathless little voice, long red hair, and a sweet, broad, friendly face. "Go ahead," I said. She slipped off the sandals. Her feet were clean, a little ridged where the straps went. Stepped out of the hip-huggers and folded them across the back of Conrad Hilton's standard armchair, took off the blouse and folded it, ducked out of the medallion and draped it over the blouse, down to red lace bra and red bikini panties. Then she turned back the bedclothes, got in, sat up, snapped off the bra, snuggled down, kicked the panties out of the side of the bed, and pulled the covers over her. "Any time, honey," she said. But I didn't lay her. I didn't even get in the bed with her, not under the covers; I drank some more of the Scotch, and that and fatigue put me out, and when I woke up it was daylight, and she had cleaned out my wallet. Seventy-one minutes left. I paid the bill with a check and persuaded them to give me carfare in change. Then I headed back for the kennel. All I got out of it was clean clothes and a hangover. I think I had scared her a little. Everybody knows how we purchased people came to be up for sale, and maybe they're not all the way sure that we won't do something bad again, because they don't know how reliably our owners keep us from ever doing anything they don't like. But I wished she hadn't stolen my money.

The overall strategies and objectives of the star people, particularly the people from Groombridge star who were his own masters, were unclear to the purchased person named Wayne Golden. What they did was not hard to understand. All the world knew that the star people had established fast-radio contact with the people of Earth, and that in order to conduct their business on Earth they had purchased the bodies of certain convicted criminals, installing in them tachyon fast-radio transceivers. Why they did what they did was less easy to comprehend. Art objects they admired and purchased. Certain rare kinds of plants and flowers they purchased and had frozen at liquid-helium temperatures. Certain kinds of utilitarian objects they purchased. Every few months another rocket roared up from Merritt Island, just north of the Cape, and another cargo headed for the Groombridge star, on its twelve-thousand-year voyage. Others, to other stars, peopled by other races in the galactic confraternity, took shorter times—or longer—but none of the times was short enough for those star people who made the purchases to come to Earth to see what they had bought. The distances were too huge.

What they spent most of their money on was the rockets. And, of course, the people they purchased, into whom they had transplanted their tachyon transceivers. Each rocket cost at least $10 million. The going rate for a healthy male paranoid capable of three or more decades of useful work was in the hundreds of thousands of dollars, and they bought them by the dozen.

The other things they bought, all of them—the taped symphonies and early-dynasty *ushabti,* the flowering orchids, and the Van Goghs—cost only a fraction of 1 percent of what they spent on people and transportation. Of course, they had plenty of money to spend. Each star race sold off licensing rights on its own kinds of technology. All of them received trade credits from every government on Earth for their services in resolving disputes and preventing wars. Still, it seemed to Wayne Golden, to the extent that he was capable of judging the way his masters conducted their affairs, a pretty high-overhead way to run a business, although of course neither he nor any other purchased person was ever consulted on questions like that.

By late spring he had been on the move for many weeks without rest. He completed sixty-eight tasks, great and small. There was nothing in this period of eighty-seven days that was in any way remarkable except that on one day in May, while he was observing the riots on the Place de la Concorde from a window of the American Embassy on behalf of his masters, the girl named Carolyn came into his room. She whispered in his ear, attempted unsuccessfully to masturbate him while the liaison attaché was out of the room, remained in all for some forty minutes, and then left, sobbing softly. He could not even turn his head to see her go. Then on the sixth of June the purchased person named Wayne Golden was returned to the Dallas kennel and given indefinite furlough, subject to recall at fifty minutes' notice.

Sweetest dear Jesus, nothing like that had ever happened to me before! It was like the warden coming into Death Row with the last-minute reprieve! I could hardly believe it.

But I took it, started moving at once. I got a fix on Carolyn's last reported whereabouts from the locator board and floated away from Dallas in a cloud of Panama Red, drinking champagne as fast as the hostess could bring it to me, en route to Colorado.

But I didn't find Carolyn there.

I hunted her through the streets of Denver, and she was gone. By phone I learned she had been sent to Rantoul, Illinois. I was off. I checked at the Kansas City airport, where I was changing planes, and she was gone from Illinois already. Probably, they weren't sure, they thought, to the New York district. I put down the phone and jumped on a plane, rented a car at Newark, and drove down the Turnpike to the Garden State, checking every car I passed to see if it was the red Volvo they thought she might be driving, stopping at every other Howard Johnson's to ask if they'd seen a girl with short black hair, brown eyes and a tip-tilted nose and, oh, yes, the golden oval in her forehead.

I remembered it was in New Jersey that I first got into trouble. There was the nineteen-year-old movie cashier in Paramus, she was my first. I picked her up after the 1

AM show. And I showed her. But she was really all wrong for me, much too old and much too worldly. I didn't like it much when she died.

After that I was scared for a while, and I watched the TV news every night, twice, at six and eleven, and never passed a newsstand without looking at all the headlines in the papers, until a couple of months had passed. Then I thought over what I really wanted very carefully. The girl had to be quite young and, well, you can't tell, but as much as I could be sure, a virgin. So I sat in a luncheonette in Perth Amboy for three whole days, watching the kids get out of the parochial school, before I found my second. It took a while. The first one that looked good turned out to be a bus kid, the second was a walker but her big sister from the high school walked with her. The third walked home alone. It was December, and the afternoons got pretty dark, and that Friday she walked, but she didn't get home. I never molested any of them sexually, you know. I mean, in some ways I'm still kind of a virgin. That wasn't what I wanted, I just wanted to see them die. When they asked me at the pre-trial hearing if I knew the difference between right and wrong I didn't know how to answer them. I knew what I did was wrong for them. But it wasn't wrong for me; it was what I wanted.

So, driving down the Parkway, feeling discouraged about Carolyn, I noticed where I was and cut over to Route 35 and doubled back. I drove right to the school, past it, and to the lumberyard where I did the little girl. I stopped and cut the motor, looking around. Happy day. Now it was a different time of year, and things looked a little different. They'd piled up a stack of two-by-twelves over the place where I'd done her. But in my mind's eye I could see it the way it had been then. Dark gray sky. Lights from the cars going past. I could hear the little buzzing feeling in her throat as she tried to scream under my fingers. Let's see. That was, oh, good heavens, nine years ago.

And if I hadn't done her she would have been twenty or so. Screwing all the boys. Probably on dope. Maybe knocked up or married. Looked at in a certain way, I saved her a lot of sordid, miserable stuff, menstruating, letting the boys' hands and mouths on her, all that . . .

My head began hurting. That's one thing the plate in your head does, it doesn't let you get very deeply into things you did in the old days, because it hurts too much. So I started up the car and drove away, and pretty soon the hurting stopped.

I never think of Carolyn, you know, that way.

They never proved that little girl on me. The one they caught me for was the nurse in Long Branch, in the parking lot. And she was a mistake. She was so small, and she had a sweater over her uniform. I didn't know she was grown up until it was too late. I was very angry about that. In a way I didn't mind when they caught me, because I had been getting very careless. But I really hated that ward in Marlboro where they put me. Seven, Jesus, seven years. Up in the morning, and drink your pink medicine out of the little paper cup. Make your bed and do your job—mine was sweeping in the incontinent wards, and the smells and the sights would make you throw up.

After a while they let me watch TV and even read the papers, and when the Altair people made the first contact with Earth I was interested, and when they began buying criminally insane to be their proxies, I wanted them to buy me. Anything, I wanted *anything* that would let me out of that place, even if it meant I'd have to let them put a box in my head and never be able to live a normal life again.

But the Altair people wouldn't buy me. For some reason they only took blacks. Then the others began showing up on the fast radio, making their deals. And still none of them wanted me. The ones from Procyon liked young women, wouldn't ever buy a male. I think they have only one sex there, someone said. All these funnies are peculiar in one way or another. Metal, or gas, or blobby, or hard-shelled and rattly. Whatever. And they all have funny habits, like if you belong to the Canopus bunch you can't ever eat fish.

I think they're disgusting, and I don't really know why the USA wanted to get involved with them in the first place. But the Chinese did, and the Russians did, and I guess we just couldn't stay out. I suppose it hasn't hurt much. There hasn't been a war, and there's a lot of ways in which they've helped clean things up for us. It hasn't hurt me, that's for sure. The Groombridge people came into the market pretty late, and most of the good healthy criminals were gone; they would buy anybody. They bought me. We're a hard-case lot, we Groombridgians, and I do wonder what Carolyn was in for.

I drove all the way down the coast, Asbury Park, Brielle, Atlantic City, all the way to Cape May, phoning back to check with the locator clerk, and never found her.

The one thing I did know was that all I was missing was the shell of her, because she was working. I could have had a kiss or a feel, no more. But I wanted to find her anyway. Just on the chance. How many times do you get an indefinite furlough? If I'd been able to find her, and stay with her, sooner or later, maybe, she would have been off too. Even if it were only for two hours. Even thirty minutes.

And then in broad daylight, just as I was checking into a motel near an Army base, with the soldiers' girls lined up at the cashier's window so their boyfriends could get back for reveille, I got the call: Report to the Philadelphia kennel. Soonest.

By then I was giddy for sleep, but I drove that Hertz lump like a Maserati, because soonest means soonest. I dumped the car and signed in at the kennel, feeling my heart pounding and my mouth ragged from fatigue, and aching because I had blown what would have to be my best chance of really being with Carolyn. "What do they want?" I asked the locator clerk. "Go inside," he said, looking evilly amused. All locator clerks treat us the same, all over the world. "She'll tell you."

Not knowing who "she" was, I opened the door and walked through, and there was Carolyn.

"Hello, Wayne," she said.

"Hello, Carolyn," I said.

I really did not have any idea of what to do at all. She didn't give me a cue. She just sat. It was at that point that it occurred to me to wonder at the fact that she wasn't wearing much, just a shortie nightgown with nothing under it. She was also sitting on a turned-down bed. Now, you would think that considering everything, especially the nature of most of my thinking about Carolyn, that I would have instantly accepted this as a personal gift from God to me of every boy's all-American dream. I didn't. It wasn't fatigue, either. It was Carolyn. It was the expression on her face, which was neither inviting nor loving, was not even the judgment-reserving look of a girl at a singles bar. What it especially was not was happy.

"The thing is, Wayne," she said, "we're supposed to go to bed now. So take your clothes off, why don't you?"

Sometimes I can stand outside of myself and look at me and, even when it's something terrible or something sad, I can see it was funny; it was like that when I did the little girl in Edison Township, because her mother had sewed her into her school clothes. I was actually laughing when I said, "Carolyn, what's the matter?"

"Well," she said, "they want us to ball, Wayne. You know. The Groombridge people. They've got interested in what human beings do to each other, and they want to kind of watch."

I started to ask why us, but I didn't have to; I could see where Carolyn and I had had a lot of that on our minds, and maybe our masters could get curious about it. I didn't exactly like it. Not exactly; in fact in a way I kind of hated it, but it was so much better than nothing at all that I said, "Why, honey, that's great!"—almost meaning it; trying to talk her into it; moving in next to her and putting my arm around her. And then she said:

"Only we have to wait, Wayne. They want to do it. Not us."

"What do you mean, wait? Wait for what?" She shrugged under my arm. "You mean," I said, "that we have to be plugged in to them? Like they'll be doing it with our bodies?"

She leaned against me. "That's what they told me, Wayne. Any minute now, I guess."

I pushed her away. "Honey," I said, half crying, "all this time I've been wanting to—Jesus, Carolyn! I mean, it isn't just that I wanted to go to bed with you. I mean—"

"I'm sorry," she cried, big tears on her face.

"That's lousy!" I shouted. My head was pounding, I was so furious. "It isn't fair! I'm not going to stand for it. They don't have any *right!*"

But they did, of course, they had all the right in the world; they had bought us and paid for us, and so they owned us. I knew that. I just didn't want to accept it, even by admitting what I knew was so. The notion of screwing Carolyn flipped polarity; it wasn't what I desperately wanted, it was what I would have died to avoid, as long as it meant letting *them* paw her with my hands, kiss her with my mouth, flood her with my juices; it was like the worst kind of rape, worse than anything I had ever done, both of us raped at once. And then—

And then I felt that burning tingle in my forehead as they took over. I couldn't even scream. I just had to sit there inside my own head, no longer owning a muscle, while those freaks who owned me did to Carolyn with my body all manner of things, and I could not even cry.

After concluding the planned series of experimental procedures, which were duly recorded, the purchased person known as Carolyn Schoerner was no longer salvageable. Appropriate entries were made. The Probation and Out-Service department of the Meadville Women's Reformatory was notified that she had ceased to be alive. A purchasing requisition was initiated for a replacement, and her account was terminated.

The purchased person known as Wayne Golden was assigned to usual duties, at which he functioned normally while under control. It was discovered that when control was withdrawn he became destructive, both to others and to himself. The conjecture has been advanced that that sexual behavior which had been established as his norm—the destruction of the sexual partner—may not have been appropriate in the conditions obtaining at the time of the experimental procedures. Further experiments will be made with differing procedures and other partners in the near future. Meanwhile Wayne Golden continues to function at normal efficiency, provided control is not withdrawn at any time, and apparently will do so indefinitely.

Gertrude Atherton (1857–1948)

THE STRIDING PLACE

"Gertrude Atherton has been the subject of more contro-
versy than any other living American novelist. England,
we are told, regards her as the greatest living novelist of
America. Many Americans so rate her," said a survey of
the American novel in 1918. "A good deal of it comes out
of Mrs. Atherton's long-standing and vigorous assault on
the literary schools of William Dean Howells and Henry
James." A bohemian in her youth, who travelled widely,
San Francisco writer Gertrude Atherton matured into a
grande dame of the literary scene without losing her verve
or distinctive style. She was the grand-niece of Benjamin
Franklin. Her most famous horror story, "The Striding
Place" (1896) was inspired by an actual locale, the setting
of a famous crime. She says in her autobiography, "I
haunted that spot, fascinated, and consumed with a desire
to write a gruesome story of the Strid, but could think of
nothing. . . . One night I determined to try an experiment.
Just before dropping off to sleep I ordered my mind to
conceive that story and have it formulated when I awoke.
And the moment I opened my eyes, there it was. I wrote it
out before leaving the bed." She first submitted it to *The
Yellow Book* but it was rejected as "far too gruesome."
She concludes, "It seems to me the best short story I ever
wrote." Today, she is remembered only for her historical
novel, *The Conqueror* (1902), based on the life of
Alexander Hamilton, and for her two collections of horror
stories, *The Bell in The Fog* (1905) and *The Foghorn*
(1934).

Weigall, continental and detached, tired early of grouse-shooting. To stand propped against a sod fence while his host's workmen routed up the birds with long poles and drove them towards the waiting guns, made him feel himself a parody on the ancestors who had roamed the moors and forests of this West Riding of Yorkshire in hot pursuit of game worth the killing. But when in England in August he always accepted whatever proffered for the season, and invited his host to shoot pheasants on his estates in the South. The amusements of life, he argued, should be accepted with the same philosophy as its ills.

It had been a bad day. A heavy rain had made the moor so spongy that it fairly sprang beneath the feet. Whether or not the grouse had haunts of their own, wherein they were immune from rheumatism, the bag had been small. The women, too, were an unusually dull lot, with the exception of a new-minded *débutante* who bothered Weigall at dinner by demanding the verbal restoration of the vague paintings on the vaulted roof above them.

But it was no one of these things that sat on Weigall's mind as, when the other men went up to bed, he let himself out of the castle and sauntered down to the river. His intimate friend, the companion of his boyhood, the chum of his college days, his fellow-traveller in many lands, the man for whom he possessed stronger affection than for all men, had mysteriously disappeared two days ago, and his track might have sprung to the upper air for all trace he had left behind him. He had been a guest on the adjoining estate during the past week, shooting with the fervour of the true sportsman, making love in the intervals to Adeline Cavan, and apparently in the best of spirits. As far as was known, there was nothing to lower his mental mercury, for his rent-roll was a large one, Miss Cavan blushed whenever he looked at her, and, being one of the best shots in

England, he was never happier than in August. The suicide theory was preposterous, all agreed, and there was as little reason to believe him murdered. Nevertheless, he had walked out of March Abbey two nights ago without hat or overcoat, and had not been seen since.

The country was being patrolled night and day. A hundred keepers and working men were beating the woods and poking the bogs on the moors, but as yet not so much as a handkerchief had been found.

Weigall did not believe for a moment that Wyatt Gifford was dead, and although it was impossible not to be affected by the general uneasiness, he was disposed to be more angry than frightened. At Cambridge Gifford had been an incorrigible practical joker, and by no means had outgrown the habit; it would be like him to cut across the country in his evening clothes, board a cattle train, and amuse himself touching up the picture of the sensation in West Riding.

However, Weigall's affection for his friend was too deep to companion with tranquility in the present state of doubt, and, instead of going to bed early with the other men, he determined to walk until ready for sleep. He went down to the river and followed the path through the woods. There was no moon, but the stars sprinkled their cold light upon the pretty belt of water flowing placidly past wood and ruin, between green masses of overhanging rocks or sloping banks tangled with tree and shrub, leaping occasionally over stones with the harsh notes of an angry scold, to recover its equanimity the moment the way was clear again.

It was very dark in the depths where Weigall trod. He smiled as he recalled a remark of Gifford's. "An English wood is like a good many other things in life—very promising at a distance, but a hollow mockery when you get within. You see daylight on both sides, and the sun freckles the very bracken. Our woods need the night to make them seem what they ought to be—what they once were, before our ancestors' descendants demanded so much more money, in these so much more various days."

Weigall strolled along, smoking, and thinking of his friend, his pranks—many of which had done more credit to his imagination than this—and recalling conversations that had lasted the night through. Just before the end of the London season they had walked the streets one hot night after a party, discussing the various theories of the soul's destiny. That afternoon they had met at the coffin of a college friend whose mind had been a blank for the past three years. Some months previously they had called at the asylum to see him. His expression had been senile, his face imprinted with the record of debauchery. In death the face was placid, intelligent, without ignoble lineation—the face of the man they had known at college. Weigall and Gifford had had no time to comment there, and the afternoon and evening were full; but, coming forth from the house of festivity together, they had reverted almost at once to the topic.

"I cherish the theory," Gifford had said, "that the soul sometimes lingers in the body after death. During madness, of course, it is an impotent prisoner, albeit a conscious one. Fancy its agony, and its horror! What more natural than that, when the life-spark goes out, the tortured soul should take possession of the vacant skull and triumph once more for a few hours while old friends look their last? It has had time to repent while compelled to crouch and behold the result of its work, and it has shrived itself into a state of comparative purity. If I had my way, I should stag inside my bones until the coffin had gone into its niche, that I might obviate for my poor old comrade the tragic impersonality of death. And I should like to see justice done to it, as it were—to see it lowered among its ancestors with the ceremony and solemnity that are its due. I am afraid that if I dissevered myself too quickly, I should yield to curiosity and hasten to investigate the mysteries of space."

"You believe in the soul as an independent entity, then—that it and the vital principle are not one and the same."

"Absolutely. The body and soul are twins, life comrades—sometimes friends, sometimes enemies, but always loyal in the last instance. Someday, when I am tired of the world, I shall go to India and become a mahatma, solely for the pleasure of receiving proof during life of this independent relationship."

"Suppose you were not sealed up properly, and returned after one of your astral flights to find your earthly part unfit for habitation? It is an experiment I don't think I should care to try, unless even juggling with soul and flesh had palled."

"That would not be an uninteresting predicament. I should rather enjoy experimenting with broken machinery."

The high wild roar of water smote suddenly on Weigall's ear and checked his memories. He left the wood and walked out on the huge slippery stones which nearly close the River Wharfe at this point, and watched the waters boil down into the narrow pass with their furious untiring energy. The black quiet of the woods rose high on either side. The stars seemed colder and whiter just above. On either hand the perspective of the river might have run into a rayless cavern. There was no lonelier spot in England, nor one which had the right to claim so many ghosts, if ghosts there were.

Weigall was not a coward, but he recalled uncomfortably the tales of those that had been done to death in the Strid.[1] Wordsworth's Boy of Egremond had been disposed of by the practical Whitaker; but countless others, more venturesome than wise, had gone down into that narrow boiling course, never to appear in the still pool a few yards beyond. Below the great rocks which form the walls of the Strid was believed to be a natural vault, on to whose shelves the dead were drawn. The spot had an ugly fascination. Weigall stood, visioning skeletons, uncoffined and green, the home of the eyeless things which had devoured all that had covered and filled that rattling symbol of man's mortality; then fell to wondering if anyone had attempted to leap the Strid of late. It was covered with slime; he had never seen it look so treacherous.

He shuddered and turned away, impelled, despite his manhood, to flee the spot. As he did so, something tossing in the foam below the fall—something as white, yet independent of it—caught his eye and arrested his step. Then he saw that it was describing a contrary motion to the rushing water—an upward backward motion. Weigall stood rigid, breathless; he fancied he heard the crackling of his hair. Was that a hand? It thrust itself still higher above the boiling foam, turned sidewise, and four frantic fingers were distinctly visible against the black rock beyond.

Weigall's superstitious terror left him. A man was there, struggling to free himself from the suction beneath the Strid, swept down, doubtless, but a moment

[1]"This striding-place is called the "Strid,"
  A name which it took of yore;
A thousand years hath it borne the name,
  And it shall a thousand more."

before his arrival, perhaps as he stood with his back to the current.

He stepped as close to the edge as he dared. The hand doubled as if in imprecation, shaking savagely in the face of that force which leaves its creatures to immutable law; then spread wide again, clutching, expanding, crying for help as audibly as the human voice.

Weigall dashed to the nearest tree, dragged and twisted off a branch with his strong arms, and returned as swiftly to the Strid. The hand was in the same place, still gesticulating as wildly; the body was undoubtedly caught in the rocks below, perhaps already halfway along one of those hideous shelves. Weigall let himself down upon a lower rock, braced his shoulder against the mass beside him, then, leaning out over the water, thrust the branch into the hand. The fingers clutched it convulsively. Weigall tugged powerfully, his own feet dragged perilously near the edge. For a moment he produced no impression, then an arm shot above the waters.

The blood sprang to Weigall's head; he was choked with the impression that the Strid had him in her roaring hold, and he saw nothing. Then the mist cleared. The hand and arm were nearer, although the rest of the body was still concealed by the foam. Weigall peered out with distended eyes. The meagre light revealed in the cuffs links of a peculiar device. The fingers clutching the branch were as familiar.

Weigall forgot the slippery stones, the terrible death if he stepped too far. He pulled with passionate will and muscle. Memories flung themselves into the hot light of his brain, trooping rapidly upon each other's heels, as in the thought of the drowning. Most of the pleasures of his life, good and bad, were identified in some way with this friend. Scenes of college days, of travel, where they had deliberately sought adventure and stood between one another and death upon more occasions than one, of hours of delightful companionship among the treasures of art, and others in the pursuit of pleasure, flashed like the changing particles of a kaleidoscope. Weigall had loved several women; but he would have flouted in these moments the thought that he had ever loved any woman as he loved Wyatt Gifford. There were so many charming women in the world, and in the thirty-two years of his life he had never known another man to whom he had cared to give his intimate friendship.

He threw himself on his face. His wrists were cracking, the skin was torn from his hands. The fingers still gripped the stick. There was life in them yet.

Suddenly something gave way. The hand swung about, tearing the branch from Weigall's grasp. The body had been liberated and flung outward, though still submerged by the foam and spray.

Weigall scrambled to his feet and sprang along the rocks, knowing that the danger from suction was over and that Gifford must be carried straight to the quiet pool. Gifford was a fish in the water and could live under it longer than most men. If he survived this, it would not be the first time that his pluck and science had saved him from drowning.

Weigall reached the pool. A man in his evening clothes floated on it, his face turned towards a projecting rock over which his arm had fallen, upholding the body. The hand that had held the branch hung limply over the rock, its white reflection visible in the black water. Weigall plunged into the shallow pool, lifted Gifford in his arms and returned to the bank. He laid the body down and threw off his coat that he might be the freer to practise the methods of resuscitation. He was glad of the moment's respite. The valiant life in the man might have been exhausted in that last struggle. He had not dared to look at his face, to put his ear to the heart. The hesitation lasted but a moment. There was no time to lose.

He turned to his prostrate friend. As he did so, something strange and disagreeable smote his senses. For a half-moment he did not appreciate its nature. Then his teeth clacked together, his feet, his outstretched arms pointed towards the woods. But he sprang to the side of the man and bent down and peered into his face. There was no face.

THE
DARK
DESCENT

Edited by David G. Hartwell

Tor Books ®

SPINE-TINGLING
HORROR FROM TOR

THE BEST IN
SCIENCE FICTION

☐	51083-6	ACHILLES' CHOICE *Larry Niven & Steven Barnes*	$4.99 Canada $5.99
☐	50270-1	THE BOAT OF A MILLION YEARS *Poul Anderson*	$4.95 Canada $5.95
☐	51528-5	A FIRE UPON THE DEEP *Vernor Vinge*	$5.99 Canada $6.99
☐	52225-7	A KNIGHT OF GHOSTS AND SHADOWS *Poul Anderson*	$4.99 Canada $5.99
☐	53259-7	THE MEMORY OF EARTH *Orson Scott Card*	$5.99 Canada $6.99
☐	51001-1	N-SPACE *Larry Niven*	$5.99 Canada $6.99
☐	52024-6	THE PHOENIX IN FLIGHT *Sherwood Smith & Dave Trowbridge*	$4.99 Canada $5.99
☐	51704-0	THE PRICE OF THE STARS *Debra Doyle & James D. Macdonald*	$4.50 Canada $5.50
☐	50890-4	RED ORC'S RAGE *Philip Jose Farmer*	$4.99 Canada $5.99
☐	50925-0	XENOCIDE *Orson Scott Card*	$5.99 Canada $6.99
☐	50947-1	YOUNG BLEYS *Gordon R. Dickson*	$5.99 Canada $6.99

Buy them at your local bookstore or use this handy coupon:
Clip and mail this page with your order.

Publishers Book and Audio Mailing Service
P.O. Box 120159, Staten Island, NY 10312-0004

Please send me the book(s) I have checked above. I am enclosing $ _____
(Please add $1.25 for the first book, and $.25 for each additional book to cover postage and handling.
Send check or money order only—no CODs.)

Name _____
Address _____
City _____ State/Zip _____
Please allow six weeks for delivery. Prices subject to change without notice.